The Target:
The ancient chalice of Melusine

The bad guys: Otherwise known as the Comitatus, a powerful group of gun-toting men bent on destroying the goddess grails—and anyone who gets in their way. They've got superior firepower, a worldwide network of resources and a dangerous reputation. Fearing that the power of the grails will threaten the brotherhood, they will use any means necessary to prevent them from being united.

The good gal: Magdalene Sanger, college professor and grail keeper, comes from a long line of women charged with protecting the ancient grails, keeping them out of enemy hands and safely hidden until the time is right. What's at stake? No one really knows what power the grails may hold, but Maggi's determined to find and preserve these legendary artifacts of woman power with all of her wits, her research…and the power of a goddess.

The Grail Keepers:
Going for the grail with the goddess on their side!

Dear Reader,

Enter the high-stakes world of Silhouette Bombshell, where the heroine takes charge and never gives up—whether she's standing up for herself, saving her friends from grave danger or daring to go where no woman has gone before. A Silhouette Bombshell heroine has smarts, persistence and an indomitable spirit, qualities that will get her in and out of trouble in an exciting adventure that will also bring her a man worth having…if she wants him!

Meet Angel Baker, public avenger, twenty-second-century woman and the heroine of *USA TODAY* bestselling author Julie Beard's story, *Kiss of the Blue Dragon*. Angel's job gets personal when her mother is kidnapped, and the search leads Angel into Chicago's criminal underworld, where she crosses paths with one very stubborn detective!

Join the highly trained women of ATHENA FORCE on the hunt for a killer, with *Alias*, by Amy J. Fetzer, the latest in this exhilarating twelve-book continuity series. She's lived a lie for four years to protect her son—but her friend's death brings Darcy Steele out of hiding to find out whom she can trust….

Explore a richly fantastic world in Evelyn Vaughn's *A.K.A. Goddess*, the story of a woman whose special calling pits her against a powerful group of men and their leader, her former lover.

And finally, nights are hot in *Urban Legend* by Erica Orloff. A mysterious nightclub owner stalks her lover's killers while avoiding the sharp eyes of a rugged cop, lest he learn her own dark secret— she's a vampire….

It's a month to sink your teeth into! Please send your comments and suggestions to me c/o Silhouette Books, 233 Broadway, Suite 1001, New York, NY 10279.

Sincerely,

Natashya Wilson

Natashya Wilson
Associate Senior Editor, Silhouette Bombshell

Please address questions and book requests to:
Silhouette Reader Service
U.S.: 3010 Walden Ave., P.O. Box 1325, Buffalo, NY 14269
Canadian: P.O. Box 609, Fort Erie, Ont. L2A 5X3

A.K.A.
GODDESS

EVELYN VAUGHN

Published by Silhouette Books

America's Publisher of Contemporary Romance

SILHOUETTE BOOKS

ISBN 0-373-51321-6

A.K.A. GODDESS

www.SilhouetteBombshell.com

Printed in U.S.A.

One queen was imprisoned by soldiers.
One queen was denounced by priests.
One queen was outlawed by a senate.
One queen was erased by scholars.
One queen was exiled by her father-in-law.
One queen was overthrown by her stepson.
One queen was betrayed by her lover.
One queen was forgotten by her son.
One queen was deserted by her husband.

As each queen found herself in danger from fear and envy, she asked her own daughters to do as her mother, the Great Queen, had instructed. She had them hide her cup, so that the powers she had poured into it could survive, waiting to be found and shared if ever the world again became ready for them.
The cups wait to be discovered.
The cups wait to be united.
The cups wait to change the world.
They are waiting still...perhaps, my daughter, for you.

The Grail Keepers' Bedtime Story

*L*ong ago, before accepted history began, there lived a Great Queen with nine powerful daughters. Their powers lay in their beauty, in their truth, in their abilities to heal and create and protect. Their powers lay in their skill at dance and art and sports and poetry.

But their greatest power lay in being women.

Because the world needed them, the Great Queen sent her daughters in nine different directions to be queens in their own right. And she gave them each a finely crafted cup.

"Pour your powers into these cups," she instructed, "and share them as you will. But if ever you find yourselves in danger, a victim of fear or envy, hide the cups so that your powers can live on, even though you be forgotten."

Her daughters agreed, and off they went. For a long, long time they ruled as beloved queens—queens of the North and the South, of the East and the West, of the Heaven and the Earth and the Underworld. They married and loved and bore children. But all things change, wheels turn, and eventually, as the Great Queen had predicted, men began to fear and envy their powers.

sponse time—and I disconnected from the nice emergency operator. I cracked my window, but the two officers only nodded in my direction before heading upstairs to check matters out. I waited, staring unfocused at my faint reflection in the car window—late twenty-something, long brown hair pulled into a wet ponytail, eyes too serious. What felt like forever later, a second blue-and-white cruised into my parking lot. As its female officer got out, I could hear her radio crackle. A male voice said, "Someone's trashed the place, but it seems empty. We'll look around to make sure."

Trashed the place? *My* place?

Weirdly, instead of feeling hurt or violated, I simply felt…disbelief. My apartment was safe. How could someone trash it?

The policewoman tapped on my car window. Despite having watched her approach, I still jumped. "Ms. Sanger? Officer Sofie Douglas. Could I ask you some questions?"

I was still tense—so much for the relaxation benefits of swimming thirty laps at the gym. But her being female made her more approachable. She was black, shorter than me and about my age.

As a gesture of confidence, I climbed out of the car.

"Is your name really Margaret Sanger?" Officer Douglas asked. "Like the lady who made birth control legal?"

"No," I said, not for the first time. "Not Margaret."

Her eyebrows arched. "Dispatch said you identified yourself as Maggie."

I saw her writing it down. "No *e*."

She scratched out the *e*. Hey, at least I don't dot my *i*'s with hearts or smiley faces.

"Maggi's short for Magdalene," I said.

Officer Douglas blinked at me. "You mean like Mary Magdalene?"

Lights appeared above us, from my apartment's bedroom window, and my head came up to track it. "That's the one."

"So what do you do?" she asked. "For a living, I mean."

Chapter 1

The light over my front door was out again. I noticed it as I carried my damp gym bag up the shadowy outer stairs. I'd have to call the landlord.

Then I climbed high enough to see that my door stood open several inches.

I knew I'd locked it.

Someone was in my apartment.

For a long, dumb moment, I just stared. Then I backed down the steps as quietly as I could. Don't get me wrong. I come from a long line of strong women—WACs, suffragettes, ladies who disguised themselves as boys to fight alongside soldier husbands in ancient wars. And, trust me, that's only the tip of the iceberg when it comes to my family and woman power.

But there's a huge difference between strength and stupidity. Our brains are our best weapon, or so my *sifu*—instructor—used to say. I reached and unlocked my car, and all but dove inside. I hit the lock button, only then using my cell phone to call 911.

Then I sat there on the phone, fumbling my key into the ignition in case whoever was in my apartment might force me to flee by automobile.

Or maybe to run them over. Who can say with hypotheticals?

The cops got there barely ten minutes later—not a bad re-

I owe thanks to many people for this book.
Thanks to Leslie and Stef and Lynda and Cheryl
and Julie at Silhouette Books, and to Paige at
Creative Media Agency. Thanks to friends who critiqued
or brainstormed, especially Maureen McKade and
Pam McCutcheon and Deb Stover, and to Toni and Sarah
and Jenn and Christine. Thanks to Matt and my friends at
TCC for double-checking my technical elements, and to
inspirations like Maggie Shayne and Lorna Tedder
and the Sisterhood of the Scribes.

This book is dedicated to all of them and more,
and to the spirit of sisterhood that,
as far as I'm concerned, is the most constant
and wonderful manifestation of Goddessness.

EVELYN VAUGHN

has written stories since she learned to make letters. But during the two years that she lived on a Navajo reservation in Arizona—while in second and third grade—she dreamed of becoming not a writer, but a barrel racer in the rodeo. Before she actually got her own horse, however, her family moved to Louisiana. There, to avoid the humidity, she channeled more of her adventures into stories instead.

Since then, Evelyn has canoed in the East-Texas swamps, rafted a white-water river in the Austrian Alps, rappelled barefoot down a three-story building, talked her way onto a ship to Greece without her passport, sailed in the Mediterranean and spent several weeks in Europe with little more than a backpack and a train pass. All at least once. While she enjoys channeling the more powerful "travel Vaughn" on a regular basis, she also loves the fact that she can write about adventures with far less physical discomfort. Since she now lives in Texas, where she teaches English at a local community college, air-conditioning still remains an important factor.

A.K.A. Goddess is Evelyn's seventh full-length book for Silhouette. Feel free to contact her through her Web site, www.evelynvaughn.com, or by writing to P.O. Box 6, Euless TX, 76039.

"I teach comparative mythology at the college."

She stared. "You can *major* in that?"

I was rolling on to and off of the balls of my feet, like a Tai Chi form about to escape. "When can I go up there?"

I wanted to see the damage for myself. I had to know if this really was random. I kind of hoped it was.

Static crackled on Officer Douglas's radio. Then a voice: "Nobody's here. It doesn't look like they took anything."

I jogged up the stairs without waiting for Sofie Douglas's permission.

The place was trashed, all right. Sofa cushions slit. Drawers overturned. Plants uprooted in dark spills of potting soil. In some corners, my carpet had even been torn off its pad. Stunned, I headed for the bedroom, which was just as bad. All my clothes…!

"Can you tell if anything's missing, Ms. Sanger?" asked a burly, red-haired officer. "Anything of value?"

"It's all of value," I said, more softly than I would have liked. "It's mine."

"Yes, ma'am. I mean—"

But I held up a hand to cut him off. I knew what he meant. As a test, I checked my jewelry box. There never had been a lot there—even when I was engaged briefly, I used to wear the too-expensive diamond—I had few family heirlooms.

"Nothing's missing." I turned and noticed my bedroom TV. It was portable, but it hadn't been, well, ported. I returned to my living room—the TV and stereo remained there, too, though they'd been upended—and looked into my office. My computer hummed steadily, monitor facedown on the floor. But…

"The CPU's running," I said. "I turned it off before I left home this morning."

Officer Douglas, who'd followed me upstairs, went to look more closely at my computer. The redhead, whose shield identified him as Officer Willis, said, "Does anybody have a key to your home?"

"My parents," I said. "Two—no, three of my friends."

He exchanged an amused glance with the other male officer, a tall, graying guy with a mustache.

"And the lady who cleans up for me once a week," I added. "Oh, and my dog walker."

Willis looked concerned. "You have a dog?"

As if I would've hidden in my car if any dog of mine had been in jeopardy! "Not anymore. She died last fall. I just never bothered to get my key back. I've also given a key to my neighbor, so she can check on things when I'm gone. But she's trustworthy. They all are."

"Maybe I should've asked who *doesn't* have a key."

There were a few.

"I prefer not to empower fear," I murmured, turning in a circle, and he snorted with male superiority. At least he didn't use that old line about "a woman as pretty as you," as if a decent appearance begs for trouble.

Trouble doesn't wait for invitations.

That's when I noticed what was left of my curio cabinet. The cabinet itself had been destroyed—lying on its side, the door yanked completely off, cherry wood splintered and every pane of glass smashed. And my collection of statues, inside…

Little more than rubble.

I took a step forward, unbelieving. Chunks of white marble were all that remained of what had once been a twelve-inch Pallas Athena, which I'd bought in Greece. Shards of lapis lazuli had been my Isis-and-Horus statue. My obsidian Shiva was many-armed rubble. My glossy, ceramic Virgin Mary had been smashed to shiny dust. Even the wonderfully fertile Venus, similar to the famous Willendorf figure and carved from granite, had been reduced to round and jagged bits.

There was no way the Venus could have broken like that accidentally. Someone must have pounded on her, hard. Repeatedly. Purposefully.

And in anger.

I'd recently read a news piece about a goddess artifact being similarly destroyed, in a museum in India, and the similarities—as well as my sudden conclusions—unnerved me.

"Wow." Willis whistled. "What were those?"

"Goddesses," I said. "I collect statues of ancient goddesses."

"Were they worth a lot?"

Monetarily? Some more than others—none were originals, thank heavens. But emotionally…

Officer Douglas, from my study doorway, said, "Goddesses? Are you one of those Wiccans?"

"Not exactly," I told her, fingering the amulet I wore under my shirt. It wasn't a pentagram, but two interlaced circles called a *vesica piscis*. I wasn't technically Wiccan. But our beliefs have surprising similarities.

It's like I told you.

I come from a very long line of *very* strong women.

The police all but moved in. They made phone calls and questioned neighbors. Specialists showed up to photograph the wreckage and to dust for fingerprints, more backup than I'd ever expected for a simple break-in. When I asked if this was normal, Officer Willis said, "We're just trying to be thorough, ma'am."

I put up with it for insurance reasons, but mainly I just wanted to clean up. Did you know recent studies have shown that while men have a fight-or-flight response to stress, women have a hormone that prompts them to tend-and-befriend? I hated to see Officer Sofie go, despite her leaving her card with me and telling me to call anytime. But I also wanted space in which to mourn my statues, to put things as much to right as I could…and to consider who could have done such a thing…and why.

I couldn't help thinking this break-in might somehow be related to the recent destruction of an ancient goblet, the Kali

Cup, a week before it could go on display. But that meant things I couldn't face. Not yet.

I'd barely managed to start straightening the mess, alone at last, when a knock at the door startled me. I don't like being scared. It goes against almost everything I believe in.

Checking the peephole and catching a glimpse of brown hair, and a familiar face in its usual impersonal mode, didn't do a lot to improve my mood…or my lingering disorientation.

Lex.

Alexander Rothschild Stuart III and I go back. Way, *way* back. Worse, he makes me question my life choices almost every time our diverse paths collide. See, he'd be the dream catch for almost any woman—wealthy beyond his unimaginable inheritance, quietly handsome and, despite nearing thirty, still something of a brooding bad boy. Hard to resist, huh?

Hell, even *I* have a terrible time resisting him, as our roller-coaster history attests to. And I have different views on money and power than a lot of women. At least—I try.

I could also no longer trust either him or his family as far as I could comfortably spit them.

Still, there was that lack-of-resistance thing, and the intimate-history thing, along with no small amount of curiosity. It had been months since I'd so much as glimpsed him, yet there he stood, too self-possessed to even look impatient while I checked him out. Him showing up on the night of my break-in couldn't have been a coincidence even if I believed in coincidences.

I don't. But I opened the door.

"Are you all right?" The question came out vague and polite, as if he were making bored chitchat at a cocktail party. Lex has always had that coolness about him—he supposedly can trace his family line back to the Royal House of Scotland, by way of England, so it's probably all that blue blood chilling in his veins. But the fact that he was here at all, much less this late, belied his nonchalance. So did the powerful energy that instantly roiled between us. "I heard about the break-in."

"From the police?" I asked. That might explain all the special treatment, mightn't it? "Or are you a part of the criminal grapevine now?"

He'd been accused of perjury the previous year. Worse, he hadn't denied it. It had contributed to our latest breakup.

Now my words wrung a hint of a smile from him, an expression that, on Lex, packs a potent punch. "So may I come in? You know I need permission to cross a person's threshold."

No, he wasn't a vampire. He was just being sarcastic.

"You might as well." I sighed. "Everyone else has tonight."

So he did, casually touching my arm as he passed me...except that nothing Lex Stuart does is truly casual. He's got a great poker face, but it's more as if he's eternally lying in wait for something, patiently still, ready to pounce.

I've only seen him pounce once. I didn't enjoy it.

"Ouch," he said, noticing my broken curio cabinet. I'd had to cruise every room before I saw it, but he took it in first thing. "They got the girls?"

"Thoroughly." I watched him cross to the rubble. I'd been straightening, but I hadn't gotten to that yet. Once I cleaned it up, I might as well throw it all away—nothing left to save. I wasn't sure I felt ready for that.

"Bastards." Lex picked up the round, faceless head of my Willendorfesque Venus—a piece he'd given me when I got my doctorate. We hadn't even been dating at the time. But he'd sent me the statue for my collection anyway, managing in true Lex fashion to choose something that, despite my best sense, I couldn't bear to return.

"Luckily none of it was original."

"This was," he said.

I gaped at him.

He shrugged, dropped the chunk of rock back onto the carpet, and brushed his fingers on his neatly pressed, thousand-dollar slacks. "You know my family collects antiques."

Yes, I knew. Beyond last year's corporate espionage trial, and his still-murky role, his family's antique collection was one more reason to distrust the Stuarts. Considering my own family's connection to certain relics, that is. Now this.

"You gave me an original piece of Paleolithic sculpture?" Not counting what something like that would fetch at auction, hadn't it belonged in a museum? Was owning it even *legal?*

The Stuarts never had constrained themselves with something so mundane as legalities.

"So did they take anything?" Lex answered my question with his avoidance. "Or was it simple vandalism?"

They were looking for something. The dumped drawers, the gutted cushions, the carpet pulled away from the corners... It was the only logical explanation. I hadn't cleaned enough of the damage for someone as smart as Lex to miss that, either. *And they hated my goddesses.* Any guesses?

"I haven't found anything missing," I said, noncommittal. "But it's hard to tell, this early."

We eyed each other, letting the silence stretch. Me, because I had theories I wanted to protect awhile longer. Him...who could tell? Maybe he had secrets, too. Or it could just be his love of a good competition.

Either way, neither of us 'fessed up to anything.

He turned away first—though it may have been a simple courtesy. "You really need a monitored security system, Mag. If you can't afford one, I wish you'd let me—"

Blessedly, my phone rang to cut him off before he tried to buy me yet again. Even during the good times, we generally argued when he did that.

Another ring. He turned away to look at other damage, giving me an illusion of privacy. It wasn't the best circumstance under which to take a phone call, but I didn't want the answering machine to pick up and broadcast anything to him.

Too bad I'd already rehooked the machine. So I answered. "Hello?"

"How soon can you get to France?" Sure enough, it was my cousin Lil—likely on business Lex shouldn't know about.

I used every bit of self-control to say, "I have company. Call you back?"

There was a long pause while she took that in. Then Lil asked, "Is it who I think it is?"

Maybe she's psychic. Maybe she's just really smart. Does there have to be a difference?

I peeked over my shoulder at Lex. He'd decided to make himself useful and was shelving some of my scattered books, scowling at the destruction.

"I think it is."

"I'll call you," she said, and hung up. Quickly. I wondered if she'd gotten off the line before a trace could be run...assuming anybody was running a trace.

She would call back from a different phone, likely using someone else's three-way dialing to confuse matters further. Just in case. We're amateurs at the cloak-and-dagger stuff, but we learn fast. And as much as I hated bowing to that kind of paranoia...well, someone *had* broken in.

Lex turned back to me, solemn, as I set down the phone. His rich hazel eyes didn't flinch. "You used to trust me."

Did he purposefully choose the best way to wound me, or was he just expressing his own pain? I didn't want to do this again. It had hurt both of us too much the last few times. Still, I couldn't *not* answer. "You didn't used to work for your cousin."

He tried a wry smile. "I never said Phil isn't an ass, Mag."

"And yet you cover for him, despite last year's trial."

"In which the charges were dropped." And they had been. Espionage. Perjury. Insider trading. Unfair monopoly.

Like magic.

"After an undisclosed settlement," I reminded him. "That you won't even talk about."

He took a deep breath. "Because I signed a contract of nondisclosure."

"Damned convenient, that. The ends don't always justify the means, Lex. Sometimes the means are everything."

"The stockholders seem happy enough."

I said, "So marry one of the stockholders."

His eyes narrowed. "I was just worried about an old friend, Magdalene. Don't flatter yourself that there's more. Marriage hasn't been on the table for some time."

I forced myself to say, "Good."

That brought him up short. It hadn't been my intention, whether he deserved it or not. And I still didn't know, couldn't possibly guess if he really deserved it.

That's the part that really sucked. Not knowing. And he'd fixed things so I would never know.

"Oh, Lex, I didn't mean it that way." I crossed to his side, torn. An enemy I could fight. An ally I could love. But what could I do with him? "What I meant was, you deserve to be happy, and it clearly isn't happening with me. I just wish—"

But he shut me up by kissing me.

I should probably have fought him off. Slapped his face, kneed him where it hurt, bit his searching tongue. I had my ways. That would teach him to be so damned proprietary.

But I'd missed him, and tonight I needed that kiss far, far too badly to risk any of it.

Lex....

We fit, somehow. Always have. He was my first date, my first kiss, my first time, my first love. He was also my first heartbreak, and second, and third, with a truckload of regret thrown in... And yet his arms gathering me to him felt right on a deeper level than good sense could counter. Such incredible power. Such unfathomable depths.

Such a really great body. The boy was ripped.

When I dug my fingers into his thick, ginger-brown hair and chewed playfully at his lip, he turned to wedge me against the door, never breaking the kiss. His body felt hard and necessary against mine. Alive. Real. *Lex*. My soul knew the taste of him, the feel of him, the scent of his breath. Our heartbeats, pressed chest to breast, seemed to fall into almost instant unison. I opened my mouth to him, slid one knee up over his hip, arched into the brace of his arms, my blood singing.

The telephone rang again, startling me back. "Crap."

Lex steadied himself with the heel of his hand, a solid thunk against the door, but otherwise regained quick control. "Don't worry," he said thickly, licking his lips and swallowing heavily. "I'm well aware this was just a momentary lapse."

That didn't make the reality of it any easier to bear.

"You don't have to work for your family," I pleaded. But I took a step toward the ringing phone as I said it. Talk about your divided loyalties! "No matter what they expect. The money can't be that good...."

He stared at me. Then, surprisingly, he laughed—if a little harshly—and ducked forward to kiss my cheek. "Someday you'll realize just how painfully naive you are, Mag. I hope to God I'm there when it happens."

Oh? "So that you can come to my rescue?" I asked. "Or so that you can say you told me so?"

His eyes crinkled, just a bit—and he let himself out. "Lock up," he called over his shoulder.

The phone screamed yet again as the door shut behind him, then rolled over to the machine. I snatched the handset up, interrupting my own recorded voice. "Yes!"

"So sorry," said Lil, her British accent adding to her sarcastic edge. "Is the need to save the world for womankind getting in the way of your date with Satan?"

"Don't call him that." Maybe I should be beyond defending him. I'm not. "We don't know anything for sure."

Lil's voice gentled. "We know enough, Maggi."

And she was right. In the end, it no longer mattered what I felt for Lex Stuart or what he felt for me.

I was still one of an ancient line of women charged with the protection of sacred, secret chalices. Chalices that could, if legend was to be believed, heal the world—male *and* female. Holy Grails, every one of them.

And Lex came from a family rumored to be bent on destroying them.

It's my first week in kindergarten. I already hate Alex Stuart. He thinks he's better than all the other kids.

When he won't let Freddy Morgan use the yellow paint, Freddy cries. Freddy's a wimp, but it makes me mad anyway.

"You're suppose to share," I tell Alex.

He looks surprised. "Only losers share."

At five, I'm pretty simple. "Give Freddy your paint. He needs to make his sun yellow."

Alex says, "You can't tell me what to do. You're just a girl."

So I hit him, right across the face. After a moment of clear surprise, he hits me back. The class gasps—hasn't he heard that boys aren't supposed to hit girls?

My cheek hurts, but I'm glad. I want to win fair. I shove him to the ground, and then we're rolling across butcher paper and through fingerpaints, pummeling uselessly at each other—and laughing. It's fun! We're purple and green and very, very yellow. But we're still hitting each other between grins.

Then our teacher pulls us apart. Alex's dad uses the incident as an excuse to send Alex to private school.

I don't see him again for seven years.

Chapter 2

"Listen," Lil said. "This is bigger than your twisted love/hate thing with Lex Stuart. Aunt Bridge is in the hospital."

"What?" Our great-aunt Brigitte was a historical sociologist in Paris. Even more than our mothers and our late grandmother, Aunt Bridge had convinced Lil and me of the truth in the Grail Keeper legends. "Is it her heart?"

"No, she was attacked in her office. Someone beat her pretty badly."

My mouth opened, but no sound came out. I wanted to sit, but most of my furniture was gutted or broken. So I sank back against the wall and slid down it, my gym shorts riding up, until I sat on the carpet, picturing Bridge's face. She was in her eighties! What kind of sick person would hurt an old woman?

"This is connected to her work, isn't it?"

"She isn't conscious yet, but the Paris police say that her laptop's gone, and some of her papers. You've been working with her, Mag. What was she writing about this time?"

"She's calling it The *Faerie Goddess in Early Gaul.*"

"The fairy Melusine?" Lil and I had grown up on that story. Just imagine *The Little Mermaid* with bat wings and a traitorous husband.

"If she's right, the *goddess* Melusine." But I was staring at the destruction around me with increased concern. "Uh, Lil? Don't freak, but someone just broke into my place, too."

"What?" Even without the phone, I might've heard Lil's shout all the way from England. "Are you all right?"

"Yes, but I haven't looked at my files yet. The computer was on, and I always turn it off when I leave."

Lil said, "You'd better check, Mag."

I did. But I took Lex's advice and locked the door first. Sure enough, my latest backups were missing.

"I've got to go to my office," I said, grim, when I picked up the phone. "On campus."

"Why not just call security?"

"And say what? My aunt at the Sorbonne was robbed, so I'm worried about Connecticut? We're between semesters. They only have a skeleton staff. I'll go myself. Then I'll go to Paris."

"Be careful, Maggi," Lil pleaded. "I hate when you do this stuff alone."

But, picking up the business card Officer Sofie Douglas had left on my desk, I suspected I might not have to.

Beside her home number she'd doodled a simple *O*.

Secret societies are a bitch.

It doesn't help that the scattering of women called Grail Keepers aren't organized enough to actually be an organization. Most still don't even know there are others out there. We have few written records, no official roll of members, no regular meetings and no inner sanctum.

That's by design.

Our information comes from word-of-mouth, mother to child; from truths hidden in superstitions, fairy stories and nursery rhymes. It's only been in the last few years that Lil and I, spurred on by our *grand-mère*'s dying wish, started using the Internet to find and coordinate some of the diverse women who make up our roster.

Or who would, if we kept a roster, which we don't.

Even before that, though, Grail Keepers had an ancient technique for recognizing each other. It's similar to how early Christians used to self-identify, back when their beliefs could get them fed to the lions—one person would draw an arch in the dust, and the other would draw an intersecting arch, and the result would be that simple fish design you now see on the back ends of cars. Scuff out the design, and nobody but those two people would be the wiser.

We do something similar with circles.

One woman draws a circle. The other draws an intersecting circle, and *voilà*—you have an ancient design, like a sloppy number eight, that represents the overlapping of worlds. Not that we knew this as children. Back then, it was just a rhyme game our mommies taught us: *"Circle to circle, never an end, cup and cauldron, ever a friend."*

Now that I'm all grown up and educated, I know the symbol is called a *vesica piscis* or a "chalice-well" design, after the famous version at the well at Glastonbury Abbey. Like on wedding-ring quilt patterns. Like on my pendant.

Hence my interest in Officer Sofie's card.

Jogging to my blue Mini for the second time that night, I wished I'd had time to draw the second circle on Sofie Douglas's card and hand it back to her. That would've been subtler, safer. I didn't. So I phoned her on my hands-free mobile as I sped down the highway and simply said, "This is Maggi. From tonight?"

"I remember." She sounded carefully noncommittal. It being after midnight, I couldn't blame her.

"I found your card and, well…" Talk about feeling awkward. "Circle to circle?"

For a moment I feared my connection had cut out. Then—

"Never an end," she whispered, surprised. Not that I blamed her. The first time's like learning the Tooth Fairy's real.

"I thought you should know I'm heading to Turbeville Hall on campus, and that there might be trouble."

When I arrived she had already parked outside the four-story building that houses the academic offices. I felt a twinge of concern when I saw the unfamiliar car, but then she got out, still wearing her uniform. And her hip holster. Carrying a monster flashlight.

I liked this woman.

As I got out of the car, she shone her light onto the asphalt at my feet. Her voice shook slightly against a background of crickets and a jet flying overhead. "'Circle to circle, never an end?'"

Relieved, I switched on my own flashlight and slid the pool of light partially across hers, stopping when they overlapped halfway. "'Cup to cauldron, ever a friend.'"

Vesica piscis. Drawn in light on the pavement. Our version of a secret handshake.

"I can't believe this really works." Sofie shook her head. "I thought it was just a fairy tale my grammy made up."

I shifted my keychain so keys stuck out between my fingers, just in case, and strode toward the building's front door. Final exams had ended last week, and we'd turned in grades yesterday. The place looked dead, so I assumed it would be locked. "Follow me, and I'll explain what I know."

She quickly caught up. "Why?"

Why explain, or why follow?

"Because knowledge is power," I said. "The kind of power that just increases when you share it. And because someone I know was attacked in her college office this week."

"Good..." Her voice fell softer as the door swung open into the empty lobby.

I hadn't used my key yet.

"...reason," she finished grimly. "I should call this in."

"I need to check on something first." My whisper echoed.

Sofie said, "Just keep talking, Maggi Sanger."

So I did, heading for the stairs instead of the elevator. "Your grammy told you a story about the Great Queen, right?"

Lil and I hadn't met a Grail Keeper yet who hadn't heard some version of that story.

"The one with seven daughters?" she asked.

"Sometimes it's nine." I sprinted up the stairs. "I've heard it with as few as three and as many as thirteen. But the queen always sends her daughters off into the world, and she always gives each one the same gift."

"Her own magic cup," Sofie finished, pacing me. "The older I got, the more lame a going-away present that seemed."

"Yeah, well, that's allegory for you." Both Sofie and I were in good shape; our breathing stayed regular. "Did you read in the paper last week about an ancient goblet that was destroyed in the National Museum of New Delhi, India?"

"Nope."

"It wasn't a big news item, so it would be easy to miss—"

She stopped, right there in the stairwell. "A *goblet?*"

"The Kali Cup," I said, breathing just a bit harder. "Or chalice or grail. Scholars believed this cup was used in ancient ceremonies worshipping the goddess Kali. But it was destroyed—smashed—before it could go on display."

I'd felt actual pain, deep in my gut, when I read that.

"And you think that was a magic chalice sent out with some great queen's daughter?" Sofie blinked. "Reality check. That's just a fairy tale."

"I used to think that, too. But if you had to pass along information in a way that would seem harmless to the people in power, what better form than fairy tales and nursery rhymes?"

She started climbing again, absorbing it all. "You're saying the Great Queen story was true."

I said, "All I know for sure is that since my cousin and I started looking, we've found a lot of women who were raised the way you and I were—'circle to circle.' With the Kali Cup gone, we're starting to wonder if some people weren't raised to hate or fear those chalices."

"Why?" she asked. "Unless they're really magic, I mean. History can't hurt anybody."

I held up a cautious hand as we emerged onto the third floor. Emergency lights cast the long hallway into shadows, brightened only by the red eye of an exit sign.

I whispered, "Tell that to my great-aunt Brigitte."

We made our way down the dark hallway, past the occasional row of plastic chairs. My office stood at the far end, so we got to pass all the other doors—all the possible hiding places. None of the doors had a window, even a peephole.

Taking a deep breath to slow my pulse, I slipped my key into the lock and turned it.

Sofie caught my hand. "Let me."

Since she was the one with the gun, I nodded. I stepped back while she pressed a shoulder against the doorjamb, crooked her arm so that her pistol pointed toward the acoustic ceiling tiles, slowly turned the knob—

And burst into the office in one abrupt, practiced move. "Police!"

Her shout bounced back down the hallway. Nothing.

I peeked around the jamb, relieved. It was just my office, darker than usual and straightened up for the summer break.

No books strewn across the floor. No computer monitor lying on its face. No mysterious bad guy lurking in the darkness.

With a last look around the office, Sofie holstered her weapon. "That plays better when there's a perp waiting."

I went in, turning on the light. "Better you than me. I never much liked guns. Weapons are too patriarchal."

She grunted, stepped inside, and examined my décor—a framed illumination of Chaucer's Wife of Bath from *Canterbury Tales;* stone fleur-de-lis over the window; an imitation suit of armor in the corner with a mortarboard balanced on his tin head.

Above the inside of the door hung a slim, sheathed sword, not quite Asian enough to clash with the rest of the office.

Sofie looked meaningfully back at me.

I shrugged. "Well, we do live in a patriarchy now."

I reached for the power button on my CPU, to check my files—then abruptly stopped, opening my hand to splay it across the computer case.

Wait a minute.

Warmth tickled my palm. "Someone's been here."

"What?" Even as she asked it, Sofie's head came up and she was on guard again, glancing more closely at the filing cabinets, the bookshelves, the knight.

Anything that might hide an intruder.

"It's warm." I straightened, leaving the computer alone. *"Someone was just here."*

I switched off the lights and went to the window. My office overlooked the campus quadrangle, not the parking lot. Still, the walkways were wide enough that service vehicles could use them for maintenance.

And sure enough—

"Son of a bitch," I whispered, staring down at the dark car that waited smugly, not fifty feet from the building.

In a moment Sofie stood beside me. "Plymouth. Current model. Looks empty. I can't see the license from this high up."

"Then we need to get back down." Now. A few minutes ago.

"Let me go first," she said, heading for the door.

She stopped when I opened the window and said, "No."

My office was too far from the stairway. It made sense to hurry. What if the car left before we made it down?

Leaning out, I had to really stretch, balancing on my stomach across the sill to reach the drainpipe I knew was there. Good thing I'd stretched out by swimming laps tonight.

"Are you *crazy?*" demanded Sofie.

I'd seen students climb this pipe more than once, despite regulations and safety concerns. I knew it would hold my weight. Probably. Then again, here I was grasping a copper drainpipe as I eased my knees out a window into sheer air, three stories up. So *was* I crazy?

Who knows? I've been wrong before.

I centered and balanced in order to slowly raise myself, then precariously stand on the windowsill. I touched the top of the sash for balance, then slowly shifted my center of gravity across to the drainpipe, my chest brushing ivy-laced brick. Just before the step of no return, I remembered that I was wearing sandals. I caught the heel strap of each on the inside of the windowsill to pull them off, one at a time.

One fell into the office. The other slid out the window, spinning in freefall down into the hedge at the base of the building, three floors below me.

Yeah. *Gulp*.

Not that I could've gotten back in if I'd wanted to. By now, gravity had pretty much committed me. Tightening my hold on the pipe, I swung my feet and knees across to straddle it. My toe caught on an edge of ivy. Stone bit into my soles. For a brief moment I simply clung there, deepening my breathing.

I'm in pretty good shape, but there's a reason chin-ups measure men's strength better than women's.

Aunt Bridge, I thought firmly, breathing strength into my arms as I glanced down at the mysterious car. *Sons of bitches*.

Holding the pipe with my knees, I let go with one hand to reach down. I slid some—*mostly controlled*—then reached down with the other hand. The copper pipe felt cool and coarse under my palms as I descended, hand under hand. My arms vibrated with the strain, and my knees dragged against brick and ivy. I looked up and saw my window empty; Sofie had vanished. I looked down and couldn't see where my sandal had landed.

Within ten feet of the ground I thought, *Close enough*. I probably could have slid—like a fireman's pole but with ridges. Instead I pushed away in a leap and landed in a low, shock-absorbing crouch.

My bare feet safe on manicured grass, I straightened and spun for a better look at the dark car's license plate. X1—

Then something hard pressed against the base of my skull— something like a gun—and my priorities shifted accordingly.

Chapter 3

"That's better," murmured a deep, muffled voice.

Not from my side, it wasn't. I don't like guns.

For a moment I couldn't breathe. Not good.

"Fairy tales aren't real, lady," the man said in a smooth baritone. "And little girls break very easily."

Breathe, damn it! You'd think, after training for years in Tai Chi, I wouldn't clutch like this. Admittedly, some see Tai Chi as the Hello Kitty of martial arts, but you'd be surprised at its uses on the expert level. Unfortunately, Tai Chi requires a little thing called breath.

Then the man said, "That's a good girl."

I snorted with disbelief—which got me breathing.

Which made me dangerous.

I didn't just have my balance—I owned it. I dropped my center of gravity. I spun, raising a hand, readying to redirect baritone's gun into a safe direction as I took it, and—

"Police! Freeze!"

Damn. Sofie's command surprised both of us. Worse, she stood where I'd planned to divert the gun. Using her distraction, I rerouted my movement into a full turn, stepping free from baritone and out of Sofie's line of fire.

My new friend stood, dark and deadly, pistol pointed.

More guns. Goody. But I got a look at my attacker—tall,

broad-shouldered, nice suit. *Very* nice suit. I should know, what with the company I've kept.

Interesting choice for breaking and entering.

It didn't go with his black ski mask at all.

"Ladies," warned baritone, glancing between Sofie and me, "You do *not* want to go there."

Sofie said, "Put down the weapon and back away."

Apparently not one to take orders, he swung his gun toward her. But I stepped smoothly back into Sofie's line of fire and slipped his legs out from under him as he shot.

Four ounces of strength against a ton of force, as my *sifu* says. *Appear, then disappear.* You just have to sense your opponent's weakness and know where to tap.

Baritone landed on the concrete with a surprised grunt and his shot—to judge by a crash of breaking window glass—went wild. Sofie lunged forward, shoving her pistol into his face. "Drop the damn gun!"

His fingers opened. His pistol clunked to the concrete.

Then I heard the sound of an engine, behind us.

"Down!" With a leap and a twist, I tackled Sofie to the walkway and rolled us behind a bench. More windows in Turbeville Hall exploded in a barrage of thorough gunfire.

The Plymouth hadn't been empty after all.

"Damn!" Sofie yelled over the chaos, while baritone snatched his gun and ran. Maybe she could still have risked shooting him—if she wanted to shoot him in the back. He wasn't our immediate threat anymore. Instead, she fired at the car once, twice, again.

The Plymouth's passenger door opened, baritone leaped in, and it peeled down the service walkway. The last of the gunfire came from us.

"Damn!" Sofie repeated into the otherworldly silence that followed. We both sat up slowly, blinking against the heavy haze of gunsmoke. Nearby, from the hall, an afterthought of glass crashed from a broken window onto the ground. "If you'd gotten his gun, we could've printed it."

That had been my idea, before she showed up with her admittedly expert grasp of the patriarchal value of weapons. I said, "X146."

Sofie stared, then grinned. "You got the license?"

"The first four characters, anyway."

"You go, girl!" She removed her radio from her belt, but I touched her wrist. "Don't even think it," she warned.

"I know you've got to call it in, and I know I've got to stay here for the report," I assured her. "But do me a favor. Don't mention my name on the emergency band."

"Because…?"

"Because I know someone who might be monitoring it. Or has other people doing the monitoring for him. I don't want to see him a second time tonight."

Her dark eyes whitened. *"Lex Stuart?"*

That was no psychic hunch. "I *knew* it. He *was* behind all the attention the police gave me tonight, wasn't he?"

"What've you got that has a man like Alexander Stuart throwing his weight around over a simple break-in?"

"It's complicated."

She grinned, clearly sensing a good story. "Let me just make this call," she said.

"'Little girls break very easily,'" I said, after Sofie disconnected.

She eyed me dubiously. "Come again?"

"That's what our gunman said. Not, 'real easy,' but 'very easily.' He's got a formal education…and an expensive tailor."

"So you're thinking he wasn't just here to tag the building and maybe rip off some vending machines?"

"I'm thinking he was here to get my information on Melusine."

"Meli-who?"

"A French fairy-goddess my aunt and I are researching. Either someone with a lot of clout doesn't want us finding it, or they want to find it first so they can destroy it."

"'It' being…?"

"The Melusine Chalice," I clarified. "Her 'holy grail.'"

We could hear sirens in the distance. This was going to be a long night, wasn't it?

"I thought there was only one Holy Grail," said Sofie.

"That's in the classic version." I wiped my palms where I'd scraped them on concrete, glanced toward the glass-littered bushes, and decided my shoe was history. "The Christian grail, there's only one. Goddess legends aren't so exclusive."

"And some guys with a lot of clout would care because…?"

I was having trouble with that one, too. "Because they feel threatened? Or maybe…" My logical side winced. "Maybe they've heard the legends, that if enough of the goddess cups are brought together, woman-power in this world will increase a hundredfold?"

"Now that," said Sofie, as several blue-and-whites sped into the parking lot, "would be sweet."

We both raised our hands to show we were unarmed, and I nodded toward the mostly male police officers who clambered out of the cars.

I nodded toward her colleagues. "Ask them sometime if they agree it would be sweet. They'll think we're talking about power over them."

Which made it our problem, even if they were mistaken.

Over the next four hours I filled out reports, gave statements and reassured my suspicious college president of my minimal involvement. My office was fingerprinted and, thanks to my "after my files" story, my computer taken as evidence.

Somehow, amidst it all, I managed to book a flight to Paris the next day. I got home with barely enough time to pack some necessities, like my passport and my emergency cash, before the airport shuttle picked me up.

I hated leaving my apartment in a mess. But at least

carrying just a backpack meant I wouldn't have to check luggage.

By the time I made it through the extensive security check and was jogging down the International Terminal, I felt the exhaustion, hunger and stress of the previous night's events.

The last person I needed to hear calling my name as I dodged travelers in my sprint for the gate was Lex Stuart.

"Maggi?"

It was too huge a coincidence to ignore. I turned in the terminal and, sure enough, he was striding toward me. The crowd seemed to part for him, as if instinctively sensing his importance. He looked good, tall and fit and collected. It didn't hurt that his eyes brightened just for me.

He could be a bad guy, my head warned me.

Or he might not, insisted my heart. *Not Lex.*

"This is a surprise." Lex slowed as he reached me. Even after years with him, I wasn't sure.

And I still had a plane to catch.

When I started walking again, reluctantly taking advantage of the clear space around him, he paced me.

"Are you all right?" he asked politely.

"Why wouldn't I be?"

He didn't quite shrug, but it was implied. "Because your apartment got broken into last night?"

Oh, yeah. That. "I'm fine. How are you?"

He ignored my formality. "I regret how I behaved."

The kiss? Or the argument? "Oh…"

"That's one reason I've missed you so badly this last year. You've always been my touchstone."

"So your own moral compass is still on the blink, huh?"

That wrung a hint of a smile from him. "I only mean to say, you were already having a stressful night. Please accept my apology for complicating matters."

Proper and polite to the end. But I'd helped, with the argument and the kiss both. Fair was fair. "Apology accepted."

Except that we were approaching my gate—and he was

slowing down too. Just out of courtesy, right? To see me off? Except—

He drew a boarding pass from his jacket pocket. "You're going to Paris, too? I'm guessing you're in coach."

I stared. I wasn't ready for proof that my suspicions were warranted. But this couldn't be coincidence…could it?

What the hell. "Have you ever heard the name Melusine?"

He glanced toward the gate, making sure we had time. "Isn't she some kind of medieval mermaid?"

My heart flinched. He *had* heard of her!

"You mentioned her in your report on the women of Camelot, in the seventh grade," he continued easily; if he was covering his guilt, he was really, really good. "You compared her to the Lady of the Lake, right?"

"You remember that?"

"We *did* work on it together, Mag." We'd split the workload by gender. His report on the men of Camelot had lingered on the subject of the Holy Grail. He'd compared an Irish legend, Nuada of the Silver Hand, to the Fisher King of the classic grail quest.

"There weren't a lot of high points to the seventh grade," Lex said, sounding heartfelt. "But you were one of them. Let me upgrade your seat to first class, and you can tell me all about Melusine and your research and your trip—"

"No." I hated the suspicion that kept me from saying yes. Foolish or not, I still liked him…or more.

But he wasn't just a Stuart. He was a Stuart on my flight, feeling me out about my research.

Did *he* have to pull a gun on me before I learned caution?

"I'll use my frequent-flyer miles," Lex offered, pushing it. "You know how many of those I rack up."

I shook my head, hesitation hard in my throat.

"For God's sake, Mag, I'm not trying to buy you."

A gate agent announced that they were boarding first-class passengers and passengers in need of assistance. I was neither. "Enjoy your flight, Lex."

His eyes narrowed, suddenly dangerous. "I don't know what's happened to you this last year, Maggi, or what kind of crowd you've gotten involved with. But whatever and whoever it is, it sure isn't an improvement."

At my resolute silence, Lex turned away and offered his boarding pass to the gate agent. Maybe ten minutes later my section was called, and I boarded with the other peons, carefully not looking at him...

Just enough of a glance to tell that he, comfortably settled in an oversize leather seat with a cocktail in his hand, wasn't looking at me, either. The seat beside him was empty, spacious and inviting.

I continued past, found my seat and manhandled my backpack into an overhead compartment, glad for an excuse to vent my frustration. I slid into a middle seat, between a large businessman and a teenager bobbing to his Discman.

I dug my cell phone out of my purse to turn it off.

One missed call, it read.

I thumbed a button and read my aunt Bridge's mobile number. The screen then read, *1 new voice message.*

While other passengers boarded, I retrieved the message.

"Lilith says you're coming here," my aunt Bridge wheezed, weak from more than her years as a smoker. Much of my frustration melted under my gratitude that she was even conscious. "I thought you would. My assistant will meet your flight. Be careful, *chou.* It may be worse than we feared."

That was it? I checked the display, to make sure I still had a signal. I used the code to replay the message.

That was it.

"Miss?" It was the flight attendant. "We ask that you turn off all electronic devices during takeoff, and keep your cell phone off for the duration of the flight."

I switched my phone off while she turned her attention to my neighbor's Discman. Then, before stowing my purse beneath the seat in front of me, I exchanged the phone for the one set of notes that nobody had gotten—because they were handwritten.

And because I'd had them on me—a pile of scribble-filled index cards wrapped in a rubber band—the whole time.

"Melusine," I read, ignoring the flight attendant's safety presentation. "Goddess of Betrayal."

The plane taxied awkwardly, like an albatross, back from the gate.

I read right through take-off, searching for something. Anything. Had someone stolen mine and Brigitte's notes just to learn about Melusine? Or was it more likely that they hoped to find her grail, like with the recently destroyed Kali Cup? If so, they wouldn't find the most useful clues in our notes. Writing down the rhyme we'd been taught as children would seem as silly as writing down the words to "Little Miss Muffet."

"Three fair figures," the rhyme starts. *"Side by side…"*

No, I didn't need my notes for that. Nor did I need them to understand how Melusine had gone from goddess to fairy tale. Few things just vanish, after all.

But how she could also have changed from a kick-ass symbol of female empowerment to a woman whose man had done her wrong…. That made less sense. Frustrated, I put my seat back and closed my eyes, meditating on it…accessing my Grail Keeper knowledge, passed down mother to daughter for centuries.

Mom had told me the Melusine story from my infancy. Grand-mère and Aunt Bridge had elaborated on it as my cousin Lil and I got older, adding some of the naughty parts.

"Once upon a time…"

The basic story is this. Melusine was a fairy of such beauty that, when a French count came across her bathing in the river, he fell instantly in love. But she'd been cursed with a secret, so she would only marry the count if he agreed to leave her alone, every Saturday night, and never ask about it. He gladly agreed.

They married. She magically built whole castles for him overnight, and they had ten children. Legends vary on the family that resulted—the Lusignans of southern France are the top contenders, closely followed by the Angevins who later became Kings of England and even the royal family of Luxembourg. No matter how you slice it, she birthed a powerful people.

But she had that secret curse. Every Saturday, Melusine changed. She grew a snake tail and bat wings, and could relieve her suffering only by splashing around in a bath, safe in her solitude, until the episode passed.

You can guess the rest, right? The count broke his promise and saw her secret. And Melusine flew out the window, cursed by his betrayal to remain in her serpentine form for eternity.

They did *not* live happily ever after. In fact, legend holds that every time a Lusignan count was about to die, Melusine could be heard screaming, banshee-like, outside the tower she'd once helped build. Until someone tore it down, anyway.

A fascinating story. But…had she really once been a *goddess?*

Until this week, my main purpose for researching Melusine remained academic. I wanted to compare her tale with other legends, in hopes of finding an unchanging base myth to all of them. Aunt Bridge was advancing her research on medieval goddess cults by focusing on the group of French women who had worshipped the Mother Goddess in the form of the fairy Melusine.

The idea that those women had really hidden a chalice, much less that we could find it…that had been an amusement. We were Grail *Keepers,* as our mothers' mothers had been for centuries. Keepers of the secrets of the goddess grails.

We weren't Grail*getters.*

Now someone was after our information. And if what

had happened to the Kali Cup in New Delhi was any warning…

We had to find the cup first. The chalice that Melusine worshippers would have used and which they would have hidden by the time of the medieval witch burnings.

Edit that; *I* had to find the cup.

I'm embarrassed to admit that the next thing I knew, I was drawing a deep breath and waking to an announcement, in French, that we had started our descent toward Charles de Gaulle. The previous night must have wiped me out, for me to sleep through six hours and at least one meal service.

I cracked my eyes open and saw that at some point I'd been covered with a thick, rich blanket. Mmm; nice service on this flight. Except…

A few other passengers also had blankets, and theirs were fairly thin and flimsy.

Mine was a first-class blanket.

Suspicion contracted my chest. Did that mean…?

My notes! I clenched my hand instinctively, sitting bolt upright. My fingers closed on rubber-wrapped index cards. Maybe Lex hadn't come back here. Maybe the flight attendants just ran out of coach-class blankets.

Then something small and hard slid off my lap.

It was a small box of gourmet chocolates. The kind they give out in first class. The kind Lex had always passed on to me after his business trips…back when we were together.

In the seventh grade, Alexander Stuart inexplicably returns to public school. He's no longer a bully; instead, he keeps to himself. I'm one of the few people he'll speak to, maybe because I stood up to him in kindergarten.

When he sits out PE, we think he's getting special treatment. Same with all his absences. None of us guesses he's sick until the day he comes to school with his head shaved.

This, of course, is when kids stop calling him Alex and start calling him Lex Luthor. He ignores them.

Our teacher does not. One afternoon when he's gone, she tells us Alexander has leukemia. He could die. That's why his parents want him home with them. We must not tease him.

Kids can be cruel. But not all kids. Not most of us.

Lex notices the change, the sympathetic looks, the students who hang back as if leukemia—or mortality—are contagious. He notices the return of his name. "Hi, Alex." "How are you feeling, Alex?" "Hey, Alex, what's up?"

I see his sharp hazel eyes go from confusion to to realization to fury at becoming an object of pity. Finally, during English, he stands up. "Miss Mason? I want everyone to call me Lex."

Miss Mason doesn't understand. "Now, Alex..."

"That's what I want." There he stands with his military-school posture, a twelve-year-old outsider, skinny, bald. I suspect just how exhausted he must be, how sick he must feel. But he prefers mockery to sympathy.

"No, Alex," says Miss Mason. "I won't allow it."

He continues to stand, demoted from sick to helpless by her condescension. An ache grips my throat. It doesn't seem right.

So I say, "Fine, Lex. Just sit down and shut up, okay?"

Several students turn to me in amazement, but I don't pay attention to them. I'm watching how Lex's quiet, hazel eyes slide toward me.

"Did you hear me?" I challenge. "Lex?"

And with a nod of quiet satisfaction, he sits.

"Maggi Sanger!" protests Miss Mason.

"As long as he's going to act like a jerk, why not let him be an archvillain?"

Of course I'm sent to the principal. But I also get a glimpse of Lex Stuart's rare smile. He's waiting outside the almost empty school building when I get out of detention. A black limousine owns the parking lot not five spaces from my mother's minivan.

"We're doing group reports for social studies," he says. "I chose Camelot. Will you partner with me?"

I wait. I know I am not a particularly attractive twelve-year-old. I'm chubby, and my hair is usually messy from running and playing.

He looks intrigued. "Please?"

"Sure," I say. "Lex."

He almost smiles. He has preferred "Lex" ever since.

Alex was a victim.

Lex is a survivor.

Chapter 4

Standing in line for customs, my backpack slung comfortably over one shoulder, I caught glimpses of Lex's long suit coat half a line ahead of me. Surely he was just being chivalrous with the blanket and chocolate? He wasn't *spying*, living up to his archvillain moniker, was he?

Could he possibly do both?

It wasn't lack of time or opportunity that kept me from asking. Nor was it cowardice or embarrassment. We'd been lovers at one time, remember?

Nope. I held my tongue because I couldn't think of a way to confront him without tipping my hand. On the very low chance he'd seen my notes, at least he hadn't taken any; I'd checked that on the plane. Better to err on the side of discretion.

Especially while guards stood by with automatic weapons.

By the time I left the secured area, Lex was greeting yet another reason for not trusting him.

His cousin Phil, CEO, prince regent of the family business.

Phil Stuart was stocky and harsh-featured, right down to his crooked nose. He purposefully wore his tawny hair too long. His suit was more expensive than Lex's, but not as understated. Phil was the kind of businessman who put the *filthy* back into *filthy lucre*—and yet Lex was one of his staunchest supporters.

Having someone save your life with his own bone marrow will do that.

I turned to scan the waiting crowd. Aunt Bridge's assistant would be a college-age girl, right? I noticed one young blonde, but she threw her arms wide to greet my Discman seat mate and they began making out, right there in the airport. Okay, probably not her.

I felt either Lex or Phil watching me, but didn't want to look paranoid by turning. I continued studying the crowd. When I saw my name on a piece of cardboard, I looked up.

Oh, my…goddess.

The person who held it was older than standard college age by about a decade.

He was also a guy.

Other than being tall—lanky, really—the man holding the sign that read "Magdalene Sanger" could have been the anti-Lex. He wore broken-in jeans the way only cowboys and Europeans can, and a loose T-shirt. His shaggy black hair looked finger combed, and he didn't seem to have shaved that morning. When his gaze met mine, I saw his eyes were a bright blue.

They smiled at me in welcome, even bluer. And yet something in that smile seemed unapproachable. Amiable but off-limits. Probably married…even if he wasn't wearing a ring.

Then he lowered the sign to step forward and greet me, offering a slim, bony hand, and surprised me further.

Because he wore a prominent crucifix around his neck. And his quiet greeting as he ducked his head toward me, in a thick Celtic accent, was "Circle to circle?"

"A *guy* Grail Keeper?" I asked Aunt Brigitte as soon as Rhys Pritchard politely left us alone at the Hôpital Américain de Paris. He'd said he would bring back tea.

"It is not impossible," my great-aunt murmured from where her folded bed propped her up. Her neck was in a brace, her arm in a cast. One of her eyes had swollen purple, to match the side of her face. It hurt to look at her, but I looked at her anyway, gently holding her free hand. If she could survive the beating, I could survive the evidence of it.

"His mother is from a Welsh line of Keepers," Aunt Bridge continued. "As she taught his sisters the stories, he learned them as well. Would you have had her exclude him just for being a boy? Would you have *me* do so?"

"No! I just would have thought he'd be a bit too…"

I didn't stop myself in time.

"I'd be a bit too what?" teased Rhys, peeking in the cracked door. His smile didn't falter as he carried in two cardboard cups of tea, letting the door swing shut behind him. "I would have knocked, but my hands were full."

"I'm sorry," I said immediately. "I was being nosy."

He put the other cup of tea on the rolling table that spanned Aunt Bridge's bed and retrieved her straw from a plastic cup of water. "No offense is taken."

"Not just that, but…" Might as well admit it. "I'm sorry, but I was going to say, too Christian."

Rhys and Aunt Bridge exchanged a significant look.

"What?" I demanded, immediately suspicious.

"Beliefs need not be exclusive. You know that I'm Catholic myself," said my aunt, despite how badly she'd been treated after her divorce in the fifties. "Almost every cathedral built in medieval Europe was named Nôtre Dame for a reason. Not just to praise the Virgin, but to fill a void left by the banished goddess worship."

"I know," I said. "I was jumping to unfair conclusions."

Rhys hitched himself onto a table, since I had the room's only chair. "Are you a goddess worshipper, then?"

I hated that question because I hated my own less-than-logical answer. "I'm not sure."

He took a sip of tea, clearly surprised.

"I'm still figuring it out. In the meantime…calling it research feels safer."

"You're quite the honest woman, aren't you?"

Some days I believed that more than others. "Are you studying the goddess grails along with Aunt Bridge?"

"My main interest," he admitted, "is the Holy Grail."

I could hear the capitalization, even in speech, and put down my tea for fear of spilling it. "*The* Holy Grail? The cup-of-the-Last-Supper, sought-by-King-Arthur's-greatest-champions *Holy Grail?*"

"That's the one," he said, with that great lilt of his. "Like in Monty Python, but with less inherent wackiness."

I grinned.

"Rhys believes that his grail may be hidden among the remains of the goddess culture," said Aunt Bridge.

"The church did try to suppress the Grail legends along with other heresies," he agreed. "The Templars. The Cathars. The Gnostic gospels. I'm merely seeking the truth."

Or maybe he meant, the Truth. "And you honestly think you'll find the cup of the Last Supper was hidden by old goddess worshippers?"

"British legend holds that Joseph of Aramathea brought the Grail west, after the crucifixion," he told me. "But the French have a different legend."

Ah, yes. "That Mary Magdalene brought it to Marseilles."

He nodded. "It's worth investigating."

"So it's settled," Aunt Bridge declared. "Rhys will go with you to get the Melusine Chalice."

"Wait," I protested. "The Melusine Chalice is no longer safe where our ancestors hid it, not with whoever stole our files going in search of it. But what are we supposed to do once we have it? Are we going to hide it again and create a whole new nursery rhyme for future generations?"

Somehow, even drinking hot tea through a straw, Aunt Bridge managed to look wise. "Remember, dear. The grails were hidden only until the world became ready for their return. Your *grand-mère* and I, we discussed this a great deal before she died. It is a new millennium. Women have greater power and freedom than ever in recorded history. Perhaps that time is now."

"And what if we're mistaken? What if we just make it easier for some bad guys to destroy it, like they did Kali's?"

She attempted a pained smile, crooked on her swollen face. "You think too much. Trust your heart. There may be a reason this is happening now, a reason you're involved."

I believed that, to a point. But that point ended where logic began. I still had to find the chalice. That was no longer debatable. But until I did, we needn't make a firm decision about what to do with it, right?

A lot depended on where we found it. Knowledge of the Melusine Chalice, and the responsibility to protect it, belonged to Grail Keepers, but the chalice itself...that was anybody's guess. Instead of arguing further, I said, "But why bring Rhys? I don't need a male escort."

Rhys laughed. "I don't believe I've been called *that*."

"I mean a protector." But I had to grin at his deliberate misunderstanding, as well as the face he made. Lex Stuart, even when he was being funny, came across as solemn, as if he'd taken the weight of the world onto his solid shoulders. Rhys Pritchard...

He's hiding the weight of the world in his heart. My insight surprised and intrigued me—assuming I was correct. He smiled so easily, laughed so easily. I probably wasn't.

"He has been my assistant since I began drafting my book on Melusine. He knows most of what I know," Aunt Bridge insisted, when he opened his mouth to protest. "Since I cannot come with you, and my files have been stolen, he must go. In any case, he has the keys to my car."

I didn't want to be rude. Or ruder. But I glanced toward Rhys and asked her, "You really trust him?"

"Like my parish priest," she said, which for some reason made him frown. They had some kind of secret between them. But clearly they weren't ready to share it.

Either way, her recommendation was good enough for me.

It wasn't like *I'd* been divinely chosen for this myself.

Rhys took the first shift driving. Maybe that's why I didn't notice them at first. I was busy watching dusk settle over the City of Lights, before we reached the A6 motorway.

You can see the Eiffel Tower from anywhere in the city, of course, and other landmarks like Nôtre Dame and the Arc de Triomphe are hard to miss amidst the glitter and the centuries-old bridges crossing the Seine. I loved it. I used to spend a month here every summer with my cousin Lil and our maternal grandmother. Lex once called Paris my *maison* away from *maison*.

It *was* a coincidence, him coming to Paris today. Wasn't it?

"I know to head south," said Rhys, who looked a little long for Aunt Bridge's 3-door Citroën Saxo VTR. "Have you got anything more specific in mind?"

"We might as well start in Lusignan," I said. "Since their claim to Melusine is the strongest."

"Mère Lusigne," he murmured, by way of agreement. That's where some believe Melusine got her name. So he *did* know his stuff. "The closest city would be what, Poitiers? At least we oughtn't to have trouble finding a place to stay. They have that big amusement park, nowadays. Not Disney—the futuristic one."

Good thought. "I'll call ahead for a reservation," I said, reaching for one of the cargo pockets on my pants. "What with all my overseas relatives, I got a satellite phone as soon as they came on the market."

"We can just see what's available when we get there." When I stared silent questions, he admitted, "I don't have a credit card."

"At all?"

"I haven't had time to build a credit history."

I laughed. "What, you've been in prison?"

All Rhys said was, "It's not there I've been."

I shrugged. Aunt Bridge trusted him.

And if she was mistaken, I could probably take him.

"We'll use my credit card," I said, calling Information.

"I can pay my way," he assured me. "I have cash."

This was so unlike any road trip with Lex Stuart that I had to grin at the irony. But after making a reservation at the Holiday Inn, I thought back to Aunt Bridge in that hospital bed, and my sense of humor faltered.

"Why now?" I asked, of the darkening French landscape as much as anything. "Our family has passed down a rhyme about the Melusine Cup for centuries—how did someone suddenly notice us?"

"Brigitte didn't mention her lecture to you?"

I turned to better face him. "What lecture?"

"Three nights ago," he said. "She gave a presentation on *'Le féminin perdu en archéologie du dix-huitième siècle.'*"

"'The lost feminine in eighteenth-century archeology'?"

"How they dismissed the countless goddess figurines they found as dolls or pornography. That's it. At one point, someone in the audience mentioned the Kali Cup. It had just made the news. Some of them thought its destruction was part of a—how did they put it—a patriarchal conspiracy for the continuing subjugation of women. "If destroying the Kali Cup was part of a great masculine conspiracy, I never got my ballot. Should I be insulted, do you think?"

He followed the signs toward Orléans. "I think the trouble started when Brigitte reassured the audience that there were more goddess grails, and that she and her brilliant American niece were working toward locating one in France."

I groaned. "She didn't."

But of course she had. Aunt Bridge never backed down from anything. She had to have known the danger of her announcement. That didn't mean she'd deserved the consequences.

It was the men who'd attacked her who perverted our world, who made it a darker place, not my aunt speaking the truth.

"She threw down the gauntlet, and someone picked it up."

"At the risk of sounding sexist," I said, "were there any other…?"

"Penises there?"

I choked. "Rhys!"

"There were," he assured me. "Quite a few. Assuming the attackers were men in the audience we cannot narrow it down to one or two suspects."

"It wasn't just the men in the audience," I said grimly.

Rhys glanced toward me, intrigued. "Why isn't it?"

"Because they wouldn't have had time to fly to the East Coast and break into my apartment. It has to be some kind of group or association, some kind of…"

"*You* think it's a conspiracy?" Rhys prompted.

But that sounded far too dramatic for my comfort.

About an hour later, we stopped and ate a late dinner outside Orléans—the place Joan of Arc rescued before she got burned as a witch. While Rhys refilled the tank with petrol— his word—I phoned my mother. She insisted on going by my apartment to clean up the damage from the break-in. It wasn't a battle I would easily win, so I forfeited.

When Rhys tossed me the keys to the Saxo, I slid into the driver's seat, adjusted the mirrors and merged us back onto the motorway heading southeast.

I hadn't driven ten kilometers before I noticed it.

There, in the rearview mirror, hovered a dark-green, four-door sedan made of sleek, curved lines.

Like some kind of water creature. Like a shark.

Maybe it was instinct that locked me on to it. Or maybe instinct is just our subconscious noticing something—a driver's face or a suspect maneuver—that our conscious mind hasn't caught on to. At first I hesitated to mention it to Rhys.

What if I was imagining this?

I took the Blois/Vendôme exit, just to test them.

They took the same exit. At the next cross street, I U-turned under the motorway.

They followed. *Crap.*

Rhys inhaled deeply as he sat up, unable to ignore the centrifugal force of my turn. "Is something wrong?"

I turned right, past an anachronistic McDonald's, and divided my attention between the road ahead of me and the car behind me. "What kind of car has a silver lion on its grill?"

"Rampant?" he asked, rubbing a sleepy hand across his face.

"Yeah."

"That would be a Peugeot." Yet another gender stereotype, proven out.

I made another right.

So did they.

I signaled a third right, as if lost—then turned hard left.

They followed. Worse, despite the illusion of activity given by that McDonald's, I'd somehow driven us into a dark, industrial neighborhood. No, no, no! You're supposed to stay in a populous area when you're being tailed.

"Then we're being followed by a Peugeot," I said grimly.

Rhys turned in his cramped seat to look—which is when the Peugeot behind us picked up speed, looming increasingly closer in my rearview mirror.

"Ah," he breathed.

"Yeah. *Merde.*"

I hit the gas.

Hard.

Chapter 5

"Would you prefer that I drive?" asked Rhys. The question kind of squeezed out of him. He was pressed firmly back in his seat, only partly by choice.

"No." I toed the gas pedal to the floor—after all, if the police stopped us it would be a *good* thing, right? Most tails don't stick around to talk to the authorities. "Do you think they followed us all the way from Paris?"

"I don't know. How would I?"

By looking in the rearview mirror once in a while? That wasn't fair, and I knew it. I had to focus on now.

The Peugeot was gaining on us. It was a larger car than Aunt Bridge's Citroën. It had more power.

We shot onto a bridge over the Loire—luckily, a regular, two-lane bridge, and not one of those scenic medieval landmarks. For a moment, as we left the upgrade onto the bridge, the Saxo's tires left the road.

It landed about as smoothly as the jet I'd ridden into Paris earlier today. I managed to hang on to the steering wheel and felt disproportionately proud of myself, which seemed preferable to feeling terrified.

We were leaving the industrial area behind for more open landscape and less chance of police intervention.

Who were these guys?

"Do you know where we're going?" asked Rhys, his voice not quite as tight. He was trying to stay cool, anyway.

"Away from the damned highway," I confessed. "And I want to be back on it. You're wearing your seat belt, right?"

He didn't sound encouraged when he asked, "Why do you ask?"

The Peugeot had reached our bumper. Now it was starting to pass us—rather, to pace us. I glanced to my right, to see that Rhys did have his harness on, before looking out to my left.

A tinted passenger window slid slowly downward, and a pistol appeared over its top, waving at us to pull over.

I hit the brakes.

The Peugeot whipped past us like the bullet I'd probably just escaped. Or postponed. The Saxo squealed to a reluctant stop with a horrible scream and stench of burnt rubber. My own seat belt yanked me back against my seat, hard enough across my shoulder to leave a bruise.

Rhys coughed out something that sounded like "Oofa coals." Whatever. Since the Peugeot, ahead of us, was making a 180 turn, I wasn't ready to ask for a translation.

I shifted the Saxo into Reverse and eased on to the gas. The tires had held. We started to pick up a little speed…but not as much speed as we'd need to outrun that Peugeot.

"I'd prefer we not take the bridge this way," said Rhys, his Welsh lilt more distinct the more tense he got.

"We won't," I said. "Hang on."

At least the road was relatively deserted—a benefit of late night travel. I'd only practiced this a few times, but the gun had upped the ante, so I ticked off the check list in my head.

Fix on a spot just ahead, like in yoga balance exercises.

Push the pedal to the metal. But not for long. This maneuver was only safe—relatively speaking—at under forty miles per hour. Whatever that was in kilometers.

I then did three things at once. I hit the clutch, threw the car into Drive and yanked the steering wheel to the left.

A brief grinding of gears joined the scream of tires as our

back end pivoted left and our nose pivoted right, the weight of the engine carrying us around in a perfect bootleg. *Yes!*

Before we even came to a stop, I stood on the gas to shoot us forward—the Peugeot still gaining on us. It wasn't a great improvement from a few minutes ago, but at least we were heading the right direction, nose first. We flew back across the bridge, startling some ducks out from under it. We shot back into the industrial area, but the Peugeot was quickly closing our lead. Instead of images of the *gendarmerie* finding our bodies buried in a field of picturesque sunflowers, I was now picturing them never finding us. Like Hoffa. But in France.

We weren't going to outrun these guys.

"So what's 'Oofa coals' mean?" I asked, surprised at how clenched my own words were. The Peugeot's headlights, in the rearview, drew closer. I couldn't see driver or passenger, but if I were the latter, I would be preparing to shoot out—

Yup, there was the pistol, aiming at our tires. I swerved, and the only explosion I heard was that sinister pop of gunfire. It doesn't sound as loud in real life as in the movies.

It's a lot scarier, though.

Rhys said, "*Uffach cols.* It means *embers of hell.*"

The Peugeot pulled around and was flanking us now.

"Hang on!" Again, I stood on the brake pedal, pulling the handbrake simultaneously. We skidded forward some yards, further abusing the tires. The Peugeot shot past us again, but braked faster this time—and turned, sideways, blocking our way to civilization.

Brick warehouses crowded the road on either side, without even a sidewalk to try to squeeze around the green car.

"That's some fairly mild swearing," I said, breathless.

"It is not, for me," he muttered.

The passenger door of the Peugeot opened, and a man with a pistol got out. He was wearing a ski mask.

Rhys said, "Isn't it time to back up again?"

I considered that, considered how much more abuse this

poor Citroën Saxo could take. If we ran, the Peugeot would just follow us again. Cat and mouse…and they got to be the cat.

The gunman approached us, especially ominous in the white illumination of our headlights, wreathed with foreign nighttime.

I said, "So how much does Aunt Bridge like this car?"

"She rarely drives it. She prefers the Metro."

The brake engaged and the gearshift in Neutral, I gunned the engine. Both Rhys and the gunman jumped. "Good."

The gunman wagged a gloved finger at me, a clear tsk-tsk. He came closer. At least he wasn't shooting us—yet. He probably wanted to question us first. *Then* shoot us.

Fat chance, *monsieur.*

"You cannot run him over," said Rhys, his voice firmer than at any point since this car chase started. Interesting.

I gunned the motor again, this time with less effect. "Well…I *could.*"

Damned if Rhys didn't unfasten his seat belt and reach for the door handle! I lunged across his lap, grabbing his wrist before he could do it. "Wait!"

His eyes seemed bluer in the shadows and the reflected headlights. They were determined, too. Any macho points he'd lost by not noticing the tail, Rhys Pritchard gained back in spades at that moment.

I straightened away from him, released his wrist. "Put your damned seat belt back on," I said. "I don't plan on murdering anybody, whether they deserve it or not."

He hesitated. The gunman was slowing, waving at us to get out of the car.

"Please," I said, not taking my eyes off the gun. "Have a little faith, here?"

"Have faith?" But thankfully, the familiar click of a seat belt locking into place gave me the permission I needed. I gunned the motor a third time, dropped the car into Drive and burned rubber like a teenage boy showing off at a red light.

Then I released the brake.

The Citroën shot ahead. The gunman leaped out of our path.

I wasn't aiming at him, anyway. Instead, I accelerated. Thirty kilometers per hour. Forty. Fifty—that was about thirty miles an hour. Sixty…

I rammed our Citroën straight into the passenger side of the Peugeot, behind the rear wheel. There was a crash, a jolt—but, just as I'd been taught, the car skidded out of our way.

The rear of a car is the *lightweight* end.

I flattened the gas, and the Saxo surged forward—with a nasty dragging sound that, after a few hundred feet, stopped when we bounced over our own bumper. Oops.

Behind us, the Peugeot tried to follow, not waiting for its gunman. But the car managed only a few lunges forward, unable to even navigate the turn to escape the warehouses framing them. As I'd hoped, I'd disabled the damned thing.

Yes!

Rhys sat quietly in the passenger side of the car as I retraced my turns back onto the motorway. I realized, in the near silence, that neither of us had bothered to turn off the radio. We just hadn't noticed it, our lives being in danger and all. The music seemed particularly trivial, all of a sudden.

I unclenched my hands from the steering wheel, one at a time, and practiced my breathing. Then I said, "Could you check the map for the nearest train station? We're going to be a little obvious if we keep driving this."

Rhys shook his head, not in the negative so much as to clear out the debris. "I can. Where did you learn all that?"

"An old boyfriend of mine got special training—sort of a demolition defensive-driving course. Then he taught me. The bootleg turns, anyway. We only covered the *theory* of ramming."

Lex had always been generous with the tricks he learned. We'd had a blast that week, taking turns pulling bootlegs and speeding in reverse around a big, empty QuestCo parking lot.

Funny, how all roads seemed to lead back to Lex Stuart. "And *he* took it because…?"

"Because he got tired of having drivers and bodyguards. His family's well off. It made him a pretty high abduction risk."

"That's lucky for us," said Rhys, opening the glove box to pull out a map. I glanced at the stretch of his shoulder as he rummaged, suddenly longing for human touch. Any human touch. Rhys. Lex.

You've got to admit, the whole driving-lesson thing was ironic. I had only vague suspicions that Lex might be involved with the bad guys, here. But I had absolute proof that the lessons he'd given me had saved our butts. Maybe our lives.

Damn, my life was getting complicated.

Tai Chi is a moving meditation, a choreography of ancient circular motions done slowly and with purpose. Everything resolves into its opposite—expansion into contraction, inhaling into exhaling, tension into release—and back again. Yin and yang. Softness and strength. Mind and body.

I did a few basic forms in my hotel room in Poitiers, just to ground myself for bed. Though there are older, lesser-known combat techniques involved in Tai Chi, its main focus is on harmonizing your Chi, your life energy. After the previous two days, I figured my Chi could use all the help it could get.

It helped me sleep, anyway, despite some children yelling in Italian across the hall.

The next morning I compensated with a more intricate routine, not just to harmonize my Chi but to remind myself of those ancient combat techniques. As my *sifu* has explained, their seeming mildness gives them a special power. Few people look at Tai Chi and see beyond the synchronized patterns done the world over by senior citizens, children, people in wheelchairs…blatant noncombatants.

They mistakenly equate exclusivity with strength.

As I stepped into the beautiful Wind Blowing Lotus Leaves form, I could hear more Italian shouts. I smiled—easing a blocking arm slowly up, a fisted hand slowly down, feeling the Chi. Moving this deliberately was like swimming through water—and like my regular swims, it was strengthening. Even those children could probably do this.

I turned into a double kick, finished the turn on landing, and sank into a smooth lunge and elbow strike. Then I rose into the form called Fair Lady Works at Shuttles. That, too, had martial potential…but only if I wished it. The power to do injury carries with it the power to choose against doing injury.

By the time I'd finished, turning my palms toward the floor in the original start position, I felt…strong. Calm. Confident.

And not just because I heard the children across the hall being herded off toward the elevator. Because I didn't have to sink to the level of whoever chased us last night…and because it was my choice to not sink to that level.

Choice. That's the real power.

A knock sounded at the connecting door to Rhys's room.

"Magdalene?" Rhys called softly, trying not to wake me if I were still asleep. We'd left the door cracked between us, in case there was further trouble. Only as I glanced up and saw him framed in the doorway did it occur to me that I was wearing nothing but what I'd slept in.

Yesterday's T-shirt and panties.

"I could go get breakfast while you—" he offered, then stopped, most of him hesitating between the rooms and all of him staring at me with those blue, blue eyes.

I was suddenly, stupidly glad Aunt Bridge had insisted on us traveling together.

For a long moment I just stared back. I had no desire to cover myself—why should I? A T-shirt is hardly a Merry Widow, after all. High-cut blue panties do not a G-string make.

Rhys turned away first. "Why don't I just do that?"

"A croissant would be great," I said. "With fruit. And herbal tea, if they have it. I'll shower while you're out."

"I'll have it in here." He pushed the door back to a crack.

I considered saying, "Be careful." Or even protesting that he shouldn't go anywhere without me. But it seemed overly paranoid, even after last night, and no small bit egotistical.

Instead I called, "Thanks."

A shower. That was the ticket. Shower good.

Afterward I toweled my hair semidry and combed it, and changed into clean panties and my one clean replacement shirt, a mauve camisole. I gave my face the barest hint of blush and eyeliner, not being a big makeup person, and put on yesterday's cargo pants and boots.

It's the price you pay for traveling with just a backpack.

I went to the connecting door and knocked. "Are you—"

Before I could finish, the door swung farther open and I saw that not only was Rhys back from the café, but he was kneeling by the bed, apparently...praying. In soft Latin.

I reminded myself of what he'd said—that he was after the goddess grails only to find the Holy Grail. That put us on distinct points of the religious spectrum, whether we were both ecumenical in our beliefs or not. But...

It felt weird, noticing how well the man wore a pair of jeans while he was reciting the *Ave Maria* with practiced ease.

I was raised Catholic, Catholic-ish anyway. I know the *Ave Maria* when I hear it.

It felt weird, noticing how long his dark lashes looked against his pale cheeks as he prayed. It felt *wrong*.

Not just invasion-of-privacy wrong. Deeper than that.

I started to back out. But with a murmured "Amen," he smiled toward me, almost in relief, crossed himself and stood. "The food's on the table. Let's come up with a plan of action."

"A plan for finding the Melusine Chalice?" I asked, sitting at the little table by the window. Below us we could see part of the Futuroscope park—a strange contrast to how far into the past we meant to go. "Or for avoiding gun-toting bad guys?"

He lifted croissants out of a paper sack and handed me one. "It's difficult to avoid people you cannot name."

I took the roll but hesitated—and it takes pretty heavy thoughts to keep me from a freshly baked Poitevan croissant.

"Do you have a different theory?" guessed Rhys.

"Not a theory so much as a concern."

He waited, handing me a paper cup of tea with a floral essence.

I said, "I'm worried that we've gotten involved with some kind of secret society."

Rhys sat in the other chair, eyes widening. "If we were going after the Holy Grail, I'd think you were on to something. Ceremonial orders like the Illuminati or the Priory of Scion."

I took an innocent bite of my croissant and chewed. It was still warm from the oven. Mmm! And he'd brought fruit, too—strawberries, oranges and grapes.

"You can't mean it," Rhy challenged, with a laugh. "An ancient order? For one thing, we aren't after the Grail. We're after a holy relic, perhaps even a cup, but not *the* Grail."

"You are," I reminded him.

"Not exactly," he protested. "I hope to find a connection, studying with your aunt. But as low as the chances of finding the Melusine Chalice are, the likelihood that it may lead us to the true Grail..."

I wished he'd stop making it sound like all the goddess cups were secondary. Even if he believed it, it seemed rude.

"Well," he continued, "those chances are hardly high enough to merit high-speed auto races and gunfire."

"Unless they know something we don't."

"Do they think the real Grail is in Poitou?"

"Could we just call it the Sangreal?" I asked. *Sangreal* is a classic term for the Holy Grail. To some it comes from the term *sang graal*—blood grail or blood cup. To a few it has an even more complex meaning about mythical royal blood-lines…but that really didn't apply here.

It's still about blood. Always about blood.

"The goddess chalices may not be of your particular faith," I said, with what I felt was admirable reason, "but let's assume that if they exist, they're also real. And holy."

"This is fair enough," he said. "But do you mean to imply that these…people…think the Sangreal is in Poitou?"

"No." I hated to tear down his hopes, but like he'd said, what were the chances? There was plenty of Sangreal research out there far more exhaustive than the research Aunt Bridge and I had been compiling on Melusine. "I don't think the men who chased us last night, and who hurt Aunt Bridge, and who stole our notes… I don't think they're after the Sangreal at all. I think they want to suppress the goddess grails."

"Why is that?" His gaze was unsettling. "Are they magic?"

My inner academic resisted that explanation, even as my Grail Keeper side hoped it was true. "Even if the cups have no supernatural powers, their existence could rewrite early history, reveal a more powerful feminine past. That's important."

"Again I say, high-speed auto chases and gunfire?"

He had a point. "Okay, so I don't know their motivation. All I'm saying is, there are enough of them to worry me. Unless they're racking up unbelievable frequent-flyer miles, the men who broke into Aunt Bridge's office aren't the same ones who broke into mine. They're educated enough to know about our research. And they managed to break into the museum in New Delhi—*the National Museum of India*—to destroy the Kali Cup."

"You're talking a widespread network of very powerful people," said Rhys. "Willing to go to great lengths to stop us."

"Uh-huh."

"And on our side we've got…"

"You, me and a nursery rhyme that's been in my family for generations."

Rhys stared at me.

"Yeah," I said. *"Uffach cols."*

Lex Stuart and I become friends just in time for me to watch him die. Even his willpower can't hide it. His eyelids swell. His coordination fails him. He throws up in class.

Then he vanishes altogether.

I send get-well cards and hear nothing. The normalcy of volleyball and final exams surges back as if he'd never been there. Then, over summer break, his mother calls me.

She talks about BMTs and isolation periods and platelet production resuming—I'm thirteen now, but all I really grasp is how relieved she sounds. Then she asks me to visit him.

She'll send a car. That's my first clue that I'm about to enter a whole different world. Fairyland.

The Stuarts live outside of town, with tended woods and high-gated drives. Their lawn looks like a golf course. Their house looks like a palace. Lex's mom looks like a movie star.

Only once she leads me to Lex's room and I see him, do I truly believe that he's alive.

He stands to say hello, despite his mother's protests.

Once she leaves to "arrange a snack," I fold my arms and say, "Way to keep in touch."

"I've been preoccupied," he says seriously. Not busy. Preoccupied. "Thank you for the cards."

He looks weak, but good. He's gone from wraithlike to skinny, from ashen to merely pale. His hair is growing in, a darker brown but still with ginger overtones.

"Are you back?" I ask.

He says, "I think so."

So I take over the sofa beside his chair, so that he'll sit, and demand that he tell me what it was like.

Even with his matter-of-fact presentation, without the

uglier details, it sounds awful. His cousin was a match for a bone marrow transplant, which is why he got such serious chemotherapy. His mother cried. Some days he wanted to die.

"But now…" He searches for the right words.

"Now you don't?" I prompt him.

He nods, with a ghost of a smile. But it's a friendly ghost. My smile is more free; I feel that comfortable with him. I have the oddest sensation that our spirits are also conversing, and better, if only we could listen in.

The maid arrives with a huge platter full of crackers and cheese and fruits—and candy bars with the wrapper ends cut neatly off. Almost everything tastes as wonderful as it looks.

Lex tells me he'll be coming back to class in the fall, at least until Christmas, maybe the full year. Recovery seems to be a slower process than I had imagined.

"There will be a dance, when school starts," he says, still matter-of-fact…except for a certain intensity in his hazel gaze, a catch in his breath. Except for whatever our spirits are saying behind our backs. "I would very much like it if you would attend with me. If you don't mind not dancing a lot."

I've never been asked out before. "But that's not for another month."

"I wanted to beat anybody else asking," he says.

I'm in braces, and I'm by no means slim. I'm not ugly; even I know that. But…he thinks there could be competition for me?

Lex Stuart, I decide, is wonderful.

"It will be years before we know how I'll turn out," he says, as if warning me. "Even if the cancer doesn't reoccur, I could end up not growing or getting cataracts or getting really fat. Or…other stuff."

If I think about it too hard, the warning won't make sense. I deliberately don't think about it, and it feels exactly right.

"I would love to go with you." It is an understatement.

When I get home, I can't stop talking about Lex and the Stuart mansion and the food and the fresh flowers.

"It's like fairyland there!" I tell my parents.
They exchange worried glances.
Mom says, "Just remember your fairy tales, Maggi. Fairy-land always has a catch."

Chapter 6

I was expecting Lex to call—heck, I'd half expected it the day before. This was probably his version of giving me space.

I just hadn't planned to be marinating in the destruction that powerful men so often wreak when he did.

After we checked out of the Holiday Inn, I rented a little silver Renault Clio. The train didn't stop at the small town of Lusignan, where Rhys and I were now walking. What had once been a center of power was now a rural town. And the glorious castle—one of many—which the fairy Melusine had supposedly built for her bridegroom in one night…

Long gone. Nothing left but a sunny, public walking path where once the castle had stood, and trees, and an uninterrupted view down to the River Vonne. The castle had been razed for harboring Huguenots, adding to my frustration about finding anything. Whatever the goddess worshippers might have hidden at Château Lusignan was history, thanks to devastation and religious intolerance. Thanks to dark power.

My phone trilled out "Ride of the Valkyries" at the exact wrong time. When I glanced at the caller ID and saw it was Lex, I rolled the call over to voice mail.

Trust me, Lex. You do not want to talk to me right now.

Rhys glanced at me and my phone, then said, "Any goddess cult that worshipped Melusine would have gone underground by the thirteenth century—fourteenth, at the latest. Would they not?"

I fingered a little purple flower beside the path. "Mmm-hmm."

"And Lusignan was torn down, stone by stone, in 1574?" Over religion. "A tower was torn down later."

"So what did you expect to find?" asked Rhys.

"Not the chalice," I admitted, though it would feel right to uncover it here at Melusine Central. "Just…a clue. Something. We have to start somewhere, don't we?"

He looked around us and murmured, "Three fair figures…"

That was the first line of the nursery rhyme that my family has passed down for generations, seeming nonsense with a hidden meaning—like "Ring around the Rosie" being about the bubonic plague, or "Mary Quite Contrary" being the Queen of Scots. Nursery rhymes rarely attracted the attention of people in power, so they made a great treasure map.

Ours started, *"Three fair figures, side by side…"* As a child, I'd pictured people; kids are that literal. As a scholar, I knew the "figures" could be anything, standing stones or towers or trees or buildings.

Nothing stood in threes at Lusignan. Not that we could see.

My phone rang again. *Lex.* This time I just turned it off. My inner good-girl protested that it could be important, it could be an emergency, how could I be so selfish….

AKA the Eve Syndrome, holding ourselves responsible for everything. Ten years ago, before I had a cell phone, I couldn't have stressed about it. I chose not to this time, either.

Instead, I raised my face to the blue sky, breathing in the fresh air. "This isn't where we need to be looking."

"I was afraid you'd say that." Rhys spread his arms to indicate the commons around us. "So where do we go next?"

"To the women," I decided, looking down the hill toward the two-lane road—and a Romanesque church that had survived the castle's destruction. "And since I'm not ready to

go door-to-door asking questions, I suggest we try St. Hilaire down there."

Why did I sense that Rhys didn't like my suggestion? He didn't frown. He just said, after a moment, "Do you want to borrow my handkerchief?"

For my head. This was Europe.

"Thanks," I said, accepting the neatly folded cloth.

"I'll get the car and meet you outside."

Once upon a time, the women of Lusignan would have gathered around the town well to wash clothes or collect water, and to bond. Wells are famous for their goddess connections.

If you've ever tossed a penny into a fountain and made a wish, some part of your soul *must* have understood their magic.

With the advent of modern plumbing, we've lost that. Now, elderly Catholic women tend to congregate at church.

The twelfth-century St. Hilaire de Lusignan had thick walls, round arches, and heavy piers instead of mere pillars. Its graying stone and blue-slate roof hinted at what the castle may have looked like—beautiful. When I pushed through one of its heavy double doors, I stepped into the scent of centuries of incense and wax and wood polish, of Yuletide greenery and Easter flowers, of continued faith. And it felt...

It felt powerful in a way few places can.

You don't have to be Catholic, much less a practicing one, to appreciate the holiness of such a place.

As my eyes adjusted to the shadows, I respectfully draped the handkerchief over my hair. In random pews, pretending not to notice my invasion of their territory, knelt three old women.

Yes.

On instinct, I strode to the front pew, genuflected, then sidestepped in and sat near the woman I assumed was most important who, kneeling, was saying her rosary. She had

A.K.A. Goddess

woven a crown out of her white braids. She wore a black shawl over that, and a black dress, and a thin wedding band.

She seemed somehow timeless. That made sense. Old women, wise women, are the most powerful brand females come in.

If I'd had a rosary, this would be easier. Instead, I unclasped the chain that held my chalice-well pendant and laid it on the wooden pew between us, in a loop.

When the woman beside me said "Amen" and slanted her gaze toward the chain, I murmured, *"Un cercle et un cercle."*

Her sunken eyes searched my face suspiciously, slid with disapproval to my camisole, then dropped to the necklace. Then, as I'd hoped, she looped her rosary across it. *"Pour toujours."*

Basically, "Circle to circle, never an end."

I'd made contact.

"I apologize for interrupting your prayers," I whispered, still in French, but she shook her head.

"St. Hilaire hears from me each day. He will not mind some peace. You have come for the fairy, *oui?*"

"I'm here for her cup."

She snorted.

"Is it not time for the cup to be found?" I asked gently.

"Perhaps…perhaps. But few daughters are worthy to find it. Few understand its power."

"Then help me to understand."

Her chin came up as she looked me over again; cargo pants, spaghetti straps. I'd left the backpack with Rhys. "You are too young and too beautiful. You will not want to understand."

Not want to? "But I do. Please!"

She picked up her rosary, dismissing me. So I added, as quickly as I could, "'Three fair figures, side by side.'"

I said it in English, but the old woman must have understood, because she lowered the beads to her lap. She crossed

herself for Saint Hilaire, turned back to me and said in English with a heavy French accent, "Go on."

I recited:

"Three fair figures, side by side,
Mother, son and brother's bride.
In the hole where hid her queen,
Waits the cup of Melusine."

The old woman nodded slowly, intrigued. "Perhaps you are one of us, at that."

"But that doesn't tell me where the figures are, what they are. It doesn't say if the hole is a pit or a cave or a well."

"Non!" My companion reverted to French. She seemed to like French better, and she was old enough to demand what she liked. "It tells more, if you only listen correctly."

"I want to." I touched her hand in supplication. "Please…"

She sharply nodded her decision. "You must drink of it."

I blinked. "Excuse me?"

"You must promise that, should Melusine's daughters help you in this, you will not forsake her. Should you find her chalice, you must drink her essence. Or you must let her sleep."

"But…" My intellectual, academic side was having major trouble with this. I was supposed to drink out of an ancient cup? Couldn't that screw with carbon dating or DNA? And how did I know what the cup had last held? The likelihood of something gross like poison or blood sacrifices was low, but still!

Still… "I will."

"Then you will regret it."

Was she trying to piss me off? "I promise to do as you ask, if you help me find the cup."

The woman beside me turned—in several ungainly lurches, her body no longer as lithe as it surely once had

been—to look behind her. I followed her gaze and saw that
the other two old women had been unapologetically eavesdropping. The three were somehow one, I realized, logical
or not. They went together like the Norns or the Fates or the
Wyrd Sisters.

They nodded in answer to my companion's silent question.

She turned back to me and said, very intensely:

"Quatre nobles avec le même coeur
Mère, père, fils, et belle soeur
Dans le tròu se cache sa reine
Attend la tasse de Melusine."

Then she nodded, satisfied.

I wasn't satisfied. From one cryptic nursery rhyme to its
cryptic translation? Still, it seemed significant to her, and I
was already noticing minor variations from my family's version.

I slowly repeated the rhyme, word for Gallic word.

My impromptu teacher—or priestess, even?—squeezed
my hand. "Perhaps you are the one. But you must remember—"

Which is when the doors at the back of the church opened,
and Rhys entered. The women took one look at him and
turned back to the altar, back to their devotions, as if the
priest himself had walked in on us.

Rhys noticed me, opened his mouth, then awkwardly
closed it. Then he pointed at himself, made walking-fingers,
and pointed outside.

Then he escaped. But the damage had been done. My
companion had reverted to praying.

I waited a few minutes, assuming she would finish. She
just kept repeating the prayers, so finally I interrupted her.
"You were about to say something. What is it I must remember?"

For a long moment I feared she'd reconsidered. Then she pressed my chalice-well pendant back into my hand and patted it, for all the world as if she were my own grandmother.

"Remember that *Melusine survived,"* she said.

When I emerged into the sunshine, Rhys stood across the road from the church, leaning against our Renault. He ducked his head while I looked both ways and jogged across to meet him. He winced up at me when I reached his side.

"I am sorry," he said, before I could speak. Not that I'd meant to. I felt strangely light-headed, like after a deep meditation, or a movie…or a nap. A nap with powerful dreams.

Still, I couldn't ignore him. "Sorry for what?"

"You had the whole nave, but as soon as they saw me…" He mimed turning a lock against his lips, then tossed the imaginary key over his shoulders, down the hill.

I grinned at the gesture, but I felt for him, too. Rhys seemed like a good guy, but just because he was a man, he came across as some kind of threat. Reverse discrimination, even unintentional, is still discrimination. "Don't worry about it."

Even though it felt weird, just how much authority they'd seemed to grant him. As if they sensed something I didn't.

Rhys simply grinned and said, "Maggi? You have a handkerchief on your head."

I palmed it off and gave it back, and he was *so* not an authority figure.

Which isn't to say he didn't have his own personal power.

"So where to?" He opened the car door and popped the locks. "Have you solved the mystery of the Melusine Chalice?"

"Nope. We're still stuck with the obvious possibilities."

"Those being…?"

I went around the car and climbed into the passenger seat. If we were doing Melusine's home tour, I knew exactly what came next. "Did you by any chance pack swim trunks?"

* * *

Deeper and deeper I swam, kicking my feet for power, stretching my hands ahead of me into the murky river. I squinted at water plants, at little clouds of billowing silt, at a turtle paddling past.

I thought I saw something—a stone? Perhaps it was the large remains of a relic or a ruin, some unlikely but not impossible hint that Melusine Was Here. Tightness built in my chest from lack of air, but I was so close. A few more silent kicks...

Now I could see it was an old barrel. Rusty and moss covered. Years, not centuries, old.

Blowing the last of the air from my nose in bubbles of disgust, I aimed for the surface. I broke into the dappled summer sunshine with a splash and a needy gasp.

Rhys, on the wooded bank, called, "Do you see anything?"

"Not yet." I was still treading water, kicking my bare feet, enjoying the gentle pull of the Vonne's current against me. I still couldn't believe I'd left my suit home. *Me!* "I'm going down one more time before we give up on this spot."

He nodded. Rhys *did* have a pair of swim trunks. Since he claimed that his swimming amounted to little more than a dog paddle, I wore them with my camisole while he kept watch from the bank. Neither of us actually said this was better than me swimming in my underwear, but it *so* was.

I took a deep breath and dove again. Deeper and deeper. Freer and freer. Free of gravity, free of whatever kernel of attraction was flirting its way between Rhys and me, free of anything but one simple goal.

Try to find, against all reason, the remains of Melusine's "fountain" in the Colombière Forest.

It wouldn't be the first time goddesses were worshipped at a spring—like in Bath, or Lourdes, or the Chalice Well in Glastonbury.

Deeper. Freer. Was that possibly a bowl of some sort, on its side on the bottom?

Tightening my throat against the need to breathe, I kicked closer—and startled away another turtle, in a burst of panicked mud.

I reluctantly gave up the peace of submersion for the surface, yet again. Luckily, the surface was a nice place too, with birdsong and wildflowers and gently stirring tree branches…and a far-too-intriguing companion for my peace of mind.

"Nothing," I called, when he waved to show he'd seen me emerge. Then I began a strong sidestroke back to shore. "If there was a sacred spring along here, it will take people with more experience than me to find the signs."

It wasn't like we'd seen either "three fair figures" or the French version, "four nobles." If they'd been sentinel trees, the likelihood of them living this long was low. If they'd been standing stones, we hadn't found them.

I waded out, my hair streaming water down my back, my toes gooshing deliciously in the mud. Rhys offered a warm hand, and I accepted it, and he pulled me firmly onto the grassy bank.

Close to him.

I noticed his gaze sink to my breasts, under a film of wet camisole. My breath fell shallow…but in a good way.

He noticed me noticing, let go and turned away.

"I'm sorry," he called over his shoulder, clearly discomfited. "I'll walk ahead, see if there are any more promising spots."

Oddly disappointed, I used yesterday's T-shirt to dry off my feet before I put on my socks and boots to follow him. Interesting fashion statement, hiking boots with swim trunks. Very unacademic. I liked it.

I rezipped my backpack, which I'd apparently left open, and shouldered it. Then I hiked happily after Rhys, through what legend had it were enchanted woods.

When he glanced a truly self-conscious welcome over his shoulder and kept walking, I had to know. "Are you married?"

He stopped, startled. "What? I am not. Why?"

Because you act like it's a sin to notice a woman's body.
It wasn't as if he'd ogled me. "Just curious," I said.

Rhys stared at me for a long moment. "I was engaged
once," he confessed. "She died last year, before we could
marry."

"Oh." Way to feel guilty, Mag! "I'm so sorry."

He shrugged one shoulder and started walking again.

"So, Aunt Bridge has been researching the goddess-wor-
ship side of Melusine," I said, to change the subject. "I'm
more into the mythology. You're her assistant, give me an
overview. How would it work? Women worshipping a goddess, I mean."

For a moment he seemed lost in other thoughts. Then he
said, "That depends on the time period. Gaul stayed pagan
well into the Dark Ages. Probably they would meet in a sacred grove."

Considering that we were in a forest, that hardly narrowed things down. "How would the scene have changed
once Europe converted to Christianity?"

"By the sixth century, ritual groves were being destroyed
in an attempt to convert blasphemers. Like Charlemagne
cutting down the sacred oaks of the Saxons."

"And that *worked?* If you cut down my sacred trees, you'd
tick me off worse than before."

He'd slowed his step, so I no longer felt like I was chas-
ing him. "Back then, power defined your ability to lead. If
your gods were so great, how could they let us cut down their
trees?"

I glanced at the trees around us, dappled greens and golds
and browns, and felt sorry for them. "You're not really saying that your god can beat up the other boys' gods?"

He grinned. "The remaining pagans would have met in
secrecy—at night, or in the woods."

"So if these people worshipped a goddess who was connected to a local spring…"

Thankfully, he picked up the thread of my idea. "Then they would have met near that spring. Their ceremonies would resemble witches' circles, complete with moonlight and cauldrons."

"Or cups. Or bowls. Or chalices." Or grails.

"That is it exactly," he agreed.

I took a moment to look around us. The banks of the Vonne were slightly rockier. It was all fairly soft limestone. One boulder looked particularly significant somehow, especially white amidst vines and brush.

"How far have we come since Lusignan?" I asked.

"I'd imagine we've come four or five kilometers. Why?"

I was noticing another bank of white limestone, near the boulder. "Do you suppose the Melusine worshippers would have come this far out?"

"If they feared the Church more than they feared wolves."

I noticed a third length of limestone. My pulse picked up. *Three fair figures?*

I sank down into an easy crouch to untie my boots.

I kicked off one boot, then the other and put down my backpack.

Then, I waded in to swim the water where Melusine the goddess may have once bathed.

Chapter 7

By the time Rhys and I signed ourselves into a small bed and breakfast in Vouvant, I was still pissed off.

Melusine's river had yielded bupkas.

"It was a good idea," Rhys insisted, not for the first time, as we paused in the narrow hallway outside our room to unlock the door. Yes, one room—two twin beds, but one room. Yes, way to invite trouble. But we'd wanted a view of the town's medieval landmark, called Melusine's Tower.

Like Lusignan, Vouvant claimed its castle was built by the fairy Melusine. But this one still had pieces standing. This little hotel had that view—from one available room—and the added benefit of not keeping their reservations on-line.

Just in case someone was looking.

I had faith in my ability to resist Rhys Pritchard, even if today's time outside had given him just enough sunburn to add an extra glow to his eyes, a windblown carelessness to his hair. And I had faith in my ability to fight him off, if he couldn't resist me…assuming I wanted to.

"It wasn't a good idea," I said, about the rocks. "It was a waste of time."

I ducked through the too-low doorway into an incredibly quaint room, complete with wood beams across the angled ceiling, striped wallpaper, antique furniture, and a gabled window overlooking a small, twilight field with a chunky, crooked tower. Fireflies, blinking on and off near the tower, added to its fairy feel.

I dropped my backpack onto the bed by the window. "Mind if I take the first shower?"

"I do not. If you'll stop blaming yourself," said Rhys.

But I didn't feel like making any promises, just now.

I took my minimal laundry down the hall to the shared bath, along with some personal items and the extralarge T-shirt I'd just bought at the café/souvenir shop next door. In a few minutes, it and my last pair of clean underpants were going to be the only dry things I owned.

I started the water in the claw-foot tub, washing and rinsing my clothes as the tub filled. Then, with the laundry wrung out and draped wherever it might dry, I slid into warm water.

For now, I was going to soak and hope no other guests needed this particular room.

My exhaustion came from more than sun and exertion. I felt tired from something a lot like defeat.

The bathroom was tiny. The roof above me slanted, the tile was cracked in several places. I sat up long enough to wash my hair, then closed my eyes and sank lower into the wonderfully deep, old-fashioned tub.

Then it occurred to me that it was Saturday night—and my eyes opened. This was exactly what Melusine had supposedly done every Saturday night, wasn't it? Soak in a tub, whip her tail around, and hide her true self from her husband?

The similarity annoyed me. It was one thing to understand the myth of Melusine, to find her chalice. But did I want to actually *emulate* her?

Not on your life—and not just because of the snake tail! I had no need to magically build castles, and I sure didn't want to expend all my energies on a man who would turn traitor. In fact...

Just to prove to myself that I wasn't a wimp, I picked up

my cell phone. Two messages. I thumbed the buttons to check my call log. Both from this morning. Both from Lex.

Now or never. I dialed into my voice mail, and selected to hear the first recording.

"Maggi? It's Lex." We both knew I would recognize his voice anywhere. His formality had to be a polite—or maybe sarcastic—nod toward my distance of late. "As long as we're both in Paris, let's get together. Dinner. Coffee. Pick a place."

I frowned. This was getting close to desperation, for Lex.

"We need—*I* need to talk," he continued, more softly. "Give me a call?"

And he recited his number, as if I would have lost it. As if I could have forgotten it in the first place.

Of course he didn't sign off the way he used to, saying he loved me. That's at least partly because I'd made it clear, after last year's breakup, that he didn't have the right to love me anymore. Not unless I gave him that right.

Against my best logic, when given the option to delete the message or to save it to archives, I chose saving it.

I could always delete it later, right?

The second message, also from Lex, was shorter. He said softly, firmly, "Please."

My heart lurched with familiar confusion. Damn it. Damn, damn, *damn it*. Why did I always let him do this to me? No. That wasn't fair—why did I do it to myself? When we were right we were *so very* right. Almost spiritually so. But that couldn't counteract all the times we were wrong. Could it?

Not permanently. And how many more times could I re-open the wounds in my heart before they would scar that way and never again heal?

But none of my internal arguments mattered. He'd already won a call-back, at the very least, with that *"Please."* I couldn't have stopped myself if I wanted to…and I didn't want to.

In fact, as I pressed his number on speed-dial, I wondered why I'd kept it. Maybe we'd never be over. My anticipation at the ring of his phone said as much. The best I'd managed to hope for, over the past year, had been a mutually agreeable separa—

"Mag," Lex answered, on the second ring. Just that. Just my name, in the caress of his voice.

I said, "Hi."

"Thank you for calling back so quickly."

At least I didn't have to feel guilty about avoiding him, but, "Quickly? You called this morning."

"It's an improvement on last time."

Oh. Yeah. The last time he'd called had been about five months ago. I'd been trying my damnedest not to get drawn back into the upper-class, cutthroat, crap-for-values world he lived in, not again. I'd agonized for a week before finally phoning him back and saying, "Don't call me again."

And he hadn't. Not until today.

"You said you needed to talk," I prompted.

I heard a wry huff of breath on his end. "You can't imagine. Are you busy tonight? I could come by—"

"I'm not in Paris."

"Oh." I could only imagine his frown. "Once I read about your aunt Brigitte's attack, I assumed…"

"I'm continuing a research project for her." It felt like a lie, even if it wasn't. I squirmed slightly, water sloshing.

"When will you be back, then? I have to be in England midweek, but other than that my schedule's—" He stopped abruptly, then asked, "Mag, are you in a bathtub?"

The way his voice dropped in pitch and increased in intensity made me laugh. "You were saying your schedule is…"

"*Shhh,*" Lex commanded, a whisper that slid down my spine, then trickled into my thighs, my arms, my breasts. I stretched out my legs in the oversize tub, splashing a little, savoring my own languid, wonderfully familiar response to his desire before I could catch myself.

"Lex," I warned, and it came out more of a plea than I would have liked. A plea for more than was wise.

"Quiet," he murmured, the richness of his voice flooding me with enough memories of enough nights to sharpen my response to something between discomfort and ecstasy. "I'm visualizing."

Tell me what you see. That was all I had to say, and he would wrap me in words so poetic, so erotic, so starkly appreciative that they would eclipse whatever little sex I've known outside of his bed. He has always traveled a lot. It wouldn't be the first time we used the phone that way.

All I had to do was ask it, and his voice would guide me through the warm water to places that he seemed to know better even than me....

And then I would be caught. Again. Just like the last time, and the time before that. Even if I *would* do that to myself again, I sure ought to make the decision with a clear head.

And wearing clothes.

Somehow, I managed to force words. Normal words. Not *Where are you and are you wearing anything?* "And here I thought you loved me for my mind."

"Mind, body and spirit, Magdalene Sanger."

I was too tired to deal with this—at least to do so while retaining any autonomy. "So what was it you wanted to talk to me about, Lex?"

He drew a deep breath, and when he spoke again his cool control had returned. Not angry. Not off-putting. Just... steady. "Matters I'd rather not discuss over an unsecure connection. Do you have a landline I can call?"

It was starting all over again, the layering of sex and suspicion. Could he want a landline because they were easier to trace? Or was I being a suspicious bitch? I hated this. I hated what I'd become around him.

"Nothing that would be convenient," I hedged. "Who do you think is trying to capture your calls anyway—*spies?*"

Frighteningly, I half believed my joke.

"Paparazzi. They're brutal around here. Not that they'd generally care about me—"

"But you dated that Italian actress," I said.

"Eight months ago," he clarified. We hadn't been dating at the time. As far as I knew, he'd never cheated on me. "This time they're interested in a princess I met skiing last February."

"So we just won't discuss the actress or the princess."

"It's not just that, Mag. I have something—things—I need to own up to. With you. Things I would rather not have publicized."

Oh? "About the trial?" I suggested. I still didn't understand much of his role in that damned trial.

His voice stayed steady. A guy who'd been to hell and back by the time he'd hit puberty didn't shake easily. "In part."

And about your family's involvement in suppressing the goddess grails?

"That's why I wanted to meet," Lex said. "But if this is going to be my only opportunity to talk to you, I'll take that chance. You need to know—"

"No." Even as I said it, I knew I'd lost some kind of don't-blink-first game, with myself if not with him. I'd been so sure I couldn't stay involved with someone who'd perjured himself. Especially Lex, my noble Lex. He'd disillusioned me more deeply than seemed possible. And yet here I sat, stopping him before he could publicly implicate himself, just in case.

So much for my own damned moral fiber.

"No?" Lex asked it softly, but his question carried weight.

"I'll be back in Paris soon," I assured him. "Not long, the way my research has been going."

"You sound like you're giving up on something."

Did I hear *censure* in his cool tone? Just who was supposed to be whose moral compass? "If I'm ready, I'll call you then."

Before he could respond to my latest refusal to commit, a knock sounded on the door. "Magdalene?" Rhys called. "You've been a while. Are you all right?"

Well…crap. "I'm fine," I called, after turning the phone away from my mouth. "I'll be out in a few minutes."

Then, wincing in anticipation, I put the phone back to my ear.

To my relief, Lex said simply, "I should let you go, shouldn't I?"

The double entendre hurt my heart. It was too late for him to let me go. Yesterday would've been fine, or the month before, or the month before that. Maybe. Probably.

But not now. He'd offered too much—a confession I needed to hear— "I'll call when I can."

"Be careful," he said. An interesting choice of sign-offs.

No way was I letting that pass. "Anything in particular I should look out for?"

"Just…be careful whom you trust." And he hung up.

What?

I immediately stabbed his speed-dial number. It rang—

And the bastard let me roll over to his voice mail.

"You son of a—" But no. I disconnected before giving him the satisfaction of a recorded rant. Son of a bitch! Whatever you want, Magdalene. Mind, body and spirit, Magdalene.

Whatever it takes to keep you on the phone long enough for me to make you an offer you can't refuse, Magdalene.

Now he had me. Worse, he knew me well enough to *know* he had me. So he didn't have to grovel anymore. If I knew Lex, he would wait until morning to return my call.

Unless he waited a week.

By the time Rhys got back from his bath, I'd channeled my energy into the chalice, cross-referencing a travel guide, roadmap and index-cards like a student cramming for finals.

I was going to find this chalice if it killed me.

But despite my new determination, when the door opened and I glanced up from the window seat, I almost burst out laughing.

Rhys wore pajamas, like in some old B&W TV-Land classic.

Something must have showed on my face because, as he put down his shaving kit, Rhys cocked his head. "What is it?"

I grinned. "Nice jammies, Mr. Pritchard."

"Lovely shirt, Dr. Sanger," he said, because that was the only thing I was wearing. Well, that and panties, but I wasn't planning to show those. It's not as bad as it sounds. I'd bought the extralarge shirt, which fit me like a dress.

Besides, he might have meant the picture. In white, on the shirt's blue background, curled the silhouette of a fairy with bat wings and two long serpent's tails—the heraldic image of Melusine. In Vouvant, the fairy is the closest thing they have to a tourist attraction.

"Here." I offered up a sheet of lined yellow paper. "I've listed fifteen important places for Melusine—or for anybody who might have worshipped her as a goddess. And I haven't even started on Luxembourg."

Rhys took the paper. "Bridge listed most of these, too." And he handed it back to me, retreating to his side of the room.

"What?"

"She made a list of the sites she wanted to investigate as hiding places for the Melusine Chalice. Lusignan was first, of course, and…was Vouvant third or fourth? I think she listed Parthenai before Vou—Why are you looking at me like that?"

"She already had a list, and you didn't *mention* it?"

"I didn't think of it right off. I can't remember even a third of the places she listed. Several were in Anjou…"

"Because the Angevins had a similar Melusine story to the Lusignans," I said, still annoyed. "Demonic, not fairy. To explain why the Plantagenets were such a wicked lot."

"Ah." Rhys sat on his bed. "Then there was Talmont. The tower of St. Maixent. The last on the list was Angoulême."

Bridge *had* been reaching. "After King John I lost most

of England's holdings in France, his widow, Isabelle of Angoulême, married the Count of Lusignan and squeezed out a whole litter of heirs before she died. By then, Isabelle was in her convent, hiding out from royalists."

Rhys shook his head, a little overwhelmed, and who could blame him? "It was quite an extensive list Bridge had."

"I'd like to see it." Preferably before I'd spent almost half an hour on mine!

"It was stolen with the rest…"

Rhys stopped, and stared at me.

I stared at him. "With the rest of Bridge's research."

"They have the list."

"They have the freaking list." I looked out the window, at the worn black hulk that was so aptly named the *Tour Melusine*.

Somehow I wasn't surprised to catch a flash of artificial light from within it.

"And they're using it."

I'm fourteen and sitting beside Lex on a flight to Paris. His mother convinced mine to "let them have a few more hours together" before we part, me to my grandmother, him to an exclusive camp in the Alps.

Lex's efforts to regain his health have worked—his shoulders are broadening, and he's inches taller. He is also leaving me. We've been to dances, to movies and spent time at each other's houses—or my house, his palace. But I've known how badly he wants to get "back to school," meaning his school.

Once summer is over, he will.

He is so oblivious, he just wants to play cards to pass the flight. "I'll teach you how to cheat," he offers at last.

"I don't want to know how to cheat," I say.

"It's the best way to make sure you're not being cheated."

"I don't plan on playing with anybody who would cheat me."

He snorts. He is healthy and happy and bound for the most prestigious prep school in the country—even this summer camp is somehow connected. He can afford to be smug.

"You would never cheat me, would you?" I ask, suddenly worried in a way that thickens in my stomach.

His answer—"Not for money"—hardly satisfies me. I know the importance of standing up for myself, even to him.

Maybe especially to him.

I say, "You can't be my friend if you cheat me."

Lex just teases me. "But if I cheat well enough, you would never know."

"And you still wouldn't be my friend!" The sharpness in my voice startles him. "Even if I thought you were. Because you would know. I wouldn't be your friend, Lex. I'd be your victim."

Now he's angry, but it's that quiet, smoldering kind of angry he gets when he's thinking very hard about something that troubles him. We hardly speak during our descent to Paris. I feel worse and worse, both because my prince has admitted to something so unheroic as cheating and because our argument has ruined what little time we have left together. But as we are waiting to go through customs, Lex turns to me and earnestly says, "I won't cheat you again."

I let him hold my hand then. I'm glad he said it.

But I wonder how I will know, if he breaks his promise.

That summer I get my period and officially "become a woman." Grand-mère and Aunt Bridge give me my own chalice-well pendant to celebrate.

The next time I see Lex—between his coming home and leaving for boarding school, he kisses me goodbye, on the cheek—before he leaves again. He asks me to his school's formal autumn dance. It's easier to let him go, the more secure I feel that our separations are only temporary.

But I still wish he'd never cheated at cards.

Chapter 8

From our room I could see bits of flashlight beam glancing out of the occasional arrow slit. Someone was definitely in the tower. *Melusine's* tower. The one that was closed until morning.

"Sons of bitches." Turning from the window, I yanked my damp jeans off the radiator and wedged myself into their tight denim confines.

Rhys politely averted his eyes. "It could be vandals. Or teenagers out for a spot of fun."

"Or little kids, scaring each other with ghost stories." Damn, but wet denim's hard to zip.

"Or tourists, too impatient to wait for official hours. Perhaps tourists with lock picks?"

"I'm decent," I announced. "Once I have my boots on, I'll be ready."

He looked over his shoulder. "Ready for what, exactly?"

To find out who they were, who they were involved with. To torture them into confessing everything before turning them over to the authorities....

Okay, so I wouldn't be torturing anybody. That's a line I won't cross. And maybe a professor of comparative mythology wasn't the best candidate for making citizen's arrests. But... "To go learn something. Knowledge is power, right?"

Unfortunately, even as I said that, I crossed the room to

my boots and almost drowned myself out with the *scritch, scritch, scritch* of wet denim. Well…crap.

"Turn around again," I instructed.

"I'll change in the bathroom," he said.

This time, as we headed out, I wore his damp swim trunks. They doubled nicely for shorts, and I was a lot stealthier that way. And far more comfortable.

"How," whispered Rhys, as we edged through the shadows, "do you propose to get close enough to learn anything?"

Vouvant's worn buildings of pinkish terra-cotta with orange tiled roofs and shutters, had looked charming earlier. So had the looming old church and the crumbling medieval ramparts that ran through town. Now the whole place reminded me more of decay and despondency, like something out of a fairy tale. And not one of the nice ones.

The Tour Melusine sat in the middle of it all, ringed with a small field. There were not enough bushes or trees to cover our approach.

"I propose that we do it very quietly." I glanced his way, saw his hesitation. "You keep watch. I'll go first."

Rhys caught my shoulder, surprising me. "You do realize that if these are the same men as before, both of them were armed."

"I do realize that," I whispered. "Thanks."

"And you realize they had firearms."

"Yeah. Too bad they aren't using swords." I meant that.

"And you'll be outnumb—"

I whirled to face him. *"You're not helping!"*

Wow. *That* was a moment. We stared, his hand still staying me, both of us vibrating with adrenaline. I may not be able to see auras, but damned if I couldn't feel mine pushed up against his, personal space warring with personal space, dangerously close to coming to a mutual agreement over the disputed territory….

Heavens, his eyes were blue. And worried. About me.

He stepped back first. Three full steps. "Be careful."

His unintentional echo of Lex's warning helped me turn away to face this latest threat, annoyed all over again. Did I give off I'm-an-idiot vibes, that I needed this advice? Or, worse…were the vibes more along the lines of *I'm a helpless damsel?*

Tower there. Me here. Time to change that.

Slowing my breath to center and balance myself, I melded into the shadows. Yep, Tai Chi again. It's the art of becoming all but invisible, substantial only when connecting with an opponent's weak point.

Appear, then disappear. Of course, my *sifu* generally said that during quiet, push-hands exercises. But I was willing to extrapolate.

Stepping as smoothly and deliberately as if I were doing forms, synchronizing my Chi to the night around me, I crept into the open. Farther. Farther…

Light flickered halfway up the tower, from inside. I heard Rhys hiss a quiet warning from well behind me. For a moment I tensed; then I breathed it out, refusing to hurry. It's the rabbit who bolts from hiding that gets chased.

The light glanced away without ever reaching me, and I made it to the shelter of a tree. Then I turned and lifted a hand toward Rhys, to reassure him.

He was hanging back, just as I'd asked.

Using the same technique, I glided like a ghost to the next tree, then the next. Like easing through water instead of a soft, cricket-filled, flower-scented night. Like Melusine.

As I reached the marginal safety of the tower's thick, blocky base, I felt downright proprietary about it.

It was an odd ruin. The bottom half was squared, with doorways opening into thin air at different heights—clearly it was once part of a larger edifice. To one of these second-story doorways someone had built a flight of stairs to a banded door, which the tourist office kept locked.

It sat slightly open.

Someone was inside. Probably there was only one set of stairs. I wasn't close enough to hear anything, but neither was I stupid enough to trace their steps, knowing they would have only one way out—through me—when they changed directions.

I mean, it's only Tai Chi. I don't actually *become* invisible. And I'd left my sword at home.

So I stood there in the flower bed at the base of the tower and looked for other options.

Unlike its blocky bottom, the top half of the tower was rounded, with framed arrow slits. Where it met its bottom half, the round tower flared wider than its squared base, shifted slightly to one side like a child's toy that had been put clumsily together. And up inside that overhanging edge, almost impossible to see through the shadows, seemed to be some kind of…shaft? Yes, almost a tunnel into the upper part of the tower. It had crumbled open toward its base, not five feet from the main door.

I frowned at the mystery, wanting to understand this before I considered taking advantage—then almost laughed to realize that it was a toilet.

A *garderobe,* they were called. Once there would have been a seat at the top with a hole in it, built over a long shaft down to the moat or river. Like a medieval outhouse. Unfortunately, those *garderobes* were lousy security risks. Richard the Lionheart's famous fortress, Chateau Gaillard, withstood a siege for who-knew how long before enemy soldiers crawled up from the moat and successfully invaded through the potties.

I hesitated. Logically, I knew this shaft had been unused and open to the cleansing powers of dust, wind, sunshine and rain for *centuries*. Lots of them. But…it was a *sewer.*

Then I thought about those sons of bitches up in the tower,

using information they'd stolen to search for evidence that women had worshipped Melusine there, and I would've climbed the damned thing fresh.

Glancing at Rhys once more, I climbed the modern stairway to the main door. That alone took me over a story high. I looked at the crumbling rock ledge that led around to the inverted corner, where once the shaft had continued.

I took my boots off, stuffing my socks inside and hiding them under the stairs. I seemed to be doing that a lot this week, didn't I? Then, barefoot and using the outside wall of the tower for balance, I stepped precariously onto the stony remains of what had probably been a curtain wall.

My toes clinging to rocks and tufts of determined grass, I stole to the ragged, inside edge of the shaft.

Then I craned my neck to look up at the looming space above me, four or five stories high. Wow. That looked pretty small. I saw darkness—but heard muffled voices.

Though I couldn't hear what they were saying, I could tell they were men. I thought I knew which ones. Taking another deep breath, I ran my hands over the rocks to find good holds—and pulled myself shakily upward.

Climbing down the drainpipe of Turbeville Hall had been a lot easier. It hadn't been as high, for one thing, and I'd been working *with* gravity. Still, I found enough niches and nooks to wedge my fingers, or my toes, or occasionally my knees—let's hear it for erosion.

Once, my foot slipped and I almost fell. Twice, I kicked small stones loose, and they clattered down the rock beneath me. I froze, unable to breathe—but nobody investigated. So I worked on that inhale/exhale business some more and dragged myself doggedly higher.

Amazing, how easily determination can stand in for skill.

As I reached the rounded upper half of the tower, the *garderobe* tunnel closed around me on all sides. That made it horribly, eerily dark. This was nighttime, I reminded myself. It had been kind of dark, anyway.

I could now use opposite walls to brace myself—especially as they leaned closer…and closer….

High enough, I thought finally, and found an uneven inch of ledge to balance against as I listened.

At first there was just shuffling. A lot of shuffling. Sometimes, a scraping noise like a file; I winced to imagine what the intruders might be doing to the historical integrity of the stone. Maybe I wasn't close enough. Or maybe Rhys had been right, and these were vandals.

Then— "This is a bloody waste of time."

Not only could I hear the man pretty well, here in the little sound tunnel I'd claimed, but he was also speaking English. British-English, with an inflection like the Beatles.

Liverpool?

"Complain if you will," chided voice number two, clearly French, but speaking English for the sake of his companion. "I won't be the one to admit I gave up too soon if she finds it where we already looked."

One of my feet, bracing me on my little ledge, started to slip. Compensating with my hands to readjust my balance in the darkness, I almost missed the next words.

"Why not let her do the boring part?" Liverpool asked. "*Then* we take the damned cup. Everyone's happy."

"You were not so confident outside Orlèans."

I grinned to myself, even as I found a new toehold. It was a strange sensation, huddled in darkness as I listened. Like I really *was* invisible. Like that invisibility gave me some kind of extra power.

"She was aiming a Saxo at me!" Liverpool protested.

Frenchy snorted. "Were I in charge, I should not count on our ability to take the cup once she has it."

"We can take what we want, if we kill her." Well, wasn't Liverpool the bloodthirsty bastard?

Frenchy's voice kept shifting in volume, giving me the impression he was moving around, still searching. At least he had as little idea what he was really looking for as

Rhys and I did. "Like you almost did with the old woman?"

"They overreacted. Our instructions were 'whatever it takes.' Well that's what it took. If she'd stayed home where she belonged then we wouldn't have had to do it."

If she'd stayed home where she belonged, you wouldn't have had any notes to steal in the first place, you idiot!

"In any case," said Frenchie, "the scholar is useful."

"Sod it!" Something metal clanged against stone—like a file being thrown?—and again I winced. Liverpool's frustration seemed even greater than mine.

Good.

"I could be in Greece with Monique right now," he whined. "We had this holiday planned for a month."

"Did you complain like this when you got that contract last year?" Frenchie asked. *Intriguing.* "Or when the authorities did not press charges against you before that? Me, I am grateful the insurance board looked the other way. I am grateful my father won the election. This is how we show our gratitude."

My breathing had fallen shallow again. This was starting to sound like the mob. I didn't want this to sound like the mob.

Liverpool avoided the question. "What's so sodding important about some old cup in the first place?"

To my frustration, Frenchie didn't answer. All I heard were footsteps and shuffling.

Goddess worshippers would not have really met in a *tower,* would they? Much less a watchtower.

But I supposed the priestesses could have *hidden* the cup anywhere. With evidence that there had once been more castle, here, perhaps there had been other towers. Three fair figures…or four nobles, depending on which edition you used.

A voice above me—Liverpool's—said something I couldn't quite make out. They'd climbed more stairs. I was losing them.

I climbed higher, too, surrounded by the darkness.

Then I put my hand on something that moved under my touch.

As I bit back a scream, it fluttered off. Bird? Bat? It took everything I had to keep hanging on to more rock instead of losing purchase to rub my hand on my hip. *Eiw. Eiw-eiw-eiw.*

Then the voices came closer again, descending the stairs.

"We're not done," Frenchy insisted, while I reluctantly felt for another hold.

"Maybe not you, mate, but I am," said Liverpool. "If they won't even tell us why this thing is so important—"

"It is important because they say so. It's enough that they've always been correct before. Correct and generous."

I found my hold and eased myself higher yet.

"But we've been doing this for a bloody week!"

"A week?" Frenchie made a disgusted noise. "Compared to generations of loyalty? Compared to centuries of power?"

My hand hit metal above me. Reaching up in the darkness, I felt across what was clearly a secured grate. Someone, somewhere along the way, had wanted to make sure tourists didn't plummet to their death.

I wouldn't get any higher. I wouldn't see their faces, either—not from here.

Damn it!

Somewhere above me, Frenchy had reached the end of his patience. "If you do not embrace this, do not believe in the Order, then why are you even here?"

"I am, all right? Isn't that enough?"

"No. This is not just a job, this is your inheritance. It is the *Comitatus.* Those idiot women do not, cannot understand, so they work to destroy us. But what is your excuse?"

"I'm not trying to destroy anything, right?"

"You are not working to uphold it, this I see."

"Enough with the sermons already!" Now Liverpool was ticked. "Look, I just wanted the damned contract! My uncle said he knew these guys who could get the bid for me if I told them who my dad was, you know? If they thought we were blood. So we did it, okay?"

Frenchy said, "If they *thought* you were blood?"

"Yeah." Liverpool laughed, sounding nervous now. "My mum was already knocked up when she married my dad, right? But he was still my dad, legal and all."

Frenchy said nothing. I hung there in my hole with an uncomfortable prickle deep in my stomach as if my body already knew something the rest of me hadn't yet worked out.

"Look," said Liverpool. "Never mind. I'm just pissed off about Greece. Let's find this stupid cup and we can—"

The diffused light above me wavered, then darted about with a clatter and stilled, as if the flashlight had been dropped. Someone grunted. Bodies thudded, hard, against rock above me. Someone's breathing rasped into a gurgle, then a strain—

And then, to my horror and relief, nothing.

Nothing?

Well…there was the steady, forgotten glow of a dropped flashlight. A scuffle of footsteps, maybe, and then a dragging sound. But the noise was moving up, away from me. I curled my fingers through the grating and pushed, unsure what I'd do—rescue? threaten?—but determined to do something.

The grate held fast. Nothingness stretched….

Then, from below, I heard one of the most unassuming, most truly awful noises in my life. Half thud. Half splat.

Goodbye, Liverpool.

It really *was* about blood, wasn't it?

I heard footsteps. The flashlight's glow moved as if picked up. It arched a slow, steady light across the top of my tunnel, grillwork casting a lace of shadows onto the stone by my hand before continuing. Then…

I moved my hand as the light slid slowly, firmly back.

Uh-oh.

At least I could finally see the stone I'd been clinging to, and the grill that had trapped me like some Dark-Ages glass ceiling. The grillwork was old, and rusty, and cemented into place—I saw it even more clearly as the light brightened, moving closer.

Time to climb down. But it was slow work, stretching downward, trying to verify footholds before I risked sinking my weight. I didn't want to go the route Liverpool had.

Frenchy murmured, "'In the hole where hid her queen.'"

This? He thought worshippers of Melusine would hide her grail in a *toilet?*

Light crept toward my hand.

I found a hold and dropped lower before it could catch me, moving my hand just in time. I dangled my foot, seeking another toehold, and found it. I reached down and under with my other hand, fumbling for another grip, hoping that—

Light suddenly flooded across me, lacy shadows and all, and I had two choices. Choice one: keep heading downward, fully aware that he had a gun that could outrun me, and let what could be my last living moments be one of flight?

I chose choice two, flung my head back and glared angrily up into blinding light, up at the murderer above me. I couldn't see anything of his face, but I could see the gleam of his gun. I tried to radiate "Screw you" with every ounce of my being.

He politely said, "Dr. Sanger, I presume?"

Chapter 9

Well...he didn't shoot me. That's always a plus.

"Here is the plan," he said, smooth as only a Frenchman can be. "You will climb down. I will meet you at the bottom. And we will come to a reasonable agreement, eh?"

"New plan," I said. "I wait here until hell freezes over, and you give up and leave before the *gendarmes* catch you with an illegal firearm."

Assuming I could hang on that long.

"You think my weapon is illegal?" He chuckled unpleasantly as that sank in. "How *charmant*. Sadly, my counteroffer to that would simply be to shoot your friend. I believe..."

For a moment the light moved away from my face, away from my stony tunnel—I realized he was checking an arrowslit. Before my eyes could readjust to the darkness, his silhouetted head reappeared, then full wattage light. "Yes, he is kneeling beside my former partner. I assure you, I have a clear shot."

Why would Rhys do something that stupid? Did he have some medical training I wasn't aware of? Did he think someone who'd been dropped off a tower this high could have *survived*?

Still, the words felt...right. Not a lie. Either way, I was less likely to risk Frenchy shooting Rhys than me.

"But if you shot him," I countered, "you would advertise your presence to all of Vouvant."

"The town is not known for its superb police squad. I could have you in my trunk and be halfway to Calais before they got close enough to discover the bodies."

He had a point. As with Tai Chi, a certain strength comes from knowing when to yield. "Then my counteroffer," I suggested, "is that if I do climb down, it's on the agreement that you put the gun away and nobody gets hurt."

Nobody *else*.

He probably wouldn't think I was stupid enough to believe any agreement of the sort. We both knew I'd heard too much. But damned if the man didn't say, "As you wish, *mademoiselle*. I give you my word. Now…after you."

So either he was stupid, or he was also pretending.

"No, really, after you."

He tapped the rusty grate with his pistol's barrel, sending a metallic echo through Melusine's tower, like a cry. "You meet with me. I put away the gun. *No sooner.*"

So I began my slow descent. But what I was thinking was more along the lines of, *Remember that word* Comitatus.

And, *He's not the man with the power. Someone else, an inner circle, has the power.*

And, *Halfway to Calais? He means to take me to England.*

What's in England?

Soon, I was edging across that last slant of rocks to the railed stairway, then pulling myself over.

I looked one last time up the sheer side of the tower. Had I climbed *that*?

Then I got my first look at Frenchy, standing several paces back from the foot of the stairway, half-lost in shadows. Still anonymous—he wore a ski mask. He was aiming his pistol at Rhys.

Rhys knelt beside the remains of what had been Liverpool, holding the corpse's hand, murmuring something. I suspected he knew Frenchy and I were there. He just didn't seem to care.

"Back away from him," ordered Frenchy.

Rhys firmly said, "I will not. Not until I'm finished." Then he went back to murmuring. Murmuring *what?*

"We had a deal," I said, as a distraction. "I come out. You put away your gun."

"It must have suffered in translation."

So I turned to go back in—body language being universal.

I stopped when I heard him chamber a round. "Another step and your friend dies."

Considering that he'd just committed murder, I wasn't going to chance it. I turned back. "Over a *cup?*"

"Apparently." He wasn't kidding.

"You don't even know what it is, do you? What it means?"

"All I must know—" he angled the gun away from Rhys to me "—is *where* it is. And this, you will show me."

"Because…?"

"Because I have the power to make you."

Damned if it wasn't Charlemagne chopping down the sacred oaks all over again. So might makes right, huh? Not permanently. Never permanently.

On the other hand, might could generally mess things up for everyone else, even if it made wrong. And Frenchy and Liverpool had been the ones with the might. They'd both had—

Oh! Suddenly I had a better plan. But for it to work, somehow I had to get Rhys's attention without Frenchy noticing it.

"Yeah," I said. "Power. Your dead friend over there is doing exactly what you want him to, right?"

As I'd hoped, Frenchy glanced in that direction, as if on a dare to look at his handiwork. As soon as he did, I waved to catch Rhys's gaze, pointed to the body and made a fake gun with my hand, thumb and index finger extended.

"Actually," said Frenchy, "my friend *is* doing what I want. He is keeping his tongue. Or what's left of it."

Rhys's brow furrowed. He didn't understand—me, that is.

Frenchy glanced quickly back, suspicious.

I immediately tried to look innocent again, with a dollop of scared, which wasn't hard. Bullies like to see you scared. "So those are my choices? Die with my secrets or betray a goddess?" Not that Melusine wasn't used to betrayal....

"Your fairy is not real," Frenchy assured me, sounding amused. "She will not mind."

"But God is real," Rhys interrupted—as his own distraction, I assumed. "Whatever face you may choose to give Him. And whomever you have mistakenly pledged your loyalties to, God is the one to whom you must eventually answer."

"Shut up," said Frenchy, trying to sound casual—and failing. He also looked toward Rhys again.

I quickly mimicked the make-believe gun and bounced it. *Bang-bang*. Didn't they play cowboys and Indians in Wales? Oh...maybe not. Bobbies and robbers?

This time Rhys did a much better job at hiding his interest in my pantomime. Which was good, except I didn't know if he understood or not. "Is pleasing your worldly masters truly worth the loss of your soul?" he asked.

He was beginning to sound like a priest.

I had a cold sense of suspicion, all of a sudden—but it wasn't something I could focus on at this moment.

"In fact," I added, to drag Frenchy's attention back, "every major religion in the world admonishes against murder. I teach comparative mythology. I know these things."

Beyond Frenchy's shoulder, Rhys pointed at himself and widened his eyes, then did a bang-bang motion with his hand, then spread it. He understood that I wanted him to get Liverpool's gun. He just didn't want one. As during the car chase, he wasn't willing to kill. Period.

"Mythology?" Frenchy sneered. "Fiction. You damned goddess worshippers would emasculate the world if you had your way."

He glanced at Rhys again, which gave me a chance to mime that he should give *me* the gun. If there was a gun. True, I didn't like them. I liked being held at gunpoint even less.

I said, "Is it any wonder people look for a better world than the one you clearly live in?" That bought Rhys a moment in which to look unconvinced by my plan. He clearly didn't want me shooting anybody, either. Well, that made two of us. Probably.

Who can say with hypotheticals?

I tried to look my most innocent for both men.

Rhys, with clear reluctance but guarded faith, gingerly reached under Liverpool's windbreaker. He closed his eyes.

Oh. Gross. Time to keep Frenchy's attention for a minute…an idea that reminded me of another weapon in my arsenal.

Talking a lot without getting to the point. I've read that men find that amazingly disconcerting.

"What is it with men like you?" I demanded. "Most men are great, but the ones that aren't…! And hey, how about war? It's not women who start the things. Unless you count Helen of Troy, and even she just wanted love."

Beyond the increasingly incredulous masked gunman, Rhys shook his head at the hope of a shoulder holster. He frisked the corpse's hips.

I took a deeper breath—and took one step downward, bringing me a little closer to Frenchy, putting him on guard. "I mean, do you ever stop to think about what you're putting out into this world with your guns and your threats and your chauvinistic attitudes? It's time you were stopped. And if it takes a magical goddess chalice to stop you, then more power to the cup!"

Just as I'd hoped, Frenchy could only take so much. "For

the love of God," he warned me, "shut up and come with me. If you behave yourself, I will leave your friend unharmed."

Behind him, Rhys triumphantly held up some kind of handgun.

"A perfect example of what I mean," I told Frenchy, taking another step. He lifted his aim from my stomach to my head, reminding me of *his* weapon.

Giving Rhys a chance to stand.

I only saw that peripherally, since I didn't dare focus on Rhys. Instead I flipped my hand in the direction of Frenchy's handgun as if in demonstration. "Why are boys so much more likely to play with guns in the first place, huh?"

Frenchy extended his arm slightly, eyes a touch wider, as if hoping I would finally figure out what he was pointing at me before he had to use it. *Hello*, had he heard nothing? I knew I was babbling—it was on purpose—but I also couldn't help wishing he might learn something.

Then again, me kicking the crap out of him would make the same point, right? Considering how, with a sneeze, he could end my existence, I thought he more than deserved it.

Rhys was edging closer to us; this would be so much easier if he were more violent himself. Ironic, huh?

I kept talking. "It's a power thing with you—the need to have power over other people. You all but force the rest of us to play, too. But you know, there's a problem with that kind of power. Sexy though power can be."

Which is when I realized that Rhys and I needed a distraction to pass over the gun. Something. Anything.

So I went from one uniquely feminine weapon to another.

I sighed. "At least promise me something?"

We both knew Frenchy's promises weren't worth the breath he used to make them, but curiosity is human nature. He widened his eyes, silently inviting me to make my request.

I licked my lips, as if nervous. Then I said, "Let's go up in that tower for a threesome, first."

As I'd hoped, Frenchy kind of, well…froze. *His* logical side had to know I was bluffing. But logic isn't everything.

I looked quickly to Rhys—and damn it, he'd momentarily stilled too, Liverpool's gun dangling uselessly from his hand.

So I lunged for Frenchy's gun instead.

He recovered his senses at my sudden movement, tightened his hold on the weapon. Calling my Chi, I clasped my two hands around his one and spun, using the strength of his own grip to wrench his wrist. He cried out, but didn't quite drop it. Damn!

"You bitch," he snarled into my face, grabbing the gun with his left hand before his right hand gave up.

Yeah. Whatever. I caught his left elbow and drew it farther, faster, in the direction he was already moving it.

He lurched off balance, shoes scuffing at cobblestone.

I danced backward, matching my direction to his, close enough to swing one foot out—and nudge his stumbling ankle even farther forward. Farther than his sense of balance could take.

He dropped. I rolled onto his shoulders to help him and gravity finish what they'd started. Riding him down, I extended one hand for the gun I knew would drop—

But with a spit of blue flame, it fired.

In his stubborn determination not to let go, the bastard had fired it blindly, and now—

I used both hands to force his head downward, like a basketball, except skulls don't bounce. He did cry out, and something—his nose?—gave. Gun clattered onto cobblestone.

With my left hand I snatched it up—it was heavy, and the barrel was hot. With my right I formed a fist, channeled all my Chi into one direction, and struck downward against his head.

One blow. He sank onto stone at the base of Tour Melusine, bloody and unconscious.

Dogs were barking. I looked in the direction Frenchy had blindly fired—the tower, thank heavens, not the town, not my friend—and sent up a quick prayer of thanks that he hadn't created another statistic.

In the meantime, lights were coming on in buildings around us. We were still hidden in shadow—but only until someone was brave enough to investigate.

I checked Frenchy's pulse before rolling off him. Still alive, and yes, I felt relief. I'm allowed to be complicated.

"The problem with power over other people," I muttered unloading his pistol, "is that as soon as they can, people then take power over you."

Then, crouched beside him, I turned spy. I wiped my prints off his weapon and pressed it back into his hand. On a hunch, I pointed it—my hand holding his—toward Liverpool's body and fired. Another blue spurt. The gun lurched.

So did the corpse.

I'd read something about a bullet remaining in the chamber.

"What are you…?" asked Rhys, sounding shaken. Well my suspicion of what he'd been doing with that corpse was pretty damned unsettling, too.

"That was so the police will hold him," I murmured, patting Frenchy down. "This is to steal a little power."

I took his driver's license, but not his money or credit cards. I took his cell phone. Information, every bit of it.

"C'mon," I said, rising easily from my crouch. I took Liverpool's gun from Rhys, before he dropped it.

"Where do you mean to go?"

"Somewhere we can hide and see if the police actually pick this guy up before he comes to."

"You don't plan on waiting for the constabulary?"

I shook my head, almost as surprised at myself as he seemed to be. But from the discussion I'd overheard between Frenchy and Liverpool, this *Comitatus* had a very long reach. "How big a sin is leaving the scene of a crime, anyway?" I asked, a touch sarcastic. "Mortal or venial?"

His eyes brightened with understanding—he knew that I knew. "It is venial," he admitted. "But a rather large illegality."

Holy crap. My instincts were dead-on. Rhys had been administering last freakin' rites!

Well, I could lose it once we were someplace safe. Our hotel was far too well lit. The bar would attract too much attention and the café or *pharmacie* would require breaking and entering. Which left…

I grabbed my boots. "Here's a wacky thought. How about the church?"

"Sanctuary it is," he said, grim.

I led the way through the shadows, from tree to tree, to the looming Romanesque church that dominated the town.

Where Father Rhys Pritchard should feel right at home.

Lex's prep school feels British. School sports include polo and sculling. The boys wear uniforms, ties, sweaters.

I visit twice a year for formal dances. This fall is my fifth time to attend. I'm beginning my junior year in high school. Although Lex and I are the same age, he is a senior.

His drive to succeed would frighten me, if he weren't Lex.

Late Saturday morning, we are out together exploring the quaint Vermont town near the academy. We don't talk much. We don't have to. We just hold hands and enjoy each other. Lex has almost reached six-two. He is quietly handsome, with a long curve to his jaw and with serious eyes and a mouth that I have recently learned was made for kissing. So whenever we find a very private place, we kiss.

Languid, intense, hard-not-to-squirm, full-mouth kissing. Fingers itchy to touch—but not yet. Not yet.

Our romance has progressed very slowly, to judge by movie standards. Or my friends at home. But Lex and I know that rushing things can cheapen them. Slowing down allows savoring. We've been kissing, when it seems appropriate, for almost two years, but it's just been this last summer that something clicked and we suddenly got the hang of making out.

We are very, very good at it. Why not enjoy that for a while, before hurrying into anything new?

This particular Saturday, we end up at a soda shop. To my disappointment, Lex's older cousin Phil—also a senior—shows up. He drags up chairs for himself and his date, Fonda Wills, assuming they are welcome.

Lex catches my gaze. He knows I dislike Phil. But we both understand that Lex has to be polite. Phil's bone marrow saved Lex's life.

I squeeze his hand under the table, understanding.

Then I realize that, despite talking about yachts, Phil is there to show off Fonda.

To show off that they're having sex.

He has a mark on his neck that I realize is a hickey. Fonda keeps sliding her hand into his lap, and he laughs each time he pushes it back. Slowly.

At first Lex looks equally disgusted with Phil and Fonda. But then he looks…angry? At Phil.

I don't get it, even when I notice Phil leering at the base of my ice-cream bowl, where I've set aside the cherry to eat last. All I know is that an energy is roiling off Lex that I haven't felt before. I don't like it.

I turn to him and whisper, "Let's go."

His nod is sharp, as if he has to force it. He stands.

Then Phil says, "Hey, Maggi. If Lex doesn't want your cherry, can I have it? Fonda let me have hers."

I realize what he's getting at, and I want to hit him—

But Lex does it for me. Except…Lex doesn't just hit Phil.

Lex picks up a tray and axes it into Phil's face, hard, right between the eyes.

Phil lets out a roar, stumbles out of his chair and back against the wall, clutches at his face. Blood gushes across the table and down his academy sweater. Fonda keeps screaming, not even stopping for breath—her screams just

*gasp in and out. Phil is staring over his blood-washed hands
at his younger cousin, horrified and outraged and agonized
and...*

And he almost looks proud.

Lex, however, looks wholly at ease.

"Shall we?" he asks me, offering his arm.

I take a quick step back from his cool violence. "No!"

*The waitress is calling for an ambulance. The shopkeeper
is yelling. Lex ignores them both and, for a moment, confusion flickers across his hazel eyes. "He deserved it."*

*"Nobody deserves that! You could have killed— Lex, he's
your family!"*

"Exactly. Come on." And he holds out his hand.

*I stare at it, fully aware of everything his hand promises.
The quiet connection we've always shared, soul to soul.*

But that connection isn't there right now.

*Then he says something he has never before said to me.
"Maggi, you're embarrassing me."*

*My heart hurting, I turn my back on him to help tend to
worthless, stupid, broken-nosed Phil—and to Fonda, who
has fainted—until the ambulance arrives. And that is that.*

Lex and I do not speak again for over a year.

Chapter 10

"*You're a priest?*"

Rhys and I paused on the church's front steps, sheltered by massive pilasters framing its looming double doors. Freakish stone creatures and wide-eyed saints, hundreds of them carved into the Norman archways, watched our arrival.

In the distance, we could hear sirens.

I'd used Frenchy's cell phone to place an anonymous call.

"It's not that simple," said Rhys, defensive.

"It's not that complicated either, is it? You attend seminary, you take vows, you become a priest. You risked both our lives to give last rites to that thug out there—"

"It's called extreme unction, now. And there was nobody else to do it."

"—and those women in Lusignan…have you been in that church before? They acted just like you were a priest."

He shrugged. "The older women who attend church every day develop a kind of sixth sense about those things. But, Maggi—"

"I was going around thinking you were married."

"I almost was!" His protest echoed from the twisting, bestial sculptures crowding over us, and not because he'd raised his voice. It echoed with anguish.

Oh, yeah. He'd said he'd been engaged. That she'd died a year ago. I asked, more softly, "Are you an *Anglican* priest?"

"I am not," he said. Then, "Look. Here's the police."

The *gendarmerie* arrived, with an ambulance. Despite not being done with Father Rhys, I left the refuge of the church's sculpted doorway to make sure that when Frenchy was rolled into the ambulance, handcuffs and *gendarmes* were involved. Excellent.

At the very least, he might be caught in red tape for a few days. Better, he might be charged with Liverpool's murder— here came the coroner's wagon now—

I backed my way up the church steps. It didn't look like the tower would be open to tourists for a few days. And the usually sleepy little town of Vouvant wasn't likely to settle down anytime soon. So much for finding clues to the Melusine Chalice here.

A police car turned down the street in our direction.

"Uh…Rhys?" I sped my step.

He tried one of the four doors behind us, two pairs of two. It didn't open. He quickly tried the next one.

I stepped back against a fluted pilaster as the squad car eased closer. "What happened to the concept of sanctuary?"

"Vandalism?" He tried the third, and I could hear it rattle, locked. "Theft? People fornicating in the pews?"

Slow as the police car was moving, they hadn't seen us. Yet. But we were pretty well trapped—

Yes! The fourth latch turned under Rhys's hand and we slipped into our second ancient church of the day, shouldering the heavy door shut just as a searchlight washed past.

This church was larger than the one in Lusignan, with massive arches and vaulted ceilings. Lit by low-wattage wall sconces and the twinkle of blue-glass votives, it felt eerie. Not dangerous eerie—not with that scent of incense and candle wax, that hush of echoes, that reserve of holiness wrapping itself around us. But somehow…*demanding*.

Like the church expected something of us.

"If the police come looking, the rector's more likely to do a walk-through for them." Rhys looked around the church with now-understandable familiarity. Then he beckoned me to the eastern transept where a blocky crypt sat near the curve of a rounded wall. We circled it—a simple tomb, without even the usual effigy—and settled into the space between it and a recessed window. "He'd have to be serious to spot us here."

I sat on the marble floor and leaned back against the tomb. And sighed. It's possible to reach a point of exhaustion where even bare rock feels like a cloud of comfort.

But I wasn't ready to rest yet.

"You're a Catholic priest," I said. Accused.

"I am," he admitted, sinking into a crouch. Then he shook his head. "I mean, not exactly. I used to be…."

Ah. Things became more clear. "You're an ex-priest?"

Rhys's blue gaze lifted to meet mine in the shadows. "There's no such thing as an ex-priest. Not in Catholicism. Only priests who have been dismissed from their clerical duties."

I squinted at him. "I'm not getting it."

"I was born to the church." With a finger, Rhys traced the patterns on the stone tiles between his knees. "True, my mother is a Grail Keeper. But we Welsh aren't like you Yanks, drawing solid lines between the old ways and the new. The old gods may have given the field, but they're hardly dead. My mum's faith may well have strengthened my own. I went straight from school into the seminary. I've never felt so complete as the day of my ordination."

I could see his passion, his truth.

"I was twenty-five when I got a little parish kirk in Cornwall, on the coast. It's what I was born to do. I still believe that."

I could believe it too. "And then…?"

Rhys sat beside me, leaned against the crypt, "And then I met Mary."

True. It's a popular Catholic name. But… *"Mary?"*

"Mary Tregaron was a fisherman's daughter. She came back from nursing school to open a clinic. She had the purest heart. I fell in love with her, and she with me, and I've never felt so sure of anything before—anything except my calling."

"Which doesn't allow you to love women."

"Like Christ, priests try to love everyone. Even gun-toting madmen. But my calling did not allow marriage."

"So you quit the priesthood for her?" At his stare, I realized what a stupid thing that was to say. "It wouldn't have been that easy, though, would it?"

"We didn't even speak of it, the connection we felt, for almost a year. Even once we did, Mary didn't want to take me from God. I thought we could conquer it, but that was my pride. She was so active in the church, so giving. One day we had a moment alone and we nearly…"

I thought he'd say they nearly had sex. I felt guilty when he said, "We nearly kissed. So I petitioned to change parishes."

I waited, wondering at the kind of personal strength their fight must have taken.

"My bishop told me it could be a year or more—there's quite the shortage of priests, you know. But he also…" He shook his head, and some of the tightness eased from his throat. "He counseled me to consider that there might be more than one way to do God's will. I wasn't so sure, but I trusted God enough to at least consider it, to pray about it, to do research."

I wanted to hold his hand. I couldn't. "What did you find?"

"I found nothing that barred priests from marriage. Nothing but church law, of course—and even that seemed suspect. Apostles were married. Early popes married. Celibacy among priests was optional until the Second Lateran Council."

"I skipped theology that day," I said. "When was that?"

"In 1139. So for over half the history of the church, priests could marry. By the time I'd learned all this, months had passed. People think the priesthood is like the army—follow one's superiors at all times or be court-martialed—but that's not true. If it were true we'd never have had Vatican II."

He paused—literally. His hands had been flying as he spoke, he'd gotten so fired up, but suddenly he fell quiet.

"That's when I realized how strongly I felt about it," he admitted with a shrug, and leaned back against the tomb. "I accepted that Mary Tregaron had been the answer to prayers I'd never even prayed, that by fighting our love I was living a lie. So I petitioned Rome to return to secular life. To marry."

A bright light tracked across the church from the outside, turning colors through stained glass, the police still driving, still looking. So far, they weren't bothering with the church.

"But you didn't marry," I said softly.

"Perhaps it was easier in the sixties, under Paul VI," said Rhys. "But now…"

"Not so much?"

His smile held no humor. "It took three years. Then one night…" The smile vanished.

"You don't have to tell me this," I said.

"One night, Mary's car was hit by a lorry on the motorway, and she was rushed to the hospital. Her injuries required surgery, and…someone made a mistake."

"What kind of mistake?"

"They gave her the wrong blood, and she went into shock…and she died. I barely got to the hospital in time. Giving her extreme unction was my last official task as a canonical priest.

"When the papers arrived, three days later, I signed them."

We sat there for a long while, in the kind of silence only churches and tragedies seem capable of creating.

Finally Rhys sat up. "In any case, if I seem vague about my status, that's why. I'm still a priest. Ordination is permanent. But I'm no longer a practicing cleric, and I quite definitely lost my job. I have no credit. No life experience outside of the church." He spread his hands. "Where else could I go but academia?"

That was a joke, right? I tried to smile. "And archeology?"

"It sounds foolish, now."

"As foolish as me suggesting a threesome with a priest?"

"It's not that foolish, no." The real smile came back—but I finally understood that edge of distance, of sadness behind his personable manner. "I began to dream about the Holy Grail. It gave me something to focus on, a distraction from my grief, and I started to think, well…I suppose it has to do with wanting to be closer to Jesus—not just the religion but the man. And perhaps it's about proving myself."

"The Holy Grail only manifests for the worthy," I remembered. "In the Arthurian stories, Lancelot is denied the vision because of his affair with Guinevere."

"But his bastard son, Galahad, receives it," Rhys agreed. "Perhaps I want to learn which of them I'm more like. When I petitioned to be laicized, I forsook my vows. Vows I'd freely taken. I understood the celibacy clause when I was ordained."

I wanted to reassure him that he had nothing to prove. But I'd known the man for two days. He probably knew himself a lot better than I did.

At least I knew him better than I *had*. "I'm *sorry*."

Rhys rested his arms on his knees, his chin on his hands. "That's all right. I'd take it as a compliment, if you hadn't included that Gallic thug in the suggestion."

The *threesome?* I pushed his arm. "That was a distraction!"

His eyes twinkled at me. "And it most certainly succeeded."

Rather than argue my innocence, I dug out the ID I'd taken from Frenchy—and got my first good look at the man's face.

Our henchman had surprisingly blond hair, squared features, light eyes, a bored expression. And a stupid-looking mustache.

"René de Montfort," I read. "Forty-one years old, from Ramonchamp." I puffed out my lips. "Where's Ramonchamp?"

Rhys shrugged, leaning closer to see the card. I felt his heat on my bare arms, bare legs. Well, we were in hiding, right? Personal space takes a hit when you're in hiding.

Except my personal space wasn't the part of me that felt concerned. My personal space kind of liked the sense of his nearness, his warmth, his solidness.

Rhys took the license, and I let him. "René," he repeated. "What could have lured you into such poor judgment?"

Which, thank heavens, reminded me of everything *I* still had to tell *him*. "The *Comitatus!*"

He looked back at me. *"Gesundheit?"*

"They seem to be called the *Comitatus*." And I explained what I'd overheard—that there really was a secret society after the Melusine Chalice. That membership seemed to be contingent on a man's lineage. That from what I knew about the word in old literature, it represented a code of conduct among pagans, particularly Anglo-Saxons. *Comitatus* had been all about strength, and loyalty to one's king.

"And," I finished, "I think they're based in England. I just don't know *where* in England."

Rhys looked both sleepy and serious. "Does it matter?"

"Of course it matters! These people are sending henchmen to beat up little old ladies and to steal the Melusine Chalice. They probably destroyed the Kali Cup, too, and who knows how many other goddess grails we don't even know about? I realize these aren't as important to you as the Holy Grail—"

"They're still important." He looked away, at the thick-silled window across from us. "They're important to Bridge, and to you."

"And they *mean something,* Rhys! The real version of history. Balance. Of course it matters!"

Rhys leaned forward with the intensity of his own argument. "I didn't say these weren't sinful, dangerous people, Maggi. But the world is thick with bad people, and the world has police and clerics to deal with them. You're a college instructor. Why does it become your responsibility?"

Wow, I disliked that argument...especially because it was starting to make sense. I'd seen a man murdered, fought with a masked gunman, and *shot somebody*—somebody already dead, but still! It had been an ugly night, and sense was not yet welcome.

Then Rhys asked, "What would you do if you found them?"

I smiled. "Walk into the middle of a solemn ceremony, flip on the overhead lights, and send the funny hats flying."

He grinned, too. Funny hats aside, I kind of liked the image of myself making them an offer they couldn't refuse.

Leave the goddess grails alone, or else.

But assuming I could get that far, would they listen to me?

"Maybe I could collect enough information to report them to the authorities," I suggested, but even that sounded weak. "Except they seem to have powerful connections."

Rhys raised his eyebrows—*see?*

"Or I could report them to the news. Hard to be a secret society when your face is on the front page."

"And the papers will listen to you because…?"

I let my head fall with a light thunk of defeat against the tomb behind us. This group might have connections to the news agencies, too. "Oh, shut up."

Rhys's smile looked sweet and, well, ministerial. "I'm sorry you feel frustrated."

"Well, I do."

"But when did going after these men become your goal?"

"When they broke into my house? When they hurt Aunt Bridge?" But again he had a point. A lot of people in this world are victimized without going on transcontinental jaunts after the people who victimized them.

There's strength. And then there's strength.

"I thought your goal was to find the Melusine Chalice," he said—and as soon as my priorities righted themselves, they went too far the other direction. I wanted to kiss him.

Uh-oh. I shut my eyes, so that I wouldn't be looking into his blue gaze. So that I wouldn't be tempted. "It was. It is."

Then I felt it. The brush of his fingertips down my temple. My cheek. Their gentleness felt so good, so very necessary, that it took every bit of my self-control not to turn my head and kiss the hand that guided them.

I didn't. I didn't even open my eyes.

Rhys cleared his throat, clearly uncomfortable. "Get some rest," he suggested. "I'll keep watch."

"Okay," I said, eyes still closed.

"I'm sorry," he said. "That was out of line. Especially after everything I just told you. I still love Mary, you know."

"Don't mention it," I said. And I meant it.

Things would be a lot easier between us if we never mentioned it again.

You know that ethereal, half-dream state when you're no longer asleep but you aren't quite awake?

Between the worlds, in neither and in both. Like that lozenge of overlapping circles on a *vesica piscis.*

As slow consciousness crept back into my sleep, comfortable and warm on the floor of Vouvant's church, I resisted the coming of consciousness. Instead I let all the little, insignificant bits of the last few days float past.

…Angoulême was last on Brigitte's list…

It's our conscious minds that need to organize everything. I took a deep breath—but not too deep—and savored being alive and rested.

…Romanesque churches. Sanctuary. Ironic, doing goddess research on holy ground, with a priest…

I didn't want to think yet.

…soldiers took the toilet route into Richard the Lionheart's Chateau Gaillard, too…

Once I started thinking, I would have to face problems and make decisions. Sometimes I get tired of decisions.

…powerful women, like Joan of Arc or Eleanor d'Aquitaine….

I squinted my eyes open, just testing. My subconscious was onto something.

Powerful women, with powerful connections.

Isabelle of Angoulême, a countess of Lusignan, had been the wife of King John of England. Making her a queen.

King John had been the younger brother of Richard I. Also called the Lionheart.

Both men had been sons of Eleanor d'Aquitaine.

After Lusignan rebelled against the French crown, Isabelle took sanctuary in a famous French convent called Fontevrault. The same place where her mother-in-law, Eleanor, had spent her final years. That's what powerful women did back then, whether they were devout or not. In a patriarchal world where religion had been everything, convents were one of the only acceptable centers of woman power.

And here was the kicker.

Richard, Eleanor and Isabelle were buried at Fontevrault, along with Eleanor's second husband, Henry II. Unlike the tomb beside me, those held effigies of all four figures.

I wasn't guessing this time. I *knew* where the Melusine Chalice was…or at least, where it had once been hidden. One of the least likely places to find a sect of goddess worshippers…and the perfect cover. *It was in the abbey!*

"Holy crap!" I exclaimed, opening my eyes.

Then Rhys, beneath me, grunted and woke—and I realized that the reason I'd been so warm and comfy on the church floor was because I hadn't been.

On the church floor, I mean.

I'd been asleep in Father Pritchard's arms.

Chapter 11

My head was tucked, warm and cozy, in the hollow below Rhys's shoulder, under his jaw. I could feel the ridge of a collarbone against my ear. One hand lay, fingers curled, near his throat, brushed by his coarse hair. The other…

Oh, heavens, my other hand was tucked, just the fingertips, into the waistband of his jeans.

I could see that very clearly, since my position had me staring down his long, lean body.

I levered myself off of him. *Quickly.*

The sliding release of his hands off *me* told me this hadn't been a one-sided cuddle. I felt a sudden, cool loss on my elbow, where he'd been holding my arm in place—the arm with the hand in his pants. I felt a similar sense of absence on my butt.

He sat back from me, knees high, trapped against the crypt. "Ah. Well." His voice sounded rough. "That was unexpected."

"We were asleep," I said.

"That's true."

"And nothing happened." Even the fingertips of my left hand, which felt very sensitive all of a sudden, had to support that. They'd been wedged *in* his waistband, not beyond it.

"Nothing did." Rhys rubbed his eyes with the thumb and forefinger of one hand, keeping his wary attention on me. Or maybe it wasn't wary. Maybe it was just…regretful?

He still loves Mary, I reminded myself.

"But," he added, "I do… I do apologize, anyway."

"Me, too," I said quickly. "Sorry about that."

Then we just sat there, feeling embarrassed and weirdly guilty. At least, I did, because I'd really *liked* sleeping in a man's arms after all these months. His body had felt solid and warm and alive against mine. Now I felt chilled and alone….

Until I remembered a great distraction. "Sun's up. Let's grab breakfast and I'll tell you what I've figured out."

He looked hesitant. And wonderfully disheveled.

"Or…?" I asked, wanting nothing more than to be on the road to Fontevrault. Now. Ten minutes ago. Well…maybe not *ten* minutes ago, considering where I'd been then.

"It's Sunday morning," he said.

Oh. He wasn't an ex-Catholic. He wasn't even an ex-priest.

I admired his dedication, even if it made me feel even guiltier. "Then let's go clean up. I'll get some food and check us out of the B&B while you're at mass. Then we can head out. I have some phone messages to check, too."

Maybe Lex had called back with more information about whom I shouldn't trust, and why.

And how he could possibly know about it.

But he hadn't called.

On the plus side, Rhys insisted Fontevrault Abbey had not been on Bridge's list. That meant we should manage to be there and gone before the *Comitatus* even knew about it. After all, how many hiding places could there be in an abandoned convent?

On the minus side—it turned out Fontevrault was the size of a small town. And turns out it was the Cultural Center for all of Western France. No complications there, right?

"At the height of its power," said our tour guide, leading us through sculpted gardens amidst neat medieval buildings, "there were over five thousand nuns living at the Royal Abbey of Fontevrault. That is not counting the monks."

"Excuse me," said Rhys, while I eyed the breadth of this place and thought—*yeah. This could hold five thousand people.* "Did you say nuns *and* monks? In the same abbey?"

The guide, a perky blond French girl, nodded. "Fontevrault was the first of only a few holy orders that allowed both men and women. Very forward of them, do you not think?"

Was she flirting with Rhys?

"It is shockingly so," he agreed with his friendly grin.

Was he flirting back?

"More unique was that the abbess, not the abbot, ruled the entire convent. She answered only to the pope and, sometimes, the king. This point was established in Fontevrault's charter, based on the Biblical instruction to 'Behold thy Mother.'"

Rhys said, "St. John, Chapter 19, verse 27."

"I am impressed," purred our tour guide.

As she turned away to point out the gardens I touched his arm. "Something going on between you and the guide, Romeo?"

He blinked, then laughed. "Her name is Claire, and I doubt we've anything in common but an interest in clerical history."

"And did you notice that this particular history reads like a 12th-century sexual revolution?"

"Surprisingly so, yes."

After trailing past the conical tower that had been part of a massive kitchen, we continued to the dining hall.

The refectory bordered a beautifully tended cloister, quartered by footpaths, with a burbling fountain in the center.

"Excuse me," I asked. "Claire? Is the fountain natural, or was it built here?"

"The fountains are supplied by artesian wells which were likely here before the abbey was built. The area is riddled with caves and underground rivers."

Like Glastonbury. Like Lourdes. Like Bath. Goddess sites.

As we continued along weathered, white-stone buildings with gray slate roofs, my theories felt all the more solid. Nothing here contradicted what I knew about goddess worship, except for one tiny thing:

As Rhys had put it in the car, *It's a convent.*

Claire listed some of Fontevrault's abbesses, like a Who's Who of power. Widows of crown princes. Granddaughters and sisters and bastards of kings, both English and French. The more I heard, the more I had to change my idea of medieval goddess worshippers as frightened and victimized, scurrying to secret meetings in the safety of the woods with their heads down and their faces hidden. If the abbesses of Fontevrault had been involved—and surely a good abbess knew what went on in her own convent—these women had access to far more resources than I'd ever guessed. And the things they'd done with it! Teaching. Nursing lepers.

They withstood quite a few efforts by the monks to put men back in charge, too.

Why did *these* stories so rarely make the history books?

From the chapter house, Claire led us into the echoing choir of the abbey church, a tall gothic structure whose height and beauty rivaled most cathedrals. Beyond, in the nave, lay the four effigies Rhys and I had come to see.

Eleanor d'Aquitaine. Henry II. Richard the Lionheart and his brother's bride, Isabelle d'Angoulême. *Three fair figures, side by side.* Except there were four, like the French version.

I edged in their direction before the rest of the group went that far. I had to see. The tombs sat on a raised dais, surrounded by a railing. Each crypt held a carved, painted effigy, as if the nobles had fallen asleep there. Eleanor even held a book in her hands, as if spending eternity reading.

Four nobles with one heart. The Lionheart. I shivered.

"Are you all right?" asked Rhys, behind me.

"It feels…" But I had no words for the power surging through me like a rush of water, a tingle in the air. *Anticipation*, I imagine. Or even…magic.

I still had to find the "hole where hid her queen"—which I now knew would be where Queen Isabelle had hidden from the French crown, after too many rebellions. But this still felt magic.

Drawing the others into the nave, Claire spoke of the four Plantagenets. I continued to look around at the faded, painted crest of English royalty on the wall beside the royal names. Intricately carved monsters and magical beasts paraded in a frieze across the tops of columns and windows. Angels. Animal heads. Rows of haloed men in the same repeated position, as if they were singing backup. And…

Melusine.

She sat at the cornice of a pilaster, her sculpture half-hidden behind a dragon. But the heraldic pose with her double tail curling to either side was unmistakable, church or no church.

I stared at her, hardly able to breathe. She, in stony silence, stared back at me, coyly guarding her mysteries.

It was still a very large church.

Claire was saying, "The very last abbess, Julie de Pardaillan d'Antin, was driven from the abbey in the 1790s. What happened to her, nobody knows."

Melusine looked even more coy. I spun away from her to stare back at our tour guide. *"Who?"*

"Julie Sophie Charlotte de Pardaillan d'Antin. The Revolution was a dark time for the abbey."

But I'd stopped listening. I'd almost stopped breathing. As Claire led the group across the soaring church, I couldn't have moved if I wanted to.

"Are you all right?" Rhys put a hand on my shoulder. "Magdalene? What is wrong?"

"That last abbess." I swallowed, unsure if I was even awake anymore. It seemed so fantastical…even more so than the creatures that clustered along the frieze above us. "Her name."

Rhys waited. "Her name…?"

"My grandmother's name was Charlotte," I said. "Her mother's name was Sophie. And her mother's name was Julie. Julie d'Antin…after her own grandmother."

"You think you're related to an abbess of Fontevrault?"

Julie de Pardaillan d'Antin, fleeing the Revolution, must have been the one who passed down the nursery rhyme about Melusine. That meant its familial sources were nowhere near as ancient as we'd all thought.

Two hundred years and change. That was all.

"How long was Melusine worshipped here, anyway?"

I looked back up at her figurine—and that's when I saw it. Really, finally, saw it. I slowly sank to my knees right there on the church floor, staring upward.

Carved into the stone wall beside Melusine's pilaster, at about shoulder height, two circles intersected to create a *vesica piscis*. And somewhere behind that, I knew, lay a hidden chamber.

The chamber of my ancestors. And Melusine's Chalice.

"The abbey closes in half an hour," a guard warned as I hurried through the gates for the third time that day.

"I'm just checking to see…" I flashed my day pass from earlier, scanning the gardens that spread out before me. Since I wasn't actually looking for anybody, I wasn't surprised to not find him. "Nope. Guess he's gone on to the car. Thanks!"

And I headed out toward the parking area.

Across the street stood a high stone wall, fronted by tall spires of cedar trees. I ducked behind them, doubly sheltered by a row of tour buses, to where Rhys waited with extra clothing.

"Have I mentioned," he said, low, "that this is an insane idea?" But he handed me the black T-shirt I'd picked up in town as he said it.

"Once or twice." Making sure the buses hid me—and trying not to breathe too deeply of diesel—I pulled the shirt on over my worn blue camisole. Rhys handed me a black ball cap.

It wouldn't mislead anybody who looked closely, not for a second. But if anybody was looking closely, we were already sunk. I'm a college professor, not a criminal mastermind—which is why I'd gotten help.

"You want to do *what?*" my friend, Officer Sofie Douglas, had demanded when I'd called her from a public phone in town.

"I want to break into a major cultural center and see what they've got hidden under their abbey church. You're the only person I could think of who might have some suggestions."

Sofie had said, "I suggest you don't do that."

"Here comes a crowd," I said. "Now, let's go." And we headed back across the street, hoping the guard wouldn't get a distinct look. I raised my day pass high, so the guard could see it over the heads of the departing tourists, while Rhys went to ask him the location of the nearest bathrooms.

My job was to keep walking, casual and confident and easy to overlook. If we were lucky, the guard would remember me leaving before, but not entering a second time.

I crossed the still-sunny gardens, climbed several stairs and stepped through the open doors into the echoing height of the almost-empty church. The other tourists paid me no heed, but the frieze that held Melusine seemed to be watching me.

Sofie had said, "I'm guessing the place is wired out the butt. And although I don't know shit for French laws, I'd say that breaking and entering is a bad deal."

Which had given me an idea. "What about just entering?"

Stepping behind a column, I tugged off the hat and stuffed it into one of the pockets of my cargo pants. Then I stripped off the shirt and tied it around my waist, reverting to the blue camisole. I wanted to look more like the woman the guard had seen leaving, for the security cameras.

By the time a recorded ten-minute warning played across the grounds in French, then English, then German, my breathing was shallow. Since taking myself through some Tai Chi forms right here in the *l'église abbatiale* wouldn't count as inconspicuous, I just had to deal with it.

Rhys was right. This was an insane idea.

So why did I feel like the night before Christmas? Not just excited. Somehow…spiritually primed?

"Five minutes to go," said Rhys softly from behind a pillar. "There's still time to change your mind."

"Not on your life."

"Nobody's followed us, anyway." He unzipped his camera bag and handed me my halogen flashlight, my cell phone, and the disposable camera we'd bought in town. Then he surprised me with a wrapped juice box and a package of vending-machine cookies. Each item he produced, I tucked gratefully into one or another of my cargo pockets. "You're safe to go in and out without giving away any secrets."

"Good." I fished out the car keys for him, but kept my passport and emergency money. On the off chance I was arrested, I might as well have my papers…and Rhys on the outside, waiting to bail me out. "Thanks."

"You're here to reconnoiter, not to remove, agreed?"

"'Thou shalt not steal.'" I believed that. What we needed was proof to convince someone in authority, someone trustworthy, that the chalice was here—and needed extra protection.

Rhys brushed a gentle kiss across my cheek. "Be careful."

But I arched upward and kissed his lips instead.

Blame it on adrenaline, or his breath on my ear, or how glad I was for an ally in this.

Except that he kissed me back.

My kiss had meant to be quick; when you're unsure of your welcome, you don't exactly go deep. His lips pressed their advantage, moved across mine in surprised welcome.

Savoring. Lingering. *Yes*.

I laid my hand on his taut back, to keep him there. No

thinking. Just enjoyment. Just the determination to keep from remembering—

But we did remember, and we pulled back at once.

"I'm sorry," I said, face flushing warm. "I…"

"Ah." And he licked his lips. "It's my fault. Really."

To complicate matters, a recording announced that the abbey grounds were now closed to the public. All visitors must leave *immédiatement*. If Rhys stayed longer he would draw attention to the fact that he was leaving alone.

He backed away, clearly regretful, then left.

I moved as stealthily as I could to the column closest to Melusine's pilaster, where the cameras shouldn't be able to see me, and sank to the floor. I had a long night ahead of me.

Sofie had said, "Let me get this straight. You're going to find it, document it, and leave it exactly where it is?"

"It will be a lot better for the chalice if someone with the proper credentials retrieves it."

"And then…"

"Then I'll wait for them to open the next morning before leaving."

"So all you're really facing is premeditated trespassing," my police officer friend had teased. "I can accept that."

What felt like forever later, I heard the footsteps of a security guard pacing slowly through the church. As I'd hoped, he didn't look behind every pier and column.

His footsteps continued on. The double doors shut with an echoing bang. The sound of locks sliding into place echoed less.

No lights went off because they hadn't been on; it wasn't even seven p.m. Evening light still filtered through the church's ancient windows, sliding down the long length of its pilasters and across the increasingly shadowed bestiary of its friezes.

So here I sat. Me and Melusine.

It felt somehow right that Rhys wasn't along. It felt right that it was just me and the goddess. In fact, the longer I looked at the intricately carved *vesica piscis* in front of me, fading with the light, the more clearly I could picture goddess worshippers making nighttime visits to this building.

For how many centuries?

Only once the shadows became so thick that I could barely see did I risk standing. No alarms went off—not that I knew of.

The pilaster was one, two, three steps away from me. I took those steps with careful balance. My logical side wanted to hesitate, maybe even give up before I left fingerprints or disturbed anything. This *was* crazy. I *was* no professional. Even if I found the secret entrance, based only on nursery rhymes, what chance was there that any locking mechanism still worked after all these centuries?

But this wasn't about logic. Logic would let whoever cut down the most sacred oaks win. Logic would give up.

This was about faith.

I reached out my hand, not thinking, just acting. It fit against the lozenge where the two circles of the *vesica piscis* design overlapped, and my fingers slipped into nearly hidden holes. Until this moment they'd looked like intricately carved decorations. They *were* that—and more.

They'd been made for a woman's slim fingers.

I curled my fingers into a solid hold—and pushed.

Absolutely nothing happened.

I pulled—and the chunk of stone in my hand pulled, as well, with an audible *click*. I heard a surprising, grating noise.

Then the two front flutes of the pilaster beside me lurched. I caught my breath.

A stone door had unlatched, just far enough for me to grasp it and swing it the rest of the way open. Goddess cultures had built aqueducts even before the Romans, so maybe they could manage some sort of weights-and-pulleys mechanism that would work even today. How sweet was that?

I stepped forward blindly, not wanting to risk the light in case this wall was visible to the security cameras. In three steps, my searching foot met only air. I put out one hand, touching the ancient stone wall for balance as I felt for more floor, and found a step downward.

Got it.

With one last glance toward the Plantagenet effigies, I grabbed the stone handle and pulled the door shut behind me.

It latched with a single, heavy grunt.

Now I turned on my light—and quickly shone it on the door. There was a latch to get back *out,* wasn't there?

Yep. Right there, beside the door.

I turned back to the dusty stairway, raising my halogen light—and slowly inhaled.

Oh...my...goddess.

This wasn't just a spiral stairway, hidden between a pilaster and buttress, curling down into the earth. It was a work of art. I'd thought the carvings in the church were fine? The ones that curled above the stairway were no less amazing. People with curving Celtic bodies and blank eyes. Knotted dragons. Cats with tails entwined. And Melusine, complete with wings and a double tail, flew over them as if leading the way.

I arched my light along the wall, then went to the steps, about to start down—

And hesitated. What if this was like an Indiana Jones or Alan Quartermain story with booby traps, anthrax, poison darts, or walls that would push in to crush the uninvited trespasser?

"No," I whispered, again meeting the gaze of the stone snake-woman carved above me. "You were a mother. I don't think the women who followed you would consider even something as sacred as your chalice more important than a human life."

The stairs had a faint dip worn into them, from centuries of use. I took a step, then a second, curling downward along the tight staircase. Nothing bad happened.

Instead of blades or arrows, I faced a tapestry.

Then, seven steps down, another. Then another.

They lined the outside curve of the stairwell, easily as large and fine as the famous unicorn panels at the Cluny and the Cloisters museums. But unlike those tapestries, these told the story of Melusine.

Here, she stood naked in a fountain with her two sisters, her hair wild and untamed. At the edge of the panel, half behind a tree, a knight stared with wonder.

Here, she sat wearing a crown and twelfth-century clothing, a child to her breast. More children sat at her feet, her knight beside them. Everyone wore the blue and silver of Lusignan.

Here she bathed in her tower, bat-winged and snake-tailed. She had a potted tree beside her tub. On the edge of the panel—the opposite edge than in the first—her knight looked on, this time wide-eyed in horror.

And finally, toward the bottom of the stairwell, hung a tapestry depicting a dragon-like Melusine flying outside her tower, her mouth wide in what I assumed was her infamous scream, exiled by her husband's betrayal.

I hardly noticed the tapestries' worth, I was so intrigued by the familiarity of Melusine's poses. I took the camera from my cargo pocket, climbed the stairs again, and snapped pictures. It was through the lens that I placed the familiarity.

Melusine in the fountain was like Boticelli's *Venus* rising—aka love goddess. Melusine with her children suggested countless pieta and Madonna poses, and statues of Isis and Horus from even further back—aka Mother Goddess.

Was Melusine in her bath a Water Goddess or a Snake Goddess? The fruit on her tree looked suspiciously like apples.

And her flying? I just wasn't sure. In the meantime, the double doors at the foot of the stairway beckoned. Their only lock seemed to be a simple stone bolt. Goddess worshippers were either naive or remarkably secure in their faith. Or both.

Over the doors read: *Soeurs Pour Toujours*.

Sisters forever. From centuries ago.

I lifted the bolt, pushed open the doors and walked in.

Chapter 12

The first thing I noticed, in that three-hundred-year-old hush, was the splatter of water.

I turned in a slow circle, shining my light across the Romanesque arches and pillars, the inverted, vaulted peaks of the low ceiling, the marble floor. In the middle of the round room stood a high altar table of white Fontevrault limestone. And beyond it, at the far end of the temple…

My light found a human-size statue of Melusine, tall and empty-eyed against the wall. Her bat wings looked somehow angel-like. Her full breasts were proud and bare, her tummy rounded out. She had wide hips, and she looked glorious. Both of her serpentine tails curved out in opposite directions, then back, to encircle the slightly raised edge of a floor-level well.

The splashing of water came from the large, thick bowl in her sculpted hands, pouring water into the pool. My light briefly reflected on the surface in bright flashes.

Had I sensed power in old churches? Even in shadows, this place sparkled with it… Real power.

Personal power.

I crossed the room to the statue, focused on the bowl. Sadly, the erosion of water pouring from it across the years, the centuries, had worn a scoop out of it. We might never know what had once been carved there. But still—*it was the chalice!*

I cleared my throat. "May I?"

Only my own voice responded—May…I may…I may…

Well, I was a Grail Keeper, wasn't I? Putting down my light, I stepped to the side of the floor-level well, reached across and took the cool rock of the bowl into my hands. I lifted—

And couldn't move it. Or pull it. Or twist it. Or push it. It was part of the statue. It wasn't the chalice.

When I looked up at Melusine's face, extrashadowy without direct light, I imagined a glint of humor in her hollow eyes.

Fine. "Cup, cup, cup," I murmured. "Who's got the cup?"

Then my gaze fixed on the altar, the hub of the round room. Retrieving my light, I went there. The round top displayed a carving of the *vesica piscis*. And its sides—yes. I found a place where my fingers slid easily in. *Click.*

The top of the altar was hinged. Swinging it outward revealed an inset box lined in worn, deep-blue brocade; I feared a sneeze would disintegrate it. A silver necklace, with a sapphire, lay in a loving circlet. And within the circle—

The most beautiful chalice I'd ever seen.

Dismissing the idea of traps one last time, I lifted the treasure. And for the first time in over two hundred years, a Grail Keeper held the Melusine Chalice in her hands.

No. The Melusine *Grail.*

It had barely three inches of height, but far more width in its bowl and flared base. It seemed to be made of alabaster, and every inch of it had been beautifully etched. Medallions had been designed onto its bowl, engraved with the same images as on the four tapestries—beauty, motherhood, watery secrets and exile. An oddly textured Celtic knotwork swooped and curled across the rest of it. Melusine's tails, I realized. They twined around the base, low stem and rim of the chalice.

I closed the top of the altar, set the grail lovingly on it—then dug out my disposable camera.

"Help me understand," I whispered, and set about taking pictures. They had to be good enough to convince a French archeologist—preferably someone trustworthy and female—to retrieve this treasure so secretly that the *Comitatus* wouldn't find out until everyone did. Whoever she was would be putting her neck on the line, arranging something so covert. She would need damned good proof.

So I shot the grail from all sides. Camera in one hand and light in the other, I took pictures of the Melusine statue and her well, of the floor and the columns. Then, holding the grail again—I loved its heft in my hand—I snapped pictures of the altar's contents.

Then I carried the grail to the fountain's edge. I sank onto Melusine's stone coils at the base of her statue, one of her breasts very near the top of my head, and laid my flashlight on the marble floor. The grail cupped between my hands, I gazed into the shadowed, seemingly depthless well.

I imagined the generations of nuns who had slipped into this sanctuary to celebrate Melusine. Surprisingly powerful women. I tried to imagine what kind of rituals they performed.

It was a good bet that they drank together. Just as I'd promised the old woman at the church.

I turned the grail in my hands. I'd be spending all night here, so I had time. But time wouldn't change the fact that now, holding absolute proof of my lineage, I was scared.

Not about where the cup had been. Not about messing up an archeological investigation. I was afraid of losing myself.

I was scared to lose Dr. Magdalene Sanger and all her logical, academic distance to the mysticism that filled this room.

It didn't matter. I'd already promised.

I knelt before the well, before the goddess. I held the grail under the trickle of water from the statue's bowl, rinsed and poured it out a few times, then filled it with temple water.

Then, determined to meet my fate with honor—I drank.

* * *

The water tasted sweet and surprisingly fresh. Spring fed, yes. But something about its coolness in my mouth, then my throat, felt even more refreshing than that.

It felt like drinking history, drinking womankind, drinking faith. It felt...

It felt like...

The waters splashing in the well seemed to swirl, sapphire blue, from more than the fountain. I felt suddenly dizzy, suddenly lost, suddenly drowning—

Save yourself, screamed my academic side. And I knew that normalcy waited for me, one protest away. But that way lay cowardice, too. So I let myself drift deeper into the sensation, safe in Melusine's coils, letting her take me to where...

Where...

Welcome, daughter.

I didn't hear the words; I sensed them. They weren't words at all, but feelings. How do you transcribe feelings?

Welcome. Belonging. Love. I felt the heat of tears on my cheeks, so overwhelming was Her soul-deep acceptance. I took another sip of Her water to keep the physical sensation from drawing me out of this....

I sensed delight and humor. *The physical is also spiritual. We women know that.*

That came in images of childbirth, a flash so real that I momentarily felt labor pains. I embraced them, as had so many women of old, not as their victim but a warrior who withstands agony for the worthiest of goals, no matter its form. *Life!*

Those were replaced with images of sex, me and Lex Stuart tangled in silky Egyptian cotton sheets and each other, surging and gasping together as we strained toward that last moment when yes, oh goddess, yes...

I cried out at a rush of pleasure, there on the stone floor of Melusine's temple—and sensed Her approval. At moments like that She seemed to say, I *was* a goddess, like ancient priestesses who brought men closer to the gods by making sex a sacred act.

"I get it," I whispered weakly, savoring my breath hot on my own lips. "The physical is spiritual…."

Listen, Melusine said—or something like it. *Look*, or *Know*.

Then, so clearly it did not need words: *We Are One*.

I nodded, but the rush of scenes and figures flooding through me seemed to insist I didn't wholly get it. Not yet.

Women forced to resort to secrecy in order to protect their holiness amidst a patriarchal world. Women hiding their talents, downplaying their true selves.

One.

Women who fell so deeply in love that they sacrificed not only their names but their individuality, their autonomy, their own dreams to that love. Whole-heartedly. Gladly. An offering.

One.

Women who were betrayed by that love. By infidelity, or distance, or condescension. The pain of having one's other half turn against them.

One.

Women who found the strength to continue loving friends, and family, and the world, through their pain. Who cherished their children despite treachery by those children's father, despite hardships that nearly destroyed them…but not quite. Never quite destroyed. Women who could look past pain to see that not all men are alike, who dared to love again.

One. One. One.

Now I got it. Melusine's legend of love and loss wasn't a cautionary tale about unworthy lovers. She was more than Her relationship. Hers was a heroic tale of survival, a testimony of spirit. Her snake self wasn't ugly any more than any woman's strength is ugly. Her refusal to conform to expectations was what got Her demonized, like so many women before and since.

We Are One.

Strong women can build, heal, love, protect. And yes, they—we—can suffer.

That's why we need to be so strong.

Some of it must have gotten lost in translation. Specifics didn't matter. Her message, Her truth filled me soul deep, cell deep—and I'd been right. I shed the Dr. Sanger I'd tried to be, objective and logical and unwilling to commit without proof, like a worn-out skin. The academic quest for myths no longer drove me.

Returning these cups, these strengths to the world—that was my quest now. Whatever Melusine was, a divine person or an idea or a universal sense of womanhood, didn't matter. She wanted me to spread Her message. It was time.

Reality lapped back around me gently. One last, lingering message seemed to flow over me: *And in return, I shall gift you....*

And then I was kneeling, staring up at the shadowy statue of a snake goddess, mother goddess, goddess of love—and a survivor.

I shivered in the wake of the messages that had coursed through me, the connections I'd felt. Ecstatic—literally—I whispered, "Gift...?"

Two things happened at once.

I heard the stone door, far above me, scrape open.

And a scream burst within my chest, forced its way up my throat until I had to throw back my head. At the very moment good sense would have me fall silent, my own voice tore out of me and screeched through the temple. Then, as my voice fell shallow, I sucked in the deepest strengthening, energizing breath of my life—

Just in time to look up and see three beams of light stream down the last stairs, followed by three ski-masked men.

Like it or not, that was Melusine's gift. She'd sent me her scream and, with it, the energy to face this latest sacrilege. It wasn't a cry of despair after all.

Melusine's famous scream held sheer, unadulterated fury.

I stood, intensely aware of the cool air on my skin, of the scent of onions off the man in front, of my own blood and bones and being. I've rarely felt so quietly assured. So strong.

"You're not welcome here," I warned the trio. *"Go."*

The man in front came as far as the doorway and cut his light straight into my eyes. Everything had to be a weapon, didn't it? I squinted against the glare, but didn't duck. I knew the layout of this temple, whether I could see it or not.

"Scream all you want, Dr. Sanger," he said, his accent...Texan? He *so* did not get it. "But you give us that cup, now."

Why? Because he thought he had power over me? "No."

He stepped into the sanctuary with his two coblasphemers.

"Give us the cup," Tex said with condescending saccharin, reaching, "and we won't have to hurt—"

I so neatly sidestepped him that at first his gaze didn't track me. He jerked around as if I'd disappeared. Finding me again, his eyes narrowed. "Fine, honey. Have it your way."

Tex grabbed at me, but his force made him as awkward as his flashlight. I evaded him so easily, we could have been playing a game of Tai Chi push-hands. Overextended, he stumbled.

I caught his elbow with my free hand and tugged.

His own vehemence sprawled him onto the rock floor. Hard. His flashlight bounced away.

The others surged forward. I turned to meet them, still calm, still clear. Hardly any thoughts about wanting to beat them senseless tempted me. We'd just call that Plan B.

Like Rhys said, my interest was the chalice. To protect the chalice all I had to do was reach the doorway.

Remember? The one with the stone bolt on the other side. But in the meantime...

Durga. Minerva. The Morrigan. There were warrior goddesses.

I tucked the Melusine Chalice against my hip, backing

quickly clear of Contestant #1 and sinking to meet #2 and #3. Number Two had almond eyes like a bull terrier's. He tried to tackle me, also full force.

I timed my pivot so that his attack flowed past me and into a stone column. He hit, hung, sank. Another flashlight escaped across the stone floor.

A third beam, erratic, telegraphed the next strike. I ducked under the third man's blow into a low body check. His own momentum tumbled him right over me.

Tex, still on the floor, lunged for me. I vaulted him, grail still safely tucked. Landing with one foot, I kicked his breath away with the other. Next!

The third man rushed me, making me dance backward, just beyond his attack. I felt or heard or sensed the second man behind me, and I neatly sidestepped.

They hit each other, like stooges—*and I laughed.*

Big mistake. It was a martial mistake—a distraction. It was a karmic mistake—overconfidence.

And it was the one thing men most fear from women.

A gunshot shattered the room, spewing several ricochets. Even the two fallen men froze in that zany, crisscross illumination of dropped flashlights. I spun, tensing.

The first man, the American, sat on the floor by the altar, knees splayed, gun shaking in both hands. His eyes burned.

Worst of all, he and his gun sat between me and the door.

Damn, I hate guns.

"We will take that cup now, Dr. Sanger," snarled the second man. He had a German accent that made me think of Nazi villains. He came toward me, reaching.

Unable to make the doorway, I backed toward the Melusine statue, raising a hand to strike him away.

He hesitated.

"You aren't destroying this one," I warned.

Tex's gun spat out another shot, blue in the light-laced shadows of the sanctuary. Melusine's stone arm broke off, splashed into the water, and sank. No!

Stunned, I watched it vanish into deep nothingness. The German, who stood nearest me, snatched at the grail—

And I kneed him in the balls.

With a grunt and a squeak, he went down.

Another gunshot. The bowl in Melusine's remaining hand shattered, so that water now poured out of an unseemly hole in her stomach instead. They were destroying everything—and they didn't even care!

"Stop it!" I yelled, my voice uneven.

"The cup," demanded Tex. His hands weren't shaking as badly now, but his fury felt palpable.

"Screw you!"

His smile had an ugly curve to it. His gaze on my bare arms and shoulders felt like an unwanted caress. "Well, now. You might have your uses outside of information, at that."

Their threats were like *Cliff Notes* on dominator values—threats of theft, of rape, of destruction. But these were more than threats. So soon after Melusine's visions of the physical being spiritual, their intentions felt even more repulsive.

"The cup." Tex looked at his two companions and jerked his head in command. *"Now!"*

The man with dog eyes—the one not curled on his side whimpering—came toward me.

I screamed a warning at him, Melusine-style. Like a jaguar. Like a dragon.

He hesitated—and I figured something out.

I held the grail out over the well and, sure enough, he took a step back. "Any closer, and I drop it," I warned. "If you didn't want it for something, you would've shot it already."

Tex said, "Now, don't you count on that."

"Her friend didn't warn us she'd be this much trouble," gasped the German. "I think we should get our money back."

He meant Rhys. "You're lying."

"And you," said dog-eyes, with a British accent, "are bluffing."

"Am I?" Even I wasn't sure. Just because they threatened

to raze the sacred grove didn't mean I could bear to burn it first.

Tex said, "You're outnumbered and outgunned, honey. Be a good girl and we'll play nice. That way you might just survive it. Do something stupid, though—"

"Like dropping the cup," said the dog-eyed Brit.

"—and we play rough, and you probably won't survive it." The *probably* is what curdled my stomach. It implied methods slower and more brutal, more personal than a shooting.

"Why do you want the cup anyway?" I asked.

"Either way," Tex said, not giving me the courtesy of acknowledgment, "we win."

Bastards. Goddamned, hard-on-power bastards. Maybe there were times when you had to torch the sacred grove, after all.

"Funny definition of winning," I said.

And with a single move backward, I stepped into Melusine's well. Water closed over my head as the grail and I sank.

Deeper and deeper into nothingness.

About a year after the ice-cream parlor "incident," Lex's mother kills herself. She slits her wrists in a Jacuzzi.

"Poor woman," my mom says, helping me into my coat for the viewing. "She gave up everything she was for that family. Promise me you'll never do that."

I ask, "What's wrong with sacrificing for your family?"

Mom holds my shoulders. "It's like giving blood, Magdalene. It's a good and noble thing, heroic even, and you should do it as often as is healthy. But never, never become so committed to giving that you drain yourself beyond your own ability to survive. Then you're no good to anybody. Do you understand?"

I don't. How is loving one's family like giving blood? But I don't want to know. Not tonight. "Sure, Mom."

"If you end up dating Lex again—"

"Mother!" I back away. "He has more important things on his mind than me. Besides, he never answered my calls or my letters. We're definitely over."

My parents let me drive alone to the viewing. The hordes of reporters seem horribly disrespectful. So does the crowd. Not all these people knew the Stuarts. Are they just publicity vultures? Worse—am I?

As soon as I step inside, I feel Lex noticing me. I approach him and his father, extending my family's sympathies from behind the safety of cardboard words. Mr. Stuart barely touches my hand; he no longer recognizes me. Lex looks drawn and pale, like a tortured poet. He holds my hand for a long moment. I briefly imagine a current between us—a soul-deep recognition.

Then he responds with cool, equally cardboard graciousness. "Thank you for coming, Maggi. Mother always spoke highly of you." He releases my hand and turns to the next well-wisher, and I feel guilty about imagining connections that don't exist.

Mrs. Stuart's bejeweled corpse looks more beautiful than I remember her, in a designer gown that leaves her arms bare, like a silent challenge for anyone to discern her wounds.

I whisper "Goodbye" and "I'm sorry," though I don't know what I'm sorry for, and I flee. I don't see Lex as I leave, but I notice his cousin Phil surrounded by other men, his nose healed crooked. I'm surprised he didn't get surgery to fix it.

The family car is across the street in the overflow parking—a long walk in my mother's high heels. I fumble keys from my purse as I approach—and nearly scream as the dome light comes on and my door opens for me.

Lex is sitting in the passenger seat. I have no idea how he got in. "Get me out of here," he asks, low and drawn. "Please?"

I drive him to a nearby park. We climb out at a deserted

playground. He wraps me in his arms and rests his head on mine, and I hold him, and we stand that way for a long time.

I haven't imagined the connection between us after all. It's as sure as the breeze rustling my skirt, as real as the sound of our breath and heartbeat. Something still links us, even after a year. Now that I'm wrapped in it, I'm glad.

"One paper called it a 'bloodbath,'" he whispers finally, his voice hoarse from so much—the loss of his mother, her own culpability, the media circus, the cruelty of strangers. I kiss his cheek, smooth his brown hair, and hold him until some small edge of the tension in his body eases.

He does not cry. I'm not sure he's capable of it, but I know he needs to. So I cry for him.

He seems to take comfort in comforting me.

"You're stronger than that," he whispers, once, and I understand. He doesn't mean I'm too strong to cry. He means I'm too strong to ever kill myself.

I think, Doesn't that depend on the circumstances?

I think of what my mother said about drowning...and giving too much blood.

Chapter 13

I sank, my hair flowing out around my head, the weight of my hiking boots pulling me downward. My hand still clutched the alabaster chalice that I would take to my watery grave before allowing bastards to misuse it.

Misuse *us*.

Then I felt the sudden pull of current—and I kicked in that direction, downstream, with all my strength.

Just because I'd *hoped* there might be an underground river feeding the well didn't mean I had any expectation of surviving. Underground rivers are notorious for being...well, underground. As in, *without a surface.* But it was either swim like mad, using the water's flow for speed, or just give up and die. I had no illusions. I probably *would* die. We all do, sooner or later.

But I'd be damned if I would go belly-up.

I shoved the chalice down the front of my camisole, like a truly awkward pregnancy, and prayed the shirt would stay tucked in. Both hands now free, kicking my too-heavy feet, I literally swam for my life. The current carried me farther from the guns. I aimed myself upward, the direction air would travel.

My insides began to slowly implode, and still I swam.

Have you ever been in a cave? You could drown in pure darkness, even without water. Only the wetness against my eyes told me they were open. I strained my head and face upward anyway, to keep my airway straight and conserve oxygen. I tried to exhale slowly, very slowly, to keep my lungs venting air. It wasn't a long-term fix.

I kicked. Stroked. Needed to breathe.

My sense of running out of air didn't hit me in the chest at first. It hit in my forehead, a pressure between the eyes. That pressure tightened into my sinuses, then my throat and then, finally, into a shrinking sensation in my chest. My kicks became wild, my strokes flails of desperation—

And then my face broke the water. I inhaled the thick darkness and, thank heavens, it was breathable. Air filled my lungs with the euphoria of life, and I laughed. I bumped my head on the cave roof, mere inches over the river surface, and laughed again. My voice echoed back at me from a million different directions, along with the sound of my splashing.

Alive, alive, alive. Goddess, life was wonderful.

After gulping more air, expanding my lungs, filling my throat, I swam crosswise to the current, blindly trying to find the side of the river. When I did, this time with a blow to my hand, I felt along the edge, expending too much energy kicking my weighted feet. Finally I found a slight ledge that the current hadn't worn completely away. It wasn't so high that I could sit on it, or so low that I could stand on it. But I could kneel, my neck strained upward to the air, and that was enough for me to work on continuing this "life" business.

Every move splashed echoes and dripping noises around me.

First step—dig my ball cap out of a cargo pocket and blindly slide it back on, to conserve body heat. Second step—grope off the boots. Unfortunately, that would make me *lose* body heat. But it's almost impossible to swim any distance in hiking boots. Hypothermia wouldn't matter if I never made it out.

I compromised by leaving on my socks.

Knotting the bootlaces together, I temporarily looped

them over my neck like a yoke. Then I untied the wet T-shirt I knew was still on my waist. Fumbling in absolute darkness, I knotted the sleeves of the shirt together to make a pouch for the boots and the grail. I tied the whole pack to my belt loops, doing square knots by feel, making the most awkward fanny pack ever.

It might be easier to swim without the boots entirely. But I had every expectation of needing footwear when I got out.

That taken care of, I pulled my cell phone from its pocket, just in case. Not surprisingly, it wouldn't turn on. I tried several times, with increasing desperation. What I wanted, even more than the very slim chance of getting a signal, was light.

Just a little bit of LED light in this pressing, crushing, suffocating darkness.

Nothing. I pocketed my phone, and that was that.

"Who would you have called anyway?" I asked myself, hugging my knees to my chest to slow any heat loss. A million echoes seemed to repeat my question, long enough for me to know the answer.

You'd think I'd want to call an SOS number, the French version of 911. Instead I thought, *Lex.* Between his money, his connections, and his general refusal to take no for an answer, Lex Stuart could do almost anything. And he would—for me.

I'd never realized how deeply I believed that until now.

No matter what organizations he belonged to, or how questionable his moral code might turn out to be, he would be there for me. If only my piece-of-shit phone worked.

Instead, I would just have to save myself. Myself, and the Melusine Chalice. Regulating my breath—see, I could breathe, despite the darkness—I launched myself back into the river's current and swam wherever it was pulling me.

Blind.

Sometimes I touched something—something that moved, against the cave wall, or something that bumped me as it swam by in the darkness. Then panic would press down on me, heavy as the darkness. I just kept swimming.

What choice did I have? I was already lost, underground, underwater. In freaking France. If I panicked, I would drown. Period.

Then something as bad as panic snuck under my defenses. I started shivering.

Damn. When you're hypothermic, mental processes are the first thing to go. I had no idea how long I'd been shuddering as I swam, muscles increasingly tense, before I realized what that meant.

Again I floundered my way to the river wall, fumbling along until I found an outcropping where I could rest—and dig out the packaged cookies and juice box Rhys had given me.

Rhys. He hadn't really told the *Comitatus* where to find me, had he? Not for money. Not after the way he'd kissed me in the chapel. Not after the heartbreaking story he'd told me about Mary and leaving the priesthood…unless that's all it was.

A story.

I'd fumbled the empty packages back into my cargo pocket before I realized that I was lost, alone and dying in the darkness—and I was worried about littering. Then I laughed. Partly because it was just too silly not to.

And partly because the food energized me—and digestion would generate a little badly needed body heat. Again I pushed off and swam. Hours passed. I began to shiver again, with no hope but to keep moving.

Then the current itself failed me.

It weakened, almost vanished—and I swam into solid rock.

Luckily, my hands hit stone before my head did. I still cried out, panic taking the lead. My cry echoed from high above me. Great—I had plenty of air, now that it was the end of the line. Nowhere else to go. Just uncontrollable shivering.

Just failure.

No. Think about this, Maggi. You're a freaking Ph.D. Think.

Okay. The current that had been my only compass was gone. Why? *I was so cold.* The water had been going somewhere. Where? *Maybe if I just rested.* It had to be escaping somehow. How?

"Melusine..." I whispered, images from her story playing through my head like a bedtime story. The spring where her lover found her, where the story began....

With a burst of clarity, I understood. I was in an underground lake now, not an underground river. But water doesn't just stop. It had to be continuing toward the ocean from some part of the lake. Just...deeper down.

Oh...goddess.

With a prayer for strength, I dove. Searched the black rock with my cold-palsied hands until I ran out of breath. Kicked upward, broke the surface, drank in the air.

Then I repeated it. Again. And again.

My swimming got more clumsy. My shivering slowed—which is a very bad sign. And then—

Finally, finally I felt the rush of water along my seeking hands getting stronger. Now I had somewhere specific to dive for, feeling along the wall, getting an idea for just how deeply the fissure where the water continued was buried. Assuming there was room for me to follow it out of this lake, who knew when or where it resurfaced...?

If at all?

But I wouldn't die here. If nothing else, I wanted my body to wash out somewhere and be found, Melusine Chalice and all. I wanted my family to know what had happened to me. I wanted a grave for Lex to visit.

So I trod water on the surface one last time, practicing my deep breathing, and then I dove. And headed for the fissure.

And swam into the close, underground tunnel.

The current picked me up. I followed it, moving as fast as I could, bumping elbows and hands on the close rock walls. I began to feel that "starting to drown" sensation again—the pressure in my head, the squeezing in my chest, the fear. Then I had to swim upward, hoping I'd gone far enough to not surface into sheer rock, hoping there would be more pockets of oxygen somewhere. My world began to blur around me. My chest seemed to implode.

I kept kicking, more and more weakly, clumsily, flailing—and then surfaced with a great, gulping breath into blessed air.

Air, and trees, and fading, end-of-the-night stars.

I'd escaped the caves. With the Melusine Chalice.

Somehow I made it to the water's edge and staggered out. Somehow I managed to tear boughs of leaves off some trees before I collapsed to the ground, drawing them over me.

I still wasn't out of the water—metaphorically speaking, this time. If the hypothermia had progressed to the point that my body's core couldn't warm itself, I would still go into shock, shut down and die. But at least I would die under the stars.

Instead I woke in leaf-dappled sunshine—warm, summer sunshine.

"Thank you," I whispered upward, at the tree branches and the blue sky and the rest of my life. I used the grail to drink from the spring that burbled out of the river beside me, then washed off as best I could. There had been no second vision.

Then I walked, found a road and hitched a ride. The businessman who stopped for me told me he was heading to Chinon, so I asked that he drop me off at the train station.

En route, I tried to decide whether to call Rhys to meet me, or to go on to Paris alone. He was probably innocent.

On the other hand, last night hadn't exactly shown the male of my species in the best light. I'd given far too much for this cup—including turning into a thief of antiquities despite my best efforts—to risk it now.

At the station, I purchased a telephone card at a vending machine. But before I could insert it into the public telephone, I caught the word "Fontevrault" on a television newscast and turned to look at the waiting room's television set.

Fire.

Film footage showed the interior of Fontevrault's church, which had sustained smoke and water damage. According to the anchorwoman, firefighters were called to the abbey when alarms sounded and discovered smoke seeping out from one wall. After some debate with the historians, they broke through what turned out to be a stone doorway and discovered a hidden vault—and wreckage. Some sort of cloth hangings had burned beyond recognition. Hidden carvings and monuments, previously unknown, had suffered destruction unlike any seen since the mobs of the Revolution.

I sank onto a bench, there in the waiting room. *Now* I felt sick. The *tapestries…?* The *statuary…?*

I'd done this. Of course I hadn't set the fire, or smashed the carvings. And yet, by figuring out the nursery rhyme, I'd led the *Comitatus* to Melusine's sanctuary—and look what had happened.

But the real blame lay square at the feet of three evil men who got their jollies by ruining something they could not begin to understand.

Like damned Charlemagne cutting down the damned sacred groves of the damned Saxons.

It made those people my enemy. Every last one of them.

And it made the tiny, guttering hope of Melusine's grail, with its message of creation and strength and partnership, all the more crucial in this poor, broken world.

Had I felt guilty for stealing the grail? If I'd played by the rules, look what would have happened.

The news camera panned a concerned crowd outside the Fontevrault Abbey, showing support for this grand historical site—and I saw Rhys. The camera did not focus on him, only skimmed past, but it was him.

And he was standing beside an average-looking man whose build and suit and bull-terrier eyes I recognized from my fights last night. One of the *Comitatus*.

Screw that.

I called Aunt Bridge's hospital room. They said she'd been released, so I called her apartment, waking her up. I asked her to find someone trustworthy who could put the Melusine Chalice on display without a repeat of the Kali Cup disaster. I told her I would call her later and arrange a safe place to meet.

"Is Rhys with you?" she asked.

Rhys. I shut my eyes against my confusion. "No. If he calls, you can tell him I'm all right, but don't say anything else for now. Nothing. I've got to go. Bye."

If anybody was tracing the call, hopefully I'd been brief enough to stop them.

I bought a ticket on the TGV to Paris. With two hours before it left, I went out into Chinon long enough to buy some basics. A waterproof gym bag to carry the grail. A towel and other toiletries. Breakfast. I was exhausted, so I let myself nap in little spurts for the barely one-hour train trip.

With the gym bag wedged safely beside me.

When I got off the train in Paris I wasn't feeling much more competent, but at least I could relax a little. There's a wonderful anonymity that comes with large cities. Despite my fatigue, it wasn't difficult to catch the Metro to a station I vaguely remembered from my early twenties, then find a hostel where I'd once stayed with my cousin Lilith. Lex and I had been broken up at the time. Again.

This was about as anonymous as I could get without walking into someplace blind.

Like most hostels, The Four Geese catered particularly to kids backpacking Europe, but it wasn't exclusively for youth. I didn't need to meet an age requirement, and they were happy to give me a separate room for a friendly bribe. It wasn't luxury—the size of my bathroom at home, with one set of white iron bunkbeds, one metal-and-plastic folding chair, peeling pink wallpaper and one small window with a stained white curtain. To use the phone I would have to go to the lobby—or, better yet, a public phone somewhere else. To use the bathroom or shower I would have to go to one of the portables that sat in the middle of a plain little courtyard, serving all the guests. Neither bunk had sheets or pillows, just a thin, striped mattress.

That's laying low for you. I locked the door, climbed onto the top bunk, used the wrapped Melusine Chalice as my bumpy pillow. I thought of what I'd helped the *Comitatus* do to Melusine's sanctuary. I cried.

And finally I slept.

When I woke, I felt great. Stiff, from my alabaster pillow and my marathon swim. Deeply saddened about Rhys and Fontevrault. Hungry. But it's amazing the difference a good sleep will make. Being alive was a nice upper, too.

And I had the grail.

Even more than food, I wanted a shower. I didn't dare think about what might've been swimming around in that dark cave with me, but I knew I wanted it *out of my hair*. So I took my gym bag with me, locked the door behind me and crossed the courtyard to the portable shower.

This was why I'd made sure the gym bag was waterproof. I wasn't about to let the grail out of my sight even long enough to bathe! I locked the door, turned on the shower and, waiting for the water to warm up, brushed my teeth and my hair. Only then did I climb under the warm spray.

Bag first.

It stayed between my feet while I sudsed myself up and scrubbed myself off—hair, skin, everything. This was another of life's luxuries, like a good sleep, that we don't always appreciate until we've had to go without.

Along with the grime, some of my despair washed away.

Things were looking up. I wouldn't have to keep the grail for long; just until we arranged for it to be safely displayed, living proof that supposedly ancient goddess cultures had lasted well into the eighteenth-century. *Then* I could figure out all the other confusing aspects of my life.

Like how to become someone powerful enough to go after those sons of bitches *Comitatus.*

By the time I shut off the shower, I felt better. Stronger.

Then, as I reached out past the worn curtain for my towel, someone grabbed my wrist.

Chapter 14

With one slick twist, I freed myself, dove out of the shower at whoever had grabbed me—

And pulled my punch a breath from Lex Stuart's nose.

He backed quickly out of reach. Holding my towel. When his wide, hazel eyes drifted down my wet, bare body in appreciation, I regretted pulling the punch.

"You're a hard woman to find, Mag," he said calmly. "Nice to see you're staying in shape, though."

Son of a—

"What the hell do you think you're doing here?"

"I could leave, but if I open the door, someone might see in. Not that I'd blame them for looking…"

"This is way beyond acceptable, Lex. You have no right to invade my privacy like this. And stop staring at my breasts."

Classic blunder. Obediently his gaze drifted lower. His lips hinted at a smile.

I snatched the towel he held. He didn't pull it from my reach—cramped as this portable was, he didn't have room to. But as I tugged it to me, he came with it.

Brave, foolish man, to get in striking distance.

And yet I didn't want to hit him. Resorting to violence seemed its own kind of failure, especially considering how I felt about the damned *Comitatus*. Especially when Lex was more annoying than threatening.

I mean—he was *Lex*.

"This is breaking and entering," I told him, wishing my words could cut deeper against his Stuart sense of self-entitlement. "You just crossed a major line."

Instead of apologizing he said, "The same line you crossed that time you invaded my hotel room in Manhattan?"

Oh. The memory of that disoriented me just long enough for him to draw the towel slowly across my wet shoulder, gently past my shoulder blade. Long enough for him to lean even closer and murmur, "I don't remember protesting. As a matter of fact, weren't you naked then, too?"

"We…were dating then." The towel continued its long, slow stroke into the curve of my spine. I shivered in reluctant appreciation.

Lex's voice, so near my ear, became a whispery purr. "No, we weren't. That's what got us dating again. That time."

"It's still not—" But the towel had reached my butt, and I bit my lip instead of continuing.

"What's sauce for the goose," he teased, circling the terry cloth across one of my hips and forward. Lower….

"Don't quote adages."

He whispered, "I know what adages do for you."

That touch of silliness, in the midst of his seduction, gave me the breath of clarity I needed. I snatched the towel from his hand before he could go any lower with it.

And felt instantly cold, despite the steamy warmth around me. Lonely, even. Damn it.

So I'd done something similar, a few years back. These were different circumstances. "Well, we aren't dating now, so you can just look elsewhere until I'm dressed. Got it?"

With a lingering look of appreciation, Lex turned away.

"Not facing the mirror," I warned.

"You still don't trust me?"

"Not lately." And, double-checking his angle from the mirror—which, fortunately, was small and rusted and steamed over—I finished drying off. "How did you find me here, anyway?"

"You've mentioned the place before," said Lex. "We argued about staying here once, remember? At the time, I won."

That was the problem with having dated someone with such sharp recall. "You said it sounded like a dump," I chided, now that he'd prompted my own memory.

I pulled on the panties I'd washed in the shower with me. I'd wrung them out in the towel and hung them on the curtain rod, but of course they were still damp.

I really wanted to go shopping.

Lex said to the corner, "No offense, Mag...."

Oh, sure. Just because we were standing in a portable, communal shower set up in the middle of a scrubby courtyard, he thought the place was a dump?

"So, what, you just staked the place out?" I pulled my camisole on over my humid skin, then paused. "No! You don't have that kind of spare time. *You hired someone to stake it out.*"

Lex tipped his head back to stare at the ceiling, still not turning to look at me. What a nice guy he was, following my instructions like that.

I smacked him on the back of the head.

"Hey!" Now he did turn back, surprised—and apparently amused. I doubt he gets smacked often. "I was worried."

"It's not your job to worry."

"Well then, consider it my hobby. An addiction, if you must. You're in a foreign country—"

"So are you."

"Your apartment was burglarized, your aunt was attacked, and you're involved with God-knows what kind of people."

"Excuse me?"

"I was afraid you wouldn't call when you got back to town."

"Wouldn't that be my choice?"

He scowled. He wore scowls well. "Not if it puts you in danger."

"Actually, yes. Even if it does put me in danger. Even if I'm, oh, facing off against masked gunmen or driving like a maniac or swimming underground rivers without equipment, that would be my choice. Not yours. Not anyone else's."

Lex said, "Be serious for a minute, would you?"

He honestly thought I was joking—which, weirdly, delighted me. I laughed from sheer relief.

"It's not funny, Mag," warned Lex. But I'd been through way too much over the past few days to just dismiss this moment of respite. Lex was still being Lex—spying on me, making decisions for me, breaking into my shower.

I stopped laughing. "I locked the door. How'd you get in?"

"It's a cheap lock," he said. "Cheap places like this have cheap security. I could have been anybody, Mag. I worry."

"That's your problem." Though I supposed his spying and intrusions made it partly mine.

"You think I'm being paranoid? If some pervert grabbed you in the shower, what would you have done about it?"

I folded my arms. My skin still felt sticky from the steam. How Lex could wear even a light, Italian suit coat and look so cool, I'd never understand. "You don't really want to test that theory, do you?"

In answer, he slid his gaze down me again. I was only wearing panties and a camisole so far, after all. My wet hair stuck to my back.

Amusement pulled at his mouth, as if usurping his otherwise cool demeanor. "Are you suggesting some kind of kinky role play, Magdalene? Or do you just want to kick my ass over keeping an eye on you?"

"Definitely the latter." I stepped into my cargo pants. "What you call 'keeping an eye on me,' other people call 'manipulation' and 'stalking.'" But hell, he was *my stalker*. "Come on, pervert. Someone else might want the shower."

"I'm sure this place has a high germ quota to fill."

"That attitude won't win you any points, buddy," I

warned, reaching into the shower for—oh, yeah. The Melusine Chalice. How quickly we forget.

I hesitated. If Lex *was* somehow involved, then we—the grail and I—were in major trouble.

But, damn it, my worst suspicions about Lex were based on ancient Stuarts showing up in conspiracy books as being decidedly antigoddess. My distrust came from an accusation of perjury which I still didn't completely understand.

Yes, I wanted to keep the grail safe. Nothing wrong with that. But I'd also spent so much of my lifetime with this man.

It would be one thing if I were blindly in love. But whether I loved him or not, it wasn't blind. I knew Lex could be proprietary and willful. I even knew he had the capacity for violence—and that he generally controlled that. I also knew he'd developed an almost Machiavellian attitude about certain laws, business ethics and society—hence our most recent breakup.

But on top of all that, I knew—as I'd realized in the river—that Lex would do almost anything for me. He'd loved me through braces, weight issues—"scales" and all, you might say. He'd once promised never to cheat me and, as far as I knew, he'd kept that promise. Even the time he'd sliced that tray into his cousin's face, he'd seemed to think he was doing it for me.

Oh, we clearly had issues to resolve…or not resolve, as I chose. But the immediate question, whether to bring him to my room to talk or to knock him unconscious and run away with the grail was pretty clear.

I retrieved my gym bag and dried it off with my already-damp towel.

"You shower with your *luggage?*" Good. If he hadn't commented, I might've thought he was faking ignorance.

"Hostels have a slight theft problem," I admitted, shouldering the bag and reaching past him to open the door. The afternoon air might be warm, but at least it wasn't steamy. I sucked it in gratefully, especially after last night.

Lex followed me out. "It's a shame you never went into

advertising, Mag. Any second now, you'll have me wishing we'd spent a nice fortnight here after all."

"Snob," I said—but I smiled. It's not like he was wiping everything with a handkerchief before he would touch it. He had *that* much class, anyway.

Actually, class had never been a problem for Lex.

"Flake," he countered, equally good-natured—and it was such an unclassy thing to say that I almost laughed again. Damn it, I'd missed him. I usually did. Why was that?

As I reached my little room, I stepped back. So he'd learned to pick locks, had he? "Demonstrate."

Lex shrugged, pulled a key from his pocket and opened the door. My mouth opening, I immediately patted my pants—

And felt a hard plastic key ring. He hadn't taken my room key, anyway.

"I can see why these places have a theft problem." Lex held the door open for me, eyes bright. "Never underestimate the power of a bribe."

Shaking my head, I went in and slid the bag, with the grail, under the bottom bunk. "So what the hell are you doing here, anyway?" I demanded, turning back to him.

In my most paranoid fantasies, he would be holding a gun on me, or opening the door for black-clad, ski-masked *Comitati*.

Instead, Lex closed the door and stepped forward, sliding his strong arms around me, all fine fabric against my bare skin, for a wholly different fantasy. "Right now?" he whispered, leaning close. "I'm giving you more reasons to kick my ass."

Then he kissed me. Proprietary. Willful.

Whatever connection we'd shared, familiar from over half our lifetimes, clicked solidly into place. My body recognized him in a hot rush. My *soul* recognized him with something like the delight of homecoming.

After the week I'd had, I downright *welcomed* him.

Issues or no issues, I turned him against the bed, murmured, "Watch your head," around his tongue, and laid him down so that I could kiss him far more fully.

He went willingly, his critique of the hostel forgotten. I straddled him, cradling his head as I folded myself down and we reacquainted ourselves with each other's mouths and tastes and hungers. He slid his arms back around me. One of his hands followed my spine upward, into my wet hair. One headed downward across my behind.

Good. He really had incredible hands.

Finally things felt right. My world had gone crazy over the last week, what with break-ins and murder and priest kissing and goddess bonding. But Lex was a constant. The feel of his hands worshipping my body with intimate knowledge, of the eager hardness in his Italian pants, was equally certain. Challenges and even danger still waited outside of this hovel of a room. But together we created a kind of emotional stillness and safety, like a time-out.

A time-out full of ragged breathing. Tongue kissing. Exploring each other's bodies to see how much we'd changed in the past year. Learning that everything was just about where we'd left it…from what we could tell through clothes, anyway.

I wasn't just straddling his hips, now; I was riding his hardness through my cargo pants and the fine fabric of his slacks. Leaning over him, my hair curtaining our faces with heavy dampness, I brushed my camisole-covered breasts across the front of his suit coat and drank in his low, appreciative moans as greedily as I'd drunk goddess power the night before.

I wanted this. Him. I wanted to celebrate being alive—and what's more alive than sex? Especially after the confusion with Rhys, I wanted to flaunt my femininity, my sexuality.

Only one thing I *didn't* want.

I pushed up off Lex's chest, so that I could keep from kissing him for a few critical seconds. But I didn't stop moving on him. "This doesn't change anything," I gasped.

"Anything," he repeated, his thumb sliding between my legs and sending a jolt of promise shuddering through me.

Oh, how I wanted this! But he could have just been parroting me. "Us. Your family. Last year's—"

My own gasp of pleasure interrupted me, and Lex's eyes, which had darkened toward brown, crescented with satisfaction.

Then I said, "Last year's trial."

The corporate espionage trial. The one in which he may or may not have lied on the stand—something I would have a hard time forgiving. Especially from him.

Now Lex's eyes closed with something other than ecstasy. Something closer to annoyance. "I hate it when you bring up that damned trial."

I rose up on all fours, no longer riding him. "Oh, do you?"

"Although *hate* may be too strong a word." But when he opened his eyes, I saw that he was joking. Or half joking. Hard to tell with him. Either way, we'd just hit a stopping point, damn it, damn it, damn it.

Maybe we could hit another starting point. "So tell me you were innocent."

Lex scooted backward, sat up against the faded wallpaper at the edge of the bed. He looked like an advertisement for casual elegance amidst bohemian squalor. "You know I can't."

I rolled onto my hip, my head beside his ribs, and arched my neck to better see him. "Because you were guilty?"

"Because I signed a confidentiality agreement."

"Awfully convenient, that."

He searched my face for a long moment, then shifted his gaze to the space between us, to the bulge in his trousers. "Not really. No."

"Why did you sign it?"

He raised his knee on my side, protecting his vulnerability. "For the company."

There was a good reason for you. "Your father's business. Cousin Phil's company."

"The *Stuarts'* business, which makes it *my* company. We couldn't just settle—" But he pressed his lips together. That, too, was apparently confidential, and it pissed me off. It was one thing not to talk about work with competitors. It was another not to be able to talk about it to his lover.

Well, I'd certainly been right, hadn't I? Us getting it on a few minutes ago hadn't changed anything. Would it ever? Was this where we were stuck, after so long?

I thought a moment. "Are you sorry you signed it?"

Lex lifted a heavy strand of damp hair off my face, studying me as he might a fine painting. "I thought it was the right thing to do, Mag. I still think so. But after losing you, I wish I'd thrown the pen in the damned lawyers' faces."

Had he known he was using the exact right magic words? *The right thing to do.* Even if QuestCo had bent some laws— and I didn't even know that for sure—the deal had satisfied his own internal sense of honor. When had I stopped trusting him? When *had* I stopped believing in that strange, solid honor of his?

I slid my hand under his raised leg to his inner thigh, then slid it upward toward where he'd started to regain control of himself and his desires.

My touch reversed *that* pretty quickly. His breath fell ragged, just as fast.

"Mag, unless you're measuring my inseam…" His gasp sounded like a warning. And it was only fair. Like I've said before—I draw the line at torture.

"Just be aware," I warned, shifting hands so that I could push his inside knee gently down, out of my way, "that this doesn't change anything."

"I don't see how it could," he agreed thickly. "I've wanted you for so long any—*yes*. Oh, Mag…"

I was sliding between his legs now, unzipping his fly, touching his arousal with my nose as I breathed in the scent of him. I wanted more than a taste of him. I wanted to devour him whole. But…

I hesitated. Maybe I'm more into torture than I think. I pushed myself up with my hands, my stomach and legs on the bed between his knees.

"First," I decided, "*you* get naked."

I've never seen fine Italian men's wear so mistreated. In moments, Lex was undressed—from Armani model to *Playgirl* centerfold. He'd been staying in shape, too—chest, shoulders, tapered hips. Hard thighs and harder abdomen and even harder…

Mmm. And he was reaching. I drew him to me, so very gladly, but when he started to palm a spaghetti strap of my camisole off my shoulder, I shook my head.

"I stay dressed," I warned. "What's sauce for the gander…"

Lex groaned good-naturedly.

I said, "Let's see how—mmm—" He'd just started licking my nipple through the fabric of my camisole, his hair soft on my arm. "How creative you can be," I finished, almost needlessly.

Then I gave myself up to him. To it. To us.

Aphrodite. Venus. Freya. They were goddesses of sex.

His hands on me, all over me, wherever he could reach under my shirt or up my pants legs or into the waist of my panties. Him under my own hands, all flexing muscle and rich, clean skin and soft, thick, gingery hair—except when it was short, wiry gingery hair. Lex and I had all the familiarity and ease of a long-term relationship, and all of the uncertain need and excitement of a new fling. Forever later— after I'd already climaxed around his fingers a couple of times—he half laughed, half sobbed, "I'm not this creative."

I decided to be lenient and pulled my pants down far enough that we could make use of one of the gold-wrapped condoms he always carried with him, even if that did mean rolling under him for the first time that afternoon.

I would have to strip, if *I* wanted to mount *him*.

That could wait until later. This was too incredible, too necessary to be the last time. I think I'd known it all along. There would *have* to be a later. There always had to.

For now it was enough for him to cover me, to slide into me hot and thick and familiar, to make me cry out my satisfaction with his first solid thrust. I coiled my legs over his naked thighs, capturing him inside of me, my pleasure no longer an ebb and flow so much as the unrelenting surge of breakers. I burned out my screams and fell into sobs, into total, full-body release. Someone pounded on a thin wall and yelled at us in what sounded like Lithuanian. I laughed until Lex reached between us during his final, shuddering thrust, sending me over yet again as he shouted out his own burst of completion.

I caught him, held him through it all. He sank gradually onto me, full body, like a penitent making obeisance. "Maggi," he whispered against my neck, his breath humid and his voice ragged. "Maggi, Maggi, Maggi…"

Like a mantra. And something that had seemed lost and confused in me since our last breakup, no matter how legitimate our reasons had been, seemed to heal and ease.

We lay like that for a while, until I tried to move under him and hardly could. I pushed at him to roll over, then cuddled back on top of him and rested.

Rested on so very, very many levels.

In some ways, this was its own heaven. Lex's heartbeat under my ear. Our bodies entwined, his naked, mine with my camisole up under my arms and my cargo pants down near my knees. Him still praying my name, every few breaths, and me so glad for the hope that I might be able to trust him again, after all.

Maybe I slept. I'm positive he did. But once we were both regaining our strength, and kissing each other, I had the sense to pull back long enough to ask, "So what was so important that you had to stake out my room for fear of missing me?"

Lex stopped worshipping my neck, midkiss. When he turned his face toward mine, his was surprisingly solemn. Even for Lex. Especially postsex Lex.

My throat tightened. I wasn't going to like this, was I?

"I think you're in danger," Lex said. Then he reached out and hooked the chain of my necklace with one finger, drawing it from the folds of my camisole to reveal the *vesica piscis*. "You, and that strange girls' club you think I don't know about."

Within months of Mrs. Stuart's funeral, Lex and I are going steady. But suspicions have taken root, something about his confidence, his kisses, the certainty of his hands.

One weekend he takes me in his Ferrari to a drive-in movie revival. The movie bores me, so I turn down the sound and say, "You aren't a virgin anymore, are you?"

For a long moment Lex says nothing. Then, "No. I'm not. I thought we were through last year and...no."

"We were through.*" But despite logic, my body's angry. This feels like punishment for having broken up, which isn't fair. I had every right to stay at the soda shop after he broke Phil's nose. He was the one who hadn't returned my calls. "Does she know you're here?"*

"We broke up. I kept thinking about you." It doesn't come out at all romantic. He sounds embarrassed. He should.

"That was rude."

"Yes, it was. To both of you. I'm sorry."

We continue to sit together in his car's butter-soft leather seats, the movie dancing past the windshield. His arm was around me before I spoke, and he hasn't moved it in either direction. I listen to how our breathing weaves together. I consider our mingling warmth. I'm disappointed more than angry.

He's a college student now. And we really were "on a break." But I'm also, well...curious. "Tell me about it?"

"No."

"At least...I mean, guilt aside, was it...?"

He slides a searching glance toward my face, in the shadows of the car, and understands.

"You're not ready," he assures me, passing the popcorn.

"We're eighteen." Eighteen feels very mature.

"Our first time has to be perfect. No back seats. No grungy dorm-room mattress or anonymous motel. It has to be...holy."

"Not to put any pressure on us or anything," I mutter.

"That's why I've been practicing."

I hit his shoulder. He laughs and kisses me. His lips are more enticing than ever, and his hands...his hands have been learning a lot at Yale. I love his touch under my sweater, on my breasts, under my miniskirt. Soon the popcorn's out the window and I'm fully under him, writhing ecstatically on the butter-soft seats. This is about as basic as man-woman relationships get. Not just man-woman. Lex-Maggi. This is deeply right.

I have my first for-sure orgasm against his hand, safe in his sweatered arms, at the drive-in movie revival.

"What?" I ask drowsily, sated, while his gaze caresses me.

"God, you're hot." He kisses me again, his tongue boldly mimicking what his fingers have been doing.

I feel his hardness through his pants, against my hip. I'm more sold on sex now than when I was just jealous. Maybe I've been waiting for him to come back. "Then let's do the rest."

"No, Mag," he whispers, between kisses. *"But thank you."*

"That wasn't an offer, Lex. It was a request."

"We have to be absolutely sure."

"I am absolutely *sure."*

"Good." More kisses. *"Hold that thought."*

I push him back, frowning. "How come the other women get a bad boy and I get a Boy Scout?"

"It has to be perfect," he says again, stubborn.

When we finally do get there, over Spring Break of my first year in college, it is perfect. Holy. After almost a year of foreplay, why wouldn't it be? We have a Manhattan hotel suite, candles, rose petals. The word love is used copiously.

Unlike what I've heard from other couples, love has slipped so easily into our conversations it was almost a non-event. Almost. As if it had been there all along.

Either way, neither of us is surprised.

I doubt we could escape this love even if we wanted to.

Chapter 15

I rolled back, completely off him, banging my elbow into the wall as I pushed my camisole down. *"What?"*

I hoped my question came out as dangerous as I felt.

That damned, protective coolness fell over Lex's face again, despite him having seemed so vulnerable moments before. "I can't say how I got my information—"

"Try!"

"I knew you were going to freak out about this. That's why I couldn't tell you over the phone."

That, I thought darkly, *and cell-phone captures.* "So you just let me wander around in danger until I happened to come back to your side of France?"

The coolness of his expression faltered as he sat up. "Oh, Christ—something happened?"

Just a car chase. Scaling a tower that would put Rapunzel's witch to shame. Witnessing a murder. Being held at gunpoint a few times. Getting ambushed in a secret goddess sanctuary that was later completely destroyed. Nearly drowning. That's all.

Information is power, and I wasn't about to give him anything just yet. Anything *else,* anyway.

"Nothing I couldn't handle," I said.

"Damn it!" Lex looked worried anyway.

"It's nothing compared to the danger you'll be in if you don't start talking. What do you mean, *that weird girls' club?"*

I knew he meant the Grail Keepers. But did he?

He slumped gracefully back against the wall. "Christ, Mag. You've worn that pendant since we were fourteen."

"And yet you never asked about it."

His jaw set, stubborn now. "I figured if you wanted to tell me about it, you would."

Uh-huh. "And you already thought you knew what it was. So what do you think it is?"

"So what is it?" he countered.

I rolled off the bottom bunk and pulled up my pants. Now I *really* had to go shopping. *Soon.*

"If I wanted to tell you about it, I would have."

His bare shoulders sank with annoyance at my answer. But he also gave. Just a little. "It's a symbol of feminism, right? Some kind of old, hereditary feminism."

I stared. If that was all he knew, that was okay. But how could I tell? "And why would hereditary feminists be in danger?"

He then pressed his lips together and scowled, clearly fighting with himself. It occurred to me that he was still in bed, albeit sitting up a bit. He was still completely, totally and gloriously naked. And he didn't even seem to care.

Was he that conceited, or that stupid?

Or did he just trust me that much, even now?

I didn't want to think like that. Him trusting me made me want to trust him back, the way I used to, and I had a freaking *goddess grail* hidden beneath the striped mattress he lay across.

Then again, just because Lex knew about Grail Keepers—and maybe the *Comitati* who threatened us?—didn't yet make him a bad guy. He hadn't known I'd already been attacked. Was I going to continue fleeing my involvement with him every time I scented a hint of treachery? Or might I finally accept that I could handle whatever happened? What if I stayed put long enough to gather some informational power of my own?

Slowly I sat on the plastic folding chair that the hostel so kindly provided its residents. "Lex," I said, a touch less confrontational. "I really want to know. I'm the one you say is in danger, so how did that happen? Who's endangering me?"

He sighed—but he seemed to come to a decision. He swung his feet off the bed so that he could sit up too, leaning forward, hands clasped between his bare knees. I tried not to think of the Melusine Chalice so close to his feet. "Try to hear me out?"

I raised my eyebrows, but waited.

"There are some powerful men—I mean, powerful *people* in this world, right?"

You should know. But taunting him wouldn't exactly move this along. "Riiiight."

"They don't all get along. But, understandably, they share a vested interest in keeping what power they have. Right?"

So did he mean personal power, or power over other people? I had my suspicions. "Most of them," I hedged.

His lips tightened with that annoying edge of condescension he sometimes lets slip. The one I'd first met in kindergarten. "All of them, Mag."

Again, it wasn't worth the argument. Yet. Not when I had more to find out. "So we've got a group of mob-boss wannabes clinging desperately to their tenuous illusions of power." We definitely weren't talking about personal power, since that can't be taken…only abdicated. "Gotcha."

Lex blinked at me. Then he continued, choosing his own battles as well. "One thing anybody in power has to watch for—in business or politics *or* organized crime—is future threats," he continued. "We've got to identify threats before they become problems, and make preemptive strikes."

"You know I hate military metaphors."

"Stop the trickle so it doesn't become a flood," he tried as an alternative. "And rumor has it there are some people out there who have decided that a group of hereditary feminists pose some kind of future threat."

"Who?" I asked.

Lex shook his head, spread his hands, shrugged. *"People."*

"Not good enough," I snapped.

"All you're getting," he snapped back. "Maggi, I'm telling you everything I can."

We glared at each other—and took deep, releasing breaths at the same time.

I tried, "Okay, so how do you know about them?"

He seemed surprised by the question, as if that part were obvious. "We move in the same circles. You'd be surprised what gets discussed on a golf course."

"If you know they're doing something illegal, why not contact the authorities?"

His brows came together in what looked like honest confusion. "Who said anything about illegal?"

"You think these are the guys who broke into my apartment and who attacked Aunt Bridge, don't you?"

The confusion faltered into chagrin. "I have no proof of any of that, nothing to act on. Just suspicions."

"Suspicions enough to warn me that *I'm* in danger."

"You're the one who's always talking about the importance of following your instincts."

He was *so* avoiding the question. Several of the questions. I just wasn't sure which ones or why. His naked, lightly haired legs and the dip of his shoulders and the elegant line of his forearms and wrists weren't helping. He kept in such good shape.

"Okay then," I tried, dialing back my annoyance yet again. "What is it you expect me to do to stay *out* of danger?"

He looked intensely relieved. "Keep a low profile, is all. Whatever you're in France to do, maybe you could let it go."

"You're joking."

No, he wasn't. "Otherwise, you're just inviting trou—"

I didn't let him finish before I grabbed the nearest piece of Armani and threw it at him. "Get out. Now."

Lex found his briefs and pulled them on as requested. But he also slanted a confused glance up at me that somehow pierced my chest. "What did I say?"

"Inviting trouble? You mean if someone holds me at gunpoint, that's my fault because *I invited trouble?*"

"Of course I didn't mean that!" Wisely, he kept dressing, pulling on his pants next. They were wrinkled now, and a bit dusty from the floor, and despite everything, I hated to see his legs vanish into them. "No excuse in the world would justify holding you at gunpoint…and why did you use that example?"

Lex zipped his pants and stood there, looking confused and concerned.

"I'm talking about blaming the victim, Alexander Stuart. Whatever the hell I'm in France to do is my own business. Mine, and maybe that 'weird girls' club' of mine, and I have *every* right to do it, and these powerful people you're talking about have *no* right to stop me."

"God *damn* it!" Lex turned to thump both forearms loudly against the ugly pink wall, fists clenched, and stood there for a long moment with his head bowed and his bare back tight. When he turned back to me, he angled just his head. "Magdalene, you do not live in a utopia. Nothing's about who has the *right*. It's about who has the ability, and if I'm correct about these particular people—"

"Whom you can't seem to name." *Why won't you name them?*

"—then they have the ability to do any damned thing they want to you, and neither of us will see it coming until it's too late. You could hire bodyguards—"

"*No.* And not because I can't afford them." Though I doubted I could.

His face, in the shadow of his arm, sharpened. "So you leave yourself open. What am I supposed to do if someone hurts you?"

I'd never seen him sustain this kind of raw upset. Lex was all about control, and pretty good with silence, but this…

"Sure, I could do more than most people. I don't need the police. I can afford to hire all the justice I want." He turned to me, spread his arms and hands as if to encompass the breadth of his reach, even as he shook his head. "But it would be too late. I could hunt people to the ends of the earth and I could make them pray they'd never heard of either of us—"

"But you wouldn't," I said firmly.

"Like hell I wouldn't." But he bent to pick up his shirt and slid his corded arms into it, one at a time. I'd asked him to get out, and by goddess he was getting out.

I said, "You're not my husband or father or brother. You're not even my boyfriend." Okay, so *boyfriend* sounds juvenile. But to say he wasn't my lover would be untrue—at least this moment, with our damp bodies and our smells all over each other and our tastes in each other's mouths.

My body still felt so aware of his presence, it mourned every piece of clothing he donned.

"Not through lack of trying," he noted archly. Lex-like.

"You have no right to go around *avenging* me."

"And you don't listen." Cool again. Calm. "It's not about rights, it's about ability."

"If you honestly believe that, thank heavens I never married you."

It was a hurtful thing to say—hurtful to him and to me. This afternoon had proven how much I still wanted this man in my life and, now, how ill I could afford it. Even if he wasn't involved with a secret society, which it seemed he was not.

We'd broken up often enough before I'd heard of the *Comitatus*.

Lex stared at me a long moment, buttoning his shirt. Then he looked down to tuck it into his slacks. He said evenly, "I just want you safe, Maggi. Why does that make me the bad guy?"

"Because it's my body, my life, my safety."

"And my—" The protest rasped out of him, surprising us both. He clenched his jaw against it, opened his hand as if to fight it, then gave up and turned the hand toward his chest. "And *my heart*, Mag! If something happens to you, it's not just you who gets hurt. It's everyone who loves you, everyone whose life will become a sucking void if you're taken out of it, and knowing that you were *right* won't mean shit!"

I stared, breathless. How did I answer *that?*

He shook his head, as if to let me off the hook. He looped his tie loosely over his head and scooped his jacket off the floor with one finger under its collar. You'd never know he'd just shouted. "I know my happiness is not your responsibility. You didn't ask for it. Hell, lately you've been doing everything you can to escape it. I'm sorry I've made things difficult. I just wish…"

He shook his head, headed for the door. "I apologize for complicating matters today."

And I couldn't let him go. Not like that. Yes, he'd complicated matters. But I'd sure as hell helped.

I caught his arm. "What is it you wish, Lex?"

He drew a long, deep breath before looking at me. I almost flinched from the raw need in his gaze. He didn't know what to do with it, and I wasn't sure I could or should advise him. "I wish you would let me help. Even if you are some hereditary feminist, what's so wrong with letting someone who has the ability *help* you now and then, unless you're worried…"

Then he glanced toward the bed, where he could probably envision what we'd just finished doing there as easily as I could. His lips tightened. "Of course you'd be worried I'll expect more."

Emotions beyond words struggled in my chest, my throat. Love, even. Like it or not, I still loved this man more than was sane. More than I wanted to. Maybe even more than I should. But…maybe not more than that, after all.

"I'll be careful," I promised him.

He laughed. Lex rarely laughs, and this one was neither

pretty nor amused. "Mag, the guy at the desk gave me your room key for ten American dollars."

"I only came here because I was so tired when I reached Paris. I'll go somewhere that even you won't be able to find me. Will you believe I'm safe if even you can't find me?"

"Safe or dead." He looked grim. "I wouldn't be able to find you if you're at the bottom of the Seine, either."

"Then we'll just have to meet somewhere," I said, glad for the excuse. "Didn't you promise me dinner when I got to Paris?"

Now Lex looked wary. "I did. Do. But don't you—"

I pressed my fingers to his lips. "I said it's a good thing we aren't married. I never said I don't want to see your sorry butt again. Especially…"

Okay, so as I lowered my hand, I also lowered my gaze toward his tight behind, beautifully framed in his smudged, tailored slacks.

Lex said, wearily, "Magdalene, I have never been so confused in my life as when I'm with you."

"Should I take that as a compliment?"

"No. Maybe. Where do you want to meet?"

I considered it. "I'm not sure what part of Paris I'll be in. Keep your phone with you and I'll let you know. Okay?"

"What time?"

I checked my watch; it was already after two o'clock, and I had a lot to accomplish. "Seven?"

"Seven." He fished out his wallet and handed me a card. At first I thought it was a credit card, and almost protested. Then I recognized the tasteful insignia of the Hotel Valmont, one of the more exclusive addresses in Montmartre. It was his room keycard. "In case you want to use my bathtub. Give me an hour, and I won't even be there."

I cupped his cheek, breathed his breath. "You being there wouldn't be what keeps me away."

He lowered his gaze, almost as if shy of whatever he was feeling now. He had such pretty lashes. "I'll let the concierge know that you're welcome any time. You need the keycard in the elevator, too. It's on the executive level, Suite #3."

I whispered, "Maybe I'll see it after dinner."

"Never so confused." But he pressed close to say it; his words kissed across my neck. Mmm.

"Does it help to know that I'm still working things out?" But I did pocket the card, as I said that.

"Absolutely. Misery loves company."

I nudged his shoulder playfully. "Stop with the adages or I'll never get anything done."

"Mag." He lifted his gaze to mine again, more serious now. "What did you mean earlier, when you said nothing happened that you couldn't handle? What were you able to handle?"

Uh-oh. I tucked his tie under his shirt collar for him, giving me something to focus on other than his searching face. "Don't worry about it."

Even a brief glance showed me that his eyes had narrowed in understanding. "Someone really did hold you at gunpoint?"

I tightened and straightened the tie, smoothing it down onto his chest. Because of him, over the years, I've become quite a fan of a well-worn tie. "I'm fine, Lex."

I should have been relieved when he let that go. Maybe it was the sheer unlikelihood of it that made me uncomfortable. All he said was, "If you don't call by seven, I start dragging the Seine. Don't think I'm joking."

"I never think you're joking. You aren't very good at it."

He definitely wasn't joking when he kissed me again— hard and intense and needful, as if he were trying to regain every lost kiss since our last "on" period. I didn't mind helping. Languid, intense, hard-not-to-squirm kissing. We were very good at it. We may have made up for a whole month, by the time he opened the door and headed out.

Slumped against the doorjamb, I watched him go. When I realized I was all but praying—*please let it work out this*

time, please let him be on the level—I frowned and pushed
back inside for my bag, my still-damp towel, my toiletries.

I'd been this close to having him out of my life for good.
Instead, here we went again. I was the one who'd kept him
from leaving. I was the one who'd suggested we might go
to his room after dinner.

In fact, I was very much looking forward to it.

But *what if I was wrong?*

On the other hand, maybe my own inability to commit
was what had messed us up so far. There, Lex never had a
problem. He'd proposed four times; I'd accepted twice. Once
I broke it off within the week. The other time we argued before the night was out and he rescinded the offer.

But I'd helped pick the fight, for some reason I couldn't
yet face. Maybe I was afraid Lex would turn out like his father, or his cousin. Worse, maybe I feared ending up like his
mother.

In the meantime, I desperately needed another shower.
And to gargle hot water, since for some reason my throat
hurt. Then I would walk away from this quaint but less-
than-secure "dump," just like Lex had suggested. But not because he'd suggested it.

Because he'd been right.

By five o'clock the grail and I were safely ensconced in
a private room at the quiet Des Jardins hotel on the Left
Bank. I was soaking in a tub, bathing for the third time that
day—not counting the underground river. It's a good way to
relax. The last twenty-four hours had been physically tax-
ing on so many levels.

And I did have a big night ahead of me.

I was pleased with myself, and not just because of either
the mind-blowing sex or the promise of more tonight.
Though that sure didn't hurt.

No, I was pleased because I'd secreted myself away so
well that even Lex couldn't have found me. First, after my

second shower of the afternoon, I'd taken a labyrinthine route on the Metro to make sure I wasn't being followed. Then I'd gone to an Internet café and done several data searches, only one of them to locate a trustworthy hotel. I shopped for fresh clothes, including an outfit for tonight. Then, with more switchbacks for caution, I arrived at the home of an old friend from my semester at the Sorbonne.

I hadn't seen or talked to Nadine for nine years. She was married now, so she had a different last name, and we hadn't known each other long enough that anybody would find her in an attempt to find me.

Turns out she was glad to see me and thrilled to help, no questions asked. So I'd checked into the hotel as Madame Nadine Lamballière, complete with a credit card and a Parisian driver's license showing a woman of my age and general coloring. Nadine herself was safe at home with her children and her husband, holding on to one of my credit cards as security.

Sure, there was always the possibility that she could somehow screw me over. I could mess up her bank account pretty badly too, if I tried. But there's a time to share vulnerability.

My last purchase of the day was a pay-as-you-go cell phone. I bribed the boy at the kiosk out of checking my ID, and so used completely false information for the paperwork. I left messages for my mother and cousin in French and used a fake name. If I was really lucky, the bad guys still thought I'd drowned outside Chinon. They only had to believe it long enough for me to unveil the Melusine Chalice—now tucked into a new leather backpack from Printemps, beside the tub—before they saw it coming.

Before they could make any damned *preemptive strikes*.

And once the grail was safe, I still had the whole summer ahead of me, free from classes and searching and men with guns. Even if I decided to research more grails, I suspected Lex might play a significant role in my vacation.

Had Melusine enjoyed her baths anywhere near as much as I did mine? I suspected, from our link the previous night, that she had. The tower room had been her version of a "room of one's own." A place where she could be wholly herself…as long as her husband wasn't destroying both their lives by spying on her….

Like Lex had spied on me in the shower this afternoon? I smiled at the irony. After all, *I* wasn't under any kind of curse. But oddly, my throat began hurting again.

My cell phone rang, startling me from fleeting thoughts, and I wiped my hand on a towel before answering it. *"Bonjour, c'est Véronique."*

"Hello, *Véronique*." It was my mother. She would recognize my voice even if I spoke Gaelic and called myself Boudicca. "I was so pleased to get your message. It's been too long."

Two days, Mom. But Véronique couldn't say that.

"Far too long, yes," I said, accented. "I have been, how do you say, busy as a pea?"

"Something like that." I'd just noticed how tense Mom sounded when she said, "You know, Véronique, as much as I would love to talk, I'm trying to find my daughter."

"Madeleine?" I've been called Madeleine all my life.

"Magdalene. I was straightening her apartment for her yesterday—did you know she'd been burglarized?"

"Mon Dieu. This is terrible."

"I found something odd there—a little box, the size of a pager, but it wasn't a pager at all. Maggi had given me the number of a friend of hers, a police officer, to call if there was trouble." I had. My partner in crime. *Sofie.* "Officer Douglas came over and looked, and said it was what I thought."

"What?" I was sitting up in the tub now, clutching its porcelain side. My throat clenched so tight that I could barely breathe past it, much less talk.

"A state-of-the-art listening device," said Mom, gently.

"Officer Douglas did some checking, and she says it wasn't there when the police searched Maggi's apartment the night of the break-in, so someone must have left it afterward."

No. I didn't want to know, really I didn't, but some ugly, bat-winged determination forced me to ask. "Left it where?"

"In Maggi's bookshelf," said my mother.

The books Lex had reshelved for me. *Lex.* The only person, other than Mom, whom I was sure had come into my apartment since the burglary…and who had coincidentally been on the same flight to France as me, the following morning.

I barely submerged my head underwater in time to drown out another powerful, furious scream at even the possibility of such a betrayal.

Chapter 16

I now had a good idea why the heraldic Melusine was shown with two tails. I've never felt so divided in my life as I did getting ready to meet with Lex.

The words *son of a bitch* screamed through my head as I splashed from the tub. I couldn't even imagine such a calculated, premeditated betrayal without some good, solid fury. I definitely needed fury to stick with the frustration of blow drying my long hair.

Lying, sneaking, manipulative son of a bitch.

Then, unwrapping my new underwear from its label-sealed tissue, I regretted lapsing into suspicion so easily, so soon. I'd bought these matching tap pants and bra, a dusky blue edged with silver, with such high hopes. Had I been an idiot?

Don't jump to conclusions, I advised myself. *It may not have been him. The police could have missed the bug, or the* Comitatus *could have planted it since then.*

But as I clipped silk stockings to my new garter belt, I remembered more. In the airport Lex had said he regretted his behavior the night before; had he meant more than the kiss? And just today he'd argued that a person's rights meant nothing against someone else's ability to ignore those rights. Like, oh, the right to privacy and the ability to plant illegal bugs?

I slid my new dress, a dove-gray silk, over my head, my arms, my body, like sliding into a whole new skin, a whole new cynicism. Worse than his betrayal would be falling for it.

And yet, as I put on new makeup, my blush brush faltered on my cheek. *No. Slow down. Don't let anger outweigh love without being absolutely sure.*

You don't want to live in that kind of world.

It wasn't just that I still loved him; lovers have been wrong before. But he loved me, too. He'd said so, and the way he'd made love, and the way he'd kissed me, and his concern for my safety…

He wasn't faking those. I knew that, with a certainty that refused to be contradicted even by fear or hurt.

It was time to call him. Instead, I unzipped the leather backpack and took out the Melusine grail, held its white stone curves, contemplated it. *Love. Betrayal. Triumph. Loss.*

And, as if it were whispering to me, *Realization.*

I'd always thought of the husband in Melusine's story as a one-note bad guy. But she'd given him ten children. He'd been goaded into spying on her by fears of an affair. He may even have thought he acted out of love.

But he'd been wrong. And his fears destroyed them.

Maybe Lex did love me. But he thought that gave him the right to control my life. To call the police and demand I get special treatment. To stake out my hostel. To bribe a desk clerk for my room key and sneak into my shower, as surely as Melusine's husband had snuck into her bath chamber.

None of that was even in question. *He'd done that much.* For what he thought was my own good, he'd done all of it.

Whether he'd planted the bug or not.

I wrapped the grail in a towel to protect it and slid it back into the leather backpack. Then I stepped into my high-heeled sandals, which I'd bought to match the dress, hefted the backpack, and headed out for the nearest Paris Metro station.

Tonight wasn't a time to retreat. From anything. But this conversation required a hell of a lot more than a phone call.

"I'm here to see Mr. Stuart," I told the *concièrge* at Hotel Valmont, flashing my keycard, my passport and my sweetest smile. "I'm trying to surprise him."

Then I strode to the ironwork elevator as if I owned it, fully aware of several pairs of eyes following me. They did not feel like threats. They felt like sexual nuisances.

I looked really good.

The elevator took me to the executive floor. I stepped out onto impossibly plush carpeting, found #3, and used the keycard to enter without knocking. *What's sauce for the goose.*

"—doesn't matter what he says," I heard Lex insisting from beyond the baroque foyer. "No."

I followed his voice and found him in the suite's high-ceilinged den with a phone to his ear and his back to me. He wore a dark pair of tailored pants and a white shirt, bisected into a Y in back by dress suspenders. The outfit matched the expensive room, with its suede-covered walls, rich draperies, fresh flowers and dark, Louis XVI furniture. One thing about hanging with Lex; the setting was usually delicious.

He said, "If anything has happened to her, if any of your boys were involved, you'll see exactly what I'm capable of."

Then he slammed the phone down. The coiled cord swung. He'd been using a land line. And oh, goddess, I knew.

He was involved. "Funny that you'd have the phone number for someone whose identity eludes you."

He spun so fast, it was…no. This would never come close to being funny. His naked relief was just salt in my wounds.

"God, Mag!" Lex exclaimed, checking his watch. I already knew it was seven exactly. "Cutting it close, aren't you? I thought you were going to call. You look beautiful."

He came to my side while he said that, touched my shoulder, kissed my cheek. I already knew what great smokescreens those little polite rituals could be, multipurpose, suitable for weddings, funerals and everything in between.

He smelled so good. He looked like a prince in a fairy tale, proud and well groomed and earnest. Even now, my heart ached to believe it. Maybe in some alternate universe, the two of us were still headed out for a magical Parisian night of dinner and not just sex but lovemaking.

Not in this universe. Some fairy tales *weren't* real.

But not all little girls broke easily.

"So who were you just threatening, Lex?" I asked, tight.

He backed away a careful step, clenching his teeth in a sort of hesitating grimace. Casual, even now. Controlled. "Sorry, Maggi. I can't really talk about business."

"Was it someone involved with, oh, trying to kill me?"

"I've been told your life was never deliberately in danger. If I'm misinformed, set the record straight. What's going on?"

"The *record?*" More business he probably couldn't talk about. "By what definition are guns and high-speed car chases and arson considered safe? Thank heavens no innocent by-standers were hurt. Not everyone gets the Stuart mantle of protection."

"Maggi, you've never accepted my protection."

"Not against your own men I haven't! That's called a protection *racket,* Lex."

"My own...no!" Lex shook his head. "Those *weren't my men.*"

"So who were they?" That got me silence. I had a hard time imagining his involvement in any group he wasn't helping to run, but let's say I believed that much. "How are you involved with people who beat up old ladies, who murder their own part-ners, who pull guns on priests? And on me? How is that, Lex?"

His ducked his head. "I can't talk about that."

That's when I lost it. I flew at him, pushed him backward, hard. He stumbled back without protest, setting his jaw, so I did it again. Then again, until he hit the suede-covered wall. "This is just like that stupid trial, just like that damned con-fidentiality agreement—"

Click. That's *exactly* what it felt like. Too exactly.

"Is what's happening now connected to last year's trial?"

He started to shake his head before he could stop himself. Then he did. Stop himself. "I can't talk about the trial."

"But that isn't the only confidentiality agreement you've signed, is it?"

"Maggi, if you'd just calm down—" His eyes pleaded with me to understand something he'd abdicated his ability to explain.

Now I had to back up or I was going to hit him for real. "No, not an agreement," I whispered, more pieces clicking into place. "You've taken some kind of oath of secrecy, haven't you?"

And that meant we were either swimming in enough secret societies for a farce, or I already knew which one he'd pledged.

Bloodlines. Power. The goddamned *Comitatus*.

Lex looked away, lest I see something in his eyes.

I said, "You belong to a secret society, and you gave an oath of secrecy. How long ago, Lex? How long has it been that I haven't even known who you are?"

Now he looked back—surprisingly angry. "You're one to talk! You were *fourteen* when you started wearing that necklace—"

"Of my own choice!"

"Do you think I've *ever* made a choice that wasn't mine?"

"Mine never required an oath! There's no vow of secrecy among my *'hereditary feminists,'* just simple, common sense. We aren't about any one person having power over others, but apparently you and your *Comitatus* demand it."

Lex's chin came up.

Very quietly he asked, "Where did you hear that word?"

He meant *Comitatus*. "What word?"

"He scowled."

"You can't even say it to me, can you? Is it because I don't have the right blood, or because I have breasts?"

I didn't want to be the only one losing control here.

It worked. "Don't play the feminist card, Maggi! Not when you don't know what you're talking about."

"I never thought you had a problem with feminism," I said.

"A problem with…? I don't!"

"But you've involved yourself with people who do, right? Oh, wait. *You can't talk about it,* can you?"

"It's more *compli*—" But of course he stopped himself, because he *couldn't* talk about it. Not to me. "I promise you, Mag, I *swear* that I'm doing everything I can to keep you safe."

"Everything except tell me how to keep *myself* safe."

When he paced across the room and glared out at the still-sunny view of Paris, he resembled his father. Had his mother ever felt this way? If so, no wonder she'd slit her wrists. But *that* I didn't say to him.

I had that much kindness left in me, if not much more.

Lex turned to face me. "Give me the benefit of a doubt."

I didn't want to feel sorry for him. But I did.

Especially when he whispered, "Please."

But sympathy wasn't enough. I needed reassurances. "Just tell me you aren't protecting the *Comitatus* with your silence."

He looked desperate. "Mag—"

"Tell me you're involved in some other secret society, working to stop them. One with its own vows of secrecy. You don't have to name them even, just nod. Cough. Touch your nose."

But that was just another fairy tale.

"You don't understand," he protested, grim.

"And you've ensured that I never will, haven't you?"

Lex shook his head, not at me so much as protesting what was happening, what we were losing, right here in this Parisian suite. "If you could just trust me…."

"For how long? Another few days? A month? Our lifetimes? Can't you see that you're asking me to abdicate my power too?"

"I love you."

Those words had never sounded so sad. The only thing sadder would be for me to repeat them. That, and the fact that some part of me would still mean them.

But it wasn't a healthy part of me, and I wasn't feeding it anymore. "Tell me this, then. Did you plant a listening device in my apartment, the night of the burglary?"

Lex stared at me, tall, handsome—and defeated. "Yes."

The last of my hopes for us died, then and there. "That's how you knew to go to France."

"I did have business in France."

"That morning."

He set his jaw. "Yes."

"Didn't you know I would hate you if I ever found out?"

"I hoped to God you wouldn't."

"Find out or hate you?"

"Both. But I had to do something. I was afraid for you, Mag. Don't you get that? I didn't know what you'd gotten yourself involved with. Accidents *can* happen. I was *afraid*."

So it was for my own good? Bastard. "You weren't afraid enough to tell me. Or call the cops."

He said nothing. Of course.

And now, for the game point— "So you already know why I'm in France, right? What I'm after."

The Melusine Chalice. Maybe I could stave off the heartache that waited just outside that door, if I remembered the grail.

Lex said, "Yes. I know."

"Do you know if I've found it yet?" My designer backpack, over one shoulder, felt heavy.

"Not for certain. No."

"Are you lying?"

He frowned. "I promised never to lie to you."

"You promised never to cheat me at cards."

He moved one shoulder, as if to say, *same thing*.

It wasn't. "You didn't think bugging my home was cheating?"

"That depends on which game we're playing, Magdalene."

"I guess I never wanted to play games as much as you did." I turned to walk out. Pain waited outside the suite's door. I knew that. A life more without Lex than I'd ever imagined, because it was a life in which the Lex I'd loved had been erased. He'd become an illusion.

He followed me to the door. "Mag, if I could explain I would. Don't you think I've wanted to? I've lost count of how many times I wished I could tell you, tell my best friend what's going on. I've hated having this between us."

Part of me wanted to wheel on him and scream, *Having what between us? You're the only one who knows for sure, because you're the one who put it there. YOU DID THIS TO US!*

The fact that I wouldn't accept it didn't make it my fault.

I didn't dare open my mouth, or I would probably have started screaming and not stopped—and it would be completely my own scream, not Melusine's. My own anguish. My own loss.

I gripped the porcelain doorknob, turned it and walked into my future without him.

"You *know* me," he insisted, following. "You know I'd never do anything to hurt you."

Now I spun on him and shouted, *"So what's this?"*

"I'm sorry," Lex whispered. Honestly, I think. Despite everything, I felt the old connection. I sensed the depth of his regret—and it didn't do anything for either one of us.

I jabbed the button for the elevator. "So am I."

Then, as long as it was taking its time, I turned back to him to set some ground rules. "Do not follow me. Do not call me. Do not have anyone spy on me. Understood?"

"I've been watching out for you," Lex countered. "You're the one who won't be careful. If you just stayed home, minded your own business—or cut me in on it—I wouldn't have *had* to spy on you."

I stared at him for so long that I heard the elevator arrive behind me, heard it slide open.

"I guess I just like to invite trouble," I hissed, and turned and stepped in.

I made it as far as the street, vaguely aware of the *concièrge* bidding me a polite good evening, before the pain hit me. I'd known it would, from other breakups. I felt sick. I felt dizzy. I felt suffocated. As if with every step, pieces of me were dying miserable deaths in light of this new truth.

Every time I'd ever hoped Lex and I would someday end up together—dead. Every memory of our happiness, our rightness, our bond—decimated. Almost every time I'd made love—ruined.

I somehow managed to point myself toward the nearest Metro station, somehow managed to keep my feet moving despite the dress heels. The Hotel Valmont, not far from the Basilica Sacré Coeur, was several blocks away from the nearest stop, probably because residents of the Hotel Valmont rarely took public transit. But I didn't want a cab. Cabbies keep records.

After timeless walking I reached the *Metropolitain* station entrance. This deep in Montmartre, it was marked by an art-nouveau arch bearing its full name in a curving, Toulouse-Lautrec font. No simple, circled M for us tourists.

Normally I love the Metro's street performers, long escalator rides down to the platforms, tubular architecture and clean, European lines. Almost everything inside the tunnels was tiled white, with bright-red benches and ten-foot-square advertising posters hugging the curve of the walls. Tonight I could barely see, could barely hear. I just wanted to get somewhere private.

Other things mattered more than Lex Stuart. The Melusine Chalice, safe in the backpack on my shoulder. Aunt Bridge's arrangements for its surprise exhibition.

If only I could glue enough shattered pieces of my world together to care. I looked down the tunnel, impatient to be home—and damned if my throat didn't start to hurt. Again.

If this was another scream coming on, I didn't want it. If I started screaming now, I might batter everything around me into little, ugly pieces. The grail. Myself.

Everything.

"Your timing," I now muttered, either to my sore throat or maybe to my stupid, broken heart, "sucks."

But my throat thickened and tightened anyway, beyond even the misery of my aching heart. Like last night, as the *Comitatus* arrived. Like this afternoon in the bathtub, as I found out that Lex had bugged my apartment. *Timing.*

Finally, stupidly, I thought to look around me. To *really* look around me. I'd told Lex not to follow me, but would that matter to him? This being summer, the subway platform held an eclectic crowd. Families. College students. School groups. Senior citizens. Couples out on dates, just as I'd hoped to be.

And businessmen, with a few suit-clad women among them. Some read copies of *Metropole Paris* or *Le Monde*. Some glanced at their watches. One frowned at his Palm Pilot.

Several grinned flirtatious hellos at me.

And one, standing by the bottom of the escalator, was watching me. He was a big man, with surprisingly blond hair and a mustache. His nose had been taped, and both eyes were swollen purple, and he could have been an extra in any war movie. I knew him from the *Tour Melusine* in Vouvant—and his driver's license.

Had I thought I hated the *Comitatus* before?

This was not a night for retreats. I headed back down the platform, toward him. He stood still for my approach. He even seemed to be checking me out.

I stopped far enough back from him to be out of immediate reach, increasingly conscious of the chalice's weight slung over my shoulder. "René de Montfort, I presume?"

"Dr. Sanger," said the man who'd killed his partner, the one I'd knocked unconscious and had gotten arrested. He'd been released pretty damned quick. Just how powerful *was* this group?

I smiled and asked, "How's your head?"

He asked, "How's your friend?"

Crap. *Rhys*. I still hadn't checked on Rhys.

I almost wished this son of a bitch would try something that would justify the infliction of major, spike-heeled pain.

Either that, or I needed a more elastic moral code.

"What do you want?" I asked, since *he* was the one following *me*. I could feel a faint breeze on the back of my neck, the first sign of a train approaching through the tunnels.

"Just to watch," he said, his smile widening.

Hands caught me from behind, too many. Before I could react, they hurled me off the edge of the platform and onto the tracks. I landed, hard, on my shoulder. Then I rolled to my feet, backpack in hand, amid cries of concern—

Just in time to see the train hurtling at me.

Once Lex and I take our relationship to a sexual level, it's an addiction. He's attending Yale, and I have a scholarship to Bryn Mawr. Different states. But we still get together at least twice a month.

Usually we stay in the city, at his father's Fifth Avenue town house. It's a four-story mansion with an elevator, a garden, and an honest-to-God rotunda. We put in appearances at museums, restaurants and art galleries. We jog in the park. But mostly we get naked with each other to exercise in a far more intimate manner.

"Do you ever feel like you're leading two lives?" I ask him one morning, my limbs useless, my head pillowed on his chest to ride his breath.

I'm surprised to feel him tense at my question. I'd thought he was as washed-out as me. "What do you mean?"

"There's my life with you," I say, "which is incredible."

"Mutual," he assures me happily, fingering my hair.

"And then there's my life at school. Studying, and grades, and...plans. Do you ever wish we went to the same school?"

It's as close as I've ever gotten to asking if he wants me to transfer or, even less likely, if he'll transfer himself. Do I want to hear the answer? I'm not sure I can respect him if he leaves Yale for me...and I love Bryn Mawr.

Just not as much as I love him.

I would hate to have to choose between them.

I'm still surprised when he says, "No."

"Not at all?"

He has relaxed, again. "If we went to the same school, I wouldn't be able to focus on anything but you. Ever."

Now that's better. Except...

"So what is it that requires so much focus, Mr. Stuart?"

"Someday, I hope to tell you."

I like this uncharacteristic playfulness. "Can I assume you're going to accomplish big things?"

Lex's gaze holds mine. "Huge things," *he promises.* "Epic."

"With an executive MBA?" *I laugh.*

"Once the church held all the power, Maggi. Then the royalty. Then the intellectuals. Now it's the businessmen."

"What a scary thought."

But he sits up in bed, which rolls me partly off him, and leans closer with his intensity. "How about it, Maggi? Would you be willing to help me do something epic?"

I momentarily wonder if it's all play, after all. "As long as you use your powers for good...I could be convinced."

Instead of making any promises, he kisses me...one of his better kisses. Full of promise. Excitement. And yeah—power.

His lovemaking almost wipes the conversation from my mind.

Almost.

Chapter 17

The train's one huge, halogen eye expanded to encompass my whole world. I sure screamed this time. And with the scream came focus. Power.

I hurled myself over the third rail, the electric one, and onto the opposite track.

The rush and roar of the train hurtled past me, a blur of lights and cars—but I didn't have time to feel relief. Instead, on the second set of tracks, I felt vibration beneath my feet and a familiar rush of wind from the opposite direction. *Crap.*

The screams of onlookers mixed with the screech of a train whistle as a second headlight caught my dilemma.

Opposite platform? Too high. Too slow.

Between the tracks? Mere inches in clearance.

No alcoves. No wall to press against. *No more time.*

I spun for the platform that I would never manage to climb, even with a few brave people reaching desperate hands toward me. Instead, I dove, rolled myself beneath it and slung the chalice over my head, safely against the concrete wall—

Dust and cinders hit my eyes, my face. Then the heavy wind, more debris. Heat. I squinted my eyes, but couldn't close them. With death so close, every second became precious for no more than being alive.

I didn't mean to die with my eyes closed.

Metal wheels on metal tracks shot sparks at me, a blur of movement inches in front of my face. I tried to flatten myself farther backward, to be absorbed by solid concrete, sure that at any moment I would be caught, dragged, crushed...

But the wheels continued, slowing.

Amidst all the screaming—the crowd's, and the train's, and maybe my own—the wheels slowed. The train stopped. And I was still lying there, stretched as long and thin as possible, squeezed between platform base and subway car.

I've never been so glad to be a B-cup.

Above me, muffled, I heard chaos—people shouting out what had happened and calling for help, the warning beeps of the other train readying to leave the platform, someone sobbing to have witnessed such a thing. And before me—

I could see under my train—so much weight and metal and size, I'd never imagined—to the other track, where the first train was slowly pulling out.

Still on instinct, I crawled on my knees and elbows, pushing the backpack ahead of me. I tried not to imagine more beeps, not to imagine this train moving out while I was beneath it. I slithered out the other side and dove over the third rail, to surprised cheers from the first platform.

Rolling to my feet, I ran in that direction, to the crowd where I'd started. A surprising number of bystanders, more concerned with a stranger's safety than their schedules, waited and reached for me. I reached back, and a group of skinny soccer players, still in their jerseys, lifted me to safety.

Suddenly I was being hugged and kissed by all of them. They were, after all, European.

"The men who attacked me," I called in French, too grateful to be alive to push anyone away. "Where did they go?"

Several people pointed at the escalator. From down the track, a police officer with a powerful flashlight circled the back of the second train. In a moment, he would see—or hear—that I wasn't caught under the wheels.

I didn't want the attention.

So I bolted for the escalators. One of my heels had broken—go figure—so as soon as I was gliding upward, I stood on one foot, then the other, in order to slip off my sandals. I tossed them toward the soccer players, who were still savoring their moment of heroism. *"Merci!"*

They caught and held up the shoes like trophies.

Then I ran up the moving stairs, as fast as I could.

Of course de Montfort and his friends were long gone when I reached the street level. Long gone…or secreted away and watching me. I stood there under the arched *Metropolitain* sign, looking through the crowds of Montmartre, and came to several quick conclusions.

One—either they didn't know I had the grail, or they wanted it demolished in a subway tragedy.

Two—Lex had played some part in this. Maybe he'd not only rescinded his "protection" but pointed me out. Or maybe de Montfort and his hench-jerks had just been watching his hotel.

And three—I had to find out what had happened to Rhys. *Now.*

Well, as soon as I reached some less conspicuous place. Call me crazy, but my love of the Metro had diminished. I still didn't want to go on record with a cab. Most of the buses driving by were for tours, not something I could just hop onto. And I was barefoot.

So I ran for the closest intersection where, amidst a tangle of traffic, a vaguely Asian girl with orange hair and multiple piercings straddled a Vespa, waiting for the light to change. She startled when I caught her handlebars. But when she saw my hair and clothes and shredded stockings, her expression turned to concern.

"'Circle to circle,'" I said, breathless, in French.

She said, "Huh?"

Oh, well. It had been worth a try. "I've been attacked, and I don't want to go to the police. Can I have a ride?"

She said, "Climb on."

I did, the light changed, and we buzzed away, easy as that.

That's when I started shaking.

Lex had said nobody had been actively trying to kill me before.

But they sure were now.

After a mile or two, my wheelwoman pulled over long enough to introduce herself and make sure I was all right. Her name was Edmee, she worked at McDonald's, and she didn't trust the authorities, either.

I didn't think it polite to ask why.

"Where will you go?" she asked. "My friends and me, we have a flat if you need to hole up."

Between her generosity and the help of the Metro onlookers, I was in danger of crying for a completely different reason than I'd worried about before.

Lex and the *Comitatus* were clearly *not* the majority. There really were good people in this world. A lot of them.

"Nôtre Dame would be fine," I said, instinctively naming one of the greatest monuments to divine feminine energy in all of Europe. "But if you can…make sure we aren't being followed."

"A-okay," said Edmee in enthusiastic English, and off we zipped. She spun me through more tiny roads, alleys and twists than I'd known Paris even had. By the time she dropped me off at the square before the cathedral's famous facade, even I felt lost.

I tried to pay her, but she shook her head. So I lifted the *vesica piscis* pendant from around my neck—the one Grand-mère had bought for me when I was fourteen—and pressed it into her hand, along with one of my business cards. "If you ever see a woman wearing one of these, say 'Circle to circle,'" I instructed. "If she says, 'Never an end,' you can trust her."

Edmee looked delighted, before buzzing away on her scooter.

"E-mail me if you want to know more," I called.

Then I crossed the square to the shelter of the cathedral's

intricately carved doorways, calling Aunt Bridge on my cell phone.

De Montfort had asked, *How's your friend?* I had a sick feeling that my suspicions about Rhys—Father Pritchard!—had been as misplaced as my trust in Lex Stuart.

"Have you talked to Rhys?" I demanded when Bridge picked up. "Is he okay?"

"He's right here," she said. "I'll put him on."

Before I could respond, the receiver changed hands.

"Maggi?" That was him all right, Welsh accent and all. *He was okay.* "Thank God you're safe. What happened to you?"

"To *me?* What about to you? They said you helped them, but then today they asked how you were and I was afraid—"

"Today? You ran into them again?" He paused. "Maggi, you thought I was helping them?"

In the background, I could hear Aunt Bridge's protest. She'd always trusted Rhys. But she'd known him longer.

"Not completely!" That sounded inadequate, for all that it was true. "But…not enough to contact you right off, either. There were extenuating circumstances, but…I am sorry, Rhys."

"You're forgiven," he said. "They tracked the phone."

"What phone?"

"The one we took off the murderer in Vouvant. It seems to have had a GPS chip in it. When I got to our hotel, they were waiting for me."

Oh, no. "Rhys! Are you all right?"

"I am. They mainly postured about, took our maps."

I didn't want to be paranoid anymore today. I preferred to live in a world where strangers helped strangers off subway tracks or gave them Vespa rides, no questions asked. A world where even laicized priests were the good guys.

"So they didn't tail us after all," I said. At least I could stop wondering how I'd missed them.

"They did not. But clearly they had some connection with abbey security, to get in as they did. I was so worried."

Which made two of us. I sat down on the steps of the large left door—the *Porte de la Vièrge*—before my legs gave way. Rhys hadn't betrayed me. "But you're all right?"

"I am. But keep asking me that, and I'll think you doubt my survival abilities," he chided. It sounded so much like something I would say that I laughed, which felt good.

Rhys said, "Your aunt found, um, *someone*. You know— a professional? To take care of that matter we discussed?"

James Bond, he was not. But if he meant some kind of trustworthy museum curator, willing to accept, protect and display the Melusine Chalice, I didn't care.

"That," I said, aware of the weight of the grail in its backpack, "I want to hear about. In person."

We made arrangements—using personal references only my aunt and I knew—for him to pick me up. Bridge assured me that she would be safe with her lover, Sergio, who'd fought in the French Résistance. "Worry about yourself, *chou*. Let me worry about me."

I didn't have a long wait at the spotlit *Cathédrale* before a car pulled up to the curb across the square—a wonderfully familiar, horribly dented Citroën Saxo VTR. From what I could see, nobody seemed to be tailing it. Rhys ducked his head to see out the passenger window, and waved.

Pigeons scattered as I ran to the passenger door and climbed in. "You brought Aunt Bridge's car home—thank you!"

"Maggi, what happened to you?"

I jerked my leg away when Rhys extended his hand, uncomfortable to have any man touch me just now.

"I'm sorry," he said, gesturing instead to the huge rip in my silk skirt. One of many. Oh.

"You remember René de Montfort?" I asked, stretching out my legs—as best I could in a Saxo—to get my first good look at what had recently been new, sexy stockings.

"The murderer," he said, taking a good look as well.

"He and someone I didn't see tossed me onto the Metro tracks. I'm okay," I added quickly, glancing up—and gasping.

Rhys had a black eye and an abrasion across one cheek.

"What happened to *you?*" I demanded. "You said they were just posturing when they found you!"

His grin came out lopsided, because of the swelling. "I'm alive, aren't I? And I'm okay, as well."

"Those sons of bitches—you're a *priest!*"

"That depends on whom you ask," he said, judging the traffic before pulling into it. "And they didn't know it. And it ought not have mattered."

But *I'd* known it. "And then I didn't trust you. I didn't even call you when I got to a phone."

"You left a message for your aunt," he reminded me. "She's the first person I called when I didn't hear from you."

"But if we hadn't drawn you into all this—"

"Maggi," insisted Rhys, far more patient than I felt I deserved. "I'm glad to be involved with this. With you."

Oh.

"And with your aunt, of course," he continued, before I could read more into that. "I'm as determined to see this through as anybody."

I clutched the backpack to my gut, like a bumpy teddy bear, and felt bad anyway. Once we left the Ile de la Cité behind, there were a few—very few—more parking spaces along the curb. God must still like Rhys, because he found one and nosed the Saxo into it, killing the engine before turning to better face me. "Maggi, how long has it been since you started this?"

"This?" I'd heard legends my whole life. I'd known there really were Grail Keepers since I got my first period. Lilith and I began our Web site just over a year ago.

"Since you came looking for the Melusine Chalice. A week?"

Oh. "My apartment was broken into five days ago."

"And you've been running full-out ever since, haven't

you? Give yourself permission to misjudge a person now and then." When he grinned, easily showing more teeth than I may have ever seen on Lex, his hurt eye vanished behind the swelling. His grin became a wince. "Assuming you did misjudge me, of course."

"Don't even say it! I couldn't stand it if you morphed into one of the bad guys, too."

His eyebrows went up. "Too?"

"I ran into an old boyfriend," I admitted, needing to tell someone. "Actually, he found me. Alexander Stuart?"

Rhys looked completely blank—and I could have hugged him. Him, and his jeans, and his faded black T-shirt. He hadn't grown up in Connecticut. He clearly read neither the financial pages nor the gossip columns. Lex was nobody to him.

"He's very rich," I clarified. "I had reasons to suspect his family was involved in old conspiracies against the grails. But Lex and I…we've been close since childhood, and I believed he was different, and we…"

Okay, so maybe I'd leave out the details about me, Lex and the old iron bunkbed. But I edited myself as much because I felt ashamed—for my stupidity more than the sex—as because it would qualify as oversharing.

"You…?" prompted Rhys, sounding strangely wary.

"We planned to go out tonight," I said, to explain the silk. What was left of it. "But…he's with the *Comitatus.*"

"Ah, Maggi…"

Damn it! At Rhys's sympathetic *Ah, Maggi,* all the hurt I'd tried to fight back as I left the Hotel Valmont, all my shock at being thrown in front of a train, found the weakness it needed to burst through. It drowned me in one overwhelming wave. Tears filled my vision, and my throat ached without threat of screams. "I thought I *knew* him," I said, an awful warble in my voice. "But he's involved in some horrible, murdering secret society, and he bugged my apartment when I thought he was there to check on me, and oh, God, Rhys, I've loved him so long…."

That was the true tragedy of tonight. My heart didn't have a return policy. Even when I'd thought Lex and I shouldn't be together, a large part of me had continued to love him for everything he'd been to me. And now…had it all been a lie?

I could barely see through my own tears, especially parked between streetlights, but I heard the click of a seat belt unfastening, then felt a fumbling at my own hip. Then Rhys was pulling me into his arms, and I went gladly.

Crying like an idiot.

"Shhh," he soothed, petting my back, rubbing his jaw on my hair. "It's all right, Maggi. Go ahead and cry."

"I don't want to cry."

"Don't be a goose. Everyone cries. It's good for you."

Goose? I cried harder.

"Shhh," he repeated. "The deeper you love, the deeper it hurts. Surely you know that. I'm even told it's a good thing."

A *good* thing? My tears were turning to sobs—ugly, wet, openmouthed sobs against his shoulder. "But I…was…so stupid!"

"I doubt you have it in you to be stupid. This man kept his involvement a secret, didn't he?"

Hence the term, *secret society*. But I'd had concerns about his family. And he'd been on the same damned flight to Paris!

"Maggi Sanger." Rhys pushed me back from him and wiped my eyes with what felt like a paper napkin. Then he wiped my mouth, and my nose. Yeah, some defender of goddessdom I'd turned out to be. "Never regret love. Loving each other brings us closer to God than anything in this world."

"Not when you love the wrong person."

"God loves everybody." He shook his head. "It's true that sometimes we make poor choices."

Oh. Everything in the world wasn't about me, was it? I sniffed, hard. "Do you regret the choices you made with Mary?"

"Absolutely. But which choices depend on what day you ask."

I had no argument left in me, only exhaustion, only tears. Rhys drew me back into his embrace, and I sobbed against him until his shirt's yoke was damp. Once I ran out of tears, I still stayed where I was, struggling to breathe, struggling to collect myself. I was so tired of this. So damned tired.

Rhys continued to hold me, pet my hair, make comforting sounds until finally, blessedly, an edge receded from the ache in my chest. The void in my soul where the Lex I'd known had been wrenched away—had wrenched himself away, through his secrecy and lies—seemed a hint smaller.

If just a hint.

Slowly I returned to an awareness of things other than pain. An awareness, in particular, of strong arms around me. Of a solid shoulder supporting me. Of a friend, unexpected and necessary and so wonderfully *there*.

His fingers softly massaged the back of my neck. *Mmm.* I found myself remembering how, just last night in Fontevrault's chapel, he'd kissed me. This could be something good.

And the timing was so horribly wrong, on so many levels.

"So," I said. Snuffled. "You get that I'm on the rebound."

"Are you?" he asked thickly. "I hadn't noticed."

I pushed back from him, because cuddling wouldn't make this any easier. "And I don't imagine that, after waiting so long for Mary, and how badly that ended…you're looking to leap into the dating scene just yet either, right?"

He was looking at me the way a man looks at a woman he wants to kiss. But he said, "I've not asked a girl on a date since I was in school. I'm not even sure I remember how."

"It will come back to you," I assured him fervently.

"She ought to be Catholic," he said, at the same time.

I stared, and he shrugged, eyes bright. "I've not even considered other women until you came along, Maggi, and I suppose I should thank you for that. But…wouldn't I be a fool to date someone I didn't feel I could marry? And to marry in the church, wouldn't she have to be Catholic?"

Him being the expert, these had to be rhetorical questions.

"As opposed to a goddess worshipper," I said. Because as of last night, I *was* one. "Who's only Catholic-ish."

Rhys touched my face. His touch felt gentle, healing. He drew his fingers down my cheek, his thumb across my lips—and I could see that he still wanted to kiss me. Even if he wouldn't do it, if I wouldn't have let him, the wanting meant something.

"As opposed to anyone who's only Catholic-ish," he admitted. "But you certainly do complicate matters."

I felt a pitiful smile pushing at my lips, and I welcomed it. Blessed him for it. "So you're saying that if only I weren't upset about Lex, and if I weren't a goddess worshipper, and if I were Catholic, and possibly if I didn't live across the Atlantic Ocean from you, you might someday be interested. Right?"

"I'm already interested," Rhys said, simple as that. "But if it weren't for all that, I'd most certainly be acting on it. Fasten your seat belt."

And he started the car, to take me to dinner—and to tell me about the museum curator whom Bridge had found to help us.

Dr. Catrina Dauvergne, a curator at the Musée Cluny.

"This is a much better fit than the Louvre," said Aunt Bridge the following evening, after her lover, Sergio, dropped us off at the high-walled entrance of the Cluny. "Don't you think?"

Rhys, holding her good arm as we walked, caught my gaze over her head. "It is. The chalice would be lost in a place the size of the Louvre."

The Cluny, like the Cloisters in New York, specialized in medieval artifacts. It *was* almost a perfect fit.

Catrina Dauvergne, a former student of Aunt Bridge's, had a double major in archeology and business, a master's in the art of Medieval France, and a Ph.D. in museum studies. She already knew about the Kali Cup and wholly supported our plan to keep the Melusine Chalice from meeting a similar fate. We were bringing the grail to her now, as the museum closed, so that she could lock it in her personal safe and arrange its launch with the utmost privacy. Unlike with the Kali Cup, the *Comitatus* would have no advance notice.

I'd spent all day with the grail. I'd photographed it. I'd drunk from it again—with less dramatic but equally peaceful results. I hated to let it go.

But other women deserved to experience it, as well.

"And the Roman baths of the Hôtel de Cluny were built atop a site of ancient goddess worship," continued Aunt Bridge.

Fine. So it was the perfect place. The fifteenth-century "hotel" was its own fortress, safe behind crenellated stone walls, accessible through only one set of high double doors, thick and wooden and fronted with iron bars. It had quiet dignity.

And it shared a Metro stop with the Sorbonne, which mean Aunt Bridge could easily visit the grail whenever she liked.

Passing through that one open doorway, we crossed the cobbled courtyard, not to the tower entrance but around to the back offices. We knocked, the door opened—and I met the woman who would introduce the Melusine Chalice to the modern world.

Dr. Dauvergne, in her midthirties, had a sleek beauty about her. Her hair was a honey-gold knot, her glasses hung on a chain around her neck, and her suit was conservative. She'd taken an endearingly plain picture for her ID tag.

She also held Aunt Bridge's hands between hers for a long moment, with delight to see her old teacher. And she told Rhys and me to call her "Cat." "We're working together, after all."

The administrative stretch of the museum looked like the abbey the building had once been, its small offices literal monks' cells. Like most ancient buildings, it had exposed pipes and inadequate lighting. But the room into which Cat led us was larger, with brighter overhead lighting and steel tables holding different *objets d'art*.

In particular, I noticed a framed tapestry stretched on an easel, depicting a standing unicorn. My step slowed. "That's not one of *the* tapestries, is it? I mean, I know it's not a panel from your standing collection."

"*La Dame à la Licorne?*" clarified Cat, and I nodded.

"We are in the last stages of acquiring this," said Cat. "Clearly it is not one of the original six panels. But it is from fifteenth-century Flanders, commissioned through Lyons, and so may be related. I harbor particular theories that *La Dame* secretly references the Royal House of Stuart."

Wow, did I ever want to sit down and talk shop with *this* lady. But of course, we weren't there for the guided tour. We were there for something even more important.

"There were tapestries in Fontevrault, too," I said, by way of transition, and offered her the photos I'd had developed that morning. It turned out that since I'd finished the film before going down Melusine's well, all but the first few pictures had survived the water. "Before those bastards burned them."

Catrina looked at the first of the photographs I handed her, then the next—and slowly sat down, her face blanching.

"*Mon Dieu,*" she murmured, wholly getting just how vast a cultural massacre the *Comitatus* had committed. She forced herself to continue through the shots. "They were beautiful…."

"They really were," I agreed, my throat thick with loss. "I wish my photography could have done them justice."

"It is appalling, that such a thing could happen in this enlightened time."

"The people who have been trying to stop us," I said, "are all about destruction. But they didn't get this."

And I unzipped the bag, and lifted out the grail.

Cat inhaled slowly, appreciatively. "*Magnifique!*"

Passing over that chalice was one of the hardest things

I've ever had to do. I could barely breathe around the lump in my throat. But I also felt immensely proud of myself.

If Cat was as competent as she seemed, this could work.

And once the grail was safe, I meant to put my considerable research skills to work—hunting down the *Comitatus*.

"Well," said Rhys, as we left the courtyard through the doorway to the street. "A job well done, eh? How does it feel not to be solely responsible for the chalice anymore?"

"The *Comitatus* may still think I have it," I reminded him, around a lump in my throat. My backpack felt so light! "As long as we're buying Cat some time, maybe we can trick them into giving away more about themselves."

He shook his head, but wisely withheld any critique of my latest plan. "So…you'll be in Paris for a while longer?"

I smiled, liking the sound of that, even if I was still having trouble breathing.

Aunt Bridge, between Rhys and me, said, "Is your throat all right, Maggi? I believe I have a lozenge in my purse."

My step slowed. My throat *did* feel sore. Not with the screaming intensity I'd felt over the last few days, but…what if this wasn't mere emotions at ending my grail adventure?

That thought allowed other instincts to flow over me, nauseating suspicions that had to, *had* to be mistaken.

I looked back at the Cluny—and saw that someone had shut the barred gates and doors across the courtyard entrance since we'd left. Someone far stronger than Catrina Dauvergne…which meant our visit hadn't been a complete secret, after all.

That alone wasn't enough—but combined with my tight throat, I suddenly just…*knew*.

"Oh, my goddess," I whispered. "Something's wrong."

Chapter 18

"What do you mean, something's— Maggi, wait!" called Rhys. But I was running along the museum's fortress wall, racing back to its barred and blocked entrance. Walking more slowly, with Aunt Bridge on his arm, he fell behind.

I slammed my forearms against the doors, between the bars. I barely made noise, they were so thick. Each stood twice as high as me, flush to the carved stone jamb. They were locked.

Oh, no. *Cat!*

"Try her cell phone," I said, backing up deliberately.

"Why—" began Rhys, but stopped as I took a running start—and leaped upward against the rise of the sculpted doorjamb. Like so much medieval architecture, it bore stone decorations—and my only hope for a handhold.

"We have to warn her," I gasped, climbing it like a tree.

"Warn her about what?" warbled Aunt Bridge. "Magdalene, what are you doing?"

I was topping the jamb and reaching for the carved hood molding that arched over the stone portal, that's what I was doing. Hopefully the ancient rock would hold me long enough to top the parapets. Haste made me clumsy. One foot skidded. I nearly fell to the sidewalk beneath me.

Clutching close to the wall, I looked down.

Rhys stretched a hand upward, eyes wide, as if he hoped

to catch or steady me. Only when I saw that he couldn't reach me did I realize on a gut level just how high this wall was.

Aunt Bridge had her cell phone out and was squinting at its display, pushing buttons.

I hooked my inside knee over the hood molding and accessed all my leg strength, all my balance, to ease myself upward, upward, until—yes! My hand reached the bottom edge of the crenellations. Reached, and knocked hard against them.

The battlement thrust outward, over the sidewalk. I would have to push away from the wall, away from the molding that held me, if I had any chance of scaling the top of the wall.

"It's ringing," Aunt Bridge called, beneath me. Beneath, and to one side. I wouldn't risk landing on her.

I edged my outside foot precariously up, onto the hood molding in front of my inside knee. Now I crouched against the wall, between doorway and crenellations, like Spider-Man without the handy web.

"Maggi," Rhys warned. Too late—not that I would've heeded him. With a final lunge, I rose up and outward. It was a move that, if I didn't catch the embrasure between the upthrust stone merlons, would launch me into a dramatic back flop onto the pavement far below.

My hands met air. Flailed forward. Caught stone. Then I clutched gratefully to the edge of the toothy parapet, steady.

"It's transferring me to voice mail," relayed Aunt Bridge. "What should I tell her?"

"I think she's in danger." I dragged myself across the embrasure on my stomach, glad for something solid beneath me. "She should lock her doors and call security or the police."

Assuming the *Comitatus* hadn't already gotten her.

Levering myself the rest of the way into the embrasure between the crenellation's stone teeth, I looked down at the long drop onto cobblestone inside the wall—and felt momentary despair. Bad enough to lose Melusine's grail, but to have put an innocent woman, not even a Grail Keeper, into the line of fire...

To my relief, a security guard jogged across the courtyard toward me, waving. "You must not do this!" he yelled in French, making a shooing motion. "You will be injured!"

"I need to get in!" I called, also in French. If he could just catch me, break my fall....

No—that would risk yet another innocent.

My accent must not have been as good as I'd thought, because this time he used English. "The museum, it is closed. Get down, or I will call the police."

"Call them. One of your curators may be in danger."

That got the guard's attention. "What is this?"

"Dr. Dauvergne," I explained, frustrated with just talk. But when I extended one leg downward, ready to drop myself toward the inside doorway's hood molding, the guard pointed a warning finger at me. I suspected I wouldn't get past him without a fight. "We were just in her offices, and I'm very afraid something has happened to her. You have to let us in."

He shook his head. "No, this is impossible."

"Then check on her yourself. But hurry!"

"No," he insisted. "I mean, you cannot have only now spoken to Dr. Dauvergne. The museum offices, they are also closed."

"She let us in the back door. Over there." I pointed. "Look, we aren't trying to get in."

He tipped his head back, eyeing my perch on the wall.

"Other than to help her, I mean. Check on her, now, or I'm calling the police myself." *And going in without you.*

A woman's voice said, "Surely we do not need the police." And the museum curator herself approached across the cobbles, her gaze a mix of confusion and amusement at this scene.

"Cat!" I exclaimed, glad to see her safe.

From the street side, Bridge said, "Cat? Thank goodness."

"Paul, it is all right," she was telling the guard. "Please, open a door for me? We can leave the gates locked."

After a moment's hesitation, he did as instructed.

"I'm afraid you really must get down," she told me, and pointed as I shifted my weight to join her. "No—*that* side."

"Cat, I think you might be in danger."

"I trust Paul implicitly. But unless you wish to draw even more attention than you already have…?"

I glanced toward the street—and saw that I had quite an audience, some with cameras. I didn't like giving up. But she was here. She was safe. The man beside her—whom she trusted—had keys to the gates as well as the doors.

So I repeated my climb in reverse—feet dangling past the bottom edge of the battlements, swinging in search of first the molding and then the bars. I jumped the last ten feet to land into an easy, shock-absorbing crouch.

Onlookers applauded, but I wheeled to grasp the iron bars. "Cat, our visit was supposed to be secret but someone shut the gates behind us. Was it Paul? Did you know he knew?"

And Cat said, "I'm sorry…do I know you?"

It's as if the world froze, right there. Or as if I wanted it to, because part of me was starting to figure this out, faster than the rest of me could keep up.

I already suspected I was *not* going to like this.

Rhys stepped closer behind me, his hand on my shoulder relaying how much my climb had concerned him. "Mademoiselle Dauvergne, we were just in your office."

Bridge said, "Catrina!"

Cat leaned closer—though she did not stand near enough to be grabbed through the bars. "Dr. Taillefer?" she exclaimed, then turned to the guard. "*C'est bien*, Paul. This is my old sociology professor. Dr. Taillefer, what are you doing here?"

"Are you sure, *mademoiselle?*" asked Paul, clearly torn. "They spoke of danger, and being in your offices. They demanded that I let them in, but I told them it was impossible."

"I'm fine," Cat assured him, touching his hand and winning a slave for life. "Thank you for watching after me."

She turned back to us. "As Paul has explained, it is impossible to have visitors after closing. But if you would like to set an appointment, Dr. Taillefer, I would be glad to give you and your guests a personal tour of the exhibits during our regular hours."

"You…" I protested as Paul went to speak to another security guard who'd shown up. "You're with them, aren't you?"

Cat blinked at me, searching. "With…?"

"With the *Comitatus!*"

She scrunched her mouth in what looked like real confusion. "Norse war bands?"

Aunt Bridge said, "The men we warned you about."

"Ohhh." She nodded even as she said, "No. Assuming there even is such a threat, I am not what you would call a 'joiner.' Now run along and stop causing trouble. You would appreciate the complication of the *gendarmes* even less than would Paul."

"Try me."

She blinked, all innocence. "And whatever would you tell them, strange woman whom I've never met before?"

Rhys's hand tightened on my shoulder, advising caution. I thought of Melusine's cup, *my* cup, and desperately needed his steadying presence. "You know exactly what I would tell them. We brought that grail to you in good faith, Catrina."

"Grail…" She shook her head, smiling at her own feigned confusion. "You're claiming to have brought me an artifact?"

I lunged at the bars and managed to wedge a shoulder between them, reaching desperately for her. The hell with personal power—I wanted the power to smash her face into the cobblestones! Getting her keys so that I could retrieve the grail would just be gravy.

She tsk-tsked at my fury, taking another step back. "Should I report this harassment to the police, and you told them some similar story, would they not ask where you found such an item?"

Rhys's hands closed on my waist now, trying to pull me back from the bars. I wouldn't budge. He said, "You know full well, Dr. Dauvergne, that we rescued it from Fontevrault."

"Ah, yes," she said. "The abbey that was so badly vandalized. I'm surprised you wish to be connected to that."

Only then did I let go, strength slowly seeping from me. I let Rhys pull me back. He wrapped his arms around me, but I wasn't going to lunge again. I didn't have the heart.

Because goddess help me, she was right.

Who would believe our story against hers? Assuming the authorities would check inside for the grail—and I wondered if it would get that far—would they believe us? A Welsh laicized priest and an American post doc—me—carried less clout than the curator of one of the most respected museums in the world. Even Aunt Bridge was in her eighties. And she hadn't been at Fontevrault.

We'd walked right into Cat's trap.

Actually, no. *We* hadn't done anything. *I'd* done this. I'd lost the grail. I'd trusted the wrong person…in part, I was afraid, because she'd been a woman.

She was at fault. But I'd sure as hell helped.

Aunt Bridge said, "Catrina, why are you doing this?"

"But I have done nothing at all, Dr. Taillefer. Although, if I had," Cat conceded, "it might be to dissuade vandals who go about raiding medieval sanctuaries from playing archeologist. That room beneath Fontevrault's chapel could have been the find of the *century!* Instead, it is mere ashes and stone fragments."

"That wasn't us," I protested. "That was the *Comitatus!*"

"A secret society," she challenged.

It wasn't the most credible story, true or not.

"That was the work of the men who are after the Melusine Chalice," I managed to ground out. My hatred had to be secondary. Protecting the grail had to come first. "The men we warned you might try to destroy it. They may still come after it."

"So you were only an innocent bystander at Fontevrault?"

I tensed, partly from guilt and, more, from a second wind of fury. Rhys's arms, still around me, tensed in response.

Compromise, good, I warned myself. *Rock-throwing, bad.*

"At least tell us you can keep the grail safe," I said. "This isn't about credit for us. Say you'll put it on display, like you promised, so other women can experience it."

"I am afraid that would be difficult," said Cat. "To feature an artifact in the Cluny, we would need far more than your notes and snapshots as evidence of its authenticity. Assuming such an item even existed outside this conversation."

I took a shuddering breath. "What's going to happen to it?"

Cat studied me, like some kind of specimen. "Do not worry, strange woman whom I've never met before. Private buyers snap up unique pieces with far less authentication. Their collections are generally quite safe. Now, if you will excuse me—"

"You *bitch!*" Now Rhys *did* have to hang on to me, because I was going *through* those bars, or over, or under—whatever it took to get at Dr. Dauvergne and vent some fury.

She vanished from sight, heading back toward the offices—but I heard her call, "Paul? Shut the doors. If they are not gone in five minutes, let's do call the police."

While I struggled, my head connected with Rhys's face, and he made an *oof* sound. Oh. The face that had taken a beating because of me and my personal grail quest.

I fell still in his arms, panting and guilt-ridden. *Nooo.*

He leaned closer to my ear. "Maggi," he murmured, low and steady and Welsh. "It's over."

Even with my head hanging, I wouldn't take that. *"No!"*

"What do you suggest we do—break into the *Cluny*, this time? We don't even know if the chalice will still be there, and we *do* know that she will be watching for us."

The heavy wood door swung shut. I barely got my arms out of the way in time as they set in, flush against the iron bars.

I couldn't give up yet, damn it. "Then we stake the place out, watch everyone who leaves."

"They get quite a few visitors," warned Rhys. "All she needs to do is wait for the museum to open tomorrow."

"Then…then we break into her place and take something that's precious to her, to force a trade."

He turned me, held me at arm's reach. "You can't mean it."

"Even an ice queen like that has to care about *something*. Her grandmother's pearls. Her photo albums. Her cat."

"This isn't you, Maggi!" Rhys was right.

Damn it. I didn't want to become the *Comitatus*. But…

"But she's wrong," I said weakly. "And we're right."

Someone moaned, and we both turned to Aunt Bridge. She looked so small and pained, leaning against the wall.

"Brigitte!" Rhys immediately went to her, looped an arm around her. She shouldn't have been standing this long, not so soon after her release from the hospital.

"Let's get you back to the car, Aunt Bridge," I said, catching her hand. "Sergio can drive you home."

Aunt Bridge shook her head. "I thought we could trust her."

"We all did," I said. "This isn't your fault."

"She was such a good student." *Her* student.

"I know." I swallowed back misery. "People can fool you."

"Now that beautiful cup…" And Aunt Brigitte began to cry.

If I hadn't been struggling to stay strong, I might have cried, too. How long had our family passed along the rhyme about Melusine? I imagined centuries of babies in their mothers' arms. Bedtime stories to little girls. Quiet words over sewing or cleaning or cooking. All of it in order to protect one magical grail....

Only to have me dig it up and give it away.

Bad enough that Aunt Bridge had been physically attacked last week. Now her heritage was being decimated, as well.

"I'll get it back," I said grimly. *"I promise."*

From the other side of Bridge, Rhys said, "Maggi, leave it be. You will not break into the woman's house. You will not threaten her or her cat. You are out of options."

But I wasn't out of options. I had one more wild card to play, one that only an hour ago would never have borne consideration. Not in a million years.

But that had been before I made my aunt cry.

I said slowly, reluctantly, "I know somebody who has dealt with stolen antiquities before."

The line rang only once. Then, "This is Lex. I'm unavailable. Please leave a message." *Beep.*

I quickly stabbed the disconnect button.

Across my hotel room, where he sat by the nighttime window for moral support, Rhys looked concerned. "What's wrong?"

"Either he's busy or he isn't taking my calls."

He shrugged. "Good."

"Not good. I have to do this." But I looked at my phone the way Cleopatra probably looked at a certain asp.

"Not with him, you don't."

"Do you have any other ideas for getting the grail back?"

"Yes." I don't know if I've ever seen Rhys this adamant. *"Don't* get it back. Not at this price."

"Would you say the same thing if it were *your* grail that had been stolen? Your cup-of-Christ Holy Grail?"

He scowled. "I might, after seeing you cry over him."

Oh. I went to the chair across from his and sat, squeezed

his hand in silent thanks. He squeezed it back, looking sad. This hadn't been a good night.

But I still wasn't giving up. "Well, there's the problem. What little you know about Lex Stuart is what I told you last night, while I was brokenhearted and crying like a baby."

"And you're quite over him today?"

I sincerely doubted it. But… "This is for the grail. And Aunt Bridge. And women I don't even know."

Rhys did not look convinced. "You said he was *Comitatus*. They want the grail, too."

"Good point." And it was. But…he was also Lex.

"The thing is," I added, slowly, "despite his faults—his many faults—Lex has some consistencies. And one thing that's been consistent since we met is, there's very little he has ever denied me, if I just asked. Even when his family disapproved. *I've* always been the one denying me, especially when it came to his money or connections. So even if the *Comitatus* is like a family to him, there's still the slightest chance…"

"It sounds like a deal with the devil to me."

To me, it sounded like years of therapy in the making. As soon as I'd convinced myself that I didn't really know this new, secret-keeping Lex, I was now hoping I did. But I was desperate.

"What are the chances that the *Comitatus* won't learn the grail was stolen, won't get it off the black market?" I asked. "And what are our chances of finding out where and when it will be sold without the help of someone who's done this before?"

"Low," said Rhys, "but what good would that knowledge do? You can't steal the chalice from professional art thieves."

"Wasn't planning on it." Fontevrault pretty much proved my limitations in that area.

"And you can't afford to buy it, even if you did find it."

"I've called my cousin Lilith, and she's already raising money. Her mother does that professionally, you know, and she's a Grail Keeper, too. If we include our combined retirement money, and everything else we can get…" I didn't like this part. I feared my aunt would mortgage her home rather than let me lose the grail, which scared me. But it was her grail, too.

"And it will involve you with that man. Again." Which I suspected was Rhys's main argument.

"Not the way that sounds. I know not to trust him now. I'll be on my guard." Assuming I went through with this.

I looked at the phone. I thought of Aunt Bridge, and my cousin. I thought of my dead grandmother, and her dead grandmother, and hers—all the way back to Julie Sophie Charlotte de Pardaillan d'Antin, an abbess barely escaping her abbey ahead of the mob, perhaps creating the rhyme that would help future women someday find their sacred relic.

I thought of the daughters I might someday have, with no grail to keep. And I pressed Redial.

Rhys sighed.

One ring. "This is Lex. I'm unavailable. Please leave a message." *Beep*.

"Um, hi. This is Magdalene. I…sort of…needafavor."

I disconnected. Quickly. Then I looked solemnly up at Rhys.

It was done. And—

I jumped when the phone rang in my hand, that quick. I knew the number on its caller ID and so answered, "Hello, Lex."

"You have *got* to be joking." Why did his rich voice have to sound like such a homecoming, even now?

Rhys was right. This was a bad idea.

But the grail was even more important.

"No. I'm not joking. I need a favor."

Lex hesitated, then asked, low, "Is someone sick, Mag? Someone having legal problems? Your family's all right?"

"My family's fine."

"Then no." And the line disconnected.

No? He'd just said *no* to me? And *hung up?*

Rhys watched, curious, as I hit Redial.

"No," Lex repeated, picking up on the first ring.

"You owe me."

"For *what?*"

For breaking my heart. For keeping secrets. "For planting that damned bug in my apartment."

"I know you, Mag. You won't forget something like that for a mere favor."

"Of course I won't. But you still owe me for it."

"So I owe you. According to you, I'm one of the bad guys."

"If you belong to the bad-guy club and pay bad-guy dues and attend the bad-guy meetings, it's not that big a leap."

"Bad guys rarely do favors."

"Except in case of health or legal problems. Yeah, you're a real hard-ass."

There was a pause. Then Lex said, with careful evenness, "I'm a little confused about which side I'm arguing, here, but I'm clear about what we both said yesterday. I'm not willing to do that again. Not to either one of us. Frankly, it surprises me that you don't feel the same way."

"I'm prioritizing."

"You said you hated me."

I swallowed. Hard. "I'm desperate."

For a long moment the line was silent. I heard him murmur something in the background. Then he was back. "Tell me what you need, and I'll tell you if I'm willing to help."

Okay. This was it. The grail's last chance. "You know that item I came to France for?"

"Yes," said Lex, slowly. Warily. "I said I did."

"I found it. It's been stolen. And I need to get it back."

Silence.

"Lex?"

"You found it?"

"Had it with me the whole time." *It was under the bed.* But taunting him wouldn't get me what I wanted. "Now someone stole it, and she said she's selling it to a private collector. I need to know how that works, and what I can do."

"You found it." He seemed stuck on that part. Only after a long moment did he then say, "You have *so* got to be joking."

I think he meant about my request for help, not about me finding the cup, but who can tell? "I'm not joking."

I heard him take a deep breath. "Here's the deal. I'm in England for a couple of days, and I'm very busy, but there's a party Thursday night where we can talk further. Meet me there."

"In *England?*"

"In Kent. The FitzGeoffrey estate, outside Canterbury. I'll courier an invitation via your aunt Bridge. You'll need it to get onto the estate. If you want my help, be there."

"I don't want you sending anything to Aunt Bridge."

"I am not going to send a mail bomb to your aunt."

"Why can't you just call me back?"

"Because I don't want to make this easy for you!"

My mouth fell open before Lex said, more quietly, "Also because I may need more information from you, things you shouldn't be saying over the phone. All right?"

And if he was really going to help, despite the *Comitatus's* clear desire to keep the grail away from me, heaven knew there were things he shouldn't be saying over the phone, either.

If he was really going to help me. *If* this wasn't some sort of a trap.

I thought of my grandmothers and my daughters—and all the women who deserved to experience the Melusine Chalice.

I said, "How formal is the dress?"

I hate the society parties Lex insists on attending. I'm twenty-one. Why would I want to spend my night with stiff old powermongers who talk politics and business and ogle me as if they hope I'm for sale? Lex's family is no better, with his mother gone. His father rarely notices him, and his cousin…!

"Another hour," Lex promises, finding me on the terrace of our oil-mogul host's penthouse suite. "Then we'll go."

He and I have already argued about fossil fuels tonight. We've also argued about whether me getting into our host's face about environmentally safe alternatives will do any good. Lex has asked me to play nice. Stupidly I've agreed.

So tonight I'm a hypocrite, a fake face among fake faces. And speaking of fake….

"I had a painful chat with Phil's date," I say.

Lex is nothing if not chivalrous. "She's not so bad."

"How can you tell? Her hair isn't really blond, her eyes aren't really purple, and she's got caps on her teeth. Her breasts, her butt, her nose…someday that poor woman's going to wake up and wonder why she thought bagging a Stu-art was important enough to go all, well, Frankenstupid for him."

"He didn't hold a gun to her head." *Lex seems distracted.*

"At least they match. Why didn't you tell me about Phil?"

He turns away from the skyline, to me. "What about Phil?"

He doesn't know? "Taffy said he got a certain, ahem, sur-gical enhancement himself. She's pretty happy with it."

Lex blinks, not getting it. He can be so cute, sometimes. I silently count. I'm to four when his eyes widen. "No!"

"Yep. He super-sized. Family resemblance between you two never was strong." *I have had no cause for complaint.*

"I mean—no." *He recoils.* "Phil wouldn't do that."

"We're both talking about your cousin, right?"

"But that's mutilation."

Talk about your double standards. "Oh, so when Taffy does it, it's to be expected, but when Phil does it—"

"I've got to talk to him." *Only then do I realize how much fury is simmering beneath Lex's clenched jaw.* "I'll ask Dad to see you home."

"First? I can get home on my own. Don't you dare inflict your father on me. And second, what's wrong?"

"Just because you've started taking martial arts classes doesn't make you Wonder Woman. How about my friend David?"

"Lex." I narrow my gaze at him. "This is going to sound perverted but, what's Phil's penis have to do with you?"

"Stuarts don't self-mutilate. I'll get David."

"No. You won't. I'm out of here."

"Maggi," he protests—but only once. Before I've even managed my dramatic exit, he's gone off after his cousin.

Is it any wonder I'm wary of marrying into this family?

Chapter 19

The party was formal.

"This is incredible," said my cousin Lil, awed, as she pulled to a stop in front of the mansion where the party was being held. She'd driven across southern England to pick up Rhys, me and my new gown at the train station.

That, and to do her part for the Melusine Chalice.

Thanks to the Chunnel, we arrived from Paris almost as quickly as she made it from the Salisbury Plains.

"It's certainly excessive," said Rhys, from where he'd managed to fold himself into the Ford Fiesta's back seat.

The FitzGeoffrey estate looked like someplace the royal family would stay. Easily four stories high, it rose in grand, column-fronted majesty before arching into two separate wings ending in turrets to either side. The paved drive, wider than most two-lane roads, circled around a tiered fountain. And down the landscaped hill, near what looked like a six-car garage, a series of limousines and BMWs and Aston-Martins congregated, along with drivers, waiting for partygoers to summon them.

Lil's snub-nosed Ford, a cross between hatchback and wagon, belonged at this mansion even less than I did.

"I think he's trying to intimidate me," I murmured, turning my invitation over and over in my gloved hands.

We took in the floodlights, and the colonnade, and more

glittering beveled glass—every window lit—than seemed possible.

"I think he's succeeding," said Lil. "Uh-oh!"

The "uh-oh" came as a large man, dressed in black, crossed to our car. He looked like a bouncer.

"They let us in the gate, didn't they?" I assured her.

"I wish you weren't doing this," said Rhys, behind me.

Lil turned in her seat. "You don't like Satan, either?"

Rhys said, "Excuse me?"

By then the bouncer was tapping on my window. I cranked it down. He asked, "Do you have an invitation, miss?"

I handed it to him.

"We'll go wait with the other drivers," said Lil. "We're only a phone call away. If you need anything…"

"May I see some identification, please?" How times have changed. I handed the guard my International Driver's Permit.

"I won't need anything except a ride home." Tonight, home would be the cottage Lilith shared with her husband and three children. "But thank you."

My door opened, compliments of big guy. "Everything seems in order, Miss Sanger. Please enjoy your evening."

"I need to fluff you," Lil called, getting out.

Rhys touched my bare shoulder, from behind. "Maggi…"

"I know. You wish I weren't doing this."

"Actually, I was going to say he won't be able to resist you. But I wonder…can you resist him?"

"After what he's done?" I hesitated. "I sure hope so."

Then I put my gloved hand in the bouncer's and stood.

Lilith moved around me, making sure my skirts fell properly and my headdress wasn't crooked, just as I had for her at her wedding five years ago. But what I wore was nothing like her wedding dress. It had sleek, slim lines and showed a lot of skin. What material it possessed was a vibrant mixture of heraldic blues, whites and silver, reminiscent of the Middle Ages, but the tiny chain straps, plunging neckline, and plungier back were far from medieval. The skirt split up the front and back, hinting at long lengths of my high-booted legs, shadowed behind a material that resembled fine chain…or, if you thought about it, scales.

An understated headdress duplicated the effect with silver chain, draped over my upbraided hair like a royal elf's. Around my neck, in my ears, and on one of my upper arms, I wore heavy silver cuffs that each resolved itself into an ouroborous—a snake eating its tail, symbol of life, death and rebirth.

The whole outfit was on loan from Sergio's granddaughter, who worked at the Galleries LaFayette. If this one ended up getting rained on, spilled on, or, say, run over by a Metro train, it would cost me about what I'd paid for my first car—but it was worth that risk.

Whether or not anybody but me recognized it, I was going in as a priestess of Melusine. I was going for our grail.

Lil drew back and nodded. She's a year older and looks nothing like me—shorter, with short blond hair and round, pink cheeks. I was so glad she was here. Lil and I were like sisters.

"Sic 'em, love," she said.

And with a deep breath—though not too deep, considering the gown—I turned and mounted the twenty-something stone steps that led up to the main verandah that opened into the high, front foyer of the FitzGeoffrey mansion.

I'd attended similar parties—silent servants, men in tuxedoes, women draped in jewels, and a live orchestra in the gallery. Very likely there *were* royals in attendance, or not-so-distant relations, and certainly members of parliament. I wouldn't be surprised to run into the prime minister.

But I didn't expect to stroll right past old Mr. Stuart.

If he recognized me—and I suspected the geezer was sharp enough—Mr. Stuart did not say so. I felt coiling unease, to hear his voice and see him holding forth with two men who looked like politicians. What in the world was Deuce doing here?

That's the name he went by, being Alexander Rothschild Stuart II. Classier than "Junior," you know. I'd always felt gratitude to the man's wife that Lex had never become a Trey.

Making a mental note about where Deuce was and whom he was with, I accepted a glass of champagne off a tray and continued farther into the house, toward the back gallery with its refined music. I sensed eyes on me, but refused to turn and look.

That's when I heard Phil, though not from where I'd sensed my hidden watchers. I'd recognize his obnoxious laugh anywhere. Sure enough, when I rounded a corner into the high-ceilinged, dark-paneled gallery, there he stood with his second wife, holding another man's arm with the intensity of his latest joke.

His wife, Tawny's, bored gaze found me. Her eyebrows arched, but she did not come to say hello. We knew each other from the occasional family function, and I'd attended her wedding as Lex's date, but we were not close.

Again I felt eyes on me. I scanned dancing couples and clusters of conversation at the edges of the room. Some men's gazes were checking me out. Others weren't so admiring.

Something about one watcher's eyes bothered me. I couldn't place the color from across the room, and I was sure I hadn't met this balding bear of a man, and yet his eyes, almond shaped like a bull terrier's....

It clicked.

It was one of the men from Fontevrault. He'd been wearing a ski mask then, but I knew those eyes. And if one pair of the eyes I felt watching me were his...

What had I just walked into?

A familiar presence stepped close enough to warm my back, leaned over my shoulder, and a familiar voice murmured in my ear, "Welcome to the shark tank, chum."

I was so stunned to be surrounded by *Comitatus* that I didn't speak. Lex aimed a bitter air kiss toward my cheek, palmed my shoulder and turned me firmly toward the dance floor.

For a moment I went with that. Speaking took thought; dancing with Lex could be done on instinct. Even if he was not the man I'd thought, our bodies had a powerful acquaintance.

And he did look unfairly good in his tall, debonair, literally born-to-wear-a-tuxedo way.

But not as good as I looked.

As we stepped into the Gershwin piece and moments passed without assassination attempts, I noticed that Lex's fingers, leading me, felt unusually hard against my spine. He gripped my gloved hand surprisingly tightly. His usually cool gaze...

Was icy.

True, it's hard to tell with someone as composed as him. But was that anger I saw in his hazel eyes? His cheek and jaw were clenched. And his possessive grip—

With silk gloves on, it took no effort at all to slide my hand from his. "What have you done?"

"Me?" He reached to reclaim my escaped hand, but I drew it back and stopped dancing.

"Play nice, or I'm out of here," I warned.

"And *that* would be a first." He said that as if this had anything to do with our previous breakups.

We glared at each other. No matter why *he* might be angry, I wasn't backing down. Not even if it brought certain henchthugs down on me. Not this time. Not with secret-society guy.

Lex gave in first, with a slow exhale that eased the worst of the ire from his gaze. He held out his hand in request, instead of demand—still tight-jawed, but compromising. Barely.

I let him have my hand, and we began to dance a little less like wrestlers and a little more like, well, ex-lovers. Not great progress, but a marginal improvement.

"What the hell have you done?" I repeated beneath my breath, letting him lead me through both the music and the posh handful of dancers. I knew better than to say the C-word around here; there's a reason secret societies don't have company picnics or matching caps. "You brought me behind enemy lines?"

"No," Lex murmured. He wasn't one to feign innocence, but neither did he look at all guilty. "I sent you an invitation behind enemy lines. You came of your own free will."

Careful not to glance toward the watcher from Fonte-vrault, I asked, "So is this a test or a trap?"

"That might depend on what happens upstairs."

"You have got to be joking."

His stiff posture and scornful silence reminded me of what we both knew. Lex Stuart was no comedian.

It made pretty good blackmail. I felt sick, to think of what I might lose—information, assistance, my best chance to re-trieve the Melusine Chalice. But there *must* be other op-tions.

"Bite me." I turned, and I left. Began to leave.

He shadowed me, leaning dangerously close to murmur, "So you think all these bad guys will allow you to just walk out?"

"You aren't fooling me," I whispered back. I even sent a friendly wave toward Phil and Tawny. Not liking lies didn't keep me from being good at them. "Not everyone here is part of your warped little club. This party is to impress some-one—probably the politicians. If they'd already bought in, it would be a waste of money. And since kidnapping and scandal tend to make politicians nervous, you'll let me go."

I kept walking, out of the gallery and toward the foyer.

Following, Lex said, "Don't get your tails in a twist, Me-lusine. I meant that we'd go upstairs to talk."

He was almost loud enough for someone else to hear, de-spite the music and pockets of conversation. Almost.

I spun around—he stood very close, even now—and studied his posture, his handsome, angry face. "Why did you call me that?"

"Of course, you'll have to look like you're into me for us to fool anybody," he said coolly, not answering my question. "But don't worry. That's the only performance you'll have to give tonight, no matter how good you are at it."

Oh boo-hoo, did he think he was insulting me? Curiosity outweighed insult by a landslide. Sure it was dangerous. But I liked to think I was becoming more dangerous myself, lately.

I stepped closer, ducking my head for the benefit of anyone watching, as if I were apologizing. But what I actually said to him was, "Two conditions."

"You called me for a favor. What makes you think—"

"One, you keep your goons away from me and my friends. I'm here under a flag of truce, or I'm not here at all."

"And your second request?"

"My second *demand*," I clarified, "is that once we're in your room tonight, the illusion of romance is over. No touching. No kissing. No romantic expectations."

"Not a problem."

"Swear on it," I warned.

His eyes searched mine. "You really don't trust me, do you?" he marveled. "Well, don't worry your pretty little head about it, Mag. I agree to your terms."

I made a mental note to smack him, once I had what I wanted, for that sarcastic, "pretty little head" comment. But what I said was, "On your mother's soul."

Now he stiffened, full poker face. When I simply waited, he asked, "When did you become such a bitch? Or was I just too stupid to see it before?"

Him? He was upset at not knowing secrets about *me?*

"Maybe it was when one of your club mates threw me on the Metro tracks the other day. So swear."

Did I detect a flicker of shock at my close call? Maybe it was some naive part of me still stuck in wishful-thinking mode, wanting my old, imaginary Lex back. He said, "Yes, Magdalene. I swear on the soul of my mother."

That victory was tempered by the fact that the way he was looking at me—think mongoose vs. cobra—nobody in their right mind would believe we wanted to go upstairs together.

So I laughed. That startled him, but it also gave me a chance to lean into him as if he'd just said something winning and to whisper, "You wanted to dance, Captain Evil. Dance."

He still didn't look excessively happy. Luckily, Lex rarely looks very happy, even when he is. *Content* is a victory. So when he drew me back out onto the dance floor, and I pressed into him for what had become a lilting Rodgers and Hammerstein piece, it probably looked convincing enough.

Especially when I pillowed my cheek on his solid shoulder, like I used to. It didn't take much to melt into either the dance or his body, another moving meditation. My own body's memory didn't bother with little matters like trust. My body just liked him. A lot.

It knew his thighs, brushing mine, and how he moved. It knew the brace of his chest. It knew his tension-hard back, beneath the fine weave of his tuxedo jacket. My body had no complaints…as if physical familiarity meant something.

Lex tipped his face near my hair as if praying to me, also a move from better times. After some time to establish a facade that already felt too real, he murmured, "Someone threw you on the Metro tracks?"

Instead of answering, I said, "Do you know of a place in France called Ramonchamp?"

"Yes. It's near the German border. Why?"

So much for still wishing I could trust him. "No reason."

"René de Montfort threw you on the Metro tracks?"

So he knew de Montfort well enough to recognize the man's hometown. "It will take more than that to stop me."

"Unfortunately for you, Mag, there's a lot more than that out there. There's more than that just at this party."

I lifted my chin to nose up his clean-shaven throat—oh,

but he smelled good—and to nibble his earlobe. His thick, ginger-brown hair tickled my cheek. Even over the horn section, I heard his sharp intake of breath.

"If you're playing with me tonight, Alexander," I murmured, "I will hurt you. Badly."

"I know you, Mag. Your threats don't carry a lot of— Ow!"

That last, because I'd bit his ear. Just hard enough *not* to draw blood. He jerked back, eyes widening down at me. Several other dancers glanced at us in concern.

"Oops," I said innocently.

Lex forced an iffy, all-is-well nod toward our onlookers and returned his leading hand to my back. Warily.

When I began to nuzzle him again, I could feel his neck and shoulder muscles tense in expectation. This time, though, I licked his earlobe, refusing to feel guilty.

It's not like I'd even broken skin.

"I have had a week, Lex," I warned, low, into the crisp collar of his dress shirt. "Do. Not. Push. Me."

"I don't even know who you are anymore." He sounded as affronted as he'd looked.

"Welcome to my world." Except that I didn't want him in my world anymore. "I want to get this done with. Don't you have to look as if you're into me, too?"

His fingertips slid slowly, seductively down my bare spine, hitting at least three major chakra centers en route and seriously interesting a fourth. "How's that?"

That was sending dangerous jolts through my central nervous system, is how that was. You'd think I would be better able to resist him, knowing he was such a lying bastard. Not to mention, having gotten such a thorough Lex-fix just a few days earlier.

Instead, it's as if Paris had only whetted my tastes, as if the challenge of his secrets and threats added something to our already strong attraction. Maybe I was kinkier than I'd thought.

No, I wasn't going to sleep with him. But…was there any reason not to enjoy the prologue?

"Before we go upstairs," I murmured, close to his lips, in what I hoped looked like love talk. "Tell me that you have information for me there."

Over his shoulder, I saw Phil watching us.

Lex's family had never exactly embraced me. Had they known I was a Grail Keeper all along? Was that part of the problem?

"Yes." Lex's breath heated my bare shoulder in dangerous ways. "I've got something. Whether I share it or not…"

I pressed myself closer against him, to hurry things along, and felt his firming interest against me. "Oh," I murmured—still talking about the information, of course. He was smart enough to know that. "You'll share it."

"Don't flatter your—"

I shut him up with my tongue as I covered his mouth with mine, flaring gloved fingers into his hair, all but pasting myself against him. I felt him shudder, attempt resistance…

Then he gave up and drew me closer—especially the hand that was claiming my bottom, pulling me against his obvious interest.

More important, he danced me—awkwardly—out of the gallery and toward the main foyer with its sweeping staircase.

This was a new brand of kissing for us. It wasn't loving. It wasn't worshipful. It was competitive, and yes, I was clearly kinkier than I thought, because it was also incredibly hot. Lex's leading had gone to hell. He bumped us into another couple, then an archway. I smiled satisfied triumph. Then his seeking hand, already inside the back of my dress, slid over the curve of my breast and I stumbled into someone, too.

"Well, really," complained whoever it was.

Lex and I laughed into each other's mouths and steered each other toward the stairs. At least we were convincing. If we were really sneaking upstairs to play spy/counterspy, no way would we be this obvious, right?

I didn't feel dizzy with it; I felt energized. Hungry. Powerful. Even knowing nothing would come of it.

So to speak.

When we reached the steps, we did our best not to actually race up them, Lex's hand on my waist, mine feeling across his tight butt in a way I never would have dared when I hadn't wanted to embarrass him. Not caring somehow freed us. Every landing we would kiss some more, deep and aggressive. Practiced—we each knew what the other wanted, and even flirted at giving it—but dangerous, too. New. Uncertain. Excited.

The need to put on a good front made a hell of an excuse.

I lost count of landings. Then a hallway, with a glimpse of suits of armor and a huge flower arrangement. Then Lex framed me into a doorway, kissing down my shoulder, down the plunging neckline of my gown, between my breasts…oh goddess, yes….

I slid a chain-draped knee between his legs, up his inner thigh and higher toward other promises, and he groaned.

He also managed to gasp, "My room." Even as he nosed a chain strap off my shoulder, kissed the cup of my gown off my breast to give it some one-on-one tongue bathing.

My breast was as eager as the rest of my body, even while threads of good sense—though muffled—screamed that this was bad, bad, that I had business to take care of.

"How nice for you," I gasped. "Your room."

He was pushing against me, pledging, longing, me between him and the door. What was it, with us and doors?

"Nothing—" the effort of words seemed a breath away from beyond him "—happens."

At first that made no sense. Not with another chain strap conquered and the rest of my bodice sliding to my waist. I didn't just know that this would be hot. It was already hot.

This would be scorching. Forest-fire level. Burn-off-everything-and-start-the-forest-over hot.

Then I figured out what he meant. "No touching in the

room," I panted, despite the bliss of what he was doing to my oh-so-appreciative breasts. "You swore."

At that, a little clarity trickled through me, drops of coolness amidst the inferno. I'd had a reason for demanding that promise, whatever his reasons for keeping it.

Lex grunted something that sounded like "Out here...." But *mmm*, he was talking with his mouth full.

I arched my back, luxuriating in what he could do to me. It was a deliciously shocking compromise, sure. Sex in the hallway. Standing up. Pushing aside the tuxedo and expensive gown. Seeing what he felt like through silken gloves....

Clarity, Mag.

"No," I gasped—and sidestepped out of his embrace.

That's all it took, like a deep breath of fresh air. Oh, sure, my body still demanded his—hot currents stormed through me, pooling in sensitive, discomfited parts, but this was too important to risk.

Lex slumped, front first, against the empty door where I'd just been, eyes momentarily closed.

Besides, I thought, sliding my bodice back up over my damp, hungry breasts and readjusting the gown's chain straps. If we had sex, and then he helped me, I would feel like a prostitute.

Guess I'd found another line I wouldn't cross.

"No," I said again. Not that he was pushing it.

I almost felt guilty. Almost. Then I remembered all the *Comitatus* downstairs. That he'd known the rules. That this "into each other" pretense was his idea in the first place.

At that, I was marginally more okay with this.

Without looking at me, Lex dug a key out of his pocket and unlocked the door, then opened it for me.

I went in, politely not looking at him either, and sank into an upholstered chair near a table where he'd set up his briefcase and laptop computer.

I crossed my ankles. My body was starting to realize it was out of luck tonight. It was complaining.

"Make yourself at home," Lex managed to murmur—noblesse oblige, and all that—as he passed me to open a second door. When he turned on the lights, I saw it was a private bathroom.

He shut the door wordlessly behind him—and locked it. I heard a faucet turn on, running water.

I bit my lip, torn between the guilt I refused to feel and the mischievous temptation to ask if I could help by making lustful, *oh-baby* noises from my side of the door.

I chose courteous silence.

That, and searching his room.

Chapter 20

Lex's guest room offered enough paneling and bookcases for a myriad of hidey-holes. Since we didn't live in a game of Clue, I checked the wardrobe instead. Clothes for his visit hung neatly inside, but there was nothing in his pockets. No guns or technogadgets filled his case on the wardrobe's floor.

Nothing under the bed. Nothing under his pillows.

Quickly I returned to his laptop, portable printer and file-stacked briefcase. As soon as I touched the computer's *space* key, killing the screensaver, I faced an administrator's log-in screen demanding a password. Damn.

That left the files. Despite his wealth, Lex has always overworked himself—it didn't stop once he graduated early from prep school and Yale. I saw he hadn't changed in the pile of folders on his briefcase and the scattering of CD-Rs, some labeled, most blanks. The CDs, like the file folders, seemed devoted to the job of running his family's business, QuestCo.

I flipped through return-on-investment reports, departmental budgets and privately commissioned market-trend analyses. Stuff that, if I worked for a rival company, might be worth quite a bit.

Maybe even enough to buy the grail back?

But no. After how I'd reacted to Lex's seeming involvement in the world of corporate espionage, no way would I join their ranks. His business interests, at least, remained safe from me.

As I put the file folders back onto Lex's soft-sided brief-case, I felt a lump beneath them. I peeked into the case and saw that he also had a hardcover book. I recognized it.

Goddess Cultures of Europe and England, by B. Taillefer. So Lex had been reading up on goddess worship?

Hearing the water turn off, I sat before Lex came back into the bedroom. He wasn't wearing his tuxedo jacket anymore, and he'd loosened his tie. He smelled more of soap and water than anything else. I could have been mistaken about what he was doing in there…but I didn't think so.

Especially considering how well his trousers fit again.

He gave me wide berth on the way to the bed, where he sat and fixed me with an unpleasant stare. "Tell me about the cup. What's so important about it?"

"It's mine and I want it back, that's what's so important."

"How did you lose it?"

"A curator at the Cluny, Catrina Dauvergne. Do you know her? She said she'd find a way to display it, but she lied."

"I'm sorry to hear that," said Lex. "I don't know her."

"Not that it matters. Even if she is a fan of unicorn tapestries and Stuarts. She's looking at acquiring another one."

Lex pressed his lips together. "A Stuart?"

Funny. "You do have my information, don't you?"

"I've got it," he assured me. "How the sale takes place, when, and what prospective buyers need to put up, bona fide, to get in. But whether I'm sharing that with you…" He shrugged.

He'd never been so cagey with his favors before. In fact, he was usually downright bountiful. But that was before I'd learned his secrets and called him on them.

"Let me guess," I challenged. "You took a vow of secrecy about the sale too, right?"

He rolled his eyes. "I just want to know about the cup. And here I thought you didn't take any vows of secrecy at all."

"Proof that smart people don't need vows to keep secrets."

"Then you've wasted both our time." He stood stiffly.

I stood, too. "You have information and you won't tell me?"

He looked at me coldly. "Goose. Gander. Figure it out."

"Why do you even care about the grail? What does it mean to you and—" But I stopped, because he'd startled at the word *grail*. "What is it?"

"You mean the cup." He backed to the window. Since it was dark, I assumed his room overlooked the back of the house. "I'm not being unreasonable here, Maggi. This is Negotiation 101. We each have something the other wants—goods, services, in this case information—so we trade. *Quid pro quo*."

"Fine," I said. Reluctantly. "You start."

"You're the one who came to me. And your information has an expiration date. Ladies first. Tell me about the cup."

I'd hate to see him in Advanced Negotiation. "Okay," I said. "The Melusine Chalice is a family heirloom."

"One you've known about for how long, exactly?"

How *long?* "I've heard the legends my whole life, but I wasn't sure whether to believe them. Like the Holy Grail, you know? Nice story, but no proof? As long as the cup stayed safely hidden, there was no reason to dig deeper."

Lex glanced out the window. "And then?"

"What do you think, and then? Someone broke into my place, attacked Aunt Bridge, and stole our files. Where's the sale?"

"It's in the city," he said. I'd won my first point.

"The…?" It clicked. "*New York? When?*"

"So you only went after the chalice after you were burglarized. You haven't been hunting goddess cups all along?"

"Like I said, the cup—" I hesitated as he looked back from the window. "Why did you say it like that? Plural?"

Again, he shrugged. I disliked this game. I said, "We assumed the Melusine cup was safe until then. When's the sale?"

"This week." That didn't give us much fund-raising time.

"A few more specifics would be nice," I told him.

"What made you the champion of the chalice? There are other family members than you. Your mother is younger than Lilith's, so wouldn't it be your cousin's job?"

You first, I thought, warming to the competition…but I hesitated. I hated this game. Yes, knowledge is power. But it's a power that, as a teacher, I'd devoted my life to spreading around.

These weren't nuclear-defense plans, here.

The only way to protest a game is to stop playing it—or at least playing to win. But since Lex wouldn't respect anything I just handed to him, I said it after all. "You first."

But now I was playing a different game. By *my* rules.

His eyes widened. "It's this weekend. Your turn."

"We're not about who inherits the responsibility," I conceded, feigning reluctance. "Yes, my family descended from priestesses of Melusine. But there must be scores of us by now. We haven't kept in touch more than any other family, so I really couldn't say."

He looked incredulous. The Stuart family line was probably accounted for, in all directions, to the last bastard second cousin.

"It doesn't matter who's oldest," I continued. "Or who descends from whom…Lil's adopted, but her mom still told her the stories. We're defined by our knowledge not our blood. I've done the research, I'm off work for the summer, and I have no children at home, so…here I am."

"But who holds the documents?" he challenged. "Who guards the mysteries?"

"Mysteries…you mean our secrets? Lex, we're only secretive the way deer are. To keep from getting shot at." I was enjoying this. But he would catch on if I didn't go cagey again. "So, when this weekend should I be back in the city?"

"Saturday." Score. "How do you know you aren't being kept ignorant by more powerful…what do you call yourselves, anyway?"

"Grail Keepers," I said. "And I'm not being kept ignorant. There's no inner circle. No one person in charge. No mysteries."

He was staring at me, clearly taken aback.

"So when on Saturday, and what's wrong with you?"

He looked down quickly, his mouth working, but all he said was, "There have to be mysteries."

"A riddle here, a fairy tale there, and that's it."

"How do you even know what happens if you find this thing?"

"What?" To my surprise, Lex came to my side—and kneeled. True, there were no other chairs in the room. But he was in tuxedo pants. On his knees. Beside mine.

"Listen, Mag," he said, touching the chair's arm. "Are you *sure* you've done your research? Putting that chalice back into your hands, any of your family's hands, could carry unimaginable consequences. What proof do you have that it's safe?"

"*Safe?* It's a cup, Lex, not a bomb."

"It's powerful, or you wouldn't have come crawling to me."

Excuse me? "You aren't my arms dealer, and *I didn't crawl.*"

Something that could have been a smile flickered at the edge of his mouth. "True, but you normally wouldn't come to me at all. Especially not after our biggest fight ever. So why?"

"Because the grail—" I said, and saw his sudden blink. "It's a religious relic, Lex. Why can't I call it a grail?"

"Call it whatever you like." But *something* bothered him.

"Because the *cup*," I clarified, "represents balance."

"What proof is there that it won't harm anybody?"

"You mean that it won't harm the *Comitatus*, right?"

"I mean anybody."

For a moment I almost bought it. Then I remembered the previous week. "You mean like me getting shot at and chased and thrown on train tracks? You weren't so worried about *that* harm."

"I was so worried about that, I ruined what little trust we had left trying to keep watch on you." His desperate eyes *looked* like Lex's. He *sounded* like Lex. But damn it…

"Because you had insider information from the very group that's after me. Men whom I hate more than I ever thought was possible, and you're part of them. Talk about wasted potential."

He sat back, then stood, staring at me all the while. He wanted to say something. I knew it, and I sensed the suffering that went with his silence. But I refused to take responsibility for it, Eve's Syndrome or not. He'd taken the vows, not me.

Still, I gave him something else. "The stories say that the cups will empower women, not that they'll morph us into superheroes out to control the world. No offense, but fear and domination have historically been more of a guy thing."

Lex ran a hand down his face, then shook off the worst of whatever haunted him. "So it's not dangerous."

"I found the chalice. I held it, drank from it. I *know* it. The Melusine Chalice is an ultimate good. It shouldn't be hidden away in some millionaire's private collection. It should be displayed where it can speak to everyone, men and women."

Like that, Lex leaned to the table beside me and hit the spacebar on his computer. "I'll give you the basics, anyway," he said, typing in his password. "But it's a lot of money."

I glanced past him, to an e-mail with the header Private Auction. He turned the notebook away from me and kept typing.

"Women earn more money than we used to," I said.

"Not this much. You still need my help, Mag, and I

still…I'm sorry, but I still don't know how much to trust you."

My mouth fell open. "Me? Talk about geese and ganders!"

He slanted an accusing look at me as the printer started to softly hum. "You never took any vows of secrecy."

"Hello? Deer trying not to get shot, remember?"

"By *me?*"

"You were in a secret society, too."

"But you didn't know that." Which on one level was the most circular reasoning ever, but on another…why *hadn't* I ever trusted him with my Grail Keeper background? Was that part of why I'd never gone through with marrying him—because I wouldn't marry someone with secrets between us, and didn't want to tell?

"Maybe instinctively I knew." And, to be fair, *my* secret society was benign and life-affirming. *His* secret society seemed to be elitist, dominating and violent, whether he pretended to support that or not.

Lex signed off while the printer finished then tore the header off the printout and folded what was left. "I'll decide how much more I'm helping by Saturday."

"This is help enough, thanks." I caught his wrist. "Really," I repeated, more sincerely. "Thank you."

His gaze lingered on my hand—

But a pounding at the door interrupted us.

"Hey, Alex!" bellowed Phil. "I need to talk to you."

I tucked the folded paper into my bodice. "Crap."

"Bathroom," he said, unzipping his pants and unbuttoning his shirt. "You don't look messy enough."

He was right. Besides, I didn't relish seeing Phil even under normal circumstances. "Just a minute," I murmured, and bent to slide a kiss across the snowy bottom hem of his shirt, deliberately smearing my lipstick over it.

What lipstick was left after getting this far.

"Al-*lex!*"

"Nice touch," he muttered, kicking off his shoes. For my part, I dropped my wrap and purse on the floor before ducking into the bathroom. But I didn't shut the door all the way.

Lex yanked open his door and roared, *"What!"*

One of the first times I've ever heard him yell.

"Sorry, buddy. I know it's been a long, dry spell, but you've got some explaining to do. Where is she?" Phil even leaned into the bedroom to look the place over.

What, he wanted to see me naked?

Lex said, "That's it," and shouldered Phil back out of the room, following him, shutting the door behind him.

But I heard Phil saying, "What, don't want her to hear this?" as he did.

Hear *what?* I slipped out of the bathroom and put my ear to the door, but they were speaking low. I caught phrases, like "a problem," and "one blow job doesn't," and "can't control your men." Men, like *henchmen?* But which one had said that last bit?

Frustrated, I straightened—and noticed the computer.

The one I'd just seen him log onto.

Just how much *did* I hate the *Comitatus?* Just how far would I go to get more information about them? Lex sure as hell wasn't telling me anything....

And it's not like his friends hadn't done the same to me and Aunt Bridge, mere days ago. Besides...what were the chances I'd even get in?

Unable to hear more through the door, I perched onto the chair and tapped a space key, then faced the log on screen. I worked off my slick elbow gloves as I tried to remember what he'd typed. Fifteen or sixteen letters, I thought. The last of them numbers. Like a date?

The name Alexander was nine letters long, leaving six numbers for a date. Lex wouldn't be so foolish as to use his own name, would he? But another possibility....

Almost afraid I was right, I listened to my instincts and typed M-A-G-D-A-L-E-N-E.

Correct or not, that too left six figures. Just enough for a date. Quickly, I typed in my birthday.

The computer beeped at me. Worse, it flashed a warning: *Password incorrect. Please re-input correct password. Two attempts remaining.*

Damn it! This was one of those programs that would only allow three tries before shutting down for some prescribed period of time. And speaking of time…

I glanced at the door, typing my name again but this time using Lex's birthday. I hesitated, then hit *Enter.*

The computer beeped and flashed the same warning. This time, it read *One attempt remaining.*

Was it not a date? It had to be a date—it was six figures, and besides, it felt right. But which one? His mother's birthday? The day she died? Some historical event…but those would require four spaces for the year. I had to give it up.

Except that, as I let go, I suddenly knew.

Leaning forward, I typed *Magdalene*—and the date of Lex's bone-marrow transplant. The date he'd stopped dying.

His desktop appeared in front of me.

Knowing I had time to read approximately squat, I instead grabbed one of his blank CD-Rs and put it in the laptop's drive. Then I keyed the commands to burn a copy of his entire "My Documents" folder, his address book, and his e-mails.

I would only look at things that seemed pertinent, I assured the part of me that hated this. Then I'd destroy it all.

I clicked the button that read "burn this CD." Then, while the laptop whirred into its task, I watched the folder-names flicker past. *Letters. Memos. Proposals. Sangreal.*

I blinked. *The* Sangreal? As in—*the* Holy Grail?

Subfolders flashed past—*Genealogy, Credo, OrdCom, Succession.* And I had to see. As the angry voices outside continued, I opened the file marked *Succession.*

It would take me longer than a hurried minute to understand the list that appeared. Every name had symbols beside it. But one thing did make almost immediate sense.

Alexander Rothschild Stuart III—not Deuce, but Lex—was at the very top of the list. Phil came immediately after him:

Did this mean that Lex really was in charge?

It shouldn't have bothered me. It did. But at least I felt a lot less guilty as I closed the word processor, ejected the CD, then logged out of Lex's system. Tucking the CD into my clingy gown with the printout, I went to the door to listen.

Muffled voices still argued. I assumed that the louder voice was Phil's. It usually was. But that didn't mean anything.

Had I really thought that Lex could belong to *any* organization without eventually running it? My frustration made me daring. I cracked the bedroom door to hear better. And what I heard was clearly Lex's voice saying, "—just a good lay. Give it up. She's not going anywhere."

And maybe he was lying. Or maybe he wasn't. I'd had enough of flip-flopping, either way, and I wouldn't take that chance.

I closed the door—and locked it. Then I tied my wrap around my waist, tied my gloves around one wrist, looped my purse's chain strap across my shoulder and opened the window instead.

It would have been easy to change my mind when I looked down that drop to a shadowy, paved patio. I'd lost count of the landings on the way up, having been distracted by lips and hands and lust, but it seemed Lex's room was on the fourth floor. I saw no drainpipe, like I'd had on campus. There were no shifted rocks and pitted handholds, like at the Tour Melusine. Just seamless masonry and—on the bright side—a single ledge maybe ten inches wide.

Unfortunately, that ledge ran beneath the *third* floor windows, a good twelve feet beneath me.

But I was angry about Lex and Phil and the *Comitatus*. I was uncertain whether I'd swayed Lex, or told him too much. And I was so sick of playing by other peoples' rules that I could easily have belted out a scream to rival Melusine's.

Besides—I had an odd confidence that I could do this.

Probably.

So what the hell. I sat on the windowsill. Then I slid off.

For a moment I plummeted, my academic mind screaming, the rest of me flying. Then—thud! Both booted feet landed neatly on the ledge. My pointed toes stuck out over the edge.

Not a bad landing, Magdalene.

Now a mere three stories up, I sidled my way along the wall toward the far corner of the east wing. Without a drainpipe, my best route down would be the crenellated corner stones, right?

Unfortunately, every time I passed a window I had to carefully navigate around its two inches of sill.

I didn't look down. Though I thought I heard banging above me—some jerk trying to get back into his room, maybe?—I didn't bother looking up, either.

Instead, I dug out my cell phone and pressed the speed-dial button for Lilith.

Sidestep. Sidestep. She picked up on the first ring.

"Are you ready to go?" she asked.

A breeze chilled my bare shoulders. "Something like that."

"Was it lovely? Did you get what you wanted?"

Sidestep. Sidestep. "I certainly got more than I expected."

"Oh, love, you didn't have breakup sex, did you?"

In the background I heard a surprised noise. Like Rhys.

"No, we didn't have breakup sex." I used my free hand to judge a sill as I eased around it. Only four windows to go before I reached the corner. "Give me a little credit."

I heard her say, "She withstood his dark powers."

"Lil," I said, "I'm in a bit of a rush, here. Could you pull up in front of the manor? As close to the east wing as the drive goes? I'll be coming around the side of the building." I edged around my third-to-the-last windowsill and kept going.

"Why aren't you coming out the front door, Maggi?"

Here came the second-to-the-last windowsill between me and the corner. "It's a long story. Can I tell you in the car?"

"Meet you there. Rhys sends his love. Ta!"

I heard Rhys protesting even as the line disconnected.

Now I was able to drop the phone back into my purse and concentrate on careful steps and those last two windowsills. Far, far below me, I saw a cat trot silently across paving stones. I eased around the next-to-the-last window, having to pooch my tummy outward to make room for my butt, trying not to let the dress rub on the wall. There. I made my way slowly toward the last windowsill, and eeked my way around it…. Yes!

Then I stood at the corner, three stories high, with another problem.

The stones fit as seamlessly here as they did across the rest of the manor home's exterior. They weren't crenellated at all. Instead, they offered the same, sheer, almost forty-foot drop.

Oops.

I'm in a motel lobby and my hand is shaking too hard to dial my cell phone. If only I hadn't erased his number off speed dial when we broke up the previous summer—but I did.

I use the voice-recognition feature instead. "Lex."

The phone buzzes protest. My voice is shaking, too, which is stupid. Nothing bad has actually happened. Just something…unsettling.

I take a deep breath, hoping the clerk at the desk isn't eavesdropping on my foolishness, and try again. "Lex."

Beep. The call goes through.

"Be there," I whisper, as it rings. But it's 2:00 a.m., and he's been seeing some heiress for over a month—about as long as I've been seeing Evan. "Please be there…."

Another ring.

Then a sleepy, familiar voice. "Mag? What's wrong?"

"I…" I'm not sure why I called him, except that everything feels wrong and I need a friend even more than I need a ride and he's the first person I thought of.

The only person I thought of.

It's selfish. It's needy. It's everything I've disliked seeing in other women. But my voice shakes as I say, "Can you come get me?"

I hear shuffling on his end of the line. "Yes. Of course. Just tell me where you are."

I do. I think he understands what's going on as soon as I say it's a motel, but he just asks, "Do you want me to stay on the line with you?"

I think I hear a woman's voice in the background, but that could be projection. "No. My battery's low. I'll just wait."

"Are you hurt? In some kind of danger? This Evan guy..." I hear the ding of an elevator.

"No!" So he knows my dating life as surely as I know his, huh? "You think I couldn't take Evan Prescott?"

"Not me," he says, deliberately cheerful for my benefit. "You could wipe the floor with the guy."

He's right. I'm tough. I'm also twenty-three, and very single. We haven't talked for months, not since I refused to marry him, and he gave me an ultimatum, and I took it.

Calling a cab would have been a lot less complicated.

"Never mind," I say quickly. "I shouldn't have gotten you up. I'll be fine. Pretend this never happened?"

"No," he says. "I plan on breaking some speed limits. Whether or not you're there when I arrive is up to you."

So I wait. He gets there in under fifteen minutes, gliding to a wet stop in front of the motel in his latest sports car. I run to the passenger door, and not just because it's raining.

"Somewhere else," I plead as I tumble into the low, leather seat. "Anywhere else."

With a press of horsepower, the car takes off.

We end up parked outside the Cloisters, in Washington Heights, looking across the river at Fort Washington. The police will probably show up and ask us to leave.

Or, this being Lex's car, maybe they won't.

"I'm sorry," I say at my lap. "I shouldn't have dragged you into this. God, this is embarrassing."

For a long time, Lex says nothing. Then he tries, "Now you know how I felt at that drive-in movie."

I stare at him in the shadows. "What?"

"When I admitted to sleeping with someone who wasn't you."

"We'd broken up," I remind him.

"Exactly." Just like this time.

"So why do I feel like I've cheated on you?"

"Same reason I do." When I stare, stricken, he adds, "Feel like I've cheated on you, I mean. Every time."

Oh.

"Maybe we're just supposed to be together," he suggests.

"I can't talk about us," I protest. "Not now. Not…yet."

But we will. We always do, don't we?

"Okay, then," he says. "Maybe Evan's just bad in the sack."

"Lex!"

"Well, it sure isn't you."

I laugh. It comes out uneven, but it's better than the gut-sick confusion I've felt since my less-than-orgasmic attempt at moving on. Speaking of which… "I really should go back."

"Don't ask me to do that."

"I didn't leave a note. He'll freak. He's not a bad guy."

"If you break up with him, may I take you to dinner?"

I look at him, and he says, "Please?"

"I'm even less ready to get married than I was before."

"I know. I'm sorry. I took you for granted, then I felt rejected, and instead of owning up to what an idiot I was…"

Well, we know how that turned out. But he wasn't alone.

"I didn't have to accuse you of trying to own me."

"Unless that's what I was trying to do. I'm sorry."

"I'm sorry, too. But I do need to go back. I'll take a cab."

"No." Lex starts the car. "I'll take you."

"I need to think this through on my own. Without you."

"I know." He doesn't sound happy, but it's something.

"Thank you," I say. "You're the best friend I've ever had."

And he is. Within a month we're dating again, better than ever.

It's like we can tell each other anything.

Chapter 21

Stupid manor home. The corners had been crenellated in the front—I'd seen that much. But apparently the back of the home was where they cut costs. No columns. No bright lights. The place still had old-fashioned electrical and telephone wires running up to the roof…and within my reach.

If I were willing to reach out over the drop for them.

They sloped down to the yard, like in some kind of steep confidence course, albeit one that could incinerate me.

A bird or bat flew by. I flattened my bare hands against the cold stone wall behind me, anchoring myself to lean around the corner and check for a continuation of the ledge.

Nope. Not on the side of the building.

I looked back at those wires, wary. There was no way to tell which lines were harmless cable or telephone lines, and which ones carried electrical death, except to hope the power lines were the highest. Would any of them even hold my weight?

It was a stupid gamble. But was I imagining it, or did I hear a faint bang from behind and above me?

Like, say, a door being kicked in?

I was pretty sure I heard Lex call, "Maggi!"

I read somewhere that dry silk doesn't conduct electricity. So I unwrapped my silk gloves from my wrist and stood on my toes. I stretched out as far as the lowest and hopefully safest of the cables. I whipped the gloves over it, double-looped their ends firmly around each fist, started to lose balance…

And leaped outward, like launching myself into flight.

The cable held.

I slid—flew—all the way down to the yard. And it felt wild. Free. *Magic.* As soon as my feet touched grass, I strode around the corner, far below Lex's next, faint call of, "Maggi?"

Lil's Ford idled at the eastern curve of the drive, waiting for me. It took all my willpower not to race for it. Instead, I strolled over and let myself in sedately.

"Drive," I said, waving pleasantly toward the bouncer who hadn't been fast enough to see me and get my door.

Frowning, he said something into his wrist.

I waved again, gloves frayed in my hand. *"Now!"*

Lil hit the gas, and we hurtled out of the FitzGeoffrey estate like a shooting star.

It's more than a three-hour drive from Canterbury, in far southeast England, to Lilith's home near Cornwall.

Within five minutes, I'd freed the printout and the CD from my gown. In another minute I'd read the note. "Crap!"

Sir: Thank you for your interest. The auction for this item will be at 2:00 ET this Saturday. $100K bona fide by Thursday. We will ship the package to your verified address.

"What's wrong?" asked Rhys, while I clawed my cell phone back out of my chain-mail dress purse.

"What day's today?" I demanded, dialing.

"Thursday," said Lil, and glanced at her dashboard clock. "Rather, we're pushing Friday. Why?"

"We may have missed our chance to put down earnest money. And there's no damned location!" I pressed the send key.

Rhys said, "Perhaps you should calm down first…?"

After all this *and* what I'd overheard in the hallway?

Lex picked up on the first ring. "Are you all *right?*"

"No, I'm pissed. What kind of instructions are these?"

I only realized how raw his first question had sounded when his voice cooled. "The same instructions I was sent."

"You said there would be a location!"

"You know my address in New York."

"Your *apartment?* No way."

"Then I just lost $100,000. Unless I decide to bid myself."

My annoyance at the threat tripped over his first tidbit. "You put down the earnest money for me? And before *talking* to me?"

"You weren't showing up until tonight. And speaking of tonight…Mag, my room is on the fourth floor."

"No kidding."

"Wouldn't stairs have been more appropriate?"

"I overheard you talking to your cousin."

After a moment of silence, Lex asked, "What did you hear?"

"That I apparently wasn't going anywhere."

He sighed. "I meant not going anywhere as in, I'm still dating you."

"But you're not still dating me." I shook my head at Lil, whose eyes widened in concern, and pointed to the road.

"And I didn't want him to know that," said Lex.

It was possible, considering the ruse we'd used to snag private time. *Just a good lay* could even have been preceded by the word, *not.* But that was the problem with conspiracies and lies. Once you start doubting, it's hard—and unwise—to stop. "I hate this," I said.

"I know. But this isn't a secure line, so can we table this discussion until our erstwhile date?"

"We don't have a date." The car swerved slightly.

"Not a romantic date," said Lex. "A datebook date."

"And did you just say *erstwhile?*"

"If you're going to no-show, tell me now. There's work I could be doing here in England."

And I should trust him *why?* Because I wanted the Melusine Chalice. He was my best chance at getting it. *QED.*

Some risks are worth taking.

"We do this alone," I warned. "None of your hench-thugs lurking around. No Cousin Phil pounding at the door."

"The apartment will be empty. Come alone yourself, and you can check." Which wouldn't do me a lot of good in an ambush.

"Then it's a datebook date," I said anyway. Risk. Woo-hoo.

"Good. And Mag?"

"What?"

"Steal from me again and we're through."

I blinked, then reacted. *"We're already—"*

But he'd hung up. If I weren't afraid of scaring Lil at highway speed, I would've screamed. Instead, I muttered, "I really wish we could still hang up phones by slamming them. Pushing a button doesn't even come *close*. Maybe if I just whack it on the—"

Rhys reached forward from the back seat and took the phone out of my hand. "Could you perhaps fill us in?"

So I relayed a G-rated version of my evening. Lil kept sending me suspicious looks from her right-hand driver's seat. Rhys, in the back, seemed so intrigued by my mention of the Sangreal file from Lex's computer that I passed him the CD.

When we parked at a truck stop, so that I could change into something a little more comfortable and far less expensive, Lilith loaned him her laptop to check it out.

"We look at the files, then we destroy them," I instructed as we all headed inside. "It doesn't go beyond us. I know the *Comitatus* stole *my* files first, but…I still feel kind of yucky about taking his." I'd always hated eye-for-an-eye thinking.

"That's a good sign," Rhys said, sitting at a booth and opening the laptop. "It means you have a conscience. We could just destroy the files now, you know."

"No!" I caught his wrist, in case he was serious. "I need to know if he's a bad guy, Rhys. For the grail and for me."

"Of course he's a bad guy," said Lil.

"I'm getting mixed signals. Since *he* can't say anything…"

Rhys nodded, solemn. "I'll see what I can find."

As Lil and I went on to the ladies' room, she said, "Rhys likes you. And I like him a lot better than Satan."

"Don't call Lex that." Once we pushed through the swinging doors and saw we were alone, I turned so she could unfasten the chains running across the back of my dress.

"How bad-guy does he have to get?" she demanded.

"Actually…" I sighed in relief as I stepped out of the gown. "I think Lex might be the head bad guy."

"Which absolves him how, exactly?"

"I'm not sure, but it seems that if we're going to turn the snake, we turn its head first. And if anyone can turn Lex…"

The dress seemed to have survived the evening unscathed. I traded with Lil for the T-shirt she handed me from my bag.

"So, Mag," she said innocently, as I pulled the soft knit material over my head. "If you abstained, how'd you manage that hickey on your breast?"

Oh. I drew my most professorial dignity about myself as I stepped into a pair of shorts, aka Rhys's bathing trunks. They looked even trashier with dress boots than they had with hiking boots. "We didn't have sex. We just…came close."

I peeked under my collar to see. It was barely a hickey.

"Oh, Maggi," she moaned. But instead of feeling defensive, I relaxed into the ease of having my cousin here, at last.

It was one thing to face guns, thugs and subway trains alone—but this was man trouble! "I don't know what it is about him, Lilith! I see him or hear his voice, and it's as if my body says, *'Hot damn, time for sex!'*"

"After a year? You poor frustrated thing." Then she squinted at me, suspicious. Her eyes widened. *"When?"*

"Three days ago. In Paris, before I knew he was *Comitatus*. It was…" I spread a hand, searching for words that didn't exist for what we'd done in that little room.

"Awful?" she suggested for me, but she was clearly teasing. "Old hat? Nothing worth ringing *me* about?"

I reached for the dress bag. "You hate him," I reminded her. "Something you never have adequately explained."

"I explain it every time you ask." She held the bag open while I threaded the dress's hanger up into it.

"Not with the same reasons. You've hated him because he's so rich. You dislike fraternities. He made me cry. I was only dating him out of pity—which was ridiculous—and just because."

"And clearly I was correct on all five counts." She shouldered the dress. "As it turns out, I also hated him because he was running a secret society out to get goddess grails and their Grail Keepers. We'll call that Reason #6."

"Uh-huh." I slumped against the wall, beside a towel dispenser. "I figured that knowing his involvement would make me immune. But tonight the attraction felt even more powerful. *Dangerous*."

"Do you suppose Melusine has anything to do with this?"

I squinted at her, intrigued.

"You already told me how your body's predicting danger by tightening your throat—like Melusine's scream. What if you're also playing out her romance, choosing a man destined to betray you over and over?"

I'd already considered the romantic parallels. Hearing it from her, though... "So maybe it's permanent? Or maybe once I get the grail back, and we find someplace safe for it..."

"The attraction might stop," she said. "Goddess willing."

It was worth a try.

When we left the bathroom, Rhys didn't look up from the laptop. Only his eyes and his page-down finger seemed to move.

"I'm getting a lemon shandy," said Lil. "Anyone else want something from the machine?"

Rhys looked up. "Maggi!"

"Sorry," said Lil. "They haven't bottled her yet."

Rhys looked back down. "Maggi, it's the bloodline."

"I know. The *Comitatus* are all about blood."

"No," he insisted, flushed. "This is about the *Sangreal* bloodline."

One breath, my world seemed marginally normal. The next—I understood. He didn't mean the *Sang Grail,* or blood rail, but the even more mythical *Sang Real,* or royal blood. More noble than any one family. More momentous than any kingship or crown.

I caught at the Formica table with one hand before plopping down, lest I collapse onto the truck-stop linoleum.

"What?" demanded Lil. "What's a Sangreal bloodline?"

Rhys said, "It's a rumor—heretical, but still compelling—that certain powerful European dynasties trace their bloodlines through the immediate families of Jesus Christ and King David, and as far back as early Sumerian kings."

"Dynasties like the Merovingians in France," I whispered. "The Pendragons in England. And I guess the Stuarts…"

"The Pendragons?" challenged Lil. "As in, King Arthur?"

The one Lex had idolized since childhood. "When you think of the Holy Grail," I said, "don't you think of Arthur?"

"Maggi." Rhys's voice shook. "Your old boyfriend seems to be the most direct successor. And if he's head of the Sangreal, good or bad, that rather makes *him* the current Holy Grail."

Oh, heavens. I couldn't swallow. Crazy or not, it *fit.*

No wonder Lex was surprised to hear I was a Grail Keeper.

Lil said, "Let's just call that one Reason #7."

Two days later, I left my friends at a nearby café and strode through Gramercy Park—one of New York's older neighborhoods—to meet the head of the Sangreal.

Sofie—aka Officer Douglas—had driven up from Connecticut. Rhys was still working on Lil's laptop. Lil, looking surprisingly pregnant, sat with Aunt Bridge and fumed about Lex. But I had to do this alone—and not just because Lex had said so.

My arrival at Lex's building, a prewar co-op, had a muted familiarity to it. It was practically home turf. Except—

"Excuse me, miss?" called the doorman, hurrying around the desk to intercept me. "Miss? You need to check in."

In the six years since Lex bought his apartment here, I'd never once been stopped entering the building. But it was a new doorman, graying but broad-shouldered.

"I'm Maggi Sanger, for Lex Stuart. I know the way."

He stepped between me and the elevator—the security here had been a selling point. "I'll need to see some ID, miss, and check your name at the desk. Please step aside for a moment."

"It's all right, Ed," said a rough, friendly voice. "I can vouch for Ms. Sanger here."

"Sam!" Turning delightedly, I surged into the big, black man's arms for a hug. "How are you? It's been too long."

"Now, Ms. Sanger, if you would just marry Sir Silver Spoon upstairs, we wouldn't have such an on-again off-again association ourselves, now would we? Let me take a look at you."

Sam held me at arm's length, as if the sight of me brightened his day. Despite the weight of grails and secret societies, seeing him brightened mine. I'd known Sam for over half my life—he'd once been Lex's bodyguard. Later, when Lex bought the penthouse apartment here, he'd recommended Sam for a job on their elite security staff. And now…

"Chief of security," I read off his nametag. "Impressive."

"I do what I can, Ms. Sanger."

"I'm sorry, Mr. Truman," said Ed-the-doorman. "Even if you vouch for the lady, regulations say I need to check her name…."

"You go ahead and do that," conceded Sam. "She's at the top of Mr. Stuart's list. Though it has been too long since her last visit." That last, he directed pointedly at me.

"You know why I stopped coming," I reminded him.

He snorted. "Now Ms. Maggi, you know that boy upstairs etter than anybody. He'd as soon cut off his right hand as o something he thought was dishonorable."

"He thought" being the operative words. Just because ex didn't think something was dishonorable didn't mean it asn't.

Showing Ed my ID, I just said, "I hope you're right."

But I didn't want to get my hopes up.

I pressed PH on the elevator, got off on the twelfth floor, nd knocked at 12A. Lex answered the door dressed in his ersion of casual-pressed jeans, loafers and such a soft-look-ng green jersey that it took all my self-control not to touch . "Come on in," he said. "It's just me. You're welcome to earch the place to make sure."

I'd always loved Lex's apartment. It had a simple, open loor plan, with one long stretch of dining and living room ll the way from the kitchen to the spiral staircase up to the errace. Clear sunlight washed through arched, mahogany vindows onto gleaming floors and high white walls Lex ad promised to paint once we married. Three bedrooms and wo baths took up less room along the inside, eastern wall.

I went in, but instead of creeping throughout and peek-ng into every closet, bathroom, and nook of the terrace, I ust relaxed into the apartment's familiarity…and listened.

All I heard was Lex shutting and locking the door behind ne—hardly sinister, in this city. All I sensed was his quiet, owerful presence and a whole lot of questions. Mostly nine.

"It had to be my place," he said, answering one of them, 'because this is where they courier the laptop."

On the kitchen table sat an unopened box the right size or a notebook computer.

"You've got your own laptop," I reminded him. When he ave me a dirty look—oh, yeah, that would be the one I'd bro-ken into—I raised my chin and stared back. I'd had my reasons.

"Yes," he said, glancing at his watch. We had more than half an hour yet. "But not one hard-coded with the IP address we need. Do you want something to drink? I've got that juice you like."

"Okay." I followed him to the kitchen. *"Your Grace."*

He might as well know I'd read the files, right?

"Correct me if I'm wrong," he said easily, getting a pitcher from his refrigerator, "but aren't I helping you, here?"

I watched him pour two tall glasses of juice. "I'm not always sure, lately."

"Could you at least give me the benefit of the doubt and lay off the snotty honorifics? It's been over three centuries since the Stuarts were deposed."

"I know. I did some research." While he put the pitcher away, I helped myself to a glass. Then I hesitated. "Most books say the line died out with Bonnie Prince Charlie, but a few…"

"A few report that he had children by a second wife." He came to the opposite side of the counter from me, took the second glass, then squinted at me as if taken aback. "What?"

"It's just…you actually told me something."

"I can't talk about my family tree?" Well…duh. Any vow of secrecy he'd taken related only to *Comitatus* matters.

But I had to push it. "Okay, then. Do you think you're related to Jesus directly, or through his brother James?"

His jaw set. Tight.

"Oh," I said softly. "Only the *recent* family tree."

He took a drink of his juice, still annoyed.

Maybe he had a point. I *was* being snotty. "So why's your family so quiet about their ties to the throne of England?"

"Because we barely *do* have ties. James II was deposed. Neither his son nor his grandson—pretenders, they were called—managed to restore the Stuarts to power. By then royalty was on its way out as a world power. The intellectuals knew it. So they looked for power in democracy, and…"

I saw the moment he noticed my full glass.

"Aren't you going to drink that?" he asked pointedly.

I looked at the glass, too, and felt guilty.

"Oh, for Christ's sake." He took my cup and drank a few swallows, then thunked it back onto the counter—and glared.

"I didn't really believe you would drug me," I protested.

"But you weren't sure. Maggi, it's me. I know I screwed up planting the bug. You made your point, I apologized, that's it."

I opened my mouth to protest—we hadn't even touched on his involvement in the *Comitatus!*—but he interrupted.

"You're only here because you have to be, because you want my help. Fine. It's better than nothing. But I'm not going to let you crucify me over my mistake every time it comes up."

I took a sip of juice, watching him vent. It was a really good drink, a papaya-mango mix they made fresh at a deli a few blocks down. I suspected he'd gotten it especially for me.

Suddenly more relaxed with him, I grinned.

Lex looked wary. "What?"

"*Crucify* you. I mean, considering your family lines…"

"Oh, for Christ's sake—"

Now I laughed. Lex scowled at me, then went to the table and tore open the box. Sure enough, it had a laptop in it.

We still had awhile, but I was glad he was getting prepared, even if my mockery had chased him into it. "So…everyone who puts up earnest money gets a laptop?"

"Yes. It's part of the expense of this kind of business. Come on." He took the computer into the middle bedroom, which served as his home office—or, as we jokingly called it, the War Room. He crouched beside his main desktop.

"And it's 'hard-coded' with an 'IP address'?" I wasn't sure exactly what that meant, but he'd said that much, right?

"And the VPN settings we'll need. The auction server only

accepts incoming messages from IP addresses it recognizes, so only people who've been vouched for can join the auction."

"Unless they get hold of one of the laptops." I watched him connect the computer to what looked like a DSL cable. Nice wrists.

"And even then they would need passwords." He straightened, opened the laptop and turned it on. It booted up smoothly.

"When the note said they'd ship the package to the verified address, I thought they meant the grail. I mean—the cup."

Lex looked vaguely amused. "No. If we win the auction, they'll e-mail us with a location. We set the amount up to transfer to their account, with our own password. When we arrive, they show us the cup and a computer. We type in the password, the money is transferred, and we leave with the cup."

How…efficient. "You do this often?"

"Isn't that why you came to me? Sit down." Gesturing toward his luxurious task chair, he vanished out the doorway.

I looked around his office, at why we called it a War Room. He'd decorated it with antique weapons—a battleax, a halberd, a mace and a whole wall of swords. Rapiers and longswords and sabers. A bastard sword and a katana. A six-foot-long claymore.

"Most of them are legal," said Lex, seeing what I was looking at as he returned with a kitchen chair.

"But some of them aren't." The sadness in my voice clued me in to how much this bothered me, and I shook my head. "Which is stupid. Why should I care if you deal in stolen art?"

"Because you're an idealist." When he pulled his chair up to the desk, beside me, our knees bumped. I moved mine.

"I think part of me suspected you had secrets, all along," I said. "That could be why I never stuck with an engagement."

No matter how desperately I'd thought I loved him.

He typed, saying nothing. I knew from experience that him saying nothing meant he was more upset than usual.

"That," I said, "and that I was keeping secrets, too."

He nodded, then slanted a searching glance toward me, then went back to typing. "For what it's worth, I don't *deal* in stolen art. I buy it—and yes, there is a marginal difference," he added, before I could protest. "It's not stolen specifically for me. And if I didn't buy it, it would just vanish into someone's private collection, never to be seen again."

I looked pointedly at the armory around us.

"Most of the really good stuff, I donate to museums. Anonymously. Or occasionally I give it to a girlfriend."

"I want to believe that," I admitted.

"I suppose it's my fault you can't." But he said that with quiet resignation, this time. Then he leaned back from the computer, turned the screen toward me. "There. Is that it?"

I looked at the screen—and pressed a hand to my new *vesica piscis* necklace, recognition flaring within me. "It's my grail!"

Whoever had done the digital photography had taken pictures from all angles, then set the display so that the white cup slowly rotated, revealing each piece of the carved Melusine story as it turned past. I could use the mouse to turn it faster or slower, to look at the smooth top or tail-knotted bottom.

"It's beautiful," said Lex, very close to my cheek.

"It's perfect," I whispered. Beside the picture were links—*history, background, appraisal,* and *bid.* I clicked on *history* first, and gasped. "The bitch used my notes!"

The very notes I'd given Catrina Dauvergne, to prove the legitimacy of the Melusine Chalice, were now neatly posted for prospective buyers! The *background* link offered some of the photos I'd taken with my disposable camera, in the Fontevrault Sanctuary before its destruction. And under *appraisal*...

"It says it's worth no less than $300,000," I whispered.

Lex quietly asked, "Do you have that much?"

Only then did I remember that he'd already put up a third of that in *bona fide*. I dug into my purse for the cashier's check I'd brought with me and, equally proud and worried, handed it to him. "Lil's mom has raised $600,000 so far."

He looked impressed. "That's a lot of investors."

"Not investments. Donations." I smiled at his surprise. "She knows a lot of well-off people—mostly women—who took her word that some underfunded scholars needed it."

Admiration became suspicion. "That's crazy."

"A surprising number of women will gladly risk being wrong on the mere possibility that it could end up wonderfully. So is this enough money?"

He looked at the computer, at the clock beneath. Five minutes left. "It depends on who else is out there bidding."

"So we have a chance?" At his nod, I could have kissed him.

I deliberately didn't, focusing on more important matters. I might actually get my chalice back! Sofie, Lil and I already had a plan for getting it out of the country, and where to hide it once we did. Since our putting-it-on-immediate-display plan had turned out so badly, we'd needed one.

The clock said 1:57 p.m. "Click on the *bid* link," said Lex, and I did. A message appeared stating that the auction would not begin until 2:00. "That's okay. We're just testing it."

"I don't think I could have done this without your help," I admitted. "I'm partly grateful and partly annoyed."

1:58 p.m. "Why annoyed?" he asked, his tone nonchalant but his close, hazel gaze caressing my face.

"Because I wanted to be able to do this myself. Not just because I'm connected to a powerful man." Then again, the priestesses at Fontevrault had been well connected *and* strong in their own right. Was I thinking too either/or, here?

He sat back. "Maggi, you found it in the first place. You and your…Grail Keepers…raised the money yourselves. How do you think I feel, being relegated to tech support?"

Now I did kiss him—on the cheek. Wise or not, I wanted to do more. From his long, shaky inhale, he wanted more, too. But we both had more self-control than that.

I smiled into his eyes, and felt hope for him.

Then the laptop clock turned to 2:00, and I clicked on the link to *bid*.

Chapter 22

A box opened up, like an Instant Messenger screen floating over the larger picture of the grail, with a name in brackets. *[Percival.]*

"That's us," said Lex. "Cute."

"You didn't choose it?" In Arthurian legend, Percival is the classic Grail-quest knight.

"Each laptop has its own sign-in." Then Lex said, "This is good. If we're the only ones in the auction…uh-oh."

Another name appeared—Lancelot. Then Galahad. Then Kay.

Letters typed across the screen. *[Kay] 1*

"That's not one dollar, is it?" I asked grimly.

"No. We're dealing in hundred thousands. They'll clarify that on the final bid, to make sure nobody was confused."

"What if I wanted to bid in between—"

[Lancelot] 1.5

"Oh," I said, and typed in my own bid of *2.*

[Galahad] 2.5

[Kay] 3

I quickly tried *3.5* and hit *Enter.* There.

[Kay] 4

When Lex lightly touched my fingers, to keep me from typing more, I glared at him. "What are you doing?"

"Don't appear too eager," he advised. "They'll give us

three chances before a sale is made, and we might as well
see how far it goes first. Look. Lancelot has already dropped
out."

[Galahad] 4.5

[Kay] 5

[Galahad] 5.5

Then the number sat there, on a quiet screen, unchanging. $50,000 less than the Grail Keepers had raised. Kay had
apparently given up. When I moved to type my bid, Lex
didn't try to stop me.

[Percival] 6

I held my breath. This was *my* grail. I'd found it, I'd rescued it, and I was a Grail Keeper. *I* should decide what happened to it.

After a long moment of waiting, a new log-on name appeared.

[Administrator] The bid is $600,000. Going once.

"Yes," I whispered, all but praying.

[Galahad] 6.5

No! Lex's steady voice cut through my upset. "I already
put down a hundred *bona fide*. Use that. Go to seven."

"And owe you a hundred thousand dollars?"

"You think Lilith's mother can't raise that much more?"

[Administrator] The bid is $650,000. Going once.

I didn't like it. It felt wrong in too many ways, including
a tightening in my throat that may or may not have been Me-
lusine-inspired. But when the words *Going twice* appeared,
I couldn't have stopped myself.

[Percival] 7

I leaned closer to the screen, then closer yet…

[Galahad] 8

"I *hate* Galahad!" But I pushed the laptop away from me,
my heart aching. That was it. I was done.

"He has good taste, anyway," mused Lex, looking at the
screen when I refused to. *"Going once."*

"That's all I have. *More* than I have. Almost a million dollars." Damn it. "I fought the good fight, anyway." Crap.

Lex turned the laptop toward himself and typed something. I didn't have to look to see that he, as Percival, had just bid *8.5.* I looked anyway.

"Don't do it," I warned him. "I don't want to owe you."

[Galahad] 9

[Percival] 10

Lex hadn't even stopped at the halfway mark, that time—he'd just barged over the million-dollar line. "So don't owe me," he said. When Galahad bid *11,* Lex upped it to *12.*

Double what the Grail Keepers had raised.

[Galahad] 14

"He's suspicious," noted Lex softly, typing *14.5.*

"Don't owe you?" I watched over his shoulder. *14.7* "This is too big for a gift."

"It's not a gift." *15. 15.3.* "We aren't dating, remember?"

[Galahad] 15.5

I shook my head, wary. "You're buying it for yourself?"

[Percival] 16. For a long moment, nothing happened.

[Administrator] The bid is $1,600,000. Going once.

"Maybe I have my own uses for it."

"You? It's *my* chalice!"

[Administrator] The bid is $1,600,000. Going twice.

"I've got a million more than you that says—damn it."

[Galahad] 16.3

[Percival] 16.5

"Will you donate it to a museum?" I demanded, uncertain.

"Out of the goodness of my heart?" When Galahad went to *17,* Lex typed in *17.3,* increasingly grim. "Not this time."

I'd hated him getting this way—competitive to the point of cutthroat—even before I'd known he was with the *Comitatus.* Now...

I slid my foot toward the DSL modem on the floor, to hook my toes under the cable. If worse came to worst, I could always—

Lex's foot knocked mine away. "Don't do it," he snarled.

I looked at the screen. Galahad had just bid $1,750,000.

"If you destroy this cup," I said, "I might just kill you."

"Screw this," he muttered, and typed in *18*. "You might try. What makes you think Galahad isn't the one out to destroy it?"

I *hated* this! I hated not trusting him. I hated him not listening to me. I hated being made powerless because I didn't have endless money. All that kept me from imploding was my Tai Chi and goddess training.

Yielding overcomes unyielding. Don't always meet force with force. Everything doesn't have to be a competition.

I didn't have to play his game. I only had to sit back and figure out what it was—then go around it.

[Galahad] 19

No decimals. The boys were getting impatient, were they?

[Percival] 20

Lex had just bid two million dollars.

For a long moment, nothing happened. Then,

[Administrator] The bid is $2,000,000. Going once.

We were both holding our breaths.

[Administrator] The bid is $2,000,000. Going twice.

Lex glanced at me coolly. It made me wonder how much of this he'd already set up…though surely if he'd, say, hired Galahad, they wouldn't have chased the price *that* high. Would they? Unless he was making a different point, maybe showing off.

[Administrator] Sold for $2,000,000. The auction has ended.

The IM screen vanished and the laptop beeped as Lex received an e-mail.

I slumped while he read it. He accessed some kind of online bank account and rapidly typed arrangements.

When he logged off, the silence between us was suffocating. He broke it first. "I couldn't let him get it."

"You don't even know who he was."

"At least you'll know where the cup is," he said.

"So you did it for me? I already told you I wouldn't take it as a gift, so why did you want it?"

He spread his hands. "Leverage."

"Leverage…" I had a bad feeling about this. "With *me?*"

"Just because I won't donate it anywhere doesn't mean we can't come to a business arrangement."

"Right. What have I got that you would pay two million dollars for?"

Lex took a deep breath. Then, squaring his shoulders, he said, "Marry me."

I hit him—and this was no "four ounces of strength against a ton of force," calculated Tai Chi strike. This was a backhanded smack across his handsome face, swinging his head to one side, as hard and as personal as I could make it.

Maybe he'd half expected that. Other than turning back to face me, his hazel eyes cold, he didn't move.

I did. I was up and out of that damned War Room in an instant, striding toward the kitchen table for my purse. "You spoiled, selfish bastard. You can't take no for an answer, can you? You just can't stand it that there's anybody in this world who won't give you just what you want just because you want it."

"It's not that," he said softly, and I spun to face him. He stood outside the den. A wash of sunshine gave him a deceptively angelic aura. "It's bigger than that. Bigger than us."

"What is?" My whole body was clenched with fury. "No, wait, you *can't tell me* can you? What a great basis for a marriage. How could I possibly refuse?"

"It…" He swallowed hard. "It doesn't have to be permanent."

"Even more tempting! You know what? I'm *not* going to kill you. Along with finding and saving every single goddess grail out there, and putting them together into an, an *arsenal of empowerment that you people can't even imagine,* I'm devoting myself to something else. I'm going to uncover every single sick secret you and your *Comitatus* have vowed to keep hidden."

I spun for the door, flipping open my cell phone, pressing the speed-dial for Lil.

"It's about feminine power," said Lex. "About balance."

I spun back, alert. He looked deliberately at the phone, but I didn't disconnect, not for him. When Lil picked up, I said softly, dangerously, "Come get me downstairs."

Then I hung up. My own person. Leaving his sorry person.

"What I need to do," he tried quietly, intently. "It's important. I wish I could tell you more, but God, Maggi, it's so very important. And I've found I can't do it alone. No one man can. No one *woman* can. There has to be balance. I need you."

"Without any idea what you need me *for?* Go screw yourself."

"Then date me. Just for a year or two." Something in my expression must have worried him, because he added, "Not for real. We don't need to…I mean, no sex. Unless you wanted it of course—okay, no sex," he edited quickly. "But we'd be a couple."

"And in return for my escort services, you give me a two-million-dollar goddess grail," I challenged.

"It's the only thing I've found that might tempt you."

Go figure. Another line I wouldn't cross.

I flipped him off. Then I turned away, my throat tightening unbearably….

My throat tightening unbearably? Danger!

I spun back, ready to dodge, expecting to find him aiming a gun or throwing a knife. A movement from the spiral stairway above him told a different story. *I wasn't the one in danger.*

I screamed my warning as I ran toward him. "Lex, look out!"

He turned, eyes widening, raising a defensive arm even

as a figure in a black ski mask leaped down on to him—and shoved a blade deep into Lex's ribs.

I drilled my cell phone at the attacker. It ricocheted off his head, distracting him. Lex elbowed him in the throat, then punched him in the face, one-two, and the man dropped. As he fell, his bloody knife threw droplets across the white wall.

Lex bit back a cry of enraged pain as the blade sliced free. He clutched at the gash, stomping viciously downward—

I didn't have to watch that; I saw a second black-clad figure on the stairs. I lunged forward, vaulted the wrought-iron banister, kicked outward with my swing before he could leap on to Lex. Both feet connected hard with his face. He stumbled.

I landed, crouched, on a wedge-shaped step above him.

Then someone heavy landed on me. *Crap.* They were coming down off the terrace. The very large, very private terrace.

I ducked under and past this attacker, swinging my foot around, tripping him as I passed, then kicking him from behind. Balance gone, he rolled over the railing and plummeted.

"Mag," grunted Lex, below me. "Get *out.*"

Right. I raced upward, flowing under and around another masked attacker in my need to reach the top. I felt him surge up the stairs behind me, saw a fifth figure filling the doorway—

I hit the door hard, knocking it and him backward. From instinct alone, I kicked out at the man behind me. I connected.

I heard the faint clang of him falling against the stairs.

The man on the other side of the door bulldozed forward, his brute strength more powerful than mine. All I had was the ability to use my body as a brace between the ground and the door. I did that, despite the threat from behind which…

Which was ignoring me. Oh no. *Lex!*

A line of flame traced across my shoulder—another knife, wielded blindly, trying to *cut* me away from the door. Making a point by squeezing my fingers together, I jabbed at an exact spot on his exposed wrist.

He yelled—and his hand reflexively opened, dropping the knife. Shoulder still holding the door, trembling legs bracing against the floor, I slowly slid downward, reaching for it. My boots were starting to slide, with reluctant squeaks, on the wooden landing. Finally, crouched almost in half, I caught up the weapon with my fingertips. I flipped it in my hand—heavy, a seven-inch fixed blade, serrated at the bottom.

If this was what they'd hit Lex with...

No time to worry. I struck outward from my crouch, through the open doorway, and hamstringed my attacker's near leg. It felt like slicing a piece of steak. He fell away from me.

I shut, rose and bolted the heavy wooden door.

Immediately, the pounding against it began.

Who had unbolted it? How did it get open? How did they get on the roof? Did Lex know about them all along?

Darting to the top of the stairway revealed that, if Lex had known, he'd been murderously misled. They had him down. One man rolled with him, leaving smudges of blood across the gleaming floor. That one had been disarmed; they were wrestling. Another pushed himself to his feet. A third crouched over them, ready to deliver a final blow with another death knife. The fourth, the one I'd dodged past, watched it all from the stairs.

Four against one? Against *Lex?* I didn't think so.

The pounding above me continued, but that could wait. I vaulted the top railing, bypassing the middleman to land on the guy crouched over Lex. I rode him to the floor, defaulting into protective, deeply instinctive rage.

Anyone who thinks females aren't naturally violent never

met a mother bear. Women rarely fight for fun, but we can still be the most dangerous creatures in the animal kingdom—and I was channeling that. No, Lex wasn't my child; nothing like it. But he was mine. On levels beyond understanding, *he was mine*.

Morta. Hecate. Kali. There are goddesses of death, too.

It was easy to catch this assassin under the chin with the crook of my elbow. It was simple to slide the borrowed death-blade across the front of his throat, deep and deadly.

It stopped him, didn't it?

If a cry escaped my own throat as I did it, that was the price I paid. His head lurched farther back in my grip. A wave of red fountained across the wrestling confusion at our feet.

"Maggi!" grunted Lex, half plea, half warning.

Hearing the fourth man—now the third?—land behind me, I spun and dodged, danced backward. He followed me. I caught his wrists and pulled. He fell forward, hard, with his momentum.

I kicked the knife from his hands, toward Lex. "Lex!"

Lex, straining beneath his attacker, caught the weapon midskid, then expertly thrust it upward. The man fell off him with a soggy grunt. The second tackled him.

"The panic room, Maggi!" Lex yelled. "Please…"

He was a billionaire in a New York penthouse. Of course he had a panic room. And of course I knew where it was.

Its entrance lay through the den.

The pounding above us sounded crunchy, as if the door was giving. Lex's second "Please," a sobbing groan, decided me.

I ran for the den, a black-clad figure close behind me. Hands caught at my waist, but I twisted free. I pushed through the door into the panic room, slapping the red button to alert building security and the police of a problem—

—and turning—

—and catching the top of the doorjamb to swing through, kicking my pursuer solidly in the head.

He fell hard while I landed catlike. Instead of ducking back into the panic room and shutting the impenetrable door, I ripped a saber off the wall and stepped after him.

As if I would've hidden with my old boyfriend in jeopardy.

He crabbed backward, eyes widening behind his ski mask.

I grabbed the katana with my other hand, still walking.

He twisted over into a crawl, found his feet and ran.

I followed into the carnage of Lex's living room. A second body lay sprawled next to the man whose throat I'd slit. Lex had regained his feet but swayed, barely staying there. He'd hooked his left elbow through the wrought-iron stairway to hold himself up as he wielded his knife. Blood drenched half his body.

His attacker, though injured, darted in for quick stabs which Lex was deflecting—so far. With that blood loss, he couldn't keep it up. The man I'd chased from the den hesitated.

I worked to free the saber from its old scabbard.

"What if he *is* the one…?" the man asked, panting.

"Then we're already dead," warned his companion, stumbling back with a groan. "Do it!"

So he attacked—while my blade slid free.

"Here!" I threw the saber, hilt first. Lex dropped the knife, caught the sword and skewered the man who lunged at him.

Just in time to hear a crash above us as the door gave way.

"Why aren't…?" he gasped, glaring upward through blood and messy hair, clearly furious. At me.

Three more black-clad figures poured down the spiral staircase, reinforcements for their remaining comrade. And Lex was mad at me, just for being here. *Why wasn't I hiding in the panic room while he fought to the death?*

"Because," I called, charging up the stairs to meet this latest onslaught with the katana, "I'm a Grail Keeper!"

* * *

"Teach comparative mythology," repeats Lex, leaning back on the railing of his family's yacht. This late at night, on the edge of the Atlantic, the air is bitter cold. But from there we have a great view of the New Year's fireworks display.

I've just told him what I'm doing with my doctorate.

"Sure," I say. "Why do you think I've been going to Sarah Lawrence—just to be closer to you?" Sarah Lawrence College—where famed comparative mythologist Joseph Campbell once taught—is only fifteen miles north of the city.

"No. Not you." His wry tone surprises me.

I've spent a semester in Paris. He's spent a year at Cambridge. At our closest, we were never joined at the hip. I ask him, "What happened to accomplishing great things? Epic?"

"That's just it. How…?" Maybe he senses that he's on dangerous ground, but he goes for it. "How do you accomplish great things as a college teacher?"

The Statue of Liberty is behind him. "As opposed to your executive MBA, degree of choice for philanthropists everywhere."

"When has creating wealth not been a good thing?"

"When people hoard that wealth?" He turns away from me, plants his hands on the railing, lifts his face to the wind.

I lean on the railing beside him, my shoulder against his. "I didn't mean to imply that you hoard anything. I know you donate to charities."

Lex says, "There are more jobs, and cheaper technology, and higher standards of living because of families like mine. What else can help as many people as business opportunity?"

I say, "Education?"

He slants his gaze toward me, searching for…something.

"It just seems…passive," he admits. "For you, I mean."

I laugh. "Just for me?"

"I didn't choose you for your passivity."

"I didn't know you'd chosen me at all."

He looks down, scowling, but I duck under one of his arms to stand between him and the railing, facing him. Wind whips my hair into both of us.

"Not that I need to explain myself to you," I say, "but I happen to think that what our world needs most right now is a sense of direction. We've lost our faith in ourselves."

"And mythology can help?" he challenges me.

"Myths give shape and...and meaning to the world around us. What if, to choose your reality, all you really have to do is choose your myth?"

He stares at me, and for a moment I think he's dismissing me as naive, idealistic...passive. Then he leans forward and kisses me. Deeply. More desperately than he's kissed me since the last time he tried to win me back, after another breakup.

Of course he did win me back. He always does.

I drape my arms over his shoulders, sinking into him, relaxing into his kisses and his apparent adoration of me. He unbuttons his long coat and draws me inside it, and we kiss some more until the first blast of fireworks draws our attention away from our shared warmth and strength and identity.

I turn in the cocoon of his embrace to watch the show. Lex's cheek presses against mine from behind. Surrounded by a profusion of bright blasts and falling sparkles, he calls into my ear, "I'll love you forever, you know."

I've never hesitated to say I love him, except during breakups. But I've often hesitated to commit to a time frame. This moment feels so powerful, so magical, that it's easy.

"Me, too," I shout. Vow. "You. Forever and beyond."

He ignores the fireworks to kiss my ear, which allows me to arch back into the sensation and still enjoy the show. "I'll hold you to that," he warns, voice husky and happy.

I think, There are far worse fates.

Chapter 23

While Lex held off the last of our original attackers, I faced off against the reinforcements.

You have to practice Tai Chi for at least a year before you get to use a sword. I'd been working with a sword for four years. Not a *katana—katanas* are Japanese. But in this serious a fight, such a supersharp blade sure wouldn't hurt.

It's still Tai Chi, almost like push-hands with props. Instead of the dramatic clank-clank and thrust-parry of a pirate movie, this kind of sword fighting was almost... sinuous.

I touched my blade to the fighting knife of the first man on the stairs. When he tried to push it aside, I let the blade wind around his. He stumbled. His arm, as he caught at the banister to keep from falling, blocked his two companions.

"Who are you?" I demanded, letting my blade flow across his, diverting his thrust. "Why do you want Lex dead?"

A heavy scream gargled to silence, below us. *Don't be Lex. Please, don't be Lex.*

"Out of my way," growled my opponent. With a hard parry, he tried to push by me.

His parry only dispersed his energy, not mine. Instead of falling aside, my sword circled his knife and stayed where it had been. In his downward lunge, he impaled himself. Heavily.

His fall jerked my sword and wrenched my wrist. *Crap*.

"The hell with this!" exclaimed the man at the top of the stairs, and jumped the banister. That left me with one masked intruder—and a wounded man crumpled awkwardly across the stairs between us, still weighing down my sword.

Double crap. I backed up—as in, down. Stepping deliberately on the wedge-shaped steps, I yanked my blade free. "Lex?"

I heard metal strike metal, never so glad of a sound in my life. It meant he was still alive. He was still fighting his own attackers—in a more classic, fencing style, à la Yale.

"Mag…" His voice wavered, probably from blood loss. "Go…." But then he growled his frustration, with another metallic clank. He wasn't down yet.

"I'm okay," I assured him. *Better than you, you idiot.*

But they hadn't come for me this time.

"That's what you think." The man who stepped over his fallen companion to stalk after me had a distinct, deep voice.

"I know you." I caught his blade with mine before he could lunge at me. My wrist still burned from being wrenched, but I'd live with that. "You held a gun on me at the college last week."

"You should have listened, little girl." He parried one way. My blade slithered around his, undaunted. He knocked it, hard, and I sliced his arm without even trying.

"Why? Because you're a man and I'm a woman?" I laughed at him—this time, on purpose. I wanted him angry and clumsy. I wanted him annoyed. "My blade's longer than yours, college boy."

He lunged. When I darted out of his way, off the stairs and into the living room, he nearly fell.

So did I, skidding on bloody floor. I caught my balance, kept moving. At least from here, I could see Lex again.

He still hung, still desperately anchored on the stairway to keep his feet, holding off his last two attackers. One, bent and staggering, seemed almost as badly injured as Lex. The other, fresh and fast, was clearly one of the newcomers.

Only the saber gave Lex a fighting chance—*his* blade was longer, too. But I heard a dangerous gurgle to his breathing, saw a glazing in his eyes.

"Why," I repeated loudly, "are you after Lex?"

"What's it matter to you?" College boy lunged.

I stepped out of the way, elbowed him hard in the nose as he staggered past, then whirled and sliced the katana across his knife arm. More blood splattered white walls and a window.

He clapped the opposite hand to his injured arm. Blood spurted from between his fingers. "You traitor-loving bitch!"

Traitor-loving? "Tell me what's going on," I warned him, "and I might let you keep putting pressure on that until an ambulance shows up."

"Mag…" gasped Lex from behind me, and my throat tightened in warning. I whirled, dropping into a low lunge, and struck. The man who'd just rushed my back fell on my sword. Literally.

His fall yanked it from my grip. I let it go and rolled sideways, kicking out as another one—the man who'd been crumpled on the stairs?—attacked. His ankle snapped under my feet. He fell to his knees. I stood and double-kicked him in the chin, knocking him out. Maybe killing him. I didn't bother to check.

Behind me, a heavy blade clattered to the floor—Lex was spent. I dove in that direction, slid on the blood-soaked wood floor to Lex's feet, grabbed his fallen saber in both hands.

Then I rose slowly between him and these last two threats.

"I asked you people a question," I panted. *"Why?"*

"Dr. Sanger," purred Lex's latest opponent, his French accent equally familiar. "You only delay the inevitable."

"René de Montfort? I thought we'd moved beyond masks."

"Kill her," groaned college boy. He'd stayed on his knees, losing too much blood despite putting pressure on his arm.

Lex, my heart mourned. Nobody held pressure on his wounds. He was dying, maybe dead. No matter his secrets, no matter our differences, it would be a far greater loss than any grail.

Life was more important than objects. Always.

Even his. *Especially* his, no matter what I'd told myself.

"It will be my pleasure," said de Montfort, and stepped back to take a fencing stance.

Raising my eyebows, I feigned a similar stance. It's not that I've never fenced regulation style. I just choose not to.

"En guarde," he said, allowing our blades to touch—and I just kept mine touching his. When he swung, mine swung with his. When he thrust, mine circled and unbalanced it. He did all the work. My saber's blade just rode his.

I could feel his frustration in his increasingly hard, choppy movements. "Fight, damn you!"

Funny, that he didn't even see what I was doing as fighting. "Nope," I said. "That's your game."

Furious, he lunged. My blade slithered around his—and skewered his throat, under the ski mask. *Deeply.*

I pushed harder, just to be sure.

De Montfort stiffened. Coughed. Fresh blood dripped across the saber. He fell first to his knees, staring at me through his pale, warrior eyes.

"My game," I said firmly, yanking my saber free with both hands as he fell, "is stopping you, you piece of shit."

Suddenly, the room seemed to echo with silence. Or my pulse. Even college boy lay still. I spun back to Lex, where he hung, unconscious—and still on his feet.

"Oh, no," I murmured, unhooking his arm from the rails, taking his full weight to ease him toward the floor, into my arms. I lay the sword beside me, just in case.

He was soaked in his own blood; I've never seen so much. The deepest wound was the first, under his ribs; I pressed a bare hand against it, across his blood-soaked jersey. But he was also oozing blood from a chest wound, and from defensive slices on both arms. "Don't be dead."

His beautiful, hazel eyes cracked blearily open, fixing on me. "Not...dead," he murmured. "Not...yet."

His front door burst open. "Security!" I heard Sam yell. "Everyone down! Everyone—oh, my God!"

He'd just gotten a look at Lex's bloody apartment. He continued in, sweeping with his gun.

"We need a medic!" I yelled, a surprise sob breaking in my voice. I brushed Lex's hair back from his blood-smeared forehead, then kissed it. "You'll be okay, do you hear me?"

Sam bolted toward us, saying something into his headset, followed by other gunmen. Our *gunmen*. I listened only to Lex.

"Go," he gasped, barely audible. "Before..."

He struggled to take another breath. I hadn't imagined the gurgle. I didn't imagine the bubble of blood from the corner of his mouth, either. Now that the fight was over, panic threatened to overwhelm me. Threatened—and failed.

I come from a long line of *very* strong women.

"I'm not going anywhere," I said.

His head jerked—his exhausted attempt at shaking it, *no*. "Before...police. Get the cup."

"Don't try to joke," I scolded him. "You're no good at it."

He scowled, looking annoyed when Sam opened a box beside us. Sam pushed my hands away to press bandages onto Lex's wounds. "Mr. Stuart? Are you still in danger, sir?"

"Check the roof," I said, and one of Sam's gunmen bolted past us, up the stairs. "That's how they came in. A few may still be alive. I think this is all of them, but...but I'm not sure." *Breathe.* "They didn't use guns, Sam. We wouldn't have survived if they'd used guns. I don't know why..."

Or did I? Blades have history. Blades are ritualistic. Blades spill blood. As if the death is secondary.

"Maybe they didn't want to make the noise, Ms. Sanger." Sam put my hand on one of the bandages, to keep pressure.

"I think they could have afforded silencers," I murmured.

Sam ignored that, wiping blood from Lex's mouth. "You hang on, Mr. Stuart. The ambulance and police are coming."

Lex's hand fumbled toward me; I caught it.

"Five o'clock," he gasped. "JFK. Terminal 1. Air France."

"I'm not leaving you," I warned him.

Again his head jerked a weak negative. "VIP lounge," he continued, coughing blood. "Reserved Room C. Say...expected."

Another man hurried in, wearing casual clothes but carrying a black bag. Even after a year's absence I recognized Dr. Joe Cooper from the fourth floor.

"Lucky you caught me," he told Sam, kneeling beside Lex and pulling out a stethoscope. "I was on my way out. Maggi, some people in the lobby are making a hell of a fuss to see you."

"They're my friends," I told Sam. "Send them up."

He snorted and shook his head.

I said to Lex, "See? We'll send Lil after the cup."

"Can't...protect it." His lips pressed together, as if maybe he was trying to smile. "Not like you. The password..."

Dr. Cooper eased me gently but firmly back to press an oxygen mask over Lex's nose and mouth, turning on a miniature tank. "You'll have to stay back, Maggi. His lungs are damaged. He desperately needs air."

Lex glared and pushed the mask away.

"Lex," warned Dr. Cooper, but Lex was looking at me, willing me to come closer, to hear what he had to say.

So getting the cup was worth more than even two million dollars to him, was it? What he had to do was *so very important,* he'd said. And it was about female power. *About balance.*

About everything I'd fought for all this week. Damn it.

I bent closer and kissed him. "So what's the password?"

"Nuada," he whispered back, on what sounded like his last breath. New-*what?* At first I didn't recognize the word, had no idea how I'd spell it.

Dr. Cooper pushed the mask firmly back over Lex's face and held it there. Lex's eyes looked increasingly desperate....

Then it clicked. "Nuada of the Silver Hand? From Irish mythology?" Arthurian legend, I would understand. Or Scottish mythology. Even goddess legends. But an *Irish king?*

Lex's expression eased, and his eyes fell shut.

I brushed the hair off his forehead again, trying to soothe him with my touch. It's traditionally been the role of women to sit by sickbeds day in and day out, to tend to the dying. Maybe that's why I felt such a strong, instinctive need to stay right here...despite what might be his dying wish and my living one.

But I'd started a job. Time to finish it.

"Joe," I said evenly to Dr. Cooper. "How bad is it?"

"He needs emergency surgery," he said. "But...Maggi, if you know his family priest, you might want to call him, too."

Of course! "One of my friends, downstairs, is a priest, Sam. Father Rhys Pritchard. *Please* send him up."

Sam reluctantly gave the command through his headset.

"Go," muttered Lex, eyes closed, muffled under the mask.

"Soon," I assured him. "Not quite yet."

Dr. Cooper said, "You need to stop talking now, Lex." Under his breath he muttered, "I can't believe he's still conscious."

Lex caught at Sam's arm, slanted his gaze at me. "No...police." Then, before Sam could dismiss that as impossible, he added, "Maggi. *None.*"

Sam whistled. "That's a tall order, Mr. Stuart."

Lex said something like, "...pay you for..."

Spoiled and selfish, just like I'd said. And to judge by the ache in my chest, seeing him like this, I still loved him anyway...just like I'd once vowed.

Rhys pushed inside and hurried across the room to us. "Maggi! Good God in Heaven, what happened? Are you all right?"

I surged up into his concerned embrace. It felt wonderful, for a moment, to be hugged in strong, healthy arms by someone who didn't smell like blood. But I couldn't savor it. When I glanced down at Lex, his hazel eyes had opened to scowl at us. I laughed. Possibly dying, he still had time to be jealous?

Just because I loved him didn't give him *that* right.

"Rhys Pritchard," I said, "this is my old friend, Alexander Stuart. The one we've been talking about. Lex, this is my new friend, Father Rhys Pritchard."

Lex's suspicion eased, and he blinked a wary hello.

"Pleased to meet you, Stuart," said Rhys. "Though I'm sorry it's not under happier circumstances."

"I've got a favor to ask," I told Rhys. "But it's a huge one. It would mean you not being there to get the cup."

"You want me to accompany your friend to the hospital," he guessed, too easily. "Of course I will."

"He might…" I swallowed, hard, against the possibility. "He might need you officially. If you can still do that…."

"I can, Maggi," said Rhys. "I can still hear confession."

I turned to Lex. "*Him* you can tell secrets to. That's my deal. If I go, Rhys stays with you until I get back."

Lex's lips moved weakly. I bent closer, moved his oxygen mask momentarily back and asked, "What?"

"Trust…him…?"

I smiled into his eyes, sliding the mask back into place. "More than I trust you," I told him honestly. Lovingly.

His eyes smiled back at me, then closed.

And…I couldn't leave him. I wouldn't. To hell with the Melusine Grail. Women could just go on empowering themselves the way we have over the last thousand years, one woman at a time.

But I was fooling myself. So I stood.

"Ms. Sanger," warned Sam. "If you're going…"

Rhys gave me a quick, hard hug, energy I needed. "You know it was never the goddess grails I was after, don't you?"

I knew. He wanted the Holy Grail, in any form he could find it. Including Lex and his mysterious bloodline.

Sam handed me off to Ed, who led me down the fire stairs as emergency sirens howled nearer.

I sensed her, the grail, as soon as Sofie drove us onto airport property. The sensation felt…it felt like landing in New York had, barely a day before. Like a homecoming.

I'd washed at the security station; then Aunt Bridge had tended my cut arm en route. Thank goodness we had a lot of luggage, so I could change into clothes without blood-stains! Lil had made some important telephone calls. We were ready.

We parked outside Terminal 1 and headed to the block reserved by Air France, tucked between Air Afrique, Alitalia, and Austrian Airlines. Who knew Austria had its own airline? From there I could practically follow the call of the grail, instead of the signage, to the nearest VIP lounge.

Once upon a time, all such lounges lay inside the main security check. Now that you can rarely get that far without a boarding pass, some airports have made them more convenient.

"I'm expected in Reserved Room C," I told the guard outside the lounge, as if I belonged. My posture dared him to deny it.

He checked paperwork, then moved a security rope, allowing us into the comfort and privacy reserved for public figures and first-class passengers. The chairs were more lush here. The sound was more subdued. Drinks and refreshments were laid out for the taking.

Sofie, who was a civilian today, looked around us. "So this is how the other half lives," she muttered. "And to think—last time I flew, I was happy they gave me a box lunch."

I went to Reserved Room C, knocked and walked in.

Sofie stayed outside to stand guard.

The gentleman who rose at our entrance looked supremely unremarkable. Even his expensive suit was understated. His eyes narrowed at the sight of three women.

"I expected one guest," he said, once the door closed.

"All for one," I said, with the coolness that comes from just having stared down—and dealt—death. "One for all. Do you have my package?"

"Are any of you police?" he asked.

Sofie had warned us to expect that question—it had something to do with laws of entrapment. That was another reason she stayed outside.

"No," I answered. No one in the room, anyway. "Are you?"

He smiled. "No." Then he lifted a leather case onto the room's one marble-topped desk. The laptop computer was already plugged into a data port, beside a phone.

"I trust," he said, unlatching the case and lifting out the alabaster cup, "that you will find the merchandise acceptable."

Melusine's energy washed over me, before I'd barely gotten a look—more than acceptable. I took it first, low and flared and ancient and beautiful. I turned its weight in my hands—and, oh, yes. This was it. My grail had made it back to me.

"Oh, my…" murmured Lil, who hadn't seen it before now.

I carefully handed it to her, turning back to our friendly art smuggler. "I'm satisfied."

He typed some information into the laptop, then faced it toward me. *Transaction pending,* the screen read. That transaction being the transfer of $2 million from one numbered, foreign bank account to another. *Password required.*

N-U-A-D-A, I typed carefully, and hit Enter. Why Nuada…?

Beep. *Transaction completed. Please make a note of your confirmation number....*

"Thank you," said the unremarkable gentleman, with his hard-to-place accent. He logged out of the bank site, then shut his computer and tucked it into a padded case. "It is always a pleasure doing business with your family." He meant the Stuarts.

I just nodded, shook his hand and watched him go. For once...had something gone smoothly? It hardly seemed possible.

Then again, we had four Grail Keepers here.

It was definitely time for us to celebrate our sisterhood.

We tucked the chalice back into its case before leaving the private room. Better not to linger with our smuggled property at the exact scene of the crime, right? Unfortunately, our plans meant we couldn't go far or take very long, either.

"I found just the place." Sofie nodded toward the VIP ladies' lounge.

I looked at Aunt Bridge, our official wise woman.

She nodded, smiling. So we did it.

This being part of the VIP lounge, the rest room gleamed with cleanliness and smelled of its vases of fresh flowers. We washed the changing table before making an altar out of it, amidst all the mother-caring-for-child vibes you could want. Sofie, who'd been toting our backpack, retrieved a liter-size bottle of spring water and a mixed bouquet of roses and daisies and carnations that they'd purchased from a street vendor.

Excellent.

We covered our makeshift altar with flowers. Then, after washing the grail itself, we filled it with spring water and set it in the center.

It made a beautiful tableau. Even before drinking, I felt peace settling over me. Even with announcements of arriving and departing flights. Even with the occasional woman coming in to use the bathroom, sending curious looks but giving us our space. This wasn't supposed to *be* separate from the world. This was supposed to *be* the world, for anyone who wanted it. Soon…

"So…" Sofie whispered. "Do we say something?"

"Only if you want to," I murmured—and lifted the grail and drank deeply. Like drinking sisterhood, hope, belonging, strength. *Welcome…*

My experience was hardly as dramatic as back in the sanctuary. This time I understood the glimpses of people and places that danced before me. Other women had fought and even killed for their loved ones before—some with success, some without. Other women, so many others, had faced the dreaded deathwatch. Almost all of us loved, sometimes well, sometimes poorly.

Women throughout time had gathered with their aunts, cousins, sisters for strength. This was right and necessary.

Everything that was happening was right.

"We are one," I whispered, blinking quickly against the warmth of tears, and passed the cup to Lilith.

She drank, then closed her eyes…and smiled at the images she, too, must see. It was the smile I'd sometimes seen her give her babies, when she felt especially loving, especially proud.

Now she gave that smile to herself. "We are one."

She and Sofie helped Aunt Bridge hold the chalice, since Bridge's arm was still in a sling from her attack. Bridge kept her eyes closed for a very long time, even once trails of tears began to slide down her frail cheeks. Finally, when she opened them, she simply nodded at us with a tremulous smile, indicating that Sofie should take the grail.

Apparently, she couldn't speak past what she'd seen.

Sofie drank, then put the grail down…and sighed, long and deep. "We," she murmured, then cleared her throat around her emotion and spoke firmly. "We are *so* one."

We nodded. Then, shared smiles not being enough, we

group hugged. How could spreading this feeling, this understanding, not be of vital importance for women? For *people?*

Someone cleared her throat behind us. We turned to see a
middle-aged woman watching us, overloaded with a purse, a
laptop case and a rolling suitcase. "Excuse me," she murmured.

The rest of us exchanged self-conscious glances.

"Don't mind us," I assured the newcomer. "We're about
to clean up."

"No, it's not that. I was just wondering…this is going to
sound silly, but…" She ducked her head, embarrassed. Then
she squinted at our necklaces. "'Circle to circle'?"

Oh, my goddess.

"'Never an end,'" we responded in delighted unison.

Was it a small miracle? Maybe, but why rank them? The
important thing was that Sandra Dennison from Klamath
Falls, Oregon, got to drink of Melusine's Chalice, as well.

Someday, as soon as we found a way to do it safely, other
women would also experience this grail. But until then…

"It's quarter to six," said Lilith, checking her watch once
Sandra left. "Our flights are going to board soon and, uh, I
could use some help in here."

She was edging toward the handicapped stall. With her
round, pregnant stomach, it was the only one that fit her well.

But she had more reason than that.

"Coming," said Sofie, with a been-there, done-that grin.

I poured the remaining water from the grail into its plastic bottle. Then, kissing the grail once more, I put it safely
back in its case. It was mine, but never *just* mine.

Sofie took the case with her into the stall, with Lil.

That left Bridge and me—and the perfect chance to chase
down a niggling piece of mythology. After helping her to an
upholstered settee to wait, I asked, "You know the story of
Nuada of the Silver Hand, don't you, Aunt Bridge?"

"I'm better with goddesses than gods," she said. "But
yes."

"Nuada is kind of an elfin king—warrior elves, like in Tolkein. But he loses his hand in battle and has to relinquish his throne, right?"

Aunt Bridge nodded. "The leader represents his land. As with the Fisher King. If he's not physically perfect…"

"Then the people fear the kingdom will suffer." The password had to be a message. But Lex was about as physically perfect as mortals get. He'd worked incredibly hard at it, almost obsessively, ever since…

Oh, heavens. *Ever since the leukemia.* The point at which his father had started ignoring Lex for Cousin Phil.

Phil, who would take over either Sangreal or *Comitatus* if Lex wasn't in charge…*and who already had.* I didn't understand everything, but I'd just gotten a chunk of it.

The *Comitatus* really *was* about blood!

Aunt Bridge continued. "But Nuada regained his kingship after a silversmith fashioned a replacement arm for him."

"Yeah," I said slowly. "But I bet whoever had gotten the throne in his place sure fought *that* restoration."

Splitting the loyalties of their followers down the middle.

Lil and Sofie emerged from the large stall.

"Okay," said Sofie. "Let's get this show on the road—"

But she stopped, her head coming up to stare at three male figures in the sheltered entrance to the ladies' room.

They were well-dressed men who had the stance I'd come to recognize as *Comitatus.* Control. Power. Confidence. Like Lex's.

Qualities that weren't always bad things, unless you used them against someone else. And considering these guys' timing…

Crap.

Chapter 24

"We'll take that," said the man in front, gesturing toward the leather case in Sofie's hand.

"Eat shit and die," said Sofie. Most women can be warriors by necessity. But some, like her, just excel at it.

"No," said their leader. He was an older man, balding, still fit. I guess they couldn't risk ski masks in a place as crowded and terrorist-sensitive as an airport. "Thank you."

No, thank you? That weird touch of humanity, sarcastic or not, niggled at me. How did a bunch of men associated with what many thought was a holy bloodline turn out so bad?

Unless, like Lex, they didn't think they were.

"I already helped take down eight of you today," I said. Hopefully it had been the worst eight, since college boy and de Montfort had been among them. "The men who ambushed Lex Stuart."

They tried not to let it register, but the way they blinked, the way they breathed, gave them away.

"You didn't know about the attack in Lex's apartment?"

"Alexander Stuart has been murdered?" demanded their leader with the kind of careful calm that wasn't calm at all.

"No. Together, he and I are more powerful than ever." Even if it had been a lie—us being together—I would've said it.

"Oh, Mag," moaned Lil. "Not again."

Beyond them a woman said, "Isn't this the…? Never mind."

This was one woman's sanctuary they couldn't invade for long without being noticed, and they knew it. The leader extended an impatient hand toward Sofie. "The chalice. *Now*."

"Eat shit," she began—but stopped when the stocky brunette man drew a pistol from under his designer suit coat and aimed it at Aunt Bridge's head.

They couldn't show a gun for long here. "Now," repeated the leader, heading for Sofie.

I stepped between them and murmured, "Give it to me."

She did—I felt the case's weight in my hands—while Bridge protested, "It's not worth it."

But it would always be worth it. I thought of the men I'd killed today. I'd been defending the most important thing, life. Yes, the Melusine Chalice was powerful, if not in the way some men seemed to fear. I had willingly risked my life for it at Fontevrault, and in Paris. I would risk my life for it again.

But nobody else's. And damn it, I'd hit my quota for killing today.

Face-to-face with the leader of this latest trio, I said, "Fine, you can have it."

Sofie, behind me, said, *"What?"*

"Maggi, no!" protested Bridge weakly.

But the man in front of me smiled. "Thank you."

"You're welcome," I said. "But it's conditional."

His smile faded. "We do not negotiate."

"Please, this is Negotiation 101, here. I have something you want, and you have something I want. We're both short on time. So here's my deal. Sofie takes Lil and Bridge to catch their planes—" flights we'd reserved mere hours ago, en route to the airport "—and I sit with you in the lounge. They won't call the cops, because of the grail being here illegally. Once Sofie phones to say that they're on their flights, I give you this."

The leader reached to take the case by force, but I dropped easily away from him. The sandy-haired man aiming a gun at my aunt was more worrisome.

"I'm not fighting you," I said. "But I'm not handing this over without something in return."

To my delight, I saw their leader hesitate.

Aunt Bridge said, "But, Maggi, you've gone through so much."

"There are more grails out there," I assured her, still holding the leader's gaze. "We'll find them."

The leader said, "Leave the backpack."

He meant Sofie's backpack. "Eat—"

"They want to make sure we're not smuggling the chalice out in it," I interrupted her. "You can understand that."

With a glare, she retrieved her phone and wallet—then tossed the pack to the stocky man. "I'll be back for it."

"Call me once the others are on their planes," I said.

"If that's really how you want to play it," said Sofie.

I looked at the gun in sandy-hair's hand. "That's how they're *making* me play it."

So, with one last wary glance, Sofie eased Bridge and Lil out the rest room exit. *Be careful,* she mouthed from behind them.

Then I was alone. Outnumbered.

The leader smiled again and reached for the case.

I not only stepped past him, but thumped him hard in the stomach to remind him that I wasn't completely helpless. "Did you forget the rules, or are all of you just that bad with delayed gratification? *Nobody touches the grail.* We go into the lounge, where nobody should complain about your presence, and we talk."

Glaring at me, he nevertheless signaled to sandy-hair to holster the pistol.

The stocky man said, "We have nothing to tell a woman."

"Not even a woman who helped stop an assassination attempt against your rightful leader?" I smiled at their startled gazes. "I think you do. And even if you don't, I've got plenty to tell you. Come on."

And I started for the lounge. As I passed, sandy-hair reached for the case—and found himself with a handful of nothing and two of my fingers against his eyeballs.

Everyone froze, that time.

"And here I thought you men might have some twisted kind of honor," I said. It was the only explanation I had for the use of blades against Lex, instead of guns. "Didn't we have a deal?"

Since they were a hierarchy, I looked to their leader. "If not, I can be more trouble than you can imagine."

Reluctant, he nodded and spoke the words. "We have a deal."

I went out and sat down. I laid the leather case on my lap and folded my arms across it.

Two of them pulled up chairs, as well, to look more natural. Sandy-hair continued to stand watch. This was the VIP lounge; more than one person around here had probably seen a bodyguard.

I smiled, fully in control. *For* now.

They did not smile back.

This afternoon had stripped everything down to the bone, and in my bones I believed that Lex was a good man, despite his connection to the *Comitatus*.

It was time to test whether that might be true of any of the rest of them.

"Here's how I see it," I said into the silence. "René de Montfort called you guys *Comitatus*. Like the old code of conduct for Anglo-Saxon warriors defending a king. Since your group clearly crosses borders, I'm thinking your king is metaphorical, probably the head of the Sangreal bloodline. Right so far?"

"How did—" started sandy-hair, but the leader raised a hand to silence him.

The stocky man said, "She's bluffing."

"Or Stuart told her," said the leader.

"Please. Like even I could convince Lex to break vows.
You did mean *Lex* Stuart, right? Not *Phil?*"

No answer.

"It would be easy to mix them up, if you just looked at
their genealogy," I continued. "And not their appearance,
personality, ability or worthiness to lead. But even by bloodline, Lex should be in charge. And no, he didn't tell me that
either." Technically speaking. "There are several good conspiracy books out on the genealogy of the Holy Grail. It is
information anyone can find if they look hard enough."

They seemed uncomfortable but said nothing.

"I can see how your group might have worried when he
was dying—as a child, I mean. Maybe people questioned a
sickly boy's place leading such a distinguished society. And
once his and Phil's blood mixed, after the bone-marrow
transplant... Oh, wow."

Maybe against his will, the leader looked intrigued.

"Is it possible that Lex's father *agreed to support Phil's
succession* in return for the bone marrow that saved his son's
life?" It put Deuce Stuart in an uncharacteristically fatherly
light, but it also made incredible sense.

"That's ridiculous," protested sandy-hair. So their leader-
ship wasn't something that could be bartered for.

Not openly.

"It would certainly explain the difficulty Lex seems to
have had reclaiming his position," I continued, feeling out the
truth of my words by their responses. "He's a picture of health.
He's competent. And he's not afraid of a few goddess cups."

They looked uncomfortable. Good.

"Powerful individuals must still support the Phil faction,
despite him having a dick job some years back," I mused.

Now they recoiled. It was hard not to laugh. Keep your
enemy off balance, and all that.

"But surviving plastic surgery doesn't require close to the
strength Lex needed to conquer leukemia. And he did conquer it."

I could *smell* their discomfort. I was so damned close!

"Only through his cousin's help," blurted sandy-hair, who was clearly the Talking Pooh of the bunch.

"True. But I've got to think that you boys are having some conflicting loyalties, lately. Maybe not you three personally," I admitted with a shrug. "But a lot of your brethren. On the one hand, you have Phil, who got his position by default and has men running around beating up old ladies and trying to steal antique cups for reasons he probably won't share, because in fact he's scared of them. On the other hand, you have Lex, who by blood *should* be in charge and who supports strength, balance and honor. In fact…that's why he still hasn't taken over by using force, isn't it? He's honoring the rest of you. He needs you to accept his qualifications and ask Phil to step down."

That was it. With no more confirmation than a few nervous glances between the men, I finally understood. Damn, I was good.

"When does your aunt's flight leave?" asked their leader coldly. He didn't like listening to me? Well boo-hoo.

"Since nobody's telling you what's so scary about a goddess chalice," I said, "I think I'd better explain."

All three men blinked at me, sure I was joking.

"Long ago, before accepted history began…" I started—and kept going. I told the fairy tale. I explained the difference between power over people and power from within. I didn't use the word *Grail Keepers,* but I did mention the importance of empowerment for their mothers, their sisters, their wives.

I gave them a *lot.*

If I had to, I was going to convert these bastards one man at a time. At the very least, the more I kept talking, the more real I probably became to them. The harder to kill.

Assuming they *were* human.

By the time my cell phone rang, I suspected I had at least planted doubts. It was a start, and a good one.

"I'm on my way back," announced Sofie. Most people

need boarding passes to get beyond security…but a police badge can certainly help. "Lil missed the preboarding call, but she's on her Virgin Atlantic flight. It took off without a hitch. We saw it while I walked Brigitte to her Air France connection."

"Good," I said. "Thanks. I'm about done here."

"'Cup and cauldron.'" I heard the grin in her voice.

"'Ever a friend,'" I finished. "I'll be waiting."

Then I hung up, stood and faced three men who looked downright hungry. "Here you go," I said, handing them the case.

The leader motioned for the stocky man to open it—so he was the first one who got a good look at the plastic bottle of spring water inside. "Son of a—"

"You bitch!" The leader grabbed my arm roughly. "We had a deal, Sanger. You said you'd give us the chalice."

"I said I'd give you what I had, which was the case," I said. "Read the fine print. The information I just gave you is worth a hell of a lot more to you than that cup would be."

"Where is it?" He tried to shake me. *"Who had it?"*

With an easy twist, I stepped free of his grasping hand. Then I drew myself up to my full height, in *their* faces. They thought personal power didn't matter?

Let them get a taste of *this*.

"Listen up, you bullying, power-hungry toads," I hissed. "This is me. Magdalene Sanger. You've got to have heard the stories by now. I can jump down wells and survive. I can fly out fourth-story windows. I can vanish from in front of trains. And I can damned well put that chalice wherever I want to. I can also create a world of pain for you—"

Sandy-hair reached under his coat, but a woman across the lounge yelled, "Does he have a *gun?*"

His eyes widened, but he dropped his hand.

I smiled. "Like that. You may leave now. Tell whoever thinks they're in charge that the bottle is full of goddess water, and that if they're not pure cowards, they should give it a drink. It might just help you people understand some things you've been missing for a very long time."

Their leader all but vibrated with rage. He didn't like losing—even if it was the best thing for him.

A security guard was crossing the lounge toward us. "Is there some kind of trouble here?"

"Tell your leaders," I said, even more softly, "that if you leave the innocents alone, we'll leave you alone. But if any of you ever comes after me and mine again, I can more than take you. All of you. Can you remember that?"

Sandy-hair said, loudly, "No, sir. We were just leaving."

And since nobody had actually seen a gun, the guard stood back and just made sure they did that. Left.

"Thank you," I told him after they were gone. "Some men don't realize how threatening they can come off, you know?"

"Yes, ma'am," said the guard. He looked young, but he'd still been willing to risk himself for everyone else's safety. "Are you all right?"

I saw Sofie waving at me from beyond the doorway, and I grinned. "You know—every time someone like you reminds me of how great most men can be, I'm better and better. Have a nice day."

Then I went to meet my friend. The one who'd yelled *gun*.

"You're okay," she said, giving me a relieved hug.

I hugged back, so glad to have a friend in this. "I told you I would be. They took your backpack, though."

"A change of underwear, a paperback. Nothing I can't live without. So…they never guessed that Lil isn't pregnant?"

"Not for a second."

"Men." She rolled her eyes. We headed for the parking lot.

"Thanks for getting that fake belly for us. It made a wonderful hiding place. Great mother-goddess connections."

She shook her head. "Keep talking like that, people will think you're a college professor or something."

"There's something to be said for being sneaky," I mused. "We got the grail. Once Lil has it safely in hiding…."

"Then we can collect more of them, until we've got an exhibition nobody could dare destroy or ignore, right?" She'd been hanging with us since yesterday. She knew the plan.

"For all we know," I mused, "Charlemagne may have cut down the wrong trees. What did he know from sacred groves? All the pagans had to do was jump in front of a particular stand of wood and start screaming 'No, not our sacred trees!'"

Sofie was staring at me now and maybe I *was* getting silly. The Melusine Chalice was safe again—I felt it in my bones. I'd planted some fertile seeds of discord among my latest thugs. Her car, when she remote-unlocked it and did a visual scan, wasn't hiding anybody or anything.

The sound of planes rushing overhead and the traffic in the distance and New York City on the skyline…

Everything was as it should be.

I only had one more stop to make, to call my day complete.

My visit to the hospital would have gone more smoothly if I hadn't come face-to-face with Phil Stuart in the parking garage.

He looked troubled, in the split second before he recognized me. Then he looked scared.

That could be because I'd just caught him by the throat, put pressure on a nerve that I knew hurt like hell, and pushed him back against a cement pylon. *Hard.*

"I didn't do it!" he exclaimed, his voice bouncing off cars around us. "You think I could have my own *cousin* killed?"

Killed? My gut twisted cruelly, and I tightened my hold. Not now. Not Lex. And not when I felt so close to…to what?

To something important and wonderful.

"Uh, Maggi?" asked Sofie, from behind me.

"Help me," gasped Phil in a pained whimper.

"Mmm-hmm," said Sofie. "Maybe you should talk to her."

He did. "I didn't know about this. I swear it! Ask Lex. He believes me."

As the fear in my own heart eased, I eased my grip on him. Phil took the chance to knock my arms aside and step clear, trying to recapture his usual swagger. Too little, too late.

Heady with relief, I let him. "He's talking?"

"Yeah. He's out of surgery, and the doctors say he should go home in a few days." He squinted at me, newly suspicious. "If you're back together, where the hell have you been while he's in there fighting for his life, huh?"

"I came from the airport as fast as I could."

He raised his chin slightly, probably aware of what had been planned at the airport. I didn't have time to confront him on that.

"If you didn't know what was going to happen, maybe you should reconsider your ability to lead that bunch of thugs."

"I don't know what you mean." He was an awful liar.

"Just don't let it happen again," I warned, going well around him. "Bye, Phil."

"See you at the family parties," he called, smarmy. Reinvolving myself with the Stuarts would be a joy, wouldn't it?

But as I found Lex's room—easy to recognize because of Sam standing guard—it *was* a joy. I pushed through that silent, swinging door into the cavern of beeps and wires and screens and graphs that was ICU. I saw Lex, still alive, and I felt such joy that I could have wept from the intensity of truths beyond my academic, logical side's ability to comprehend.

"...died a few days before the papers arrived," Rhys was saying, low, from his chair beside the bed. How much had we gone through together before he told me about Mary? Now, in the course of one afternoon, he was unburdening to *Lex?*

Lex looked particularly pale, particularly mortal in his hospital gown, wired for IVs and oxygen, heart and lung monitors, a blood pressure cuff, a finger clamp for pulse-ox.

"That bites," he said, his voice rough and groggy.

Rhys shrugged and tapped his fist on Lex's hand, curled across a blanket. Male bonding. Now there's a mystery for you.

I cleared my throat, and both men looked up. Both of them lit up at the sight of me, too. What a pair they made. Lex, normally so golden with health, low but not beaten. Rhys, the slighter man, with his black hair and pale complexion in full contrast to Lex's, standing in as caretaker.

This part of my life wasn't close to resolved. But what I had to clarify, they both should hear. Better to do it now.

"Six months," I told Lex. "We date for six months, like we discussed at your apartment. After that, if you've proved yourself to me…we'll talk."

Either way, I'd already sent his $2-million chalice into hiding somewhere in England.

He nodded, the relief in his sleepy hazel eyes intense.

I moved my gaze to Rhys's, where he looked…not quite stricken. But more taken aback than I'd expected. I tried to will him to be patient, tried to assure him that an explanation would be forthcoming, but we weren't psychically linked.

"Ah. Well…why don't I fetch some tea," he suggested, standing carefully. "Maggi, would you like some?"

"Sure, thanks. I plan on being here for a while."

We hugged, his embrace solid and honest. "You could do worse," he whispered into my hair.

"I'm still figuring this out," I whispered back.

He complicated matters by kissing my cheek, and headed out.

I looked after him until Lex muttered, "Just don't be obvious about it, okay? Spies everywhere…"

It took me a moment to realize what he was talking about. "If you and I are dating, Lex, then we're *dating*. Rhys and I aren't involved that way. He's still grieving over Mary."

Considering what Lex's body had been through today, I

doubted he had the strength to smile. But his sleepy eyes warmed in my direction in a way that made my heart ache.

I went to the chair Rhys had vacated, sat, and wove my fingers through his, despite the plastic pulse-ox sheath on his finger. Alive. He was alive. Thank you, gods and goddesses everywhere. "But dating or not, I'm going after more goddess grails. Get used to that."

"It could be dangerous." His voice was definitely rough—he'd probably had a tube down his throat during surgery.

"Says the man in ICU. We've all got our own grail quests, Lex. I think we'll do best if we combine them, but either way, I know where my priorities have to lie for now."

"With the goddess cups."

"With what they symbolize." Life. Love. Sisterhood. Personal power. None of it sucked, as far as worthy goals go.

"Mag—" His hesitation didn't seem to be because of the painkillers or lingering anesthesia. "I...I've been asking you to trust me. Maybe you shouldn't."

But I wasn't hopping back on the to-trust-or-not-to-trust Lex Stuart roller coaster. Not today, anyway. Melusine had survived her husband's betrayal with a continued loyalty to their legacy. She'd survived. Maybe I'd give that a try.

Squeezing his hand, I shook my head.

He frowned, fighting his sleepiness. "I could have gotten you killed today, just by being with me. I can't even talk to you about any of it. You *shouldn't* let down your guard around me. You should—"

So I shut him up by kissing him, gently, firmly. "Never tell me what I should do, Lex. Instead...just tell me about your goals."

He looked pained from more than wounds. *"I can't—"*

"Yeah, yeah. I know. Vow of secrecy. Let's just go around the obstacle. Hypothetically speaking, given the choice between helping yourself and helping humanity, which would you choose?"

He looked wistful now. The drugs robbed him of so much of his usual armor. "I thought you'd know."

Damn it, I *did* love him. A man who in a few ways was still a stranger…except to my heart. Weren't we the pair for keeping our most foolish, most important vows?

I drew my fingers across his cheek. "*I'm here,* aren't I? I just wanted to hear you say it, so that I—"

"Humanity," he whispered. "I hope."

The touch of modesty was what did it for me. "Then let's see what the pair of us can manage in six months. With your connections and my line to the goddess, who knows?"

Maybe it *would* be something epic.

* * * * *

*There are more grails out there, waiting to be found.
And it's up to Magdalene Sanger to find them!
Don't miss Evelyn Vaughn's next heart-pounding read
in her* GRAIL KEEPERS *series,*

HER KIND OF TROUBLE

*Maggi's off to Egypt in search of one of the
oldest grails of all, the Isis Cup.
And while she might have old friends to join her
on her quest, there are always
old enemies out to stop her!*

Available in November 2005

ATHENA FORCE

Chosen for their talents.
Trained to be the best.

Expected to change the world.

The women of Athena Academy
share an unforgettable experience
and an unbreakable bond—until
one of their own is murdered.

The adventure begins with these six books:

PROOF by Justine Davis, July 2004

ALIAS by Amy J. Fetzer, August 2004

EXPOSED by Katherine Garbera,
September 2004

DOUBLE-CROSS by Meredith Fletcher,
October 2004

PURSUED by Catherine Mann, November 2004

JUSTICE by Debra Webb, December 2004

**And look for six more Athena Force stories
January to June 2005.**

Available at your favorite retail outlet.

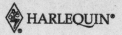

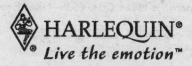